BRAVO
TOO MUCH

CHRISTOPHER DUFOUR

Christopher Dufour ◁

www.du4writes.com

Cover design by wideskystudio.com
Cover photo by Sarah Dufour Austin.

For Mom.

a.k.a. The Lone Chihuahua.

Still my best hero.

CONTENTS

PROLOGUE $\cdots\cdots\cdots\cdots\cdots\cdots\cdots\cdots\cdots\cdots$ 1

1. THE FORT $\cdots\cdots\cdots\cdots\cdots\cdots\cdots$ 13

2. JETFIRE $\cdots\cdots\cdots\cdots\cdots\cdots\cdots\cdots$ 32

3. NOT EVEN IN THE BALLPARK $\cdots\cdots\cdots\cdots$ 46

4. PLAYED THESE MINOR KEYS $\cdots\cdots\cdots\cdots$ 59

5. PARTNERS AND OTHER BROTHERS $\cdots\cdots\cdots$ 75

6. WICKER CANDLES AND BASEBALL BATS $\cdots\cdots$ 94

7. SHOE LEATHER $\cdots\cdots\cdots\cdots\cdots\cdots$ 112

8. SHOPTALKIN' $\cdots\cdots\cdots\cdots\cdots\cdots\cdots$ 126

9. THE CANVAS $\cdots\cdots\cdots\cdots\cdots\cdots\cdots$ 143

10. UM, YES. YES, HE IS. $\cdots\cdots\cdots\cdots\cdots\cdots$ 150

11. SAVES THE DAY $\cdots\cdots\cdots\cdots\cdots\cdots\cdots$ 151

12. TAYONA GONNA GETCHA $\cdots\cdots\cdots\cdots$ 168

13. HICKS IS MY FAVORITE $\cdots\cdots\cdots\cdots\cdots$ 179

14. DOTS DON'T CONNECT THEMSELVES $\cdots\cdots$ 190

15. AN INTERLUDE WITH THE DUKE $\cdots\cdots\cdots$ 204

16. MOM-AND-POP KOLACHE SHOP $\cdots\cdots\cdots$ 220

17. PARKER, AND NOT THE COOL ONE · · · · · · · · · · · · · 239

18. IT'S A CRUEL SUMMER · 250

19. LAWYERS, GUNS, AND MONEY · · · · · · · · · · · · · · · · 260

20. LIVIN' WITH WHAT I BEEN GIVEN · · · · · · · · · · · · · · 275

21. SIDES STEPPED AND SWIPED · · · · · · · · · · · · · · · · · 287

22. THE PROMISE · 303

23. STRANGE TORPEDO · 305

24. OF STEEDS AND STERNER STUFF · · · · · · · · · · · · · · 322

25. GET RIGHT, GET WISE · 332

26. FADING, FADED, AND FEYD · · · · · · · · · · · · · · · · · · · 343

ACKNOWLEDGEMENTS ·351

ABOUT THE AUTHOR · 354

PROLOGUE

"Truth is, I don't like any of these sumbitches."

"I ain't got nothin' for ya, Preach."

We were sitting—more like sprawled—on decades-old aluminum bleachers when the team in the off-colored jerseys broke through our front line and pulverized the quarterback with a three-man blitz, one that squirted the football into the waiting mitts of a rushing defensive end. Tex, Preacher, and I uttered a collective groan, one that got swallowed up in the much louder and more obnoxious squawks from the moms, dads, and high schoolers seated below us. Preacher, having just sucked a swig of Dos Equis—Lager, not Amber—dribbled and spittled when his groan released, and a slight foamy cascade of beer affixed to the corner of his mouth until it dried in the sun. Tex just shook his head, but I couldn't make whether it was 'cause of Preacher or the dim performance of the Paschal Panthers J.V. Team.

J.V. games were the best. You could catch them mostly on weeknights at Paschal's practice field, the same field where Tex and I had rung our respective bells while Preacher either cheered us on from the sidelines or sweet-talked some girl into getting naughty beneath the bleachers. The school district invested fewer resources into the junior varsity team, which meant fewer security guards and less hassle smuggling in a case of beer, cans of which we concealed in crappy paper sacks from Tom Thumb.

Today's match-up made up for a game that got canked by the Fort Worth Independent School District's sports council due to the visiting team's sudden outbreak of pinkeye, something that may or may not have been engineered by enterprising young men from R.L. Paschal High School's current crop of spiriteers. We lucked out with the Saturday reschedule. Labor Day had just passed and with it, the worst of the Texas summer heat. At three o'clock in the afternoon, the canny taste of cold beer complemented a light wind and periodic cloud cover under a warm sun.

The Panthers' varsity team played at proper stadiums like Farrington Field, complete with hot dog stands, sprawling parking lots, and Fort Worth police. Texas high school football warranted spectacle with big stages on which to orchestrate those spectacles, so practice fields didn't suffice for teams with legit booster funds. I'd often found it a little sad to get off the bus when we played at another school and their main field looked worse than our practice field.

"Jimmy Huntsacker can't keep hold of that goddamn ball," Tex said, pointing with an index finger on the hand that gripped his crinkly paper-bagged beer can. "That ain't why you don't like none of 'em, Preach."

Preacher stuck a cigarette in the corner of his mouth opposite where the beer dried, enhancing his wild visage. As he flicked open a Zippo, he said, "Tex, I don't like *any* of 'em is what I'm fookin' sayin', yeh right daft fooker. Fookin' football wankers inna first place."

"Preacher, you been coming to these damn games since high school," I said, striking up a ciggie of my own. "How can you say you don't like it? There's literally one-point-five-million other things your dumb ass could be doing."

"Well, the game's fine and all, 'specially when somebody gets his arse whipped like that Jimmy Hunstsacker there. I'm just sayin' these wee gits are all wankers and I don't like 'em. I wouldn't fookin' buy 'em a pint or light up with 'em, oi." Preacher took a drag, and I could see he was about to rankle on again.

"These fookers got whatever they want. Fookin' fancy red cars. Big-arse trucks. Stetsons, if they're so persuaded. Not those shite hats from the corner stores. Shite fabrics from Lucky Brand and The fookin' Gap. Their mums and das spoil the fook out of 'em. An' then they come out here and grab arse and shake their dicks at each other an' prob'ly split the oul' pink taco with lassies that can't say no. Church it up on Sundays and beat up fresh Mexicans on Monday." He burped. "Fookin' shite. Wank stains, the lot of 'em."

"The street preacher steeeeerikes again," Tex laughed, toasting beer cans with Preacher.

"'Sa fine observation, Texas, yeh shite."

I clinked aluminum with them. "Amen."

Preacher, capable of mean pharmaceutical feats, finished his cigarette in a couple breaths and immediately set about searching the pockets of his faded flannel shirt, itself a relic from high school. The bastard had literally not changed a whit since then. He withdrew a baggie of fine ground herb from the breast pocket, pulling it out through a hole, and unsealed it enough to stick his nose inside and breathe in a sharp inhalation, evaluating the vintage. He handed me his beer so he could prepare a proper joint.

"Shite ain't changed, Cajun," he said, eyes fixed on thin cigarette paper rolling carefully between thumbs callused by years of misanthropy and fuckery. "Same fookin' prats, different decade."

"We have cell phones now," I said, accidentally dribbling a little beer of my own. I gurgled, trying to pass it off but Tex and Preach saw and neither of them gave me shit about it. I did get a beauty of a stinkeye from one of the football moms a few rows down, the same one who had been disapprovingly glowering at us all day between plays. I'd polished off a good four or five of the Dos Equises since the game started, telling myself they're better when they're cold.

"Coz *those* are workin' out so good for us," Tex said.

"Man, we were just as much assholes as these kids and maybe even our own class," I continued, wiping the dribbled beer from my lips onto my bare wrist. "If not worse."

"We still are," said Tex.

Heights, fresh off their fumble recovery, executed a flawless option play that stymied our defense, and their linebacker picked up fifteen yards before one of our burlier safeties brought him down way too close to the end zone. The Arlington Heights families clapped and hooted and hollered, annoying their neighbors because Paschal didn't segregate the J.V. field's bleachers into Home and Visitor sections. Presumably, the bleachers integrated because of some FWISD bureaucrat's mistaken impression that few visiting teams would bring fans with them, a critical oversight made by a property planner that didn't appreciate football, the savage. As a result of that and no signage anywhere in the vicinity of the field, people who showed up for the games just mixed together. Heights wasn't that far from Paschal, so a lot of folks knew each other, making the tension even more fraught when your team did something right.

"One toke ovah the liiiiiiine, sweet birdie, one toke ovah the line," Preacher sang to himself as he prepared the spliff.

"I don't think that's how that goes," I said.

"Fook it!" Preacher displayed the perfectly twisted joint with that exhortation. "How's that fer yeh, yeh big-balled bastard?"

"You do have a talent, Preacher," Tex said, taking the proffered joint to his lips and leaning in so I could light it for him with my own Zippo, a tarnished brass hunk that would never be confused with Preacher's brushed nickel, plain-jane model. Tex didn't smoke like me and Preacher, but he loved a periodic shot of the chronic. It was Tex's turn to de-virginize the latest spliff. It was a wonder any of us could ever remember that rotation. We forgot shit all the time, but we always remembered who got to take the first hit on a fresh J.

As soon as the first waft of pot smoke found its way lazily out of Tex's mouth, the dour football mom swiveled on her ample ass to deliver her most piercing glare yet, and she opened her mouth, preparing to add some harsh words as well. However, this was the first time she got a good look at Tex, and as soon as she got that eyeful, her angry face softened to something approximating low-grade orgasm. Women *loved* Tex. Tex flashed a laconic grin at the annoyed football mom, and she instantly sweetened. Her cheeks flushed red as their eyes locked, and Tex winked at her through another exhalation of pot smoke, keeping an unthreatening yet determined gaze locked on her as he passed the joint to me. If he wanted to, he could have uttered a couple friendly words to the lady and engineered an outcome that porn producers pay thousands to capture on film.

But Tex being Tex, he just winked and looked back up at me and Preacher on the higher bleacher, laying back on that bench with arms bent at the elbow and drooped down, fingers a-splay as he caught the twist from Preacher's joint. As he stretched, unassumingly of course and not at all on purpose, the football mom's stare drew down from his face to the next most natural place: Tex's crotch, where a boa constrictor of a cock bulged against faded jeans in a ridge along his inner thigh (he tucked right). When the football mom finally turned back to the game, nervous sweat had broken out on her upper lip, forehead, and chest, and the back of her neck communicated a deep red flush.

Heights scored on us, eliciting a wave of mixed reactions in the bleachers. I clapped, doobie clamped in one corner of my downturned mouth, and hollered, "Get yer shit together, Panthers!"

"They'll sick the fookin' law on us, yer not careful, Cajun," Preacher admonished, plucking the joint from my mouth so he could suck on it. He held it the French way, a reversion that also provided cover from prying eyes. Preach inhaled in two quick bursts, saving both of his puffs for one breath and hold. One of his eyes twitched as he held the smoke in, and he regarded the field with the practiced sagacity common only to coffeehouse and jailhouse wisemen.

"'Ere," he said; "have yeh seen the hair on that front line's faces? Fookers must be collegiate already, wha."

"Designer facial hair is literally listed in the Brooks Brothers gentleman's guide, Preach," I said, scratching the black stubble on my chin, waggling eyebrows at him.

"You gotta groom though," Tex said, holding out his hand and waiting for Preacher to place the joint between his fingers. "Some of those guys are shaggy as *fuck*."

"Oi, strewth," Preach said, finally letting go the weed-breath he'd been holding. "Fookers takin' testo shots in high school now, wha?"

After a couple more rotations and crumpled beer cans, Paschal continued to underperform. As we usually found by third quarter, the Panthers were likely to lose. The families of Panther players would stick around till the bitter end, but most everyone else would shuffle out of the bleachers. The sun had exited its interruptive cloud cover into the light blue sky common to the flat plain of North Texas, temperature aggrandizing the Saturday afternoon crowd with latent summer remembrance to fight off an early trace of autumn. The boys on the football field would be feeling the swamp-ass by now, bursting exertions between torn-up yardage resulting in the grimy sweat that could never quite get bleached out of the white football pants and pads. Heights would win, as usual, and file into their bus for the short drive back to Hulen and 30 and a victory party at some affluent parent's house where rules relaxed and social contracts broke. Our boys would file into the field house next to the J.V. field, wash up, and then walk down the street to Mama's Pizza where Panther parents would spring for a consolation pizza party, which, to be fair to this 1968-founded pillar of Italian confectionary deliciousness, might have been the better deal all along.

"Need to have a right shite," Preacher announced as the fourth quarter kicked off.

"Can we get into the field house?" I wondered aloud, eyeing the ancient tin roof athletic building adjacent to the practice field where generations of Paschal Panthers had hung their pads, Tex and I included.

"Better to do it now than when everybody starts walking outta here," Tex said, crushing another empty can in his massive paws. "I'm good with a leak too, and then we can go find something else to do."

We rose and, as usual, I stumbled on something, probably my own feet, and would have killed myself falling down the bleachers had Preacher and Tex not caught me, righted me, and helped me down. I can never judge how well I can hold my alcohol on a given day, and goddamn if I don't mind acting the drunk.

Heights retained the advantage that day as we vacated the premises, and alas, the Panther J.V. squad would go home with nary a win to their name that season. The only surety in this world is that Paschal J.V. can't even beat *off* much less any of its fellow FWISD competitors, which reflects pretty poorly on Trimble Tech, the only high school I think we consistently maul on the football field every year at every level. I couldn't even tell you where Trimble Tech was, but I'm pretty sure it's nowhere near a practice field with the way those kids play.

We walked behind the bleachers to get to the field house where Tex tried the door, the cardboard case of remaining beer gripped in the other hand, only to find it locked. "Guess they're switched onto all the riffraff in the neighborhood," he said.

Preacher tried the other door and found it locked as well. "Who the fook is gonna rob a fookin' field house, I ask yeh? Does the fookin' coach think an army of Heights twats are gonna roust arses in here or somesuch shite?"

"Coach is probably just frightened of your shits, Preacher," I said, stuffing our crumpled empties into a nearby trashcan. "Tex, remember how many times we came back here after a game to find all the shitters blocked up? Yuck." I jerked a thumb over my shoulder. "'Round back?"

We circled the field house. Sneakers and boots crunched on the cracked, aging asphalt and gravel of the parking lot between the athletic building and the main school grounds. It would be another twenty years before they renovated that lot, building the multi-level parking garage warranted by an ever-increasing student body with driver's licenses. One time, in that very lot, Tex had parked his pickup not far from where we were walking right then, late for school after having spent a weekend fishing with his Pops in a river on their family's New Mexico getaway property. Within that pickup bed had lain fourteen freshly caught trout, each of which Preacher and I thought would look much better with freshly lit cigarettes smoking in their little fishy mouths. Good times.

Once we rounded the unused back side of the field house, we found a corner shaded by HVAC equipment and the lone live oak that had stood guard over the field house for decades. Preacher shrugged with upraised eyebrows and a face that said, "Fuck it!", promptly followed by the dropping of his pants and a popped squat. Tex and I flanked a few paces to either side of him, backs to each other as we unlimbered pricks for a lifesaving piss on the field house's purple, rusting tin wall.

"'The rise and fall of my sloppy love!'" I crowed suddenly, aiming urine in a painter's crisscross. "The smatterings and splatterings.'"

"'They'll getcha!'" Tex and Preach shouted at the same time.

Then, from somewhere nearby: "What is that faggot shit?"

Tex and I both looked over opposite shoulders, dicks dripping that last little shudder-precipitating bit from the tip all the way through your body. With our Spock-cocked eyebrows, we saw three dudes walking down the street behind the field house that separated the Paschal school plot from small residential homes on the other. These men had an unobstructed view of us as we deposited our leavings behind the field house on this lazy Saturday afternoon in Fort Worth.

"That fuckin' guy's takin' a *shit*!" one of the men laughed, pointing at Preacher.

For his part, Preacher did what he needed to do, wiped his ass with one of the crinkly paper bags in which he had kept his beers, and stood to refasten his jeans. Tex and I zipped up and pivoted on opposite feet so that all three of us were fully facing these intruders.

"The fook yeh daffy fook-arses want?" Preacher said.

The three men—honestly, it's a stretch to call any of us "men" given what's about to happen—stopped in the street below us. I could make out fancy patterned jeans on each of them, boots, one of them sported a cowboy hat of some kind that was definitely not a Stetson. The one in the hat threw down a crumpled beer can, and I could tell from their swagger that these guys might be as half-in-the-bag as me, Texas, and Preacher.

"What you callin' me, faggot?" said the cowboy-hatted one.

I rolled my eyes. "Well, this is gonna end well," I said.

Tex put his thumbs in the belt loops of his jeans, exuding this calm confidence shared only with Buddhist monks and badasses nicknamed Texas. He kicked at a rock on the ground, nonthreatening. "I sure do hate that word, fellas. Why don't y'all just go on your way?" he said.

"Fuck you, boy," one of the men said, this one carrying an unopened beer can in the back pocket of his jeans. "Who shits on their own field house?"

"This seems awfully familiar..." I said, eyes narrowing, searching foggy memory for teeter-totterings on precipices similar to the one on which we now found ourselves.

Cowboy Hat spit some dip in front of me, a clear signal toward combat as I'd ever seen. I fucking hate dip. And you just don't spit that shit in front of someone like that. "Y'all here for the game?" he said.

"Bitch, I *am* the game," said Preacher, taking a few steps down off the curb and into the street where the three guys were. Tex and I were right behind him, a step or two back, mostly on instinct, not judging that Preacher had a habit of inserting himself a little too lackadaisically into situations like this, but fuck it.

"Here we go!" screamed the one guy that hadn't said anything yet, a little fucker with a trucker cap that he had clearly purchased from a hipster clothier.

Tex held his hands up, palms-front, and took two quick steps to close the distance between himself and the three Heights guys, putting himself in front of Preacher in a strategic move to protect our little mad buddy.

"Fellas, I think we ought to call it day, huh?" Tex said.

Cowboy Hat eyed Tex. Like...*eyefucked* him. Then he spit another loogie of dip into Tex's path, never taking his eyes off Tex. Tex didn't look down but I could see the dip spit strike his plain brown Lucchese ropers, making a wet, slimy rope across the weathered leather from toe to ankle.

"Why don't—" Cowboy Hat started, but he never finished.

Cowboy Hat didn't wake up for the rest of the altercation. Tex didn't just jab the motherfucker in the face, he launched a knuckle-nuclear-missile that simultaneously rendered the Heights man unconscious, bloodied his nose in an exploding crack of cartilage, and set the man horizontally with the ground so fast that his fake Stetson seemed to float by itself in the air for a few seconds, like a goddamn Looney Tunes cartoon. The man hit the ground unconscious with a sack-like collapse, and a gust of dust exhaled around his body as it came to rest in the half-second it had all taken.

With attention turned to Tex's preemptive assault and Preacher—who is just so damned weird that you can't help but look at the fucker and wonder, "What is this guy even *doing*?"—the remaining two Heights guys had all but forgotten about me. Thinking I was a ninja, but obviously wrong, I tried to jump-kick the one with the beer in his back pocket…me never having ever jump-kicked any*one* or any*thing* before that moment. To my credit, I managed to get my foot and leg stretched in the right direction, but I misjudged the distance, and fell right onto my left buttock as failure claimed me like the welcome warmth greeting the man who pisses his pants after holding it for way too long.

Preacher started laughing immediately upon seeing this, even though he engaged the third Heights man—Ballcap—at the same time, so it would look like to the average passerby (there were none) that Preacher was just laughing like a madman…about on target for that fucking guy. Preach fought dirty, so he would come at people with fists like they expected then kick them in the balls and set to punching them in those very same balls as they fell, which is exactly what Preacher did to Ballcap. Ballcap howled like a little girl whose favorite RBG Barbie was taken away by Scott Kavanaugh, done.

By this time, the Heights guy with the beer in his back pocket was closing in on me, taking advantage of my misfortune by launching a couple of well-timed kicks to my midsection and back as I scrambled to get my fat ass off the ground and properly into the fight. This was Beer-butt's downfall because he doubled down on the kicks while I rolled a few times to get into some semblance of a defensive posture. I even started making KI-YAAAAHHHHH noises to distract him, but I'm pretty sure I just sounded and looked like an asshole.

Again with the familiarity.

I landed one good punch on Beer-butt's ear as he came at me with jabs before Tex, He of the Golden Glove and Thor-like

Countenance, literally grabbed this guy by the throat, picked him straight up, and punched him repeatedly in the face until the guy went limp. As Tex dropped him, he snatched the beer from his back pocket, which turned out to be a rather well-played Texas red from the Rahr Brewery. Tex popped the cap on the beer, let its fizz blast out and drip on Beer-butt's bloody face, and then took a swig. He made a face and offered the beer to me. "Too warm," he said.

I waved the beer away, embarrassed by my performance. "Maybe Preacher wants it."

Preacher, for his part, was standing on top of Ballcap like the downed man was a hill that he had conquered as part of some military campaign. Or maybe Preacher was just enacting his impression of Captain Morgan. Either way, Ballcap was curled up in a fetal position on the street clutching at battered testicles while Preacher, arms akimbo, put one topsider-encased foot on Ballcap's back.

"Jack, why does that keep happenin' to yeh?" he said.

I shrugged, sheepish. "I have not yet begun to defile myself."

"Fuckin' A," Tex said, handing the beer to Preacher who downed it in a couple swigs. "Well, that's Saturday afternoon, fellas. What are we doing tonight?"

1.

THE FORT

"Hey, man, I appreciate it," I said to the general manager, handing over six copper keys on a ring. "It's been a wild ride."

"Are you sure we can't talk you out of it?" Paul Packer fit almost every cliché of the comic book store manager stereotype except in demeanor. His three-hundred- pound bulk—clad in overlapping XXXL T-shirts to soak up inevitable sweat from the thyroid condition that confirmed his bachelorhood—belied a gentle voice and a kind outlook on a life that had consigned him to first class seats and Big 'N Tall clothiers. I'd worked for Paul a couple years now and could say few bad things about the man.

"You know you're the best we've got," Paul continued. "Nobody knows comics like you do."

"That's bullshit," I replied, fiddling with an unopened pack of cigarettes in my shirt pocket. "There's plenty of nerds in Fort Worth. Hell, Ballard's gonna make a great manager. He'll keep up what I started."

We were talking about a practice I'd employed at Lone Star Comics to feature comic book writers instead of characters or titles. Everybody knew Superman or The X-Men or name your favorite pervert-suited super-hero. The problem with most transitional comic book readers (people who just bought a comic or two after seeing a Marvel movie or some shit) was that none of them subscribed in any meaningful way to the long-term bottom line of the creators that slaved to produce those comics. Most of the best comics creators delivered their finest work in comics and characters that they owned. Big name, branded stuff from the likes of Marvel or DC usually just paid the bills in a work-for-hire model that enabled creators to craft more personally fulfilling work like *A Distant Soil* (Colleen Doran) or *Transmetropolitan* (Warren Ellis and Darick Robertson) or *100 Bullets* (Brian Azzarello and Eduardo Risso) or *Incognito* (Ed Brubaker and Sean Phillips). Creators financed stellar, independent comics like these through projects on big name comics, enabling risk-taking on lower selling but more satisfying creator-owned work.

So what I would do was rack trade paperbacks, graphic novels, and comics according to the creators' names instead of the publisher, which was the standard practice. I created big honkin' signs for names like Simone, Doran, Ridley, DeConnick, Lapham, Rucka, and more, first displaying them in a feature fashion up front near the store entrance and then slowly replacing the tired old alphabet-ical-by-publisher-and-title scheme that Lone Star had employed for decades. It prompted better conversations with regular customers seeking new stories and higher sales amongst new customers coming in for a single after the latest Spider-Man movie.

Paul made it sound like I had invented this approach, but the truth was that I chatted on comics forums where shop owners shared best practices. Nobody had done it in Fort Worth, and competition was light anyway, so what the hell, right? I'd driven up sales in three months using this tactic and pulled the store out of the red. Thanks, internet.

"Regardless, call me if you ever change your mind," Paul said. "I know the salary's nothing special, but we'll figure something out if you ever want to come back."

He shook my hand, and I couldn't help but offer up a genuine grin. I wasn't lying about the ride. It had been a good time working at Lone Star Comics. I'd fulfilled the dream of a much younger, much more naive Jack Dooley in the past two years running the Fort Worth branch of this comics and gaming enterprise, which headquartered in a warehouse-like space in Arlington and sported seven satellite locations across the Metroplex. When I'd first walked into the store, it had been bleeding money for a while, and it took me a hot minute to unravel prior mismanagement to locate all the leaks in that sinking ship. None of them were critical; some misplaced merchandise here, some incorrect accounting there. In the end, I'd had to have a handful of uncomfortable conversations with a couple of long-term employees that led to harder conversations in Arlington with Paul, a man who had yet to grow out of natural warmheartedness into the type of general manager required to issue pink slips to people who put the business at risk. After that, it had all been a matter of selling comics, man.

We were standing outside the storefront, which was wedged between a nail salon and a tax management firm that only opened for a few months of the year around America's most disliked season. Across the parking lot sat a fat, multiplex movie theater whose renovation from a dilapidated old United Artists matinee had handily coincided with my term as Lone Star's manager. Part of the winning strategy for kicking up business had involved cross-promotions with the theater, which saw much more foot traffic than our weird little comic book shop in a weird little shopping plaza tucked away off the main thoroughfare. The modern retail cliché of location and its two brothers, location and location, held firm even in the comics business.

I wore a cream colored long-sleeve T-shirt, soft from years of sweaty drunken bouts at the fraternity and faded enough so that the Sigma Tau Delta insignia on the back could not be seen through the beige short-sleeve, button-up shirt over it. The Stein-Mart special was a John McClane knock-off (*Die Hard With a Vengeance* era) and flecked with a ridged box pattern visible only up close; it just looked like a cool, beige shirt from the '50s from afar. My kinda armor. From the breast pocket of this high fashion choice, I drew a pack of Marlboro Lights and packed them onto the lower palm of my hand a few times, eliciting a sharp smacking noise. The cellophane released in a crinkle between my fingers, and I pulled out the gum-wrapper covering under the box lid, crushing all this extraneous trash in my hand and shoving it into the pocket of frayed-at-the-cuffs blue jeans. I slipped one of the cigarettes out of the box and between my lips while retrieving the Zippo, snapping open the battered brass lid, and flicking the flint to spark flame, all in one smooth motion. When I lit cigarettes, I did so with a strained expression, involuntarily afraid of the fire, perhaps; so I sometimes looked like I was mugging for a movie camera with downturned mouth and scrunched-up peepers when I drew the first few puffs. Purely instinctive. I snapped the brass Zippo closed—it had faded to a dark and orangey varnish that obstructed the engraved Spartan helmet on one side—and shoved it back into my pocket as I dragged on the cigarette and exhaled the first carcinogenic puff in some hours. Sufficiently emboldened, I stuck out a hand to shake Paul's.

"I really do appreciate it, Paul," I said. "Seriously, call me if you ever get into a jam. I'm all about side hustles right now."

"Thanks, Jack. See ya around."

We turned and parted at the same time, each of us having obeyed the social mores expected of us in that situation to the appropriate degree. Paul waddled back into the store, and I headed for the movie theater. The sun beat down a transitional spring-summer heat on the plaza, cloudless sky reflecting a blinding white glare from the light-colored pavement and the white stucco design of the plaza. I pulled forehead-propped sunglasses down over my eyes as I threaded between cars in the parking lot, making for the theater. My dirty black Chuck Taylors sidestepped a pile of freshly melted gum and a puddle of soda, both likely left behind by the same struggling single mom who eked out a living for twelve hours a day at the salon.

I got to the theater and regarded the marquee. The multiplex, thankfully, showed repertory movies alongside the latest blockbusters and middling rom-coms. The manager, a natural film buff, had figured out a way to keep the theater open all day with the right combination of films that maximized ticket sales to the right audiences. So in the mornings, elderly couples that rose at dawn would show up to catch any new movie or a Clint Eastwood marathon; in the afternoon, kids skipping school would file in to see whatever hot actioner was out; and the usual cross-section of the public would buy up everything else in the evenings, from recent favorites to also-rans. On top of that, Fort Worth's dedicated indie scene would trickle in at various opportunities to catch whatever film festival contenders that the theater had managed to acquire for limited runs.

I'd had my eye on the marquee for a couple weeks now, and today was the perfect day to make it happen. Taste-phantoms of buttered popcorn, Coca-Cola Icees, and red licorice subsumed any traces of regret left over from my Lone Star departure. Sufficiently nicotined, I stamped out the cigarette butt on the sidewalk and grinned at the kid in the box office.

"One for *Fight Club*," I said, slipping a five under the glass for the matinee price.

The route home hauled me up Hulen all the way past I-20 and I-30 to Camp Bowie. I lefto'd on the brick street and veered off in a block or so to Bryce, right next to Lucille's. Being within walking distance to my apartment, I hit Lucille's frequently for their New Orleans-inspired fare, but not as much as Kincaid's down the street. A Fort Worth mainstay, Kincaid's had slung the same incredible burgers in the same quaint location since 1946. Lucille's put a hurtin' on your wallet, but you could live off Kincaid's and feel good about your pocketbook and your life in general after every crinkly cut fry and every jalapeño-infused patty.

The sign on the side of the apartment complex read "Bryce House." Straightforward. It wasn't really a complex so much as an experimentally designed building from the sixties or seventies that had aged poorly, not unlike other apartment structures in the neighborhood. Pebble stone masonry composed the outer wall, and windows were scarce, giving the Bryce Avenue side the daunting appearance of a compound or a bunker. Ivy crawled up the edges and corners of the pebble walls where foliage crowded out alleys and hid the complex from the residential homes on either side. A small parking lot separated the building from the street, and all the residents fought for the four spaces because of the crappy carport in back. It could have been five spaces, but the complex's dumpster occupied one space, providing easy access to the Wednesday garbage pickup that invariably rumbled people awake at seven in the morning. These spaces were supposed to be reserved for visitors, but no one cared or enforced that dictum, so free-for-all rules superseded.

I turned on Sanguinet to find the alley drive behind the apartment, itself not a real street but instead two dusty, gravel-encrusted tracks for tires between ever-encroaching grass and a strip down the middle. After navigating this forest, you had to cut sharply to the left to roll your vehicle into the tight carport area attached to the back of Bryce House. There was just enough room for a standard size car to pass between the ports and the fence on the alley side, but that usually didn't stop some dickheads from forcing their monster trucks back there and sometimes scraping or bending already dilapidated carport support struts. The complex only featured fourteen units, and there weren't enough ports for everyone. I'd managed to secure mine just because over half of the units had been empty when I'd inquired about the place, and the owner had never even considered charging me a fee. Folks that moved in later hadn't been so lucky.

I could have swung the Little White Honda into my carport easily and with little to no anxiety, but that car was long gone. I had upgraded to a beige Toyota Camry with better mileage, a better sound system, and less chance of falling apart at the seams. The Little White Honda passed 150,000 miles just as it crossed the Louisiana-Texas border, and within a few miles of that, a tire had exploded and the oil pan had fallen out. I said goodbye to him in Marshall and found the Camry—a car I had wanted to own for years since my mother had shown me how fuel efficient yet comfortable they could be—in a preowned lot whose salesman gave me a huge discount for the multiple hundred-dollar-bills with which I ended up paying. The Camry was beige as beige could be with few frills aside from a high-end sound system, and that suited me just fine for stacks of CDs I kept racked in the center console.

It had taken me a few tries to get it right, but I was comfortable with backing the elongated Camry into my carport by this time. I had never scratched or dented it, at least not yet, and whenever the chance of that manifested in a drunken night out, I made sure to park on the curb out front until I could manage a sober berthing. I backed the car in, shut it down, and headed past the other cars to stairs that brought me into the complex's courtyard.

The building design put all the apartments on the outer walls with doors facing inward to a bricked-in, pebble stone courtyard where a couple of thick live oaks grew alongside enormous potted ferns and other vegetation. A fountain trickled a low-level steam of recycling water in one corner, loud enough to soothe but not so loud as to annoy. The owner had been a horticulturist in another life, and along with mismanaging the rental unit, he spent his free time curating the garden in the courtyard, watering and trimming the plants and dangling from the roof to prune live oak branches that threatened to damage the building. I never saw the guy, but I appreciated his work. He had even added a number of wrought iron garden chairs and tables to the courtyard, creating a little communal space where residents could hang out, smoke, and shoot the breeze. None of us ever did that, of course, because we were all shut-ins, introverts, and assholes.

I climbed the stairwell to the second level and walked over to Number Six, one of eight corner units sequestered in the darkness of the complex's roof overhang. As I slipped the key into the lock, I noticed that the peel-and-eat cat food containers I'd left outside had been devoured wholly, so I scooped them up for disposal. A gang of feral kittens made Bryce House their basecamp, and all us residents had silently self-organized to feed and care for them despite the no-pets rule in the bylaws. Nobody could have pets inside the units but that didn't stop us from indulging the little furry guys and girls that came to visit. I hadn't had a cat since high school, and crashing at my Mom's place for a couple months till I'd found Bryce House had reminded me of how much I liked the little critters. Mom took care of my sister's cats, Barry and Lavonne, and ended up keeping them because...well, because *cats*.

Tannish carpet covered the floor of my apartment, not unlike what you expect to find in every apartment over twenty years old that you've ever visited or lived in. Cream colored walls, old blinds, white and green linoleum in the kitchen and bathroom. Nothing special. Bryce House had been around for a long time, and the current owner had only last renovated in the 1980s. The heating and cooling unit was controlled from a central boiler somewhere, so you could only turn the fan on but not adjust the temperature inside the apartment. This generally sucked ass during transitional months between seasons because someone had to call the owner and complain about it being too hot and stuffy in the spring or too cold in the fall before he would flip the boiler from one temperature to the other. And none of us at the complex could agree on what was hot and what was cold. As such, I had a number of fans scattered about, and I regularly kept the windows open to let in fresh air.

I had come to Fort Worth with very little except cash. So I had decorated according to my very poor, mismatched, and tacky taste. A giant widescreen TV sat on an entertainment center on the wall of the living area opposite the door. On the side wall was a couch whose design could only be described as acid rock drug trip. I had arranged that so that I could watch TV lying down on the couch with no need to turn my head. A dark wood coffee table sat next to the couch with an ashtray made out of a Mack Truck hubcap and hood ornament, and it was full of crushed cigarette butts and ash. My Dad had given me a big, cushy maroon lounge chair with an ottoman that didn't match anything, and I'd set that on the opposite wall from the couch with a small side table and lamp. A stack of unread comic books rested on the side table along with four empty Dos Equis bottles and a smaller ashtray.

Behind the chair stood a massive wooden work desk and hutch, purchased on sale at a no-brand furniture store and assembled right there under my own dexterity and guesswork with Chinese instructions. Upon it rested all manner of memorabilia. The hutch had drawers, cabinets, and hidey-holes for pens, pencils, notepads, journals, staplers, or whatever else I could stash inside there. After starting at Lone Star, I had gone a little crazy and purchased a bunch of comic book statues, figurines, and action figures...replacements for things I'd lost in Hattiesburg. The problem was, after I'd started buying these things, I couldn't stop. I'd discovered eBay at one point and my first purchase was a low-number edition of the first Frank Miller *Dark Knight Returns* statue by sculptor Randy Bowen, the one with the Carrie Kelly Robin. Since then, I'd even sold some of my older comics runs to feed the habit, and it was now borderline out-of-control. The only thing that had stopped this relentless acquisition of shit had been the dwindling of badly managed finances: money mixed and mingled from those last days in Mississippi and odd jobs I'd taken in Fort Worth to put gas in the car. Even with that, I still eyed the odd Batman or Superman statue or art piece from time to time.

I'd had to dig deep to find some fortitude to quit Lone Star after realizing that my proximity to all that colorful merchandise was feeding this pricey "hobby," and I'd descended into a self-reflective funk as I evaluated whether or not the stuff even made me happy or merely served as one more thing to which I could become addicted. That was to say nothing about the Star Trek Collectible Card Game into which I'd begun pumping inordinate amounts of time and money. Also stuffed into that desk and hutch were plenty of those card decks, full of rarities and common duplicates, and I'd yet to figure out the ideal organizational schema for the hundreds of cards I'd acquired since discovering the game—and the community that played it—at Lone Star. I knew one of the things I would miss about working at Lone Star was the weird cast of characters that would get together randomly at the store to trade cards and match out against each other. We would play after hours sometimes and order pizza, wings, and beer, slinging nerdisms well into the morning, which often left me in the unenviable position of having to clean up the leavings and detritus before opening the store again. Maybe I'd show back up sometime and play.

I threw my keys and wallet on the desk, and they rebounded against the speaker setup for the desktop computer wired into the desk's computer compartment. I picked up the integrated remote from where I'd left it on the keyboard, wiped a fine layer of ash from the buttons, and powered up the TV. I cracked the window next to the kitchen. Under it sat a blue card table, which filled the space where one would ordinarily put a dining set. I used the card table as a place to toss shit that I didn't know what to do with, and right now, it was covered in bills and leftover bits of newspaper containing stories I'd not yet read and advertisements for bands coming to The Fort. Something smelled funny in the kitchen, so I stayed away. Then I remembered beer was in the fridge. So I lit a cigarette, puffed a little bit, then sidled past the dirty dish-full sink to the refrigerator where I extracted a six-pack of Dos Equis along with a noseful of moldy hamburger meat.

I shrugged out of the long-sleeve, pulling the John McClane shirt with it. It was hot. I wore the long sleeves at Lone Star because we kept it cold in the store to fight off the page-curling humidity common to the plaza's interlinked HVAC systems. I popped open the top button of my jeans, kicked off the Connies and socks, and plopped onto the couch, wriggling toes and sinking into the synthetic foam, cigarette clenched precariously between lips and emanating Marlboro smoke into my eyes. The bottle of Dos Equis I chose from the six pack made a quick squirt of air as I twisted off the cap, and I started with the sip, the one that turns into a gargle that turns into a firehose. Before I had even looked to see what was on the TV, I had polished off half the bottle.

It was about four-thirty in the afternoon, and I could smell the trace pre-summer scent of live oak and pine wafting in from the open window. A cough ejected from my throat a familiar mucus that tasted of cigarettes and beer. I found a *Farscape* marathon on The Sci-Fi Channel—they called it a *"Chain Reaction"* of the best episodes of the season that would lead up to the eventual premier of a new episode. It was the first part of "Liars, Guns, and Money," a trilogy of mad craziness that would close out Season 2. One of my favorites. Stark was back in this one.

I settled in.

———

The ringing of the phone woke me from a hazy, head-slobber of a doze. As I sat up to snatch at the handset, I noticed spillage from the sixth beer bottle on the carpet and part of my jeans. I didn't recognize what was playing on the TV as I thumbed the phone's answer button.

"Hello?"

"Jack? It's your mother. Are you hungry? I'm making dinner. Do you want to come over?"

"What time is it?" I said, searching around for a clock. It was dark inside.

"Dinner time! Come on over. It's spaghetti and meatballs."

"Ok, I'll be there in a minute."

I hung up and stood, immediately crushed by a wave of beer fog, the not-quite-nausea that hits you after you've slipped off into a drunk-nap for a hot minute. I wondered if I had time for a shower but ended up putting on other clothes and scooting.

My Mom lives out near Benbrook in a big ole' townhome regularly updated with new ideas culled from travels and a lifelong subscription to *Southern Living*. New hardwood floors with a dark oaky overtone and wide boards. A deck enclosed by a stone wall that blended into the neighbor's townhome, upon which perched a ceramic sculpture of a cherubic little angel child. Tasteful plush rugs to match immaculate furniture. Knick-knacks and souvenirs from different cultures scattered about in an orderly pattern. Snowglobes of a near-infinite variety hidden away in cabinets, ready for deployment during the next Christmas season. Multicolored Limoges boxes lining recessed shelving. Collages of pictures of family, mostly me and my sister. An old upright piano against the wall that hadn't been tuned properly in decades, her mother's transported from home to home on an inexorable decades-long journey from Meridian, Mississippi that culminated in Fort Worth, Texas.

I pulled into the circular front driveway, which comprised the totality of any semblance of yard on the townhome block. An iron gate separated the driveway from the front door, and I went in, opening the unlocked door and walking inside with a loud, "Give thanks! Thy son hath returned!"

Mary-Margaret McDowell shuffled toward me from around the corner of the dining area, thin arms outstretched, wide smile almost cracking her elfin face in half. She kept her hair short in a bob that bisected her ears, upswept in the back, bangs brushed to one side, and she didn't have a single streak of gray in that brown-tinted black yet. I got my coloring from my Mom, brown eyes to black hair, and we tanned the same: dark and quick. She had not yet engaged in much of the outdoor activity that would bring her in contact with the Texas rays this season, so her skin retained a customary fair state with a hint of last year's browning. We never got *white*-white.

Mom was in a perpetual good mood, always, even when she was pissed off and angry at you. She coined the original "Bless your heart" idiom as a young Mississippi lady, bringing it to Texas and using it to convey delight and even glee when she really meant, "Shut the hell up, you stupid son of a bitch." This was compounded by an accent that would confuse any ethnographer studying the South. Growing up in Meridian, which was about as Deep South as you could get short of the Delta, Mary-Margaret had always carried with her the lilting poise of a proper Southern belle, even though she had spoiled it thoroughly through exposure to less-than-savory characters in her illustrious life. Namely, my father. She said things like "Spraht" when she meant "Sprite," and "IN-surance" when she meant "in-SUR-ance."

Her speech got complicated, of course, by a long residence in East Texas and later Fort Worth. Having spent years raising two somewhat challenging children in Longview, Texas, where the accents turn upwards in high pitches on every word's later vowels, she had adopted a bizarre patois bridging the cultural originality of her Southern Mississippi origins and the easygoing sub-suburban-but-not-rural elan of East Texas. Like most East Texans, she stretched every syllable into two, but not so that it resembled Appalachian hillbilly or redneck. You often caught yourself wondering if you indeed heard that extra syllable, and then you get mesmerized by everything else Mary-Margaret says. She could stretch a "well" into a "way-yulllll" and a "ceviché" into a "suh-VEETCHIE," and it's goddamn endearing and I'll knock the hell out of anyone that says otherwise.

Mary-Margaret had put her vocal talents to work attaining leadership of Fort Worth's Sister Cities program. This nonprofit organization spearheaded cultural, youth, and business exchanges to Fort Worth's nine sister cities across the world. People attributed the success of Sister Cities mainly to Mary-Margaret, whose infinitely charming demeanor—always led by that accent—bridged gaps in cultural understanding, created pathways for friendship, and influenced the Fort Worth elite into opening wallets and volunteering precious time. As a result, she had visited many places in the world, from Bandung, Indonesia, to Guiyang, China. She knew more about international protocol than most of the diplos at the State Department, and had she ever the desire to apply for the CIA, she would be recruited in algorithmic seconds.

"Hi, Mom," I said, accepting the hug and peck on my cheek. I probably stunk and immediately regretted not showering, and Mom fixed me with a crooked eyebrow stare that said she knew it.

"Hi, sweeeetie," she said, spending a little too much time on the long "E." "You couldn't have cleaned up a little bit? You smell like an ashtray!"

"I didn't wanna miss all the meatballs!"

We walked over to the table where two heaping plates of spaghetti and meatballs awaited, and Mom asked, "You want anything to drink?"

"I'll take a beer of any kind if ya got one."

Mary-Margaret set down a freshly cracked can of Miller Lite, the cheapest thing she could keep on hand for visitors. She was a martini girl but kept herself limited to only one a night at happy hour right after work. I started dousing my spaghetti with Parmigiano-Reggiano, freshly grated from Mom's personal stash of this wonderful parmesan cheese produced in Fort Worth's sister city of Reggio Emilia, Italy.

"You will not believe what I've got to tell you!" she said, and you could hear the exclamation point in her exhortation.

"What's up?"

"Your sister's thinking about moving back to Texas!"

"Badass!" I said around a mouthful of spaghetti. "Fort Worth?"

"They're looking at Denton or Mansfield, but I think it's gonna be Houston."

"The fuck?"

Mary-Margaret fixed me with a hard stare. "Watch your mouth. I said the same thing though. She needs to get back *here*, not Houston. Do you want to know why they're moving?"

I gave Mom a sidelong look. "She's preggo, isn't she?"

Mom's fork hit her plate loudly, and she regarded me with an open-mouthed stare. "Aw! How did you know?"

I winked at her. "It ain't rocket science, Mom. They've been trying for a while. Is that why we're piggin' out on spaghetti tonight?"

Mom shrugged and gritted her teeth in a wide smile that conveyed her excitement, and she shrugged her shoulders up to her ears, a borderline old-lady gesture that conveyed the same. "Maybe I just wanted to see you and tell you the news, and I know how much you like my spaghetti."

"We ate spaghetti forever because it's all you knew how to cook," I said to my mother. "I'm conditioned to like it. I can't *not* like it." I hoisted my Miller Lite up in toast. "Well, that is fantastic news, and I am Superfly tickled for 'em. Very happy that's gonna be a Texas baby too."

"Amen," said Mom. It came out "ay-MIN!" "So what have you been up to?"

I shrugged and polished off the beer. "Well, today was my last day at the comic book shop."

Mom made an outraged face, mouth dropped open like she had just watched a heifer give birth to the Lord. "What? I thought you loved that job?"

"It was alright. It just had run its course."

"How many jobs have you had in the last two years? I can't keep up."

"Maybe a little less than a million."

Upon my return to Fort Worth, despite the sack of fresh cash in the trunk, I knew I was going to need work of some kind. After a few days of catching up and chilling out, I'd answered an ad for a music store in Irving that sought brass instrument repair techs, a skill still resident in my inventory. I'd done that for a while, but their band shop had never really clicked for me, and the corporatization of that service sucked compared to the easygoing fun of my apprenticeship back in Hattiesburg. I couldn't even smoke inside that band shop. Over the next few months, I'd bopped into a steady string of miscellaneous jobs that paid okay, from substitute English teacher to hand cream kiosk salesman at the mall. I had even done a couple of jobs for my Dad's consulting business as it expanded into Texas. The gig at the comic book shop had saved me from retail hell but only due to the subject matter. It was still retail, and anybody could do retail. That's why it never paid six figures unless you owned the retail store yourself. Ultimately, all a dead end.

"Have you got something else lined up?" Mom said.

"Not yet," I said. "But something'll turn up. I'm not worried."

"I thought that was like a dream job for you. You love comic books."

"Well, it turns out that selling what you love distills the love a bit," I said, wiping my mouth. "Sure, comics are awesome, but think about it. Am I really gonna work as someone else's manager in a comic book shop for the rest of my life? Look at those guys I replaced: one of 'em was ten years older than me with two kids. And he was workin' for twenty-five/thirty-K a year with limited benefits?" I shrugged. "I dunno."

"Perhaps you should start thinking about a *career* then," my Mom said, bringing up the old argument.

"I promise I will think about a career, Mom," I said, getting up to grab another beer out of the fridge.

"Until then, why don't you play some music around here? You could bring home some cigarette money at least. Have you seen any of your boys?"

Mom referred to a squad of bastards with whom I'd run in high school, musicians by talent versus accident. We'd started a blues band as sophomores, a genre of music both mysterious and scant in the Fort Worth scene. I had discovered so much of the blues thanks to those guys, from scratchy recordings of Sonny Boy Williamson screaming through his harp to Lightnin' Hopkins' amplified Guild tearing up a rubato medium in twelve bars. We had played at Fort Worth blues bars from JJ's to The Purple Pig, many of which had either turned over or been bulldozed to make way for something else. We had also run into the modest circle of Fort Worth blues musicians like Bugs Henderson and The Juke Jumpers, all of whom revolved around local legend Sumter Bruton's long-standing University Drive vinyl shop, Record Town.

"All those guys are gone," I said. "They're off savin' the world. Well, everybody but Preacher, of course."

"That boy!" Mom said, rolling her eyes. "What about him? He still around? You had some weird friends, Jackson."

I met Mom's mischievous look with one of my own. Mary-Margaret could deliver all the stories she needed to with her eyes and nothing else, and we could communicate that way solely if we needed to. "You ain't wrong, Mom. I actually ran into Preacher the other day. He's still around. We've been hanging out."

The brief recall of times past twisted inside me, egged on by dark things that Mom didn't know. I had indeed retreated to Fort Worth to remake things, to start over, to flee what had happened in Mississippi. To figure out what the hell I had done and what I was going to do.

It hadn't been going particularly well. Or at least, on present reflection, it wasn't comparable in emotional or professional maturity as my lovely sister's news. Not that we ever competed about anything: we were way too different for that. But building lives required benchmarking of some kind, and I couldn't help but feel that mine was diminishing further and further from the tentpole standard that my sister hoisted. Between jobs that I didn't much care about and funds that I readily pissed away, there was everything else that I wasn't ready to tell my mother, if ever. I flexed the fingers and bones in my right hand, feeling knuckles pop under faded bruises and old pain.

"You get enough?" Mom said, inclining her head at the empty beer can I had just drained. That one had gone a lot faster than I'd anticipated.

I burped, set the can down on the table, and grinned stupidly. "For now," I said. "But I'm coming back over here soon with a proper case of Dos Equis or Shiner or something other than this moose piss."

The phone in my jeans pocket vibrated. I slipped it out and looked at the notification. One new text message. In preview, it said:

```
From: 01934746329
Gang's all here if you want some.
```

The number was bullshit, and I knew that from prior bullshit.

I smiled at my mother and got up from the table. "Gotta go," I said. "Love ya, Mom."

2.

JETFIRE

The message had come from Deckhead, and it was time for a visit to The Jetfire Gym.

The Gym occupied a small sliver of space between a touristy gift shop and classic clothier M.L. Leddy's on Houston Street in Downtown Fort Worth. This was some of the most sought after commercial real estate Downtown, especially given the popularity of Leddy's western wear at upscale, some would say exorbitant prices. Leddy's original location stood in The Stockyards, but the outlet on the corner of Houston and Fourth had long acted as the go-to shopping source for urban business-people with its selection of luxury boots, white collar western shirts, leather and embroidered jackets, and hats. There was even a boot shine station in the window at the corner where a gentleman had dutifully scrubbed clean the boots of thousands of Fort Worth's citizens and visitors for over forty years. Steps from Sundance Square, this was one of the most trafficked blocks in Downtown Fort Worth.

So it would naturally pique your curiosity as to why one would establish in this nest of citizenry a home base for illegal activities like drugs and cybercrime. Were you in a position to ask The Gym's owners, and you never will be, you'd discover that this seeming disparity was all part of a plan.

The Jetfire Gym incorporated as Fort Worth's first internet cafe, a business that many ignored as viable in the transitional period of public internet access to private use. A couple of enterprising young individuals from Paschal High School, however, had a different perspective. Deckhead—born Domingo Reyes—and Pussy Control—born Jeri Hernández—dropped out of school following joint encounters with the Paschal Tech Lab, a bag of cocaine, a manslaughter rap, and about five-thousand dollars in cash. Deckhead and Pussy had already seen a lot of life by that time, Deck with a smalltime record stealing credit card numbers and Pussy having grown up in a household rife with abuse. When Deckhead and Pussy first met at Paschal, they instantly gravitated toward one another, hopelessly in love in that high school kinda way where everything matters right then and nothing ever changes.

Unfortunately, it *did* change. Pussy got hooked on crack, a gift from her stepbrother, a lowlife crashing in an adult-less house. The stepbrother—himself a product of the abandonment and abuse cycle in which Pussy found herself—enjoyed pushing meth, coke, and brutality on his siblings and graduated to out-and-out sexual assault. P.C. would end up having none of it.

Deckhead found out about his girlfriend's knocks in dribs and drabs, collecting cues and evidence that the world sucked in worse ways than the mere digital bits of nowhere men from whom he stole. Pussy stopped going to school and got fed up with coping. One day, Deckhead walked into her home to find that she had put a clip's worth of bullets into the stepbrother. She told him that she caught the scumbag trying to molest their little sister and that had been P.C.'s last straw and claim to agency.

Deckhead washed Pussy's hands in liquid bleach, disposed of bloodstained clothes, took her gun, and put a couple more bullets into her stepbrother's corpse. When the police arrived, he did not bother to resist arrest. The aforementioned cash and drugs were on hand for the cops to find.

Pussy was ready to do her time herself, but Deckhead wouldn't hear of it. Deck was so in love with her that taking the rap was the least of the things he would sacrifice for her. She testified on his behalf, stating that he had rescued her from her abusive stepbrother and negligent parents. The state agreed to a point, so Deckhead managed to avoid a first-degree murder rap and trial as an adult, but he still had to serve a juvie sentence for manslaughter. Neither of them would be going back to school.

Pussy cleaned up and used money Deckhead had spirited away to open The Jetfire Gym, a haven for Fort Worth hackers and crackers, named for their favorite Transformer. She visited him at the juvenile justice center as much as she could, multiple times a week, and Deckhead walked the straight path until he could petition for an early release on good behavior. Once free, he joined Pussy in running The Gym, having studied hard during his incarceration stint and coming out with plenty of legit ways to make the business work.

And plenty of not-so-legit ways, too.

The Gym didn't post open hours. It was open when it needed to be, manned by Deckhead, Pussy Control, or one of their close circle of hacker buddies. Pussy ran a modest coffee and espresso service on the front end of The Gym, a cheaper and faster competitor to the Starbucks down the street. She also worked with local foodies to bring in breakfast and lunch fare on consignment, simple dishes like chili and sandwiches that people could snag on while diving into The Matrix. The Gym posted modest enough profits to manage the staggering rent warranted by its Sundance Square location. Pussy was even a member of the local business associations that ran things Downtown, nonprofits and communications firms to whom businesses paid dues to drive more foot traffic into their brick and mortar. Most of the time, The Gym was just a public internet cafe where people could get on the internet, work remotely, read, and drink some coffee or tea.

The rest of the time, it was headquarters for one of the baddest cyber-heist crews in the country.

You see, Deckhead and Pussy had both grown up with an affinity for the art of the possible in digital technology. In the Tech Lab at Paschal, they had figured out how to hack into a local bank's server within ten days of their first exposure to basic network engineering. They learned everything they could about encryption protocols, ports, and information security. They devoured books and articles about known hackers. They experimented with zero-day exploits, spearphishing campaigns, and the advent of darknets. They had employed Low Orbit Ion Cannon strikes against Scientologist targets. They had rerouted shipments of goods from their intended destinations to places where people needed those goods more, like homeless shelters and domestic abuse centers. They had acquired embarrassing evidence of corporate and political misdeeds and shared it with journalists.

Deckhead had met plenty of ne'er-do-wells in the juvenile detention center. Those connections often called Deckhead for help when digital tech played a role in nefarious activity. Deckhead's claim to fame amongst the criminal community now was that he had never been caught and neither had any member of his crew, and none of them had even been identified as a suspect or a person of interest in any of their past jobs. They were ghosts. They eschewed black hat / white hat labels. They watched gothic movies and dressed like extras from *The Crow*. They procured original, undubbed-but-subtitled Japanese anime that had not yet been released in the United States. They argued about *The Matrix* transmedia experience. They prank called Kevin Mitnick and Chris Hadnagy. They listened to trance, house, traditional Hispanic, and classic rock. They hated on clicktivism and glorified Geocities neighborhoods. They read William Gibson and Hunter S. Thompson in beaten-up paperbacks from local book trade stores. They consumed a lot of substances. And they gathered at The Jetfire Gym.

I had met Deckhead and Pussy in the Tech Lab for the single month I'd chosen to investigate that strange, basement-level activity at Paschal. We didn't become tight friends until Pussy killed her stepbrother. That event caused a ripple effect in school at the time, shattering a lot of us whiteys' illusions about the relative safety and comfort of the picket fence life in Fort Worth. That may have coincided with the first time I watched *Twin Peaks* and the revelation of Laura Palmer's abuser and killer. I'd spend the next several years trying to ignore secret truths of the world chasing girls, playing music, and getting drunk. Had I paid more attention to those truths, maybe things in Mississippi could have been different.

I walked into The Gym around nine o'clock in the evening using a featureless RFID card Deckhead had given me that I kept secreted away between my driver's license and a credit card in the magnetic leather money clip in my front pocket. When waved in the right sequence, the RFID card unlocked the obvious front and back door locks but also the secret locks built into the tops and bottoms of the doorframe to keep out nosy jerks and The Law. Deck trusted only a few people with cards of that nature, and I was honored to be one of them.

Deckhead was behind the counter when I ambled in, and his wide face broke out into a smile when he saw me. "Jack-Attack!" he said in a deep North Texas Hispanic accent. "Whatchu up to, succotash?"

"Whataboutcha, Deck?" I greeted in return, catching his outstretched hand in a *Predator*-style levitating arm wrestle over which Carl Weathers and Arnold Schwarzenegger would have guffawed. Deckhead wore a black hoodie with a Pokémon critter on one breast and black flat-brim cap. He sported a thick goatee that did not connect, leaving space between the mustache and the chin hair right at the corners of his mouth. His face was pockmarked with light acne scars, and his cheeks became bulbous when he smiled, which was often. For a guy that had seen his kind of life, Deck was always cheerful.

"You wanna beer, man?" He said it quick like *"mayn."*

"Always. Dos Equis?"

"Gotta get you a better habit, boi." Deckhead extracted a beer bottle from the small refrigerator under the counter, cracked off the top, and handed it to me.

"I am a creature of simple pleasures," I replied with a wink. "I got your message."

"Step into my office."

Deckhead left the front counter and lead me down the length of the cafe deeper into its recesses. The walls were painted with a bright orange color on one side and a dark brown on the other. Most of the wall space, though, was covered by bookshelves hung high and out of reach, containing rows of battered paperbacks from every possible oeuvre that Deckhead and Pussy's crew consumed. Books on tech and computer programming mixed with dog-eared treatises on simulacra and simulation, cyberpunk originals, and nonfiction bombshells from journalists and madmen. To our right, rows of computer workstations lined one wall under the bookshelves:

simple desks with simple screens and blade-like desktop computers for a sleek profile. A few open cafe tables with chairs also dotted this area. In the back were more open design worktables and chairs, reconfigurable as need be.

For right now, a group of kids—I call them kids, but in reality they weren't much younger than me, which was fucked given what they were doing—had pulled together a couple tables to set up a Pokémon card game. Card games were all the rage in The Fort, and Pokémon ruled them all. Kids as young as five and adults as old as sixty had graced public areas in the playing of Pokémon, and people were weird about it. Everybody was trying to get everybody else's rare cards, and I guess something called a "Mew" was hard to find. Deck and Pussy even sold booster packs at the coffee counter because the margins were so good for the cafe's bottom line. These kids at The Gym were playing pretty quietly and seriously, eyes fixed to each player's moves and the cards in play, intensive fantasy immersion against a tide of adulthood. Fuckin' Pokémon, man.

Deckhead lead me past the Poké-tournament and to the back wall which was dominated by a large security door. Deckhead flashed an RFID badge to a reader next to the door's handle and looked up to a small, surreptitious camera built into the doorframe. A loud click emanated from the door, and he opened it, quickly ushering me inside and closing it again.

Behind this door lay The Jetfire Gym's inner sanctum. It looked like something from a cyberpunk movie, and Pussy and Deckhead had indeed built it to resemble many of their favorites. Computer terminals of the most complicated design sat in workstations that sported all manner of peripherals, from headsets to dedicated cooling systems. Gaming chairs with built-in speakers squared desks. Monitors of every size and resolution hung from jointed pedestals. The area glowed from ambient light produced by screens. A few people manned some of the consoles, not all. Power cables, ethernet cords, and other connective tissue littered the floor, snaking around desks and jutting downward from ports strung up on the ceiling. Whiteboards rested on easels near certain clusters of computers and workstations, some with incomprehensible code gobbledygook, others with simple declarations of "DARK WEB STATION—DO NOT USE!" A conference room table sat squat in the center of the room, upon it piled laptops, computer peripherals, cables, cords, microchips, motherboards, and more.

The place screamed *geek*.

"Hey, baby," came a voice from one of the gaming chairs, which was swiveling to face us. It disgorged a tall, lithe woman with taut muscles and long legs. She wore cutoff shorts and a thin sweatshirt with the faded image of a purple Horned Frog, the mascot of our local Texas Christian University. A dog collar gripped her neck, and her eyes bore heavy shadow in gray and gold. Her dark brown hair was clipped short and spiky, the grease reflecting light prisms from the monitors near her. Pussy had not let anyone other than Deckhead put their hands on her since her stepbrother died, but the unflattering greasy hairdo that would repel even the tightest of grips and the wiry musculature announced that she was ready for the next person who wanted to try. She came over to give me a hug and had to lean down to peck my cheek.

"Ahhhhhhh, Pussy Control!" I whined in falsetto, mimicking the song from which she had adopted her name. She pulled back and slapped me in the face and it stung hard and I liked it.

"Like I've never heard that before," Pussy said. "How are ya, Saint Jack?"

"Saint" was what they called me when they didn't want to use real names. Hackers are like X-Men like that. *What is your real name, youngling?* I still dunno why they chose that one for me.

"What's the occasion, gang?" I said, taking a pull from the beer bottle.

"Gear," Deckhead said. "We need a third party buyer."

I looked around. "I can see you're running low on gear."

"It's just extra stuff we'd rather not take the chance on connecting easily," Pussy said, holding up a notepad. "We've got a shopping list and cash."

"Is Best Buy okay?"

"Actually, if you could get it from about four or five different places, that would be better," Deckhead said, counting off a roll of hundreds next to me.

I looked over Pussy's notepad list whilst tugging on the beer. "You really worried about Feds connecting purchases?"

"Never hurts to be careful," Pussy said. "We've got some big stuff coming down the pike."

"And this stuff's gonna act as extra hardware that we can throw away if we need to," Deckhead said, proffering a wad of cash. "Here. Non-sequential. Well-used."

I looked over the bills. "Some of these are pesos...?"

"Whatchu got against pesos?"

"I'm just sayin'. Do I gotta go convert this first?"

"It ain't rocket science, Jack-Pack."

I gestured around to all the computer gear. "It's kinda rocket science to those of us stuck on the ground, Deck. Shit."

"The multiple currencies help vary the trail," Pussy said. "There's probably a currency exchange at the airport you can use if you don't want to go to a bank."

I took another swig of beer and pocketed the cash. "Sure, yeah. No problem. This is a lot of stuff though. You need it soon?"

"Next couple days would be great," Pussy said.

"There's more than enough in there for you too," Deckhead said. "Keep the change."

"Why, thank ya, mistuh, I's 'preciate it!" I mimed a little dance. "Y'want I should dance for ya too, suh?"

Deckhead and Pussy both cracked smiles and snickered at the routine. At about that moment, one of the others behind us snapped his fingers a couple times to get our attention. Like most of Deckhead's crew, all of 'em were so on-the-spectrum I could never have a straight conversation with them, to include this weird fucker.

"What is it, Nitz?" Pussy said.

"Somebody at the door," the kid said from his chair, enveloped by its plush technological cushion and bathed in the blue glow of his many monitors. We came over, and Nitz pointed at the camera feed in question.

"He's just knocking and there's nobody up front." Nitz meant that nobody from the crew was manning the counter up front, and these were the only people that were authorized to let people in past a certain hour.

"Aw shit, that's Preacher," I said, peering into the monitor.

"Oh, shiiiiiiiit!" Deckhead laughed. "Let's go let him in!"

The three of us traipsed up front into the public area. I hung back a bit to let Deckhead roll up to the front door and do the honors. Of course Preacher didn't get an RFID. Deckhead and Pussy were friendly with him, but it's Preacher, for fuck's sake.

"Yer the only fookin' joint I can go to roll!" he screeched as he crossed inside. Deckhead clapped Preacher on the back, and Pussy's face lit up with a smile. Everybody loved Preacher even when the only thing you could trust him to do was fuck shit up.

"Hey, buddy!" Deckhead said.

"Hiiiii, Preacher," Pussy said. "What brings you by?"

Preacher held up a paper bag next to his animated face. "Drugs! Let's get after it, lass."

He pushed past Deckhead and Pussy and saw me, offering me a wide grin with his weird eyes. "Cajun! How're yeh, yeh fooker?" He jerked his head at the paper bag. "Up for some?"

"Some of what, you weird bastard?" I said, finishing off the beer and tossing it at a recycle bin, missing.

Deckhead had locked back up and retrieved a foursome of beers from the fridge, following Preacher to a table closer to the Pokémon tournament in back. We gathered around this table as Preacher set the bag down gently, took a beer from Deckhead, and gestured importantly with it like Zeus with a lightning bolt in the direction of the Pokémon players.

"Now listen here, yeh shites. This Pokémon business is fookin' right wrong of yeh! It's a bleedin' Japaneesy conspiracy. It's fookin' savagery. *Animal slavery*, lads! Cruelty most fookin' foul, yeh twatty ballacks! Have yeh seen the fookin' cartoon? Catchin' 'em all, wha? Think about it: it's fookin' propaganda, mate. Enslavin' an entire race of beings just for their unique properties? Jaysis fookin' mental, it is."

Preacher gesticulated in a jerky, electric fashion, pointing and waving his arms around, raving like the lunatic he was. His sermon caught the Pokémon players' attention, and they looked to Deckhead for guidance on what to do about this strange cockney man. Deckhead swigged his beer with all smiles, drinking in Preacher's performance. It wasn't even that Preacher was performing so much either; he meant every word he said. It's just damn entertaining.

"Yeh can't trap these poor animals in a little red ball and have 'em live there like fookin' slaves!" Preacher shouted, turning his rancor toward the players, elevating the volume with each successive exhortation. "It's fookin' wrong! It's slavery, lads! Fookin' Peek-a-choo-choos and Snorlaxes and Squirtles, what the fook?!"

"Oh, I love Squirtle," Pussy said. "He's so cute!"

"I'm a Bulbasaur man myself," I said.

"There's a whole website on Bulbasaur," Deckhead said. "People love that one."

"Slavery!" Preacher shouted, banging a fist down on the table. He bent over the table and opened the paper bag, removing two small plastic baggies, one filled with a fine white powder and one filled with what was obviously some high-grade pot.

"Who wants what? Lines?" he said.

"If you're rollin', I'll have a toke," Pussy said.

"I'll do a bump with ya," Deckhead said. "You okay with that?" he said to Pussy.

She leaned in to kiss his check. "Do what you want, Sugar." Pussy Control wasn't one of those methadone mamas that gets uptight about others having a good time, despite the hard times from which she came.

"Cajun?" Preacher said as he swished a small mountain of cocaine on the tabletop and began chopping it up with a credit card that magically appeared between his fingers. Actually, I think it may have been an Albertson's grocery shopper card.

"It's late and I wanna get some sleep tonight, so no," I said. "But roll one up and puff-puff-give, bruh."

Preacher did a line with a tightly rolled five-dollar bill, snapping back upright from the table and shaking his head to absorb the rush. "Fookin' shite..." he whispered.

Despite indicators to the contrary, Preacher was not in fact Mancunian nor other breed of British-born cockney. Before any of us had ever met him at Paschal, Preach had gotten into the proverbial cookie jar of mind- and body-altering chemical paraphernalia via his older brothers. Bred from a hearty line of Scots, Irish, and at least one peyote-infused Navajo, Preacher's only natural aptitude coalesced in a Keith Richards-like adoption of every possible combination of substances in glorious, kaleidoscopic copulation. Now, your typical addict can never resist the urge to consume their poison of choice, always figuring out how to work it into their routine with some sense of normalcy and functionality. Preacher, on the other hand, never felt the monkey on his back, never got enslaved to dependence, and despite the volume of his consumption, no one could figure out how. It was his superpower.

Instead, Preacher's origin story unfolded over the course of years as he experimented with every possible combination of drug, chemical, and substance consumable. He was the first in our class to extoll the virtue of huffing gasoline, but when one of our less-hardy classmates emulated this behavior, he could not attain the level of tolerance Preacher seemed to possess naturally. Nor could this poor soul recover from the brain-damaging effects of long-term huffing when cut with mescaline and copious chasers of cocaine. Preacher, always generous with supply and willing to help a brother out, could never understand why the other mortals couldn't handle their shit.

These years of sex with The Substances altered only one thing about Preacher: his accent. He permanently adopted the speech of a working class cockney from Hackney or Tower Hamlets, possibly one with a Gaelic penchant for cross-cultural contamination given frequent mishmash of Scottish, Irish, and Welsh idioms. Preacher often sounded like a cross between Liam Gallagher on helium and what you would hope Cassidy the vampire from the *Preacher* comic book would sound like IRL.

Even still, that comparison does not fully explain Preacher's *nom de plume*. We started calling him "Preacher" because of his long drug-fueled rants on topics both esoteric and mundane. In a post-Tarantino, post-*Seinfeld* youth culture where caffeine-cursed conversations about nothing ate up magnificent hours of time-wasting pulchritude, Preacher ruled the pulpit. With Brad Pitt *12 Monkeys* middle fingers shooting left and right, Preacher would wax wise about anything, anywhere, sometimes prompted by a hit of The Good Stuff and always powered by the not-quite-natural in his veins. His was the *Dead Poets Society* of our little band of misfits back in the day, and everyone loved him for it.

The only other lasting effect the druggery made upon Preacher was a permanent look of madness: his right eye was perpetually open wider than the left, giving him the lasting impression that he was seeing something, confronted by a vision that no other could see or feel or hear. With his light brown hair prematurely graying and this batshit wily countenance screwing up the lifelines of his face, Preacher fit the bill for every stereotype of crazy you could imagine.

His victory, though, was in that none of this mattered to him. All Preacher was for was all.

While Deck did the other line, Preacher rolled us a joint, fired it up, sucked in two quick hits, then passed it to Pussy to get engage the circle. "Lassies first," he said.

We all pulled out chairs and sat down, kicked up feet, danced with Mary Jane, and had some frank conversations about your average Pokémon's enslavement.

3.

NOT EVEN IN THE BALLPARK

The next day, I wanted to get a jump on Deck's and Pussy's task, so I rolled over to the nearest Best Buy to start shopping. I quickly discovered, however, that their little wish list would never fit in the Camry in its entirety. So I purchased two of the requisite nine desktop PCs there, a few matching connective peripherals, and wondered what Tex and his big Ford pickup were up to. Sitting in the Best Buy parking lot with the window down, cigarette idling between two fingers and Third Eye Blind's "1000 Julys" bumping from the speakers, I dialed his phone and got no answer. I tried Preacher next, thinking that maybe they were hanging out for lunch somewhere.

"How're yeh?" he answered.

"Yo, you seen Tex?"

"I think he's Ballparkin' it today, Caje. Got a-a-whaddatheycallit. An audition or some shit."

"A tryout?"

"Yeah. A trout, wha."

"Isn't he already on the team?"

"I dunno, Caje. I only know what the oul' sod tells me. Pretty sure he's there though. Why for?"

"I need to borrow his truck. You wanna roll with me over there?"

"Fook-shite, aye. Come get me."

"You at the house?"

"Aye."

Preacher lived in Fairmount, an historic enclave tucked in between a revitalized area on Magnolia Avenue and another, more well-to-do neighborhood called Ryan Place. The houses in Ryan Place were bigger and older, and the streets were wider. Fairmount sported more quaint shotguns, duplexes, and cottages amongst run-down wooden fences and sagging porches. Both neighborhoods lay south of the hospital district and bore residents from a myriad of Funkytown gentries, from doctors and lawyers to mechanics and... well, Preacher.

Before moving to Fairmount, Preacher had laid claim to one-half of a leased duplex across the train tracks off Hemphill for damn near fifteen years. He needed little and found plenty wherever he was, and the rent house had done him solid for the period in which he'd occupied it. He'd still be there today had his girlfriend not finally kicked him in the ass hard enough to get out and find a better spot. Mikayla had been working her ass off for a long time in Fort Worth's legal community, moving from law school to paid attorney's work and making a name for herself representing corporate clients in insurance disputes, from which the spice flowed. The years with Preacher in that duplex had eventually stacked too high upon Mikayla, and one day, she demanded of him a more respectable, long-term dwelling in a nicer part of town. Preacher had suggested Fairmount only because that had been the last neighborhood he had remembered driving through that day, and Mikayla had seized upon it, finding a lovely little two-bedroom recently restored on Hurley. She had forced Preacher to shape up after they'd moved in, and now he only did his business outside on the wooden deck and cobblestone patio amongst a straight, dark green sea of Bermuda grass, where he took a perverse pleasure in decorating conscientiously with outdoors furniture from Lowe's.

They were a weird couple, and they had been together for a long time, but it worked, and really, who could argue with that?

I pulled up outside the blue-and-yellow Hurley house, honking the horn and turning up the stereo to identify myself. Preacher ambled through the open driveway gate in his weird, jerky gait, staggering as if one leg was longer than the other. He punched the keypad next to the automatic gate to close it and proceeded down the driveway. The Hurley house's front lawn had recently been clipped, and the odor of fresh-cut grass filled the air. I breathed it in, contemplating the idyllic little patch of heaven my friend had fashioned. Preacher got in the passenger seat and looked over at me.

"What?" he said.

"You got a nice place here, man, that's all," I replied.

Preacher pursed his lips and nodded his head jerkily, and I couldn't tell if he was agreeing with me or if that was just his way, his method of placating those with whom he spoke. He reached into his shirt pocket, withdrew a spliff, and set upon lighting it. I didn't mind. I welcomed the funky bunch parfumiery that would replace the standard cigarette smell that absorbed into the Camry's upholstery.

We jumped on 30 and headed east toward Dallas. Preacher fiddled with the MP3 selector till he found a song he liked. "Chevrolet" by Taj Mahal. It was around lunchtime, and Preacher talked me into the drive-thru of a Jack-in-the-Box on the way, fast food fare that our man could grub on in limitless quantity with no ill effects. I had to be careful though because Jack-in-the-Box was notorious for irritating Dooley bowels.

"What do yeh need Tex's truck for?" Preacher said through a mouthful of chicken sandwich.

"Deckhead gave me a shopping list last night, and I don't have room for it all in the Camry. I was hoping he'd let me use his truck to go pick everything up and deliver tonight."

"Aye. Yeh gonna eat that there thing o' fries?"

"Naw, go for it."

"Have yeh heard from yer da lately, Cajun?"

"Yeah, every other weekend or so we hop on the phone and shoot the shit. He's still giggin', doing his thing in Hattiesburg. He got a national customer not too long ago and does a little work out this way sometimes."

"Yeh workin' for him still then?"

"From time to time if there's something he needs done out here. Mostly trainings and paperwork drills he doesn't want to travel over here for, y'know?" I burped a mouthful of Jack-in-the-Box. "What about Mikayla, man? I ain't seen her in a while. What's she up to?"

"Same old, Cajun, same old. Killin' 'em softly at the law firm, oi. People love her over there. I guess she's good at it."

"You guess? Shit, Preacher, y'all been living together forever and you don't know if she's good at her job?"

"'S a job, Caje." He shrugged and relit his joint. "She's a lawyer, she...lawyers. She's gotta be good at it coz she's still doin' it."

"Have you *asked* her if she likes it?"

"Well...sure, we fookin' talk about it. She says it's cool."

"You do not seem convinced. You are not convincing me."

"Whaddya want me to say, yeh shite?"

"I just think that maybe you should *listen* to your girlfriend's less-than-obvious ways of communication, okay?"

"'Less-than-obvious?' Like wha? Mickey's pretty direct wi' me."

"Oh, I bet. You enjoying lighting up outside on the deck?"

"'S a nice deck. And I could use the sunshine, wha. Me poor, pale skin and whatnot."

"Does she not get all up in your business about your...business?"

Preacher exaggerated a face that said he didn't care. "Nah, she knows what's up. She's always known. That's why it works!"

"I'm just sayin', maybe one of these days she may want her boyfriend to be more than a boyfriend. And maybe when that happens, she'll also want her boyfriend to be in a line of work a little more stable than selling drugs."

"I DJ, too, yeh right bastard. Yer concern is noted." Preacher put on a bit of a pout. "Thank yeh for this therapy session, yeh fooker."

The beeping of my phone interrupted us, and I fished it from the console. The digital numbers on the screen caused me to swerve a tad, and I jerked right as the Camry's left tires made soft popping noises as they meandered over the rumble strips of the lane dividers. One hand on the steering wheel, I gripped the phone in the other hand, evaluating. Considering.

"Yeh gonna answer that?" Preacher said.

"I dunno," I replied. "Maybe not."

The number belonged to the 512 area code in Austin, and I recognized the rest of them even without looking at the name. I waited for a moment for the ringing to stop. Preacher looked on in silence, blowing smoke through the thin crack of the passenger side window. A second or two later, the phone's display resolved into a text message.

Call me ASAP. Need your help with
something.

I tossed the phone back into the console area under the dash.
Preacher noticed.

"Who's that?"

"You remember Rick Sears? Friend of mine from Longview?"

"Oi, sure do. How's he doin'? Didn't he join the FBI or some
shite?"

"He did." I gripped the steering wheel tightly with both hands.
"But he's not there anymore."

Preacher toked in silence for a few minutes, snatching a glance
at my face, which had changed.

"Some reason yer not takin' his call, Cajun?"

I could feel my jawline tighten and nerve pinch in that part of
your shoulder where the muscle meets your neck. "Just hanging
with you and Tex today."

"Plenty o' time before we get to the Ballpark, wha." Preacher
kept his gaze steady out the window, watching the brown country-
side flit by.

"*Maybe* I'd just like some privacy when I talked to him, okay?"

Preacher shrugged, still looking out the window. "Oi. Okay,
Cajun."

"We just have...a lot to talk about. That's all."

"What, yeh havenae talked to him in a while? How long? He
outta town? Phone broke?"

I shot him a pinched expression. "Would you drop it, Preacher?
Okay?"

Preacher held his hands up, still not meeting my gaze. "Okay,
okay."

A few minutes passed. The MP3 player got stuck in a cyclone
of Bruce Hornsby. Traffic on 30 intensified the more easterly we

traveled. Construction that had been in progress for decades on the interstate became visible as we crossed from Fort Worth into Arlington.

"We're just in different places these days," I finally said, aware somewhere inside that I didn't need to say this but needing to anyway. And knowing Preacher knew that too.

"Aye," Preacher said.

———

The Ballpark in Arlington occupies the same general area as a myriad of popular activities in the Metroplex. Arlington is known more as the Metroplex's middle ground, a DMZ between Fort Worth and Dallas lined with shopping plazas and any type of branded, mainstream consumer entertainment you can imagine. Nestled within the Ballpark area right off I-30 one could find Six Flags Over Texas, a few different water parks, and any number of national restaurant chains, plus Texas chains like the Pappas brands and Chuy's. From virtually any point in this area, you could look up and see the dome of the stadium reaching toward the sky in the distance, the home of the Dallas Cowboys. Arlington's mecca of consumerism extended to the Ballpark where legions of avid fans came to watch their Texas Rangers crack bats and round bases.

The regular season was still a few weeks off, so traffic around the Ballpark was light, and we found a parking spot on the street right next to the enormous red brick complex. Arlington's finest were not even ticketing for parking violations. Preacher and I bopped around the corner to the Rangers Baseball Club entrance where we jawed with the security guard about the day's schedule. As Preacher had expected, a special practice was underway within the Ballpark, this butting up against the incipient end to the club's spring training season in Arizona.

The yellow vested guard pushed back on our requests to get in to see this session, despite entreaties. He probably got that all the time, people claiming to be friends with or kin to someone on the team. I noticed a tattoo on his forearm, an octopus, and asked him about the ink. He proudly told us about his time in the Navy as a frogman, elite special operations work in underwater demolition. I told him that sounded a lot cooler than whatever it was Army special ops got up to, and we laughed. He let us in with no further hassle. Sometimes, people just wanna be *seen*.

We slipped through the deserted Ballpark to the dugouts where we could see and hear people on the field in practice uniforms. Club staff peppered the field, some with towels, some with stopwatches, all evaluating players for the variety of athletic factors required to benchmark performance on the state's premier baseball team. Tex stood out like a god amongst men, a superhero test pilot attended to by scurrying support personnel. He was swinging at home plate, decked out in an unmarked uniform and helmet. As we closed in, we could see two men in athletic coaching gear—blue caps and too-tight shorts with Rangers-branded moisture wicking polos tucked into them—watching intently as Tex swung at pitches barreling in from the practice pitcher on the mound. In the few minutes it took Preacher and I to get down to the dugout, Tex swung at and missed a total of four pitches.

There wasn't much happening in the vicinity of the dugout as we closed in, so no one challenged us as we made our way onto the field. We kept a nonthreatening distance but watched steadfastly as Tex swung again and missed. Five for five. On the sixth swing and miss, we could tell Tex was not moving naturally, his left foot coming up and going down in a staggered motion. I didn't know much about baseball, but that didn't look at all natural to me. I said as much to Preacher.

"Oi, our lad's not movin' like he should," Preacher agreed.

Tex smacked the bat on the ground, radiating frustration. One of the tight-shorted Rangers staff made a sharp cutting motion across his neck at the pitcher and walked over to Tex. They traded a couple words and then Tex listened closely, still and stolid in the midday sun. Finally, Tex took off his batting helmet, put the bat under one giant arm, and shook the hand of the staff member. A club boy ran up at that moment to retrieve both items from Tex's hands, and the big man accepted an ass-slap from a couple other players. His eyes lingered on the backs of those players as they returned to practice and as he lumbered toward the dugout. He fiddled with the Velcro snap on his batting glove as he shuffled. He didn't see us and I didn't see his eyes till he got closer to us, so I later regretted the sharp whistle I released with which to catcall him.

"*Heeeeyyy batter-batter-batter!*" I shouted.

Tex strode up slowly, a half-smile on his square jaw. "What are you two shitbirds doin' here?"

Preacher smacked Tex on the shoulder in a motion that looked like a squirrel bouncing off an elephant. "We're yer biggest fans, Tex! Can yeh sign yer rookie cards for us?"

Tex made a matter-of-fact expression and shielded his brow from the sun. "Well, I don't think you're gonna want this old lunk's autograph anymore, fellas. Looks like my days of tossin' the ball might be over."

My face fell, and that's when I started to put it all together. "What happened, man?"

"Y'all remember that twist I took last year? Got my leg hung up coming down that fire escape?"

"Savin' maidens that needed savin', if I recall correctly."

Tex lifted his left leg, stretching the muscles in calf and knee slowly before planting cleated foot back down on the dirt somewhat unceremoniously. "It's been fuckin' with my posture. And my swing. I haven't hit one goddamn ball since I walked back on for my tryout."

"Thought y'were already on the team, Texas," Preacher said.

"I was but they make you try out again after a big injury like that takes you off the roster for longer than a couple months." Tex looked at his feet, and he kicked at the dust. "My sprint time's down too. Put those two factors together, and the club sees too much risk. They ain't gonna shell out bucks for a busted leg."

"Buncha faggots," I said and obliviously missed Tex's subsequent wince. "I'm sorry, man. Are they at least gonna let you stick around for the season? Maybe do something else on the team?" I was hopelessly naive about the business of baseball. Me and sports go together about as well as oil and water: you could make a salad out of them, but you'd have to throw out the lettuce.

"I dunno yet. Coach told me to come back and talk to the admin guys next week. I gotta go turn in my gear though, which means I'm probably done." Tex looked at us. "Y'all don't know where a washed-up baseball bastard could find some work, do ya?"

At his full height of six-six, Texas was possessed of an athlete's bulk, machined every day in weight rooms and running trails. When not in uniform, he only wore plain white T-shirts, jeans, and boots, and sometimes a nondescript cowboy hat of the minimalist variety. His biceps and triceps made other shirts jealous. His chiseled jaw evoked a Space Ghost-ish, Toth-like profile at any angle and ever belied the most winsome, sincere smile you could hope to find on a good guy's face. Tex kept his blonde hair short on the sides and in back with some length to the bangs up front that were currently matted by sweat and the padding of the batter's helmet. He always knew the right thing to say, and he always said the right thing at the right time. He was gentle and soft-spoken, the first true gentleman I ever met in my own age group. No other man embodied the all-American good guy than Tex, and every true son of Texas wished to be seen in his mold, enviously or otherwise. Hence the nickname.

The guy was no-shit Captain America with the likability to match. People wrote slash fiction about this dude.

Tex and I met for the first time in eighth grade on the football field, me coming into a strange new school at the tail end of the Texas junior high experience and pursuing favor wherever I could find it. Football in any Texas town often provides a quick pathway to camaraderie, and after getting my ass kicked a couple times in regular P.E. by the local Hispanic gang, I hungered for those comrades. What I had not expected at that tender age was the same ever-escalating series of tests and taunts, tailored for the new kid on the team. I regularly got sandpapered by my new teammates until Tex came around.

At the time, Tex already towered over everyone else on the team. He lit up our opponents as an inexhaustible linebacker for the offense and two-technique for the defense. So it was really nothing for him to easily extricate me from a pile-on of tacklers in the locker room, pulling me out by the scruff of the neck like a cat. He had threatened the offending teammates with an outstretched index finger and a terse, "Nobody likes to get beat up." Tex was my first Fort Worth friend.

We played together on the freshman and J.V. teams at Paschal, but I dropped out my sophomore year to pursue a burgeoning interest in the blues. Tex kept right on dominating the football field. In addition to his ability to shake any tackle, he was faster than a prairie fire with a tail wind. This translated well when he took an interest in baseball, and Tex played for four years on the Paschal varsity team, generating an incredible amount of public interest with his unfailing ability to consistently hit homers from the most inscrutable pitchers. He got a full ride scholarship to Iowa State, and he made a name for himself on the college circuit as a short stop. He missed football though, so once his time at Iowa came to an end, he took a break from a baseball career to try out for the Cowboys back home in the state that he missed.

Tex's NFL career never really took off because he wasn't the type of guy to play politics. Tex wanted to take people at their word and assume the best about everyone, an attitude instilled by his family of Texas ranchers and military servicemen. Tex unfortunately couldn't compete with the backstabbing and the inflated egos rampant in professional football, the real world high stakes one had to ruthlessly pursue to get their money. As a result, Tex only started one season, and he was eventually benched when a more noticeable, marketable defensive end got recruited.

He had studied business in school because why not. That marketable background enabled him to bounce around and find plenty of employment selling insurance or cars, but it was only to put food on his table. When he tired of those jobs, he would take up residence back home on his parents' ranch in Aledo, trading the glitzy life of a professional athlete for the simplicity and solitude of rustling cattle. Tex hadn't wanted much out of life, and he was generally pretty happy with this arrangement. Or so we all thought.

Someone eventually realized the Paschal baseball legend had made his way back to the Metroplex. A recruiter for the Texas Rangers found Tex on the ranch one day and offered him a spot on the team if he could replicate his college record. Tex tried out, crushed it, and shipped off to the Rangers' spring training camp in Arizona. He walked on that season to a career record of twelve home runs in one game, and brought that record to twelve consecutive games, rescuing the Rangers from a years-long slump that drew DFW fans in droves to games both home and away.

Tex would never talk too much about what happened that day or even the injury that lead his coaches to make their decision. Despite his size and countenance, Tex could fade into the background pretty easily, and that was not hard to do with me and Preacher around.

Preacher was busy lighting up a cigarette, conscious enough to recognize he ought not to be caught rolling a J on the baseball field, but still oblivious to any polite customs one might expect to observe in typical public situations. One of the field hands—a boy hoping to climb the baseball club ladder the wrong way by diving into administration instead of athleticism—alternated between looks of shock and outrage as he observed Preacher. Tex caught the boy's eye, expressionless, and he sauntered off as Tex watched.

"Well, it just so happens Cajun here's got a job for Deckhead and Pussy Control he could use yer help with," Preacher said.

"Oh, yeah?" Tex said, brows upraised in question.

"Yeah, you mind driving us around to pick up some gear?" I said. "They gave me a shopping list. Also need to roll by the airport and hit a Travelex beforehand."

Tex looked around the Ballpark field for a deliberate moment. He would never return there nor would he ever find opportunity to view a baseball park from quite the same angle. He'd never again watch the sun crest behind the stadium risers from the field, quickly escaping the dusky blue and pink sky chasing it down. He tossed his batting glove on the ground and nodded his head toward the dugout.

"Let me grab a shower, and I'll meet y'all at the truck."

4.

PLAYED THESE MINOR KEYS

The great thing about the Metroplex is that you can find whatever home goods you need anywhere you want within a short drive. Within the last few years, growth in the small communities between Fort Worth and Dallas had contributed to new roads and sprawling shopping centers with every imaginable national retail outlet and eatery plus a galaxy of Texas-originating chains. DFW Airport sat right in the middle of this retail mecca, so once I converted Deckhead's foreign currency to usable dollars at a Travelex in Terminal D, we found plenty of options to complete the shopping trip. The spree went a lot faster with Preacher and Tex helping, and only a few hours passed before we had Tex's snow white

F-150 packed full of computer boxes and pallets. The truck over-flowed with so much gear in the bed and the backseat that we all had to sit up front: me squeezed between Tex and Preacher, perched on the middle front seat console, a regular triple-threat of wannabe cow-pokin'. Tex's truck was roomy though, so it wasn't too uncomfortable.

On our way back, my gut started churning something fierce. We Dooleys possess a genetic marker in our storied chromosomal makeup that sometimes manifests in what others may call irritable bowel syndrome. However, none of us have ever been diagnosed with it despite decades of Dooley men stinking up various dwellings, offices, and enclosures with the dirty, dirty stench of our insides. It didn't matter if we had eaten a banana or a pot of spicy crawfish: our asses would find some way of letting you know, by sound or scent, often both. And sometimes by sight and taste, God help us.

I struggled to contain the gastric explosion that crept up inside me and failed. The beef was both wet and horrific, instantly recognizable as such by Tex and Preacher who recoiled from me as the rancid affront assailed them.

"Jaysis fookin' wept!" Preacher coughed, rolling down his window.

"Did you just shit yourself?" Texas said, a slight tinge of panic in his voice.

"I'm sorry!" I crowed. "Something I ate's tearing me up."

"That Jack-in-the-Crack's crackin' yer jack," Preacher said, lighting a cigarette and blowing smoke inside the truck's cab, sucking tar to combat the horror and coughing like he'd been poisoned.

"*You* made me get that Jack-in-the-Crack, Preacher!"

It was almost funny how no one debated or contested who had been responsible for this olfactory assault. Tex and Preach knew me pretty well. It was not the first time I had blown ass like that, nor would it be the last. The only thing that had really changed was my drive to blame it on someone else. Better to just own it, y'know?

We stopped at a Lowe's in Keller to procure a tarp with which to tie over the gear to keep it out of sight and unexposed to the wind. We also had to air out the cab of Tex's truck, and I ran inside to check my drawers and take a massive, Jack-in-the-Box shit. *Jack-in-the-Shit.* Hah! Those Dooley insides. Preacher and I smoked another couple cigarettes in the parking lot to make sure the cab had been cleared of nasal offense, and when Tex was satisfied, we got moving again.

Back at The Gym, Deckhead and Pussy Control helped us unload the truck. We unloaded boxes of PC towers, monitors, keyboards, CAT-5 ethernet cable, and peripherals in plastic packaging. All of this went through the back loading door and directly into Deck's inner sanctum, where we stacked it nice and neat in a corner to Pussy's specification. Not a bad haul for any of us. We made out okay with the funds, too: there was about two-hundred, three-hundred left. Not enough to help Tex out with future shortages on rent, although Preacher and I tried to get him to take it all. He wouldn't, though, because he's Tex. The The dough could underwrite a helluva night out commiserating about it though. So with Pussy and Deck satisfied and a couple roadies pilfered from The Gym's fridge, Texas, Preacher, and the Cajun rode again.

I never argued with Texas or Preacher about where we settled for drinking on any given day or night. My weakness for neon lights and glitz usually pulled me toward the swankier, upscale ostentatiousness of Sundance Square or whatever they're calling the college hangouts off West 7th across from the old Montgomery Ward building these days. Tex always had a soft spot for The Stockyards and any gin-joint findable down there, tourist trap or otherwise. Preacher gravitated to TCU hangouts around University and Bluebonnet Circle where aging graduates from all Fort Worth high schools mingled across generations and roared about football. The march of time had claimed many of our favorites. Nothing slowed progress in Fort Worth. The Hi-Hat and The Cellar got chopped for new campus-adjacent apartments. The Plaid Pig got subsumed by a deli. Rumors were swirling lately that counterculture shithole The Poop Deck was on its way out, too. Sad days in post-generation Funkytown.

The Oui Lounge was always a good bet for Paschalite alumni, and we could always count on running into old classmates there whom none of us had seen in forever and a day. Those nights often led to darts, pool, and big stories about old times. I could tell from Tex's demeanor, however, that a scene of that nature wouldn't necessarily hoe his row tonight. A three-way playoff of rock-paper-scissors threw bones toward The Aardvark and not for nothing: Soviet Space was playing that night, a sure indicator of rousing spirits in the face of adversity.

The 'Vark squats on part of a Berry Street block a few doors down from Fuzzy's Tacos. This august institution—once competing band-for-band and shot-for-shot with The Hi-Hat—had staged live music and stiff pours since 1978. A perennial favorite of college kids seeking cheap beer and cheaper cover charges, The Aardvark also drew live music aficionados from all over The Fort, mixing age groups and classes in dark wooden walls and poorly lit corridors. You could catch Texas music legends like Bob Schneider or Bowling for Soup on regular rotation through The 'Vark's Thursday-through-Sunday lineups. On the off days, the bar still offered plenty of tall drinks, and you could match wits with your friends over any number of beer-spattered board games. Local church groups even gathered there Sunday mornings though how they found the verve to sing choir through the smell of that beer-soaked floor I'll never figure out.

We paid covers gladly and grabbed a high table halfway between the bar and the stage. The floor had already been cleared of most of the sit-down tables in advance of the show's start, which suited me just fine. Years of hopping around stages and mugging near amplifiers were beginning to take their toll on my hearing, and the band that night wasn't exactly easy listening. Shouting at my compatriots to speak up all night would only irritate us all and likely lead to another showdown with some crew of fuckwits seeking dominance within limited hook-up offerings. That may have been an overstatement. Soviet Space always drew good trim.

"Look, Steve Ferrone is the best drummer in music history *period*," I was saying, brandishing two extended fingers at Preacher that lightly gripped a half-smoked Marlboro Light. "Let's review: Duran Duran, *Notorious*: Check. Eric Clapton, *24 Nights*: Check. Tom Petty and the Heartbreakers, *Wildflowers* to present: Check! Not good enough? How 'bout Average White Band? How 'bout Chaka Khan? How 'bout the motherfuckin' *Saturday Night Live Band*?"

"Oi, Cajun, how can yeh classify 'best'?" Preacher was objecting. "What about Stewart Copeland? What about Neil Peart?"

"Who's Neil Peart?" said Tex.

"Rush," I said.

"What's Rush?"

"It's Canadian."

"Does that mean it's good?"

"No, that means it's Canadian."

"So what's Rush then?"

"It's a whole 'nother level, Tex, drums aside."

"Huh." Tex didn't know music at the nerd level where Preacher and I roosted, his G-major-sevenths from his tremolos, so to speak, but he was always interested.

"All's I'm sayin' is Neal Peart could run flam circles around Steve Ferrone," Preacher said. "The guy could compose drums-only fookin' music on his fookin' own, fer fook's sake! So could Copeland!"

"So?" I said. "Steve Ferrone's flams *own*, Preacher. Listen to the shit he pulls on 'White Room' on *24 Nights*. That sumbitch may not be as snazzy or as jazzy as Peart or Copeland, but he is in the pocket, baby. Every time. That guy backbones every band he plays in while *at the same time* flourishing shit like Billy Blanks doin' Tae-bo wearin' bowties."

Preacher scrunched up his face at me, exhaling dragon tooth streams of smoke from his nostrils. "The fook are yeh babblin' about, Cajun?"

"I'm just sayin'! I think you're makin' some conclusions on this whole Steve Ferrone issue here while not in full possession of the facts."

Tex interjected, Coors Lite in hand: "Tom Petty and the Heartbreakers have been putting out some good stuff the past few years, Preacher."

I smacked the tabletop with an urgent toldja-so maneuver, bouncing on the balls of my feet. "See? The voice of the common man has spoken, Preacher. I rest my case."

Preacher's one wide eye seemed to jump out of its socket while the other one narrowed, his movements spastic. "Texas don't know his Dixie Chicks from his Chick Corea! Oi, and he fookin' ain't got The Ear like you and I do, yeh right fooker. No offense, Texas."

"None taken."

I shook my head at Preacher, face non-placating and smug. "It don't matter. My point is made."

"Yer a right shite, Cajun."

"You don't love me like you used to, Preacher."

"Fellas," Texas interrupted, smacking the half-empty Coors Lite can down on the table to get our attention, one finger extended from the aluminum grip toward the door. "Y'all seein' what I'm seein'?"

It wasn't quite showtime yet, so dusk's fading light still shone a blue ray through The Aardvark's front windows, creating the only cogent pool of light the bar would see all night. Into this pool swished the heavy oaken front door, admitting a lonely pair of long legs in starch-crinkled jeans. Carefully shined Justin boots carried the legs in, not too glamorously polished so as to show off the ridges of the ostrich skin, but just so that they conveyed respect for the venue without dust or mud. A pressed blue and white checkered shirt was tucked into the Wranglers, framed by a thick leather belt with a modest chrome buckle that glinted with an inlaid pattern of engraving. The newcomer wore a weathered leather vest over his shirt, the kind you'd never catch on most of the urban cowboys flitting though Fort Worth but seemingly at home on this tall man's shoulders, dark brown and unbuttoned. A bolo tie closed the top button of his shirt to cover his neck, showcasing a simple mother-of-pearl clasp that matched the shirt's snaps. The tall man's face was obscured by the shadow cast from his gray hat, a Diamond J classic shaped to cowboy's style and bearing just enough frayed wear around the edges of the brim to prove he actually wore the thing every day, all day instead of just out to places like The 'Vark. As he walked into the bar, the dim lighting illuminated the crags and valleys of an older man's face, the droop of long jowls and the wrinkles of years outdoors. His fully silver mustache hung down with the jowls, covering his mouth and lips and giving them the appearance of perpetual sorrow and displeasure. But if you looked carefully enough beneath the brim of the man's hat, you wouldn't find those emotions at all. No, instead you'd see the twinkle of ever-observant eyes staring back at you, evaluating the space between you and he, recording and assessing everything.

His cowboy's gait betrayed bowed legs as he ambled over to the bar to order a beer. As he raised a hand to grab the bartender's attention, his vest rode up ever so slightly, and I could make out the holstered gun clipped to the back of his jeans and belt, right next to a matching handcuffs case bearing the brand of a five-pointed star with balls at the tips. The brand of another kind of Texas Ranger.

"That ain't…" I said with incredulity, despite what my eyes reported to my brain. "For serious?"

"Oi, that's him, lads," Preacher said, tapping his beer can on the tabletop with an ever-increasing tempo.

"Shit, guys, we gotta buy him a beer," Tex said, the usual serenity of his face broken by sudden wonder, like a child seeing their first bicycle by the fireplace on Christmas morning.

The man turned around to survey the bar, a bottle of Shiner in one hand. Once his scanning eyes reached our table, the three of us waved to him, exhibiting the kind of idiot grins found in bad sitcoms. The old, tall man did not acknowledge our frantic waves and simple faces, but he did start to head our way, one measured boot-step after another.

"Oh, shite, he's comin' this way," Preacher whispered, hands suddenly a-flit over his body, checking pockets for contraband. "Lads, I wasn't prepared to visit with the law tonight."

"Something tells me he's off-duty," I said with a chuckle.

The man idled up to our table and set his Shiner down next to Tex's Coors Lite, my Dos Equis, and Preacher's Miller Lite. Had it been a dick-measuring contest, we all would have folded right then. The man's face remained stolid and impassable as he inclined his neck to us, eyes regarding each of us in turn.

"Well, good evening, fellas," he said in a voice of crushed gravel and basso. "Seems like I ain't seen y'all since ya took your training wheels off your bikes."

Roger Hulen could meet Tex eye-to-eye with little more than a slight tilt of his neck, but he didn't bow up, didn't suck in, didn't put on airs that didn't already emanate from his true Texan figure. Each of us stood a little straighter in his presence, wiped our mouths, and met his eyes directly as he looked over each of us with a firm gaze. Tex was the first one to grip Hulen's hand, each of their oversized mitts clasping comfortably and not-at-all competitively, calluses in different places.

"Mister Hulen, it's an honor to see you again, sir," Tex said, clearly wide-eyed and gracious.

"Cochrane, isn't it?" Hulen said, pumping Tex's hand once and nodding twice. "From Paschal?"

"Yes, sir," Tex replied. "Thanks for remembering."

Now Hulen did smile, and he tapped the side of one brow with the fingers released from Tex's bear paw. "Like a steel trap, son." He looked over to me. "Jack Dooley, right?"

I stuck my hand out now and let Hulen damn near crush it in the manliest handshake I'd ever feel. "Yessir!" I said effusively, a little too fast and a little too loud, betraying the number of beers I'd consumed.

"I saw your mother a couple months ago at a convention bureau luncheon. Seems like she's still opening doors all over the world."

"Yessir, she sure is."

Then Hulen looked sidelong at the third member of our party, he whose mere visage begged for institutionalization and a breathalyzer test. "And you must be..."

"Preacher, sir," said Preacher, sticking out his own hand and screwing up his face in his best approximation of a smile, which ended up a toothy grimace framed by his wide-eyed, maniac's gaze. "How're yeh?"

"Fair to middlin', boys. Fair to middlin'."

Roger Hulen was another kind of Texas Ranger, the kind that carried semiautomatic weapons and evidence testing kits in the back of his state-issue Bronco. He was assigned to Company B in Garland, just northeast of us, a division held over from a time before absorption by the Texas Department of Public Safety. Texas Rangers had evolved from the special law enforcers of the state's past. Their legendary group was established in 1823 or 1835 (depending on which history you read and whether or not you were a fan of Stephen F. Austin) as a loose paramilitary unit to stave off marauding Indian tribes and Mexican banditos that raided unprotected settlements of newly emigrated Texans. In these tall times, Rangers chased bank robbers, busted up riots on behalf of incapable local law, and shot up their fair share of frontier Texas. Sometimes. Given their unique pedigree and elite ranks, only a single Ranger could be spared for any given raid, robbery, fugitive, or kidnapping. In every case, that one Ranger was enough, begetting the classic Texas saying (albeit questionably apocryphal), "One riot, one Ranger."

This particular Ranger's territory had included the Metroplex for well over thirty years. A Fort Worth native descending from the same Hulen family for whom the miles-long street is named, Roger embodied all the classic cowboy majesty one could want in their local lawmen. He gave his time freely to community groups, volunteering at Habitat for Humanity on weekends when he wasn't chasing shitheels or investigating murders. We had originally met Hulen when he came to Paschal to talk about the Rangers in a special assembly. I still remember crowding into the creaky wooden auditorium chairs between Tex and Preacher, struggling to make out every word Hulen uttered about the venerated Texas institution and the cases they prosecuted. After the main assembly, we had gotten to meet Hulen directly, and he'd given his card to every Paschal kid that wanted one, encouraging all to call him anytime about anything.

I accepted that invitation easily around the time that Deckhead went to jail for killing Pussy Control's stepbrother. I'd struggled with reconciling the things that had happened to Pussy, Deck's last resort (the turnabout for which I'd not yet been told by either), and what had happened to Deck as a result. Hulen took my call and listened to my concern over steaming mugs of coffee at The Noble Bean, interrupting nary a once and never treating me like the whiny high school snot I was. He had talked to me about the law, about courts, about the real bad things that happened in real bad ways off the TV screen. Afterwards, Hulen had stepped in on professional courtesy to put in a good word for Deckhead, understanding the situation in a way that few FWPD cops at that time could. Hulen's specialty at that point in his career was investigating and apprehending sex offenders, and he'd seen his share of shitty situations before Deckhead's revenge story reached his patient ears through repeated phone calls and meetups with one Jack Dooley. Hulen took an interest in our little crew of Paschalites after that, and he had explained to us that even though he felt for Pussy Control and sympathized for her boyfriend, Deckhead had to answer for perpetrating a man's crime. It had only been through the grace of God Almighty in Hulen's storied view that Deck had gotten the juvie sentence he did, and we should all be so thankful. But Hulen's word helped get Deck out fast, all the while oblivious to what really happened.

Somebody cut Roger Hulen from some kinda rarified Texas leather, and everybody was better having him in our lives, whether you knew him personally or not.

I'd always wonder if it had been Pussy that went down for her stepbrother's shooting, what would Hulen have said or done then?

When Deck was serving his abrogated, Hulen-wired time, Rick Sears was getting me hooked on *Homicide: Life on the Street* and Andrew Vachss novels. Comparing the hard boiling of my youth's crime fiction to an honest-to-Bob-the-Subgenius, swagger-free cowboy lawman like Hulen prompted all manner of child empowerment fantasies. I traded my *X-Men* comics for beaten-up Elmore Leonard paperbacks, the Westerns and the moderns. I made up excuses to call Hulen on the phone, which he often turned to positive purpose by proposing I volunteer for community service at Habitat some weekends even when I didn't want to. It had been worth it just to be around this Texas Ranger who would regale me with case histories of procedurals and shootouts. I'd dig up Hulen's cases in archives of *The Fort Worth Star-Telegram* and *The Dallas Morning News,* spending hours in libraries with microfiche machines, paging through the past to consume content that I'd later repurpose into projects and papers for history and language arts classes. I was so into this stuff in high school that my Mom wondered why I didn't chase a criminal justice degree at a good Texas school instead of fucking off to Southern Miss in Hattiesburg. I wondered about that too sometimes. The short story is that I just missed my Dad, and there were easier things to do in Mississippi, things that involved cheap alcohol, bandstands, and buddies.

We all know how that turned out, though.

"This is the last place I expected to find you, sir," Tex said with a grin. "What brings you?"

"Can't an old man have a musical hobby?" Hulen snickered beneath his mustache. "Got a lot of listenin' to do with retirement a-comin' on me."

"You're retired?" I said.

"Not yet." Hulen took a long, slow pull on his Shiner bottle. "But the runway's starting to clear."

"I guess we just didn't figure you for a rocker much," Tex said. "There's a pretty loud post-punk band playing in a few minutes up there."

"Oh, I know. My nephew plays on one of the guit-fiddles. The one with the four strings."

Preacher and I did a double-take, and he said, "Yer a Soviet Space fan then, oi?"

"Kinda hard not to be with my daughter all up in my business about their shows 'round here." Hulen chuckled again. "She makes me listen to all their music, but I confess I got a hankerin' for what these kids do. 'Evidence for Running Away' is a great song."

Preacher and I could not hide our astonishment. I had to test him. "'The diploma that you wear...'"

"'...Around your neck says you're done with me,'" Hulen finished. "It's a good tune."

Preacher smacked his palms on his forehead and started rummaging through pockets again to light up a cigarette, more nervous than usual with a proper, badge-wearing member of the state's law enforcement ranks present. "Oi, he's a right ringer, this one. Fookin' uncle to Soviet Space!"

"That's the kid that sings 'All Star Falling,' right?" I said. "The one where he trades the bass to play keys?"

"Yep. Jimmy. Great kid. Hope he sticks with it. He's really talented. They're all TCU kids, and Jimmy's in the political science program." The walrus droop of Hulen's mustache evened out as a smile lurked beneath its silver hairs. The pride radiated off him.

"Well, shit," Tex said, polishing off his beer. "This calls for a celebration. Can we buy you a drink, Mister Hulen? 'Nother Shiner?"

Hulen inclined his head and touched the brim of his hat. "I'd be much obliged, Mister Cochrane. Thank ya. Hope y'all don't mind an old man sidling up to your table and taking a stool. My back would oblige that too."

"Make yourself at home," I said, clinking my beer can on Hulen's bottle.

Tex left to retrieve fresh beers, peeling off a couple of the tenners on the tabletop from our Jetfire funds. Preacher excused himself with a nervous look at Hulen, headed out back to blow a J as surreptitiously as possible. That left me and Roger Hulen to watch the boys from Soviet Space file onto the stage to sound check.

"As I recall, you used to play some music yourself, didn't you, Jack?"

"Yeah, I sure did. Drums in high school. Blues band. I sang for this other band in Mississippi more recently, though."

"Really? You still sing?"

"Naw, not so much."

"You oughtta sit in with Jimmy and the boys. I'm sure they'd love to have you."

I grinned the grin of the young who appease their elders. I've had practice.

"Hell, if that were me up there," I said, "I'm sure I wouldn't want nobody interrupting my show. I'll sing along down here with you, Mister Hulen, in case I forget the words."

"Aw, hell, I don't know shit, son," Hulen said, draining his beer bottle with a curled lip that let seep a dusty chuckle.

I winked at him, my grin remaining in place but eyes no longer matching the mirth. "You ain't the only one."

Tex returned with beers at that moment, and we toasted again. Preacher came back, too, carrying with him the perfume scent of some lady from whom he'd obviously scored a couple squirts to mask the weed smell permeating his body. I don't think Hulen cared. He was off-duty and I'd never heard of him being big on pot busts. We shot the shit for another few minutes until Soviet Space got to the business of rocking out. The boys on stage wore faded T-shirts and ripped jeans, the leave-it uniform of post-punk, post-grunge passersby everywhere, shirts likely pulled for five dollars a pop at Target. They were all young, college aged, fresh faced, and possessed of sharp haircuts. Fort Worth kids had always gravitated toward the preppy, and even in a Nirvana-inspired generation, the culture held.

The movement onstage drew the attention of the crowd, eliciting "WOOTS!" and whistles, jiggled tits, and thrown elbows from claim jumpers seeking to call the best vantage nearest the band. The four fellows that comprised Soviet Space turned inward into that pre-show circle of confirmation and safety, the last prayerful moment where the multiples become one. The drummer counted two short clicks on his drumsticks and completed the measure with an introductory drumroll that would make Dave Grohl drool, launching into the opener, "Blowing Up." The excitement and drive of this song propelled even more of The 'Vark's milling population toward the stage as well-balanced JBLs exploded with double-guitar melody and a thick undercurrent of bass.

We stayed were we were, of course, sitting up to peer over heads. The Aardvark was small enough and the stage high enough that virtually everyone inside could snag a great view of the band. Preacher started headbanging immediately, not necessarily a dyed-in-the-wool Soviet Space fan but just into a good hard rock riff. Tex bobbed his head sort of in time, but his musical handicap held him back from really connecting with the song like me and Preacher. Hulen only moved when he sipped his beer, but you could see in his eyes an excitement and pride for his nephew's band that also belied true enjoyment.

Before anybody had a chance to applaud the end of the song, Soviet Space immediately pivoted into another and another, a frenetic pace of rockage mirrored from song to delivery. The tempo had picked up a half-click faster than the versions they had recorded on their self-financed album, but it didn't matter. People ate it up with a spoon. Screams, sloshed beer, college bros throwing arms around non-college bros, and girls raising arms to shake and gyrate.

They took a short break for Hulen's nephew, Jimmy, to hand his bass guitar over to one of the guitar players and take up a small Korg keyboard. The others in the band were still wiping sweat from their faces and sucking down short doses of beer and water when Jimmy idled on the opening keys of "All Star Falling," a Blink-182-ish number that had gotten some radio play around Fort Worth. I looked over at Hulen, and he was mouthing the words, prompting me to do the same with some actual voice behind it. Preacher slung his arm over my shoulder, and we swayed as the band came in on the chorus, returning to their hard rock root with shredded guitar licks and harmonized vocals on top of Jimmy's lead.

Preacher joined me in singing the chorus, and it was one verse in before my voice cracked. Nobody else could hear over the din in the bar, but Preacher could. He eyed me with strange physiognomy as I bleated, off-key and scratchy, like a retarded Speak 'n' Spell. "All Star Falling's" chorus climbs a couple steps toward the higher octave in an innovative dirge, and somehow, I couldn't do it. The song was right in my range, but I butchered every lyric. Catching onto this, perplexed, I let my craggy voice fade away into the cries of the crowd and the amplified electricity of the band's reverberations. I caught Preacher's glare, which had normalized into the closest thing he could display as concern what with his pot-potent eye. I offered him a shrug and a face that said, "Huh-wha?", indicating my own surprise.

A few more times that night, I tried to match consonance with Soviet Space, singing straight over "Evidence for Running Away" and experimenting with attaining any of the three harmonies on "Arm Circles"... failing at each attempt. My voice would not euphonize. I could not jump from major to minor, and every sustained pitched sounded flat and scratchy. I even broke down coughing at one point, covering what was only a tickled throat with deeper rasps so as not to engender concern from my tablemates. Had I attempted this in a quieter room, Tex would have patted me on the back and Preacher's suspicious gaze would have congealed further.

What the hell was wrong with me?

"Helluva band, huh? Makes ya feel like sangin', don't it?" Hulen was saying to me as he and everyone else around us applauded the close of the set. I downed my fourth beer of the evening and joined in, offering Hulen a grin that I didn't feel.

"Yeah, I s'pose," I said.

5.

PARTNERS AND OTHER BROTHERS

I woke up the next morning only because the phone bleated for attention, and in drunken stupor from the night prior, I had failed to excise it from the bed where I'd landed clothes-clad and heavy-lidded. We had stayed out after Soviet Space wrapped, crushing beers with Roger Hulen and his nephew Jimmy for a bit and then stumbling down Berry Street to get an after-hours twelve-pack at King's Liquor. Tex knew one of the stock boys, and the guy made some bucks on the side selling after hours to trusted customers. We were pretty knackered by that point, so we hung out in the alley behind the liquor store and drained the beer, Preacher jabbering the whole time about the downfall of good live music venues in Fort Worth. He wasn't wrong, and Tex and I were entertained.

Nothing mattered right then with that goddamn phone screaming at me at the crack of noon. I let it ring to voicemail, got up, stumbled into the bathroom, puked, cleaned myself up, and then squirted out some drunk shits while I tried to regain my vision. The phone kept ringing the whole time, and I finally had to concede to its signal. I splashed a handful of lukewarm water on my face to at least minimally combat the cocktail flu and answered the fifteenth call with a "WHAT?!"

"I figured if I bugged you long enough you'd answer the phone," Rick Sears said on the other end of the line. I immediately felt like shit, angry at myself for yelling at him, knowing I'd never tell him that, but also subconsciously confused by the emotion's origin given what Rick and I had been through together. I stumbled into the kitchen, sans pants, to make coffee.

"Rick, hey, shit, sorry, sorry," I dribbled, and the voice that came out sounded like I was spitting cotton. The sounds I created in the kitchen trying to get the coffee pot on made a ruckus the likes of which an epileptic burglar would have laughed.

"Well, you sound like shit," Rick said, the hint of amusement in his otherwise even-toned voice.

"Ahhh, blow me. Sorry I haven't called you back. Been busy 'round here."

"Oh, yeah? Still moving pulp at Lone Star?"

"Welllll, not exactly." I belched and it felt good. It smelled awful. "Just...doin' my thing. How's Austin treatin' ya?"

"Good. Still adjusting to the suburban life, even though this whole town might as well be one big, weird suburb. *Buckaroo Banzai's* on at The Alamo Drafthouse this month, so that's a night out I'm looking forward to."

"Cool, cool. Been a while since I seen that'n."

Silence drew from a beat to longer. Discomfort crept in, and I ignored it by filling a coffee cup and fishing the amaretto creamer out of the fridge. Rick could hear me fidgeting in the kitchen, I bet. He finally broke the detente a second before it got too awkward.

"So...I *know* you got my messages..."

"Yeah, yeah, I did, I did." I grimaced at myself. *Johnny Two-Times.* "So you said you needed help with something...?"

"Yes." I could hear in the background that Rick was shuffling papers or folders or something on a desk somewhere. "I could actually use a favor, and I figure you owed me one."

He wasn't wrong. "What kinda favor?"

"So I've got this case that's just opened up with us. Guy looking for help finding his son. He thinks the kid was kidnapped by his mother, my client's wife." A pause. "I don't have the kind of resources I used to for a thing like this."

I plopped into my maroon couch-chair, gulped coffee, and lit a cigarette. It stank inside my apartment. "Uh-huh."

Another pause. Strained silence. "Which is why I called you."

"What, you think I'm some kinda...skiptrace now?"

"Don't give me that shit. I know who *you* are."

That last bit stung at me like a copperhead snake sneaking a taste of flesh in a lightning fast strike. I exhaled a cloud of cigarette smoke and sipped on the hot coffee, prompting a mucusy throat-clearing that also relieved some pressure from the hangover headache and popped my ears.

"I guess I do owe you a favor. Or two."

"*I guess.*" Rick rarely, if ever, got angry, showed his baser emotions, but if you knew how to listen for it, it would be there sometimes. I couldn't blame him for it. He had plenty of reason.

"So what is it you want me to do for you? Exactly?"

"You can start by getting a pen and a piece of paper to write some things down."

I got up, jerkily and foggy, fumbled around at the desk for a pen and a small notebook, reclaiming comfort for my freshly-opened asshole on the cushion of the microfiber office chair. I put the cigarette to rest in the ashtray, and it traced a lazy line of smoke into the apartment air as it burned. Sloshing the coffee left amaretto streaks in the ceramic cup. I placed the mug down on a stack of random papers on the desktop. A Batman statue peered out from one of the hutch's hidey-holes, a miniature version of the original Bill Finger design with his arm pulling the cape over his face in a crouched and coiled position, slitted white eyes peering out at me.

"Okay, whaddya got?" I said into the phone.

"The kid we're looking for is one Arthur Parker, parents call him Artie. Age eight, biracial, white and African-American, resided at the client's residence in Round Rock up until the disappearance."

I scribbled this information down on a blank page in the notebook, the lines resolving into boxed graph paper to help guide the scrawl of my letters into something passably readable. "So you think his mother took him?"

"Tayona Parker, née Tayona Racquel Hattie. Age twenty-eight, African-American, originally from Los Angeles. Fairly certain she's driving a late model Acura sedan, black in color." Rick read off the license plate and VIN, and I captured it. "Couple of priors in California and Nevada for prostitution, possession with intent, small-time larceny. Shoplifting, that kinda shit."

"Who's the father?"

Rick drew a sharp intake of breath. "Before we get into that, I need to know you're in on this. All the way. Because it's client information I'm going to start sharing here, okay?"

"Then why call me at all? I don't have a P.I. license. I ain't on contract with nobody. You don't want my help—"

Rick interrupted sharply, not even willing to loosen the hook now that he had sunk it into my jaw. "I *do* want your help, but I want it done *my way*, understand? I may not carry a badge on my belt anymore, but I do have to answer to a board of directors and a client that's signed an agreement with us...an agreement that carries with it provisions of nondisclosure."

"So why not send me a nondisclosure agreement or some shit? I'll sign it. I don't care." I didn't catch it right away, but the effect of what Rick was about to say sunk into me before he even said it. I knew.

"Because you're *you*, Jack." I heard a not-quite-exasperated exhalation on the other end of the line. "And I don't necessarily want to have your name on any official paper associated with this case, you hear?"

I knew what he meant. Just because I had never been convicted didn't absolve me of the crime. Rick had been there. He'd helped make it happen. I had made him complicit in the one thing you can't come back from.

"Okay," I said quietly, picking up the smoldering cigarette and taking a long drag. "So I assume this is not a paid gig?"

Rick snickered once. It wasn't a funny snicker. More of a sound caused by amusement. Like he wasn't surprised to hear something. "I'll pick up expenses where it makes sense. If you need something specific, let me know. I'm gonna head up your way tomorrow to link up on this."

"To Fort Worth? What for?"

Patience in his voice. The same measured clip. "To link up. With you. On this case."

I narrowed my eyes as smoke got in them. "Uh, okay. When you getting in?"

"Lunchtime. That work for you?"

"Sure." The cigarette fizzled and squished as I stubbed out the butt in the ashtray, exhaling again. "Hey, wait, the father. You didn't finish telling me about the father."

"Tell you what: I'll bring everything I have on the father to you tomorrow if you can bring back a whole bunch of stuff I *don't* know about the mother. Deal?"

The clock on the desk said it was 12:24 in the P.M. "What? How the hell am I supposed to do that? I just woke up, for fuck's sake."

"Listen, I know you have friends up there, Jack. Friends with... specialties. Friends that like to play games on the internet."

The coffee was thankfully hot on my throat as I gulped it. "Why not just ask me for an intro?"

"Because I'm asking for *you*, Jack." Rick's tone turned decidedly pointed, an undercurrent of firmness that I usually never heard from him. "Because I get you, I get *them*, I get other things. I get help that I don't have down here. And I get *a favor returned*."

His last reply cut into me like the accusation that it was. An unfamiliar rumble appeared in his voice, something new, or at least new to me. Pressure dropped and rose again in my chest, the onset of the feeling that something's wrong and you just can't figure out what it is. Instinctively, I knew what was wrong. There was a lot wrong. But leaving it all unsaid between us made it worse. My throat tightened as I swallowed reflexively, working in tandem with the gut-thing to confuse me for nausea.

"Okay, okay, man," I said, and my voice wavered, catching in the wet valleys of my throat, the malfunctioning circuitry of my voicebox. "Lemme see what I can do. Where do you wanna meet tomorrow?"

"Can't go wrong with Ol' South," Rick said.

The twinge of a smile touched one corner of my mouth. "Yeah, that sounds like a plan. See ya there this time tomorrow?"

"That works."

"You need to crash while you're in town?"

"You offering?"

I looked around my bachelor's pad. The sun had begun to shine through the window next to the kitchen, casting a none-too-flattering light on the thin, invisible layer of ash all over everything.

"Sure. I mean, if you don't mind couch-surfing."

"We'll see how the day goes. See you tomorrow."

Our sign-off ended abruptly, my farewell catching again in my throat, making a stupid sound while the line on Rick's end went dead first. He didn't close out like he usually did, like we used to. I got the message. Hell, I hadn't signed off on anything with my favorite Soundgarden album in a long time either, on email or otherwise. Strange the things you shed as you grow older, accumulate more scars.

The tightness in my hand acted up right then, even though there was no trace of precipitation in the fresh air streaming in from the window. The old inflammation caught me like that sometimes, unawares and unprepared, like a Charley horse between the thumb and the center of the palm. I massaged my hand, wincing as the pain passed through me, reminding me. The grip of a snub-nosed pistol. The acrid scent of gunpowder. A circle of red appearing between pink and white wrinkles. Fire.

Fire.

Fire.

———

The day oppressed me with sunshiny heat as soon as I left Bryce House, but I needed the fresh air to get right. I traded last night's clothes for a clean T-shirt—Powdered Toast Man, a classic—and jeans with only a couple beer stains, my black Chucks, and a pair of sunglasses. If I could walk off the drunk and refill my ailing stomach with some legit Texas burger grease, I'd be okay.

The Chucks crunched as asphalt gave way to brick where Sanguinet Street crossed Camp Bowie, an old boulevard that ran from University west out of town where it morphed into Highway 377. Originally named Arlington Heights Boulevard, the city changed its name in 1919 to honor the military camp where Fort Worth soldiers had trained prior to deploying to France. The camp lived for only a few years, closing once thousands of men demobilized through its desks and tents on their way back home from the worst things they would ever experience. Once the Army left, Fort Worth built up around it and down the boulevard, eventually repaving the streetcar thoroughfare with a bricked street that remains to this day.

Across this boulevard from where I emerged sat another historical Fort Worth treasure: Kincaid's Hamburgers. Originally established as a grocery store and butcher's in 1946, it wasn't until 1964 that this quaint little white corner store started selling fresh burgers of an original recipe. People around here forget that. Everyone likes to pinpoint the oldest date on the wall to suck up a few extra decades of whatever prestige comes with age, but this joint doesn't need it. The burgers tell you everything you need to know.

Inside, Kincaid's retained the long wooden shelving utilized in grocery stores of the forties, possibly even the thirties or the twenties given Fort Worth's retro reach. These shelves sported rows upon rows of ketchup bottles, pickle jars, and cans of tomatoes that look like they died in the fifties. If you looked hard enough, you could even find some cans of authentic Popeye's spinach. No lyin'. The walls were lined frame-to-frame with photos of celebrities and famous people who had graced Kincaid's, mostly country music stars and golf pros who had tiptoed over from the Colonial Country Club between invitationals. Kincaid's always added on, never replaced. The memorabilia accumulated on the walls and shelves might have been noted by some as cluttered and divey, but most Fort Worthians respected the pride that the Kincaid family put on display there.

They had since opened five more locations in The Fort, none of which sought to imitate the old century style of the original, so the Camp Bowie flagship persevered as a lightning rod for discerning burger diners and critics. I'm sure even Guy Fieri would make it there one day if his fat fuckin' ass didn't keel over from a hair-frosted, douche-induced coronary.

I picked up my usual from the counter: a standard burger (no juniors) with crinkle-cut fries and a side of fried okra. Sometimes I'd get risky and grab a Cowtown Burger, which came with jalapeños and grilled onions, but I couldn't deal with mayo and that became a chore explaining to the counter people what to change. My stomach couldn't handle that today, so I settled with the usual and a vanilla shake. I found at spot at one of the four long, large wooden picnic tables in the front of the restaurant near the windows that offered panoramic views outside of Camp Bowie. People tended to eat communally at Kincaid's, and even if you came by yourself, there'd be plenty of conversation and chatter to overhear or be invited into. A couple butt-spots down from me, some young parents and their nuclear family giggled and squealed as they threw French fries at each other. Across from me and a table away, an old lady and an old man quietly enjoyed their lunch, neck-buttoned state of dress indicating that they had been taking that very same lunch date for decades.

I ripped into the bag, unwound the burger from its wrapping, and chomped big and hard on that bastard. I could taste the charcoal singe to the burger's edge, and I let it seep into me as I chewed. I wasn't especially hungry but I needed some medicine for that hangover. As I devoured that burger with occasional flourishes of fries and okra, I thought about Rick Sears.

Part of the worry that intruded on me involved not knowing what Rick really wanted. Oh, I was sure he was being up front about the job. But there had to be ten thousand better people in Texas than me that he could have called. Was he really just looking for me to do him a solid? With some free work tracking down a missing kid? To save his company a couple bucks?

To pay him back for helping me kill a man?

The gutwrenching twinge of obligation mixed with something that I supposed was regret, even though I kept telling myself that I regretted nothing. Life happens and every bump on the road is supposed to propel you forward, right? Right. That's some Zen logic for you right there.

Still...it was hard to talk to Rick. Even with time gone by. Even with eyes clear and hearts set going into it originally. Even with no hesitation, no questioning, and little emotion. A large part if not all of that was probably on me. But I could still perceive a nagging sense of shame in Rick every time we spoke in the months that followed Jackson and New Orleans, and we spoke less and less. Shame wasn't the greatest qualifier for it. Maybe it was enmity or simple discord. Maybe resentment. I had only seen him in person a couple times since I'd moved back to Texas, and each time I had sensed an undercurrent of something that whispered in the dark, *Look what you've made me party to.*

The guilt crept up on me like kudzu vine, slow at first but extensive and difficult to arrest. It wasn't there all the time and when it was, it mostly manifested as emotional torpor over having involved Rick in that revenge scheme.

But maybe it was more than that.

I'd have to have a drink to think about it.

I finished off the meal and said a silent prayer to whatever genetic gods presided over my family's bowels that my stomach would return to normal and settle the rest of my hangover-addled body. I couldn't wait to find out though. I had to see Deckhead.

As luck would have it, I didn't shit my pants. Unfortunately, the men's room at The Jetfire Gym didn't fare so well, and I had to apologize profusely to Pussy for making a mess in one of the stalls.

"For fuck's sake, Jack," she said in her quiet, calm voice. "Why? Why is it always here?"

I offered her a smiley face that was neither heartfelt nor ameliorating but instead clearly and ineffectively placative. I did this as I handed her back the rubber gloves and depleted roll of paper towels I had found under the sink in the restroom. "Sorry, sorry, I'm sorry! I'm pretty sure I got it all."

"Are you fucking kidding me, Jack? You're slicker than a boiled onion. You'd say that to your momma just to get her off your back." She snatched the cleaning supplies out of my hands and began putting on the gloves.

"Well...Mom would lock me in the bathroom till I could prove I cleaned it up."

Pussy regarded me with an expression that said, "Are you fucking serious?" And then she said, "Are you fucking serious?"

"Succotash, your ass so crooked you gotta unscrew your drawers every night," Deckhead said, coming up to lay an arm around my shoulders.

Pussy brandished a mop at Deckhead. "Are *you* fucking serious?"

Deckhead shrugged and exchanged worried glances with me. "Can I help you, babydoll?"

"No, I've got this. It's my turn anyway, and it can't be as bad as that little kid that sprayed diarrhea all over last month. I swear to God, we're gonna start making people sign a code of conduct before they come in here."

Deckhead gritted his teeth in a smile he didn't feel and looked at me with worried eyes. "Shall we retire to the other part of the office, sir?"

I brushed my hands off. "As you say, sir. Thanks, Pussy! Sorreeee..."

Pussy flipped me the bird.

Deck and I went back into the inner sanctum. He offered me a beer and I passed, but only grudgingly so. My hands had begun to vibrate with the telltale signs of the post-hangover shakes.

"Whatcha got, Jack?"

I tore out the piece of paper from my notebook with Tayona and Arthur Parker's information on it and handed it to Deckhead. "I need everything you can get me on this woman and her son, and I need it before lunchtime tomorrow."

Deck took the paper and looked it over. "She serious game?"

"No, this is a favor I'm doing for someone else right now. Don't know much about her other than that she may have kidnapped the son there from her baby-daddy."

"Gotcha, succotash."

"Interested in family, friends, connections, possible whereabouts, places she used to hang out, the whole sausage roll."

"Are we trackin' this girl?"

"If you find her. My guy told me she has priors in Nevada and California, so start with those and see if they lead anywhere in the Austin area. Hell, see if they lead anywhere in the state for that matter."

A small girl of indeterminate but young age glided past Deckhead on a pair of rollerblades, and Deck held out the paper to her, which she snatched in fluid motion as she skated past him. "You hear that, *niñita*?" he said to her.

"*Si, si, papi,*" the girl said, skating over to one of the workstations and plopping into the chair there. The girl was Hispanic and dyed her hair shock blue. She dressed in the casual ripped and unstylish trappings of a teenage wastrel, and a few jangly bracelets drooped from limbs too. I raised a skeptical eyebrow at Deckhead.

"Did she just call you 'daddy'?"

Deckhead put a hand over his face and shook his head. "No-no-no-no-no-no-no-no," he said in that rapid fire Spanglish-speak I love so much. "I keep telling her to stop that shit! *Poquito*! You stop that shit, hey?!"

"Maybe if you didn't call her 'little girl' or whatever the fuck that weird Spanglish shit is she wouldn't be so...Is *'programmed'* the word I'm looking for?"

"'Ey, fuck you, *ésé*. Donchu even think about it. We doin' her a favor, all right? Pussy bring her in from the shelter. Her mama don' even know who she is anymore with all the crank she tanked up on, hey? Turns out she got mad skills on the keyboards, *djoo-know*?"

The girl—who I guess is named "Poquito?"—waved at us from her workstation. "I hack you up good, baby!"

I shook my head. "Where's Preacher when I need him...?"

Upon looking around the dark and weird cockpit for Pussy's and Deck's under-the-table operations, I noticed that there were a few other new faces that I didn't recognize, many of them hard at work on some of the new equipment I'd acquired. Sure enough, the corner in which we'd stacked the new gear was empty. Little towers of ramshackle-assembled computers dotted the back wall behind the main row of workstations, and thick snakes of zip tie-bound cables wound all over the polished concrete floor. I pointed at one of them before I had a chance to trip over it.

"What're you doin' with all this, Deck?"

Deck grinned and motioned for me to sit down at the conference table. "Have a seat, Mister Dooley."

"That's not weird at all," I said, plopping into a chair. I noticed then that the majority of the table was covered by a dry erase white-board that had been lain down on its top. The whiteboard was mostly covered by papers, boxes of clips and screws, zip ties, and other hacker junk. Under that bric-a-brac I could make out the colorful zigs and zags of some kind of bubble or process chart. I tried to focus my deteriorating vision on the shapes and words as Deckhead talked over me.

"You ever heard of the name *Tr1pw1re*?"

Of course, he had said '*Tripwire*' in the King's English, but he indeed meant '*Tr1pw1re*.' I would not get the hacker leetspeak until much later in life.

"Are you talking about the first generation G.I. Joe?" I replied. "The guy who had like three speaking lines in the cartoon? And who was always tripping over shit in the comics? Despite being an explosives handler?"

Deckhead made a face at me then tried to mime something with his hands that didn't come off at all the way he had intended. "He the one with the little thing?"

"The what?"

"The *thing*! It wasn't a gun, it was some kinda—"

"Oh, you mean his *metal detector*?" I laughed. "Who fuckin' buys a G.I. Joe whose only weapon is a metal detector? Lame."

Deckhead chuckled too. "Who's the worst G.I. Joe?"

I shrugged. "I give up. Wait. It's Cover Girl, right? She only came in the tank. She was a tank driver."

"No, Cover Girl was cool as shit, succotash. She had a goddamn tank! No, it's *Lady Jaye*."

"Lady Jaye? For real?"

"F'real! Seriously, think about it: what does Lady Jaye bring to the team? *Nothing*."

"She brought some ass to Flint on the cartoon."

"And that's it! She's just there to be a girlfriend for one of the other Joes. She's useless! What does she have? Spears? And not even spears in the toy. Useless!"

I threw my hands up in mock surrender. "I'm not disagreeing with ya here, Deck. What's the point of this?"

Deckhead stopped, considering. *"Qué?"*

I cupped my hands around my mouth to shout at him like that old deaf skit on 1970s *Saturday Night Live* with Garrett Morris, drawing the annoyed stares of a couple nearby hackers. "The. *Point*. Of *THIS*. What is it?"

Deckhead shrugged his shoulders. "I dunno. You brought it up."

"You idiots," Pussy Control announced, having entered the sanctum and witnessed our ridiculousness. "Deck was talking about Tr1pw1re, and Jack brought up G.I. Joe. Like the child that he is."

"And knowing is half the battle," I said with a wink. "Yeah, so who's this Tr1pw1re?"

"We bringing him into this now?" Pussy said with a firm yet nonjudgmental tone to Deckhead.

Deckhead shrugged. "Why not?"

Pussy scowled at him. "Security maybe?"

"It's *Jack*!"

I beamed up at Pussy. "It me."

Pussy rolled her eyes. "I'm the straight man here, aren't I? I'm the guy always surrounded by idiots."

Deckhead smiled his wide smile and came over to Pussy, enveloping her with tender arms and a tiny peck on her cheek, an act requiring him to almost stand on his tiptoes to achieve. "You know I love you, baby."

"Look, all I'm saying is that the more people we bring into this, the more potential risks."

"He could help us."

"He already has."

"I'm literally right here," I said.

Pussy sat down in a chair near me and regarded me with serenity and severity, grace and firmness. She leaned forward and touched my knee. "Jack, this is pretty serious. It might be the biggest thing we've ever done."

I leaned forward, and Deckhead propped himself on the table behind Pussy, one ass cheek down and one dangling.

"Do tell," I said, reaching for my cigarettes. "But wait. Seriously, I don't need to know nothing if y'all don't think I should."

Pussy looked at Deck one more time then back at me. "Tr1pw1re is probably the most notorious hacker on the grid," she said. "He's been at it for a while. Not like some of the O.G.s in the phreak field. But he's wired. He or she—so maybe I should say *they*—ripped some of the better non-attributed hacks and cracks in the last decade."

I lit a cigarette. The flame from my Zippo threw a low warm glare on my face for a moment as it flashed and sizzled the end of the cigarette paper and the tobacco inside. Its glow contrasted against the stark blue radiance of the screens around us, which punctuated the sanctum's gloaming. With a puff of smoke from the initial inhalation, the flame died and with it the warmth.

"What makes him—them—better?" I said.

"They've never been caught. They've never been identified."

"Hell, most people don't even believe he exists," Deckhead interjected. "His hacks are loco, *ésé*. Targets don't know they've been jobbed till months after. He's like a ghost."

"Their hacks are like pieces of art," Pussy said. "Every chan on the net has a shrine thread devoted to this person, if it is indeed one person and not a crew of people, which is what I suspect is the case. One time, there was a forum thread on Tr1pw1re. Bunch of OSINTers, scrubs, and rival hackers all rubbed elbows to share knowledge on what they thought they knew about Tr1pw1re. Know what happened?"

She made a puffing motion, blowing air through long fingers and twirling them as if sprinkling magic dust before my eyes.

"The thread just disappears. No one knows how. Even the moderators don't know what happened, and they can't find an indexed archive of it *anywhere*."

"Keyser Söze," I said. "Convincing everyone that he's just a figment of their imagination."

"You said it, succotash," Deckhead said.

"Whatever methods and leads that existed in that thread could have even been totally wrong or false flags," I said. "So if you make it go away, it automatically looks like *something* in that thread was on the mark. So if all that was just bullshit, Tr1pw1re's now indirectly influenced those forum participants to keep pursuing those bad leads."

Pussy touched an index finger to her nose. "Pretty good SOP."

"They should be workin' for the Mob."

"Maybe they are," Pussy said. "One of the mobs, anyway. Russians are real into cybercrime right now. Eastern Europeans always have been. Who knows who else."

"Chinese," Deckhead said.

I narrowed my eyes at both of them. "You're going after this guy."

"Person," Pussy corrected me. "We're going after this *person*."

"Or persons," Deckhead added.

"What for?" I said. "Y'all have never been vindictive about shit before."

Deckhead leaned over Pussy and put his hands on her shoulder. She smiled, reaching up to snake one of her hands around his neck. I saw something in both their faces that I had never seen before, and it matched between them. I didn't know what it was. Maybe I wasn't supposed to.

"We're getting out the game," Deck said, a grin seeping into his face. "Going legit. Real legit this time."

"We're going to apply to have The Gym recognized as an accredited STEM academy for computer science," Pussy added. "Have kids enroll here to learn what we do and put it to good use."

"Holy shit," I said. "Mister and Missus Control, friendly neighborhood hacker teachers."

"I like the sound of that," Pussy said with a grin of her own.

"Congratulations! Wow, that's—that's..." I inhaled a hard hit off the cigarette and exhaled again, unsteady. "That's some shit, y'all."

"Thank you," Pussy said, squeezing Deckhead's hand. "Naturally, we're thinking about some changes."

"Can't be a gunslinger forever," Deckhead said.

I knew people would that would disagree with him, maybe Roger Hulen for one. But I didn't say anything. I was still taking it all in.

"So how's this legit thing gonna work?"

"Well, we've crossed the line where we can keep The Gym in the black by turning its own profit without any of the sideline ops," Pussy said.

"The Gym *was* the sideline op," I said.

"And now it's gonna help us go HAM on this STEM thing," Deck said. "Private education don't come cheap. Lotta soccer moms out there wanna pay for skills of the future."

"White hats. Y'all are turning into white hats."

Deckhead made a face like a mosquito had stung him on the nose, and he squinched up his eyes at me. "Mmmmmmmmaybe *gray hat's* a better term."

Pussy pinched his hand, eliciting a yipe. "You calm down," she said to Deckhead.

"Is this Tr1pw1re thing a heist?" I said, leaning forward, interested now as the connections slowly started coming together in my addled brain. "One last score, Donald Westlake-style?"

"I don't know who that is," Pussy said. "But you're right. It will be a last little run for the crew here."

"Why Tr1pw1re?"

"Bragging rights mostly," Deckhead said. "If we're really gonna come outta the dark, it'd be good to do it with some cred we can trade on, you know? Like as independent contractors."

"Expose Tr1pw1re, give the details to the Feds to close some cases, set ourselves up as consultants on the side," Pussy said. Then with a sly look she inclined her head slightly and added, "And maybe find a little nest egg for us in their coffers."

"They've got cash?" I said, proud of myself for getting the pronoun right that time.

"They've bilked some incredible scores over the past few years. Everything from small-time stuff like credit card skims to big financial institution bleed-offs that nobody's discovered yet. They've got to have money sitting around somewhere, maybe even in an escrow service or something that's laundering it."

I waved a hand around, indicating the sanctum's contents and staff. "Hence the plus-ups."

Deckhead winked at me. "We don't bring in all this talent back here just to play *World of Warcraft* all day."

I leaned back in my chair and stubbed out the cigarette in a nearby ashtray. "Well, I'll be damned. So what the hell can I do for you? Y'all know the extent of my internettin' stops at the Geocities neighborhoods."

"You are fairly awful at the internet," Pussy said, rolling her eyes.

"Hey. My porn game is strong, though."

Her eyeroll repeated so hard that it could have turned us to stone. Deck just tittered. They traded glances. When they looked back, Pussy glared at me with abject, unapologetic severity, an evaluative gaze that grabbed my chest and made me shudder slightly.

"Let us chop it up for a little while," she said. "We'll let you know."

"Never a shortage of work for a hump like you, Saint," Deckhead snickered.

I met his smirk with one of my own. My stomach and my asshole were feeling better.

6.

WICKER CANDLES AND BASEBALL BATS

Since 1962, the Ol' South Pancake House has delivered delicious breakfast specialties to folks hungry for a change from the usual. Photos and old newspaper articles of the famed eatery dotted the walls, each celebrating the innate simplicity and good nature common to Fort Worth's citizenry. The lot stood on University Drive right next to I-30 and Rosedale, a favorable location that attracted customers of all persuasions across Texas. Open 24/7, the pancake house—some struggled to call it a diner—hosted vast typographies of people, from truckers seeking late-night refills to families seeking the ever inscrutable yet immensely tasty "Dutch Baby." Renovation had touched Ol' South a couple times since 1962, its original single floor layout with the Kennedy-era architecture now transformed into a plainer, boxier structure to accommodate more diners and flashier signs with which to capture the imaginations of daydreaming drivers. Ol' South didn't really need to work hard to capture foot traffic, however. On any given day, and despite ample two-story seating, one typically waited at least ten or fifteen minutes to get a table. Forget about it on the weekends; families drove from as far away as Cleburne to enjoy a Sunday brunch of German-inspired pancakes after church.

I hung out at Ol' South in high school. The coffee was cheap and delicious, and the food was awesome. In that very same eatery, I once watched one of my high school blues bandmates consume an entire carafe of the house-made syrup on a dare. We were preppy kids struggling to appropriate blues culture from Chicago to the Delta, and we often invaded Ol' South after gigs at The Noble Bean or The Plaid Pig, electrified from the highs of live performance, which sometimes led to the shenanigans of syrup overdose and other gastric experimentation. You could smoke inside, too, or at least you used to could.

By the time I walked in, Rick had already grabbed a table near the windows up front, enabling clear views of the parking lot and University Drive. It was close to the same table we had always shared whenever Rick visited Fort Worth, bopping over from Longview for a weekend during high school or crashing for a few days during a holiday break. *Twin Peaks* inculcated within us a healthy respect for good coffee, and Ol' South delivered. Long, wonderful hours passed in those fading wooden booths, percolatin' over the meaning of the little dancing midget and the Red Room. I don't think we ever found clarity in any of it, but I still cherished the debate. If it's one thing an appreciation for David Lynch's work teaches you, it's that you never really find answers in any of it but you do find meditation in the palaver spurred about it.

He stood to his full six-foot-*fuck* height as I approached, clad in a typical-for-Rick plain black polo faded to textured gray from repeated washings, tucked into long legged Levis that barely touched the tongues of Reebok sneakers. He retained his government-issue haircut, smoothed to the skin on the sides, a little bit grayer at the roots than the last time I'd seen him, conservatively clipped on top to contain the mad afro that would sprout if he neglected it. Musculature that he didn't used to have grew around black forearms, indicating that he'd probably kept up with some kind of exercise regimen left over from his FBI fitness training. Rick Sears was the most nondescript of nondescript African-American men, someone who fit in wherever he went, remaining unnoticed, which is exactly how he liked it. Texas may not be The Proper South, but there were still plenty of bubbas in radio cars seeking to fill arrest quotas in their tiny townships, and those bubbas tended to pull over black men and Hispanics more than whites. Rick knew all this, of course, having grown up with it and living it still. Maybe that's why he never thought to be anything other than undistinguished in appearance. Certainly everything else about him distinguished in some way, shape, or form.

"Hey, there he is," he said, and we embraced with a customary three-round pound on each other's backs, disengaging to clasp hands.

"Whataboutcha, man?" I said, feeling the grin overtake my face.

"I'm 'bout to murder me some of this corned beef hash. You in?"

"Always."

We took seats in the booth across from each other and ordered coffees, his black and mine with more than a dollop of cream. Nobody ever carried amaretto cream, so I had to settle with French vanilla and sometimes, in the saintly case of Ol' South, hazelnut.

"How was the drive up?" I said.

"The usual. Straight shot up 35. All that construction just north of Waco."

"Didn't stop to rub elbows with any of your mates down there near the Branch Davidians?"

"It's funny you say that because I actually know a guy from Quantico that ended up there. I mean, it's been a long time since Koresh, but people still remember, from what this guy tells me."

"I couldn't possibly see why." Sarcasm becomes me, and Rick knew it.

Rick looked at me, nonchalant. I fired up a cigarette. We ordered when the waitress returned. He got corned beef hash like he said, and I settled on bacon, eggs, and a two-cake Dutch Baby with extra whipped cream and fruit toppings. What? I was hungry. The smell of coffee mixed with Ol' South's patented syrup concoctions, redolent in butter. Everything wooden in the restaurant still gave off the scent of decades-long cigarette smoke absorption. It was wonderful.

We ate in a silence that quickly became awkward, so I asked, "You readin' anything?"

"You know, Greg Rucka's been killing it lately," Rick said. "Did you ever read his Atticus Kodiak books? Great stuff, man. Real good take on the personal protection profession."

"Bodyguards? Doesn't sound like me. I did like his Batman run though."

"Well, of course you did. That run was clutch."

"Matt Fraction wrote this OGN called *Last of the Independents*. You should look that one up. It's really fuckin' good."

"Oh, yeah? Who did the art?"

"Kieron Dwyer. He did the *Torch of Liberty* short for John Byrne? In the back that *Danger Unlimited* miniseries?"

"Ahhh, that's right! I did dig that. Man, I gotta tell you: I miss that old Legend imprint."

"The *anti-90s*. So great. Remember that Hellboy short?" I waved an oversized chunk of my Dutch Baby at Rick, powdered sugar falling from the dough and coating the table. "*Pamcakes!*"

"I loved *Pamcakes*. Was it actually called *Pamcakes?*"

"I think so."

"Two pages long, that thing, and probably the best Hellboy story Mignola ever did."

"His daughter wrote it, too! At age twelve."

"You get the latest *Planetary?*"

"Aren't we still waiting for *Planetary?*"

"The latest one."

"Which issue?"

"The latest."

"We're still waiting for *Planetary.*"

"I know but I thought you'd have seen it."

"No, still waiting." I grinned through a mouthful of pancake battered dough and strawberries. "'Dreadful privation.'"

Rick looked up from his hash at me with a raised eyebrow behind silhouetted glasses. "What?"

"Nothing. We're waiting for *Planetary*. That's all." I shrugged.

"Right."

Rick, having attacked the better part of his all-day Ol' South breakfast treat, started to wipe his hands gingerly on a napkin and look at me. "So...about this Parker thing."

With my one free hand, I reached for the manila folder I had brought with me, placing it on the tabletop. "I don't suppose it's too much to hope we're talking about Richard Stark's Parker...?"

Rick made a conciliatory gesture with his hands and offered me a slight smile. "Provided you've actually read the books now instead of just watching *Payback* and *Point Blank*."

I fixed Rick with a stare and pointed my fork at him. "How is it both of those movies fucked up *The Hunter?*"

Rick folded his arms. "With *Payback*, I concede, but *Point Blank* was a great flick, man. Lee Marvin as Parker? Come on."

"Walker. Lee Marvin played *Walker* in that one because Westlake wouldn't let anybody use the name Parker in any adaptations."

"Right, but that was still a great movie."

"Awesome fuckin' movie. Didn't Helgeland do *Payback*?"

"Yep, wrote and directed, although I hear his final version got fucked up by the studio."

"Is that why it's kinda...shitty?"

"It ain't that bad."

"Well, it ain't fuckin' *L.A. Confidential* either. Helgeland crushed it with that one. Won like ten million awards."

"Yeahhhhh, but Helgeland didn't direct that one. That was Curtis Hanson. And Hanson was the magic that made most of that movie work compared to the book."

"True, true."

"*Anyway*," Rick said, a trace of impatience in his voice now as he started to eye the folder I had put on the table. Old patterns offered ample cover for awkwardness and subjects easier to avoid than confront. "The Parker case."

"I assumed you didn't want any of this stuff emailed to you, so I just made printouts," I said, sliding the folder over to him. "I can send you digital copies and links and stuff if you need it."

"I might at some point but not right now," Rick said as he leafed through the sheets of paper in the file. "Anything jump out at you?"

"Well, before we get into that, why don't you tell me a little bit about who it is you're working for." I finished cleaning my plate with a finger swipe of syrup that went into my mouth and out again minus the syrup with a loud popping noise. "Ted Parker is the father, right?"

Rick looked up at me. "That come up in your research?"

It wasn't my research at all. Deckhead rang me that morning fill me in on what Poquito had dug up on Tayona Parker. I hadn't asked where they got all the info, but after poking through it for a bit, I noticed some headers and footers on certain documents that came from police databases. Good to know a hacker when you need one. She'd gotten me family names and addresses, phone numbers, emails, all kinds of goodies, and I told Rick as much.

"I don't know how much of this you want me to restate for you if you already know it because this guy's your client," I said, letting the peeved feeling I got from all this seep into my voice reflexively. Rick caught it and eyed me over the rim of his glasses as he perused the papers.

"Go on," he said.

"Theodore Rockland Parker, age thirty-nine, address in Austin, looks like up in the Steiner Ranch area. Software engineer, runs what looks like a startup of the same." I squinted as I searched my memory. "Innovation Apps Consultants? Pretty generic. Some kind of tech spinout. Proximity to Round Rock makes sense for that, too. As do his very large bank accounts *plural*."

"Found that, did you?"

"I have my ways. Married Tayona Hattie a few years back, and they have a son, Arthur Parker."

Instinctively, I hesitated to let a key piece of information slide right then, one particularly related to the kid. Something last-minute Deckhead had dug up. I'd skimmed it in the car and only just then realized that I'd left it in the car, separate from the dossier folder. Something made me clam up about it, and I wasn't sure why sitting there in front of my friend. Not yet.

"You know all this, of course." I shrugged at Rick. "What do you *not* know?"

"I don't know where the kid is. Or Tayona."

"Does that instantly mean she took him?"

"It's the working theory."

"What for? Where she came from, sounds like she had a pretty sweet deal with Parker. Guy's loaded."

Rick took a deep breath and clasped his hands together in front of him, pinning me with a weighty stare. "Jack. I've got to know you're on board with me about this."

"What?" I said, feeling nerves creep into my hands and shoulders, prompting a lit cigarette to wave about, tracing contrails of smoke in the air between us. "I'm with you, I'm with you. What's the big deal?"

"The big deal is that Ted Parker hired KidSmart to find his son and keep Tayona at bay so he can complete divorce proceedings and retain custody of Arthur."

That about summed up everything that had filled my pants about Rick's new life in Austin. And it wasn't even that new anymore. Chasing divorcées like a sleazy private eye from some low budget Troma film and taking money where he could find it. To be fair, Rick wasn't doing that himself. Like he'd said, he worked for a firm now. KidSmart was more than an independent, non-governmental organization though. It had originally incorporated in the '90s as a children's advocacy nonprofit, a startup with plenty of V.C. money from big name Texas investors that wanted better answers to child protection issues than state CPS could give. Security for kids against exploitation and abuse. KidSmart brought in a number of high-end investigators, matched them up with expert attorneys in children's rights, and set them loose on cases big and small. The investment money enabled KidSmart to represent children who went unnoticed by the system: the fosters and orphans that slept in closets or disappeared into the night as offerings to the international sex trafficking underground.

Meanwhile, KidSmart's board and executives brought in high-paying clientele that required discretion. Adoption services that went wrong or kids that killed people. Mostly kidnappings, though. More than a few parents wanted to get their kids away from the other parent or some other kind of bad situation, and the Texas Department of Public Safety—our de facto state police organization—was poorly funded, poorly trained, and even less interested in responding to those cases. Usually, they got kicked to CPS, which had to contract out for private investigators and skip tracers to find the missing children, and none of those people were in a hurry to do anything quickly given the milk train of daily rates and guaranteed expenses with handling fees. The whole system was rife with fraud. KidSmart fixed that for the parents and the kids, the state be damned. So long as the checks cleared.

It was into this niche job market that one Rick Sears found himself applying. Not long after Jackson, Rick had left the FBI and joined KidSmart as a retained investigator. He got his Texas P.I. license and went to work immediately on child abduction cases. He had cracked a few, becoming a noted go-to for kidnapping. KidSmart's lawyers and execs loved him. It made for easy sales to high-net worth clients when you could say you had a former Special Agent on your payroll.

All this roiled around in my mind as we talked, triggering my Spidey-sense subconsciously, but I lamely waved the below-surface feeling away out of annoyance.

"Okay, so your boy Ted wants custody of his kid, I get it," I said, working on my third cigarette. "The wife finds out she's not long for the high life and zips with the kid. Is she legally wrong for that though?"

Rick tilted his head to look out the window. "That's where it gets kind of murky. It is technically kidnapping if she takes the boy over state lines, so we're trying to establish that first."

"But at the end of the day, y'all are beholden to Teddy here, right?" I tapped on the folder, pinning Rick with a wide-eyed stare even though he wasn't looking right at me. "Terms and conditions, and momma be damned?"

Rick turned back to face me in his calm demeanor. I swear. Like a fuckin' scarecrow. "I've got to do what's right for my client," he said. "That means getting his son back. So I hope there are some leads in here—" He placed a hand on the folder. "—that might point us in that direction."

I blew a smoke ring at the ceiling. "Us? Am I somehow on this varsity team now?"

"Look, resources are thin at KidSmart, okay? We're just now finding funding for a cadre of threat assessment people. People who I'd normally work with to get all this. You've got...*different* resources. So, yes, I could use the help." He looked at me more firmly than he had, eyebrows pinched together in the closest visage of irritation that Rick Sears could ever display. "How many different ways and how many different times do you want me to say it?"

I avoided his gaze and busied myself studying my cigarette, thumbing it at the ashtray so as to deposit a fingernail's length of ash. Placing it back between my lips, breathing another hit off the bad habit, emitting the secondhand smoke slowly from one corner of my mouth with enough pressure to blow it away from Rick. Did I really care about any of this? Was I just making noise to make noise? Because things still felt off with Rick? I didn't know, and eventually I had to backpedal in the quiet awkwardness of space left open by my brother.

"Okay, okay, listen I'm in, man," I said. "There's definitely enough leads in there to get started right here in Fort Worth."

Rick leaned in at that. "Here?"

"Tayona's mother has an address in Mansfield, little bit south of the Metroplex. There's also a P.O. box near that address associated with that family name. Hattie was her maiden, right?"

"Right." Rick started flipping back through the pages in the folder. "I hadn't found any direct relatives. Thought she was a Los Angeleno through and through."

I made a face at him. "People keep tellin' me the internet's got that shit. I ain't never carried no FBI badge and I know that at least."

Rick offered me his peeved glare again. "But all the things you're *not* so good at..."

"Stahp. Regardless, if you want to go down there, I'll ride with you, you're so shorthanded and all. Gotta slum with a know-nothin' bitch like me. I get it."

"Oh, you are a bitch, bunk. Just a different kinda bitch than I'm used to fucking."

"I'm gonna tell your wife that you said that."

"Be still my heart."

Something was clicking.

A long time ago, me and Rick would sit in the backyard of my mother's house on Encanto, flanking a cheap metal yard table that held a bucket of crawfish. We'd found the mudbugs at a local fish market, one from which nobody had any business buying live crawfish at that time of year or ever, really. Rick had never peeled a crawfish before meeting me, and I had only brought it to Texas from boils my Dad would take me to in Louisiana or Mississippi on the weekends. I'd had to talk my Mother into boiling them on the stove, settling for a single bag of Zatarain's crab boil seasoning instead of the multitude of ingredients that any one of my coon-ass family on the Dooley side would use in a proper boil. They still came out okay for wherever they came from (likely some Louisiana redneck transplant's creek down in Beaumont), and we got to split the whole pot ourselves since no one else could stand the things.

We sat those rare cool summer afternoons between two tall wicker candles driven into the soft, fresh earth of the sprawling backyard. Their fire purported to keep away mosquitoes and insects quotidian to Fort Worth summers, but Texas' winged monsters could not ignore the stench emanating from the bag of crustaceous shells at our feet. At either side of our lawn chairs rested a baseball bat, both wooden, both recently purchased from a local hardware store's sale rack. Neither of us would ever use them, but having them there with us completed a picture that we had always wanted to paint together, one of defiance and the type of measured hostility that we would not—could not—display to others in familial and social circles, ever small though they were. Long nights we spent talking about that setup, instruments of a youth betrayed by promises of happy-go-lucky fun that only existed between the bounds of our shared yet constrained world. That world animated in comic books, trips to the toy store to compare action figures, movies at various theaters, and phone calls that lasted hours as we unpacked the cryptic mysteries of the arcane stories discovered.

Wicker candles and baseball bats became code for a difficult adolescence, one marked by separation and anxiety, not just separation anxiety. Every Saturday, though, there was always that phone call we could look forward to; the one chance every week to catch up on what had happened to me in Fort Worth and Rick in Longview. And, for a while, that was enough.

Rick spent his entire pre-college life in Longview, a small town in East Texas nearer to Shreveport, Louisiana than any major Texas city (with the possible exception of Dallas if you put your foot to the floor). I started out there myself, but when Duke and Mary-Margaret Dooley could no longer stand to be in the same room together, my sister and I got scooped up on a one-way trip out of the Piney Woods to the plains of Fort Worth. None of us ever returned save for I, the lone member of the family pining for a pre-adolescent ideal of that naive and optimistic life. Duke went east into Louisiana and eventually Mississippi, not to mention two more marriages and a few more kids. Mary-Margaret reclaimed her maiden name and ruthlessly built a new life for her family in The Fort, all despite the idiot misbehavior of her two shithead kids.

It takes a long, long time to look back with any degree of appreciation on your childhood. Every time you do, you find new maps of heavens you once thought were hells and new ways your Mom and Pop could say, "I told you so," even though they often don't.

Always wanting more. Always believing you deserve it.

Never anything more than a sack of lumbering muscle and fat making the same mistakes as everybody else.

Rick at least had made good on walking his own path, firmly focused on criminal justice at Sam Houston State University in Huntsville, which would lead to a career as a Special Agent in the Federal Bureau of Investigation. I remember him telling me once when we'd gotten together in college—he often came to visit me in Hattiesburg where I'd lived with my father and attended Southern Miss—about his internship with the Brazos County Sheriff's Office. There, he had executed his first excursions as representative of the law, delivering subpoenas and performing other unpaid grunt work to earn his stars in a complicated state law enforcement system. Everyone always focuses on the idealized versions of themselves in their future careers, and those in law enforcement often do so with dreams of guns and badges. Rick had long known that pulling weapons meant failure to a true peace officer. He knew that the finest, most efficacious instrument of the investigator was his mind: the razor sharp tool that must be forever polished and honed on the whetstone of experience. So even as he picked up lunch orders for sheriff's deputies on stakeout or organized boxes of mismanaged evidence files, Rick paid attention and diligently applied his budding expertise to the acquisition of knowledge that would bespeak a true investigator.

Naturally, he was a lot better at this than me. So why he had enlisted me for this gig kept nagging my substance-addled brain.

Tayona Parker's mother presumably lived at an address on the outskirts of southern Mansfield, just off enough of the Metroplex suburbs to sit in a stretch of unincorporated land. It turned out to be a dusty trailer park that had sprung up some time ago if the rusty gates and dilapidated tin walls were any indication. We rolled up in Rick's Ford Explorer, its black finish acquiring a crusty sheen of soil creeping in from the southern plains. A few burned out and broken down cars sat inside the lot, testaments to the social torpor that excluded this slice of the population from newer, fancier neighborhoods on the north side of town. One trailer looked like it had exploded from the inside, possibly in a cliché of meth lab endgame. The rest looked like any other trailer park in rural Texas: too much junk scattered around each trailer, trash blowing in the wind, grass eaten up by weeds. A couple random Hispanic kids played with sticks on one side of the park, cracking each other on the back and swordfighting, yelps dissolving into breathless laughter.

"You take me to the nicest places," I said.

"This was your lead, bunk," Rick said, parking the Explorer on one side of the circle drive at the center of the trailer park.

"Can I get out now? I need to smoke something bad since you won't let me burn one in your dog-stinkin' car."

"My dogs smell a million times better than your bad habit."

"I don't know about that. Those are some stank-ass dogs, but I guess most dogs are."

As we got out, I fixed hard on the nicotine rush while Rick lead the way to the trailer. I followed, not looking anything like the Anything Man Rick could be. I had pulled on another McClane-inspired button-up short-sleever today, this one of a different pattern but similarly beige to the other six or so hanging in my closet. Just another dude.

"How you wanna handle this?" I said to Rick's back.

"I'll do the talking," Rick replied over his shoulder.

He rapped hard on the trailer door, and it rattled on its hinges so much that it almost came open on its own, secured only by a rusty bent hook inside. Commotion emanated from inside at the racket's prompt. Rick took a step back toward me as thudding steps grew closer. I could hear a baby crying inside and someone yelling something.

The door flung open to reveal a thick old black lady with breasts down to knees that looked like crumpled sausage. She wore a permanent scowl under unkempt hair and a purple smock that may have been a one-piece dress at some time.

"Whatchu bangin' on my do' fuh?" she yelled.

"Hello, ma'am, are you Sharonda Hattie?" Rick said evenly and calmly, arms straight at his sides like a serene robot.

"Sha-ron-da? Whatchu want Sh-ron-da?" The old woman drew the second syllable out as if she were daring us to tell her she wasn't Texan. "Who the hell are you?"

"My name's...Derick," Rick said, using his full name and dropping the tone of his voice in such a way that it backed into his heritage, like downshifting into a lower gear. Rick could turn on African-Americanisms when he needed to despite being raised by a very white adoptive family. No foolin': his dad literally sold cookies for Keebler.

"I just wanna talk to Sharonda, that's all," Rick said in that slower drawl.

"What, you'n that white boy behind ya?"

I waved to her with a wide, none-too-sincere-but-all-too-sarcastic smile. "I'm just here to carry *Derick's* things, ma'am."

Rick let the slight go and smiled up at the old woman, repeating his query. "Are you Sharonda Hattie?"

"Why?" the old woman said, throwing it back in his face with a whip of her hips. "Whatchu want? You from the state? I ain't got no money."

"Not here for your money. Just wanna ask you some questions."

The old woman looked Rick up and down, scowling at me over his shoulder, and seemed to come to some kind of conclusion. She leaned against the doorframe of the trailer, causing it to sag under her weight with a whine. "Well, I ain't Sharonda. I's her sistah. Latoya."

"That's a beautiful name, Latoya," Rick said, basso rising in his tone. Behind him, I rolled my eyes, turned around on the heel of one Connie, and went to smoke.

"So does Sharonda live here?" Rick continued.

"Sometime," Latoya said. "She ain't heeyah right nah."

"Do you know where she's at?"

"She got herself a man up in Southwest Arlington. Ovah by the salvage yard, you know where I'm talkin' 'bout?"

"I'm not sure I do. Do you have an address?"

I let them jaw by themselves for a bit, smoking my cigarette and stubbing one blackened toe of a Chuck Taylor into the grubby earth under us. I hated places like this. Shitholes by design. Not sure what other choice the residents had though. A lot of folks around there just inherited that life, got left behind. Sometimes trailers are all you can afford. A lot of times, they're all you need.

Rick tapped me on the shoulder after a while with his pocket notebook, a single-ring flip job you could find in any convenience store for a buck or two. He always schlepped one in his back pocket with a small pen for rando notetaking.

"Let's go," he said. "The mother's up north."

"Hi-yo goddamn Silver," I said, tossing the cigarette butt to the ground. "A-way."

"You remember the porcelain dog from Target? The German shepherd?"

"It was Service Merchandise, wasn't it?"

"Maybe," I said. "Anyway, remember that thing?"

"We were going to put it in the backseat on our road trip to California."

"Never made it to California."

"Not yet."

"I still want to do the *L.A. Confidential* set tour out there."

"I want to do the James Ellroy tour. Have you heard about this? You get on a bus *with James Ellroy* and he takes you all over L.A. talking crazy through a loudspeaker like some demented carnival barker."

"What? That can't be real."

"I checked. It's a thing, bunk."

"That guy is fucking nuts."

"That's why it sounds so cool."

"What is he taking you on tours of?"

"Basically all the places in L.A. that are famous for crime scenes and murders and such. The spot where Elizabeth Short from *The Black Dahlia* got killed. Wiseguys like Bugsy Siegel and Johnny Stompanato, where they got killed. Shit, he even takes you to the spot where his *mother* was murdered."

"Ellroy's mother?"

"Yup."

"That's fucked up."

"He's a fucked up guy."

"I guess you have to be to write that good. Are you the only person on this murder bus or is it a group?"

"Naw, it's a group, man. Who would want to do that alone?"

"Name any writer doing crime comics today. Bendis. Brubaker. Azzarello. Rucka even."

"Fair."

We cracked the windows a bit to let in the afternoon breeze.

"Fuckin' Ellroy, man..."

7.
SHOE LEATHER

The house to which Rick had been given the address turned out to be abandoned, nobody home. It looked like no one had lived there in years. So I called Deckhead to run the names again and see what he could find.

"Sharonda Hattie," he repeated to me over the phone. "Get this. She works at a car dealership down the road."

"What? Shut the fuck up."

"No lie. Some used car sales shit." He gave me the address. "Her name's listed as the contact on the website....which you could have found with a mere search on this thing called *Google*."

I hung up on him and told Rick. We jumped back in the Ford and made a three-minute swerve down the highway to the dealership. It looked like a standard Mom and Pop affair: outdated signs, cars that hadn't been washed in weeks, an office smaller than a Japanese hotel room. We pulled up, walked in the front door, and there she was.

"You must be Sharonda!" I announced, sidling up to a put-together black woman sitting at the reception desk. She wore a flowery one-piece dress and oversize glasses, indicating an age of well over fifty, I assumed. The lines around her mouth and eyes crinkled as she struggled to smile at me, loud greetings obviously not her thing.

"Can I help you, sir?"

"Yes, ma'am," I said, plopping into the seat next to her reception desk. Rick came to stand next to me, and I could feel annoyance radiating off him. "Ma'am, you are Sharonda Hattie, right?"

Sharonda looked at me then up at Rick, lingering slightly on my tall black companion. "Yes, are you looking for an appointment with one of our salesmen?"

"Actually, we're looking for your daughter," I said, kicking up a crossed leg and lighting up a cigarette.

"You can't smoke in here," Sharonda said, the facial lines deepening.

"I know. You wanna tell me about your daughter? Tayona?"

Rick put his hand on my shoulder and leaned down. "We just want to make sure she's okay, ma'am. We're trying to find her."

"She fine," Sharonda said, a highly annoyed uptick in her tone. Her eyes vibrated from left to right in a rapid buzz.

I nailed her with my best winsome grin. "You sure?"

At that moment, the car dealership's general manager walked into the cramped reception area. He was a roly-poly man, balding, mustache, wearing a tie with a short-sleeve shirt like he lived in the fifties. He started waving his hands in the air, fanning away my cigarette smoke.

"Can I help you, gentlemen?" he said in a high-pitched whine. "Perhaps you'd like to enjoy your cigarette outside?"

"Perhaps I would," I said, blowing a cloud of smoke at Sharonda. "Excuse me."

I shouldered past Rick, giving him a quick look before inhaling another lungful and blowing it into the general manager's face. As the paunchy little man started to cough, I wrapped an arm around his shoulders and gestured outside to the lot. "What you got out here, man? Huh? You got a Nissan? You got a Chevy? You got a motor-scooter?"

The G.M. sputtered trying to reply, caught off-guard. We paused in the doorway as I gestured out at the lot of used cars. Meanwhile, Rick got to questioning Sharonda.

"Ma'am, I'm with a firm that represents at-risk children," Rick was saying to her, handing her a KidSmart business card with his name, title, and contact information. "I'm trying to find your daughter before Child Protective Services does."

He let the statement hang in the air for what it was: not a threat but a reality. That snapped Sharonda onto a different level, and she leaned in close to Rick as he sat down in the chair I had vacated.

"We-we have many fine preowned vehicles," the G.M. was stammering to me in the doorway.

"No shit, you don't say," I replied, retaining my grip on the man. "Why do you say 'preowned' instead of 'used,' man?"

"Mister, I'm not sure it's anybody's business where my daughter and her son are at any one time," Sharonda told Rick, upbraiding him with a stiff-backed posture of resistance.

"I completely understand, ma'am," Rick said. "We're just really concerned about Arthur, and we need to talk to Tayona about it. Now...you know she left in a hurry from Austin, right?"

"Of course she did, son! Why, you would too if you were married to the...the...*bastard* she was!"

I heard this little bit eject from Sharonda and pricked my ears up. I had to manhandle the G.M. to do it though, and I ended up booting him out of the little office with a strong push that sent him skipping across the gravel of his parking lot. Then I flicked the cigarette at him and said, "Just browsin'." I pulled the door shut and locked it from the inside.

"Well, we don't wanna judge nobody for the choices they made," Rick was telling Sharonda. "Everybody does what they need to do for their family, right?"

"That's right," Sharonda said. "Tayona just looking out for her own, you know? That *Ted* wasn't right for her! Especially with how he treated her and that boy."

I heard the vehemence in Sharonda's tone when she said Ted Parker's name and mentally filed it away. For now, I had to lean on the door to keep the G.M. from getting back in.

"Where can we find her, Mrs. Hattie?" Rick said. "Does she live around here?"

"I can't tell you a thing because I don't know a thing," Sharonda said, sticking her chin up at Rick.

"But you *do* know something, Mrs. Hattie," Rick said, fixing her with firm, unmoving eyes. "You know something about what happened to her and Arthur."

"She just trying to get by! She just trying to protect her boy! Ain't nuthin' wrong with that!"

"I don't disagree, Mrs. Hattie." Rick paused, letting Sharonda's ire subside and the growing anxiety with the situation rise. "Where is she?"

"I don't know! She don't tell me where she is. She workin'. Gotta earn for her boy."

"Where's she working, Mrs. Hattie?"

Sharonda looked up and away from Rick with a huff, a full sigh to the Lord requesting His Divine Intervention. But she succumbed to Rick's calm, steady demeanor and big brown eyes.

"I don't frequent those places," she said.

"I'm not here to judge, Mrs. Hattie," Rick said.

"Well...I don't know which ones she goes to, but she *dances,* you see."

Stripper, my ever-pubescent mind told me. *Strip. Stripper. Titties. Nekkid. Nekkid titties.*

"Does she dance around here?" Rick asked.

Sharonda nodded, deflating a tad, perhaps glad to be unburdened of this knowledge. "Yes, she does. Anywhere she can find an opening in the Metroplex."

"But you don't know of a place specifically?"

"No."

"Are you *sure*?"

"Yes."

I walked over to Rick and patted his shoulder. When he looked up at me, I winked at him and stuck my thumb over my shoulder at the other doorway in the direction where he'd parked the Explorer. He looked back to Sharonda and grasped her hand, the one that clutched his business card.

"Thank you, Mrs. Hattie," he said quietly. "You've been a great help. And you can believe me when I tell you that no one is going to know what we've talked about, okay?"

As Sharonda nodded to him, Rick added, "And please call me if you hear anything, all right? If she's in trouble or Arthur's in trouble. If anything is wrong, I can help. Just dial the number on that card, okay?"

She continued bobbing her head up and down as Rick rose to disengage. She didn't say anything, just watched us go. We pushed through the doorway just as the G.M. was coming in, and

I purposely shoved the guy aside, causing him to stumble again and sprawl out on the lot.

Rick shook his head as I put on my sunglasses and we jumped into the Ford. "That make you feel better?"

"It did actually," I said with a smirk.

"Well, now I've got to get the fuck out of here before that guy calls the cops on you. And while we're booking, you can tell me why you pulled me off her."

"Look, if she's stripping, excuse me, *dancing* again, then she could be anywhere in the Metroplex," I was saying in the car as we bopped up 287 back toward Fort Worth. It was getting later in the afternoon and the sun was going down to the west, framing a purple-pink glow of clouded ridges in the sky.

I grabbed the folder I had put together for Rick and waved it at him. "Don't tell me you didn't already know she was a strip—*dancer* before all this."

"I knew," Rick said, solemnly driving. "She hasn't taken her clothes off though since before Ted Parker married her."

I peered at Rick over the edge of my sunglasses. "Wanna expand on that?"

"It's a pretty common story, right? Girl gets into the shady side of life up in a shady-ass town. Gets high, gets hooked. Takes her clothes off for money. Maybe sucks or tugs too for bigger paydays. Finally graduates to hookin'. Gets roughed up by a john. Has some regrets about it. Runs."

"I thought she was dancing for legit joints though. Her name's on the revue for a couple of those Vegas shows with the girls that wear peacock getups and high heels."

"Oh, she's got some high heels, bunk. Don't you be worried about that. You ever been a dancer?"

"Are you fuckin' with me right now?"

"I'm just sayin'."

"I can cut a rug when I need to, bruh."

"Only thing you can cut is cheese."

"It's gonna happen soon just to mask the stench of this gross-ass car of yours with its wet dog fragrance."

"The point is, dancing in Vegas is competitive. It ain't easy to get into those high end shows at the casinos, and there's gaggles of girls kicking each other in the can to make way for their own shot at those gigs."

"Gaggles."

"So, yes, our girl *did* in fact throw down at a few Cirque du Soleils, but she was still turnin' tricks. Sex work's a protected profession in Vegas. They'll be waiting for you at the airport and hand out cards with menus at baggage claim. You can dance for the glam, but fuckin's still gonna pay the bills."

"All right, I got all that. You knew all this too. What we're trying to figure out is where the girl goes now so we can find her. Sharonda seems to think she's dancing somewhere in the DFW area, but that's a *lot* of damn strip joints, bunk. And those are just the legal ones. There's no telling how many more unregistered titty shacks are out there past county lines. There's gotta be a hundred of 'em. And that ain't countin' if she's gone back to trickin' either."

"I'm glad to hear that you're so read up on the vice scene out here." Rick smacked my chest with the back of his hand and let a small smile grace his otherwise stolid face. "I knew this was a good idea."

"What exactly are you envisioning here? Huh? Some kinda *canvas*?" I looked at him. "Is this an excuse to go see some *girls* with me?"

This time Rick did glower at me, eyes narrowing as the retinas tightened and the irises fell to the corners. "I hope you know me better than that."

I threw up my hands in mock outrage, looking to the roof of the car and rolling my eyes with a touch of melodrama. "It's like you were an FBI agent. Do they make you sign some kind of honor code at this company of yours?"

"The employment agreement is definitely not a joke," Rick replied, and I could detect some hesitation there. Doing something for the right reasons always felt good when you could pin it on a badge. When you were forced into it because of legalese and T's and C's, that could get you feeling a bit down about the outcomes of your work. It would take me a while to figure that out, and Rick would be the one to make me.

I started punching text into my phone. "Deckhead can help us with this."

"This one of your magical internet wizards?"

"He got you that folder. And Sharonda."

"Gift horses, I guess."

There was no way we were going to make any sort of dent in a survey of Dallas/Fort Worth's less reputables, so we decamped back to The Fort proper and selected Trés Josés off White Settlement Road for an authentic Tex-Mex dinner. Rick wasn't much of a drinker, but I had a mad-on for the margaritas there, which I proceeded to gargle as quickly as they could be served. Trés Josés specialized in the cheesy multicolored variety, and sometimes I indulged in a raspberry or strawberry swirl. That evening, though, a nice salty regular on the rocks conveyed just the sort of thirst-quenching magic that would get me where I needed to be.

Rick watched as I gulped down my first one in record time and said, "You all right there, boss?"

I burped, smacked the empty mug down on the table, and waved the waitress over. "I have not yet begun to defile myself. One more, please. And how cold are your Negra Modelos?"

The young server shrugged. "Cold...?"

"Like super-super cold or just regular cold?"

She smiled at me as she collected the margarita mug and said, "Cold, sir."

"Cold it is. Set me up with one of those, too, if you don't mind, honey." I fished out a smoke as she departed and noticed Rick's calm stare. "What?"

"Oh, nothing," he said, taking a sip of water from the large plastic cup in front of him. A lemon wedge floated between ice cubes, tendrils twirling lazily in the currents like a dead jellyfish. So healthy.

"Okay, *so*...the game plan." I stretched my arms out in a rapid, snake strike-like motion, not so different from a carnival tent pastor getting his Jesus on before the pulpit, or maybe more like Reverend Horton Heat about to wrangle his Gretsch 6120 to scream out the opening chords of "Psychobilly Freakout."

"The *game...plan*, " I repeated, enunciating for effect. "We gonna go to a whole lotta titty bars, baby."

"This does not jibe with your earlier admonishment that there may too many of those to visit."

"True! But we got help. I got a couple guys that can add some manpower to the walkabout, *and* I got a connection at DPS I can go ask for a favor."

Rick's deadpan look didn't betray his skepticism but I could tell he was anyway. "Who are these...*guys?*"

"Couple buds from the old days." I widened alcohol-fueled eyelids at Rick—another margarita had come and gone by then—and pointed at him with the cigarette. "I may have mentioned them before. Tex and Preacher. Great guys. Y'all should get along great."

"If memory serves, y'all had some rather *colorful* altercations in high school."

"With the law?"

"With *life*."

"We just livin' with what we been given, brother."

"Who's the DPS connection?"

"Somebody who can get Tayona's picture shown around a lot more than we can on our own."

"I don't want to involve the police if we don't have to."

I shrugged and made a "what-can-you-do?" gesture at him. "Are they not going to get involved eventually if a missing persons report gets filed?"

"It hasn't so far." Rick raised and lowered his eyebrows quickly and looked at away, inspecting the decor of the restaurant, one we had come to call a favorite every time he'd come to visit me in Fort Worth. "Parker hired us for discretion, too."

A slow cloud of smoke seeped out of my nostrils. I threw an arm over the chair back of the chair next to me and leaned on the rear two legs of the chair in which I sat, perching. My third eye chakra was chanting about slow blades and penetrating shields. That one little bit of information I'd decided to withhold from Rick started twisting in my brain more than subconsciously.

"What's the deal with this guy, man?" I said. "You've been kinda cagey about him."

"He's very…techy. I've only met him a couple times, and he fits that weird, tech executive vibe you hear about sometimes in Silicon Valley…Austin. Guys that don't necessarily like to swim with big fish in California, find cheaper office space in Round Rock. You know the type."

"Man, Texas has been spittin' out tech money just as long as Cali. Texas Instruments was makin' calculators for nerds before Sun Micro ever thought about getting energy efficient. But I get your point. What else?"

Rick shrugged with the innocence and naiveté of someone who takes people at their word. I envied him that, I guess.

"The guy just wants his son back. He and Tayona were apparently not getting along, usual story. Wife spends too much of the husband's money, goes a little crazy, maybe puts the son at risk. Hence the cause for divorce."

I met Rick's shrug with the nervous jitter of nicotine, caffeine, and alcohol all mixed into perpetual disfavor. "See, I don't get that. He's saying that Tayona's causing harm to Artie enough to warrant sole custody?"

"Between you, me, and the fencepost, that's the way it's probably gonna go down."

"Look, I don't know the guy, so what do I know, right?" I tapped out some ash into the ashtray and shook my head slightly. "Just... who wants a kid to be taken away from his mother, you know?"

"Look at the mother though, Jack. You really think a woman with Tayona's history can take care of a kid like Artie?"

I didn't catch it right then. I should have though. I wasn't the only one withholding information.

"I dunno. What's she been doing since she married Parker? Hell, *why* did she marry Parker in the first place? How'd you say they met?"

"I didn't."

I cocked an eyebrow at Rick as the waitress returned with another margarita and our food. We both sprung for the enchiladas because Trés Josés owned those babies: chicken and cheese for Rick; three beef for me. The scalding plates overflowed with melted cheese, molé sauce, pinto beans, sour cream, guacamole, and the best damn

Mexican rice you ever did eat (dry style with nary a trace of excess oil or butter). We dug in immediately, oblivious to the radiating heat.

"What, is that attorney-client privilege or some shit?" I said through a mouthful of rice. Holy shit, I loved the Mexican rice at Trés Josés. I could eat a tub of that stuff and gamble on the starchy crap I'd have to take later. "That story wasn't in Deckhead's file. Just the marriage certificate, which looks like it originated in Austin."

"It did," Rick said with customary restraint and civility, pacing himself evenly as he ate. "But that's not where they met. She was dancing again at a club in San Antonio, making pretty good money from what I hear. Anyway, Parker sees her one night at this club and goes all goo-goo eyes. Falls for her. Offers to set her up at a more respectable place in Austin, which he does. But that only lasts a little while because he ends up marrying her." He couldn't hide the judgmental shake of his head. "Guess he got what he paid for."

"Nice. I guess he didn't specify whether he was just tuckin' bills in her garters or taggin' her in a San Antone screw shack?"

"This guy wouldn't be going to no screw shack. If it happened like that, he would have been taking her to some resort hotel on the Riverwalk." Rick spread his arms out in as close to frustration as he would exhibit. "She moved in fast. Whatever happened, that's between them."

"He a churchin' kinda guy? Bible-thumper?"

Rick pinched his nose in thought as he chewed on a tortilla smothered in cheesy mole sauce. "No, I don't think so. But I could be wrong. We don't really ask clients things like that if it's not relevant to a case, and he's not exactly offering to take us to mass every Sunday morning."

"Huh. Okay."

More things started bothering me about the story. I didn't know what exactly right then. Maybe I was just more annoyed by the dribbling of information Rick was feeding me on his case and one thing he either didn't know or didn't care about. Six, seven years is plenty of time to clean up and get right but...

"What kinda person is she?" I asked, thinking aloud. "Like, did she make friends in Austin? Hang out with any of Parker's friends' wives? Go to church herself?"

"Kept to herself mostly. Had her hands full with the son. After he gets a little older, she starts easing into Austin society and spending Parker's money. Y'know, to be honest with you, it wouldn't surprise me if the money is what prompted this whole thing."

"You mean Parker catching his new bride pissing away his cash? How much is he worth?"

"He's a modest single-digit millionaire in the Austin tech sector. Got a lot to lose."

My plate surrendered its last temptation, and I washed everything down with a final swig of the dark beer, signaling the nearby waitress for another margarita as a digestif. Gotta settle the stomach, after all.

"You thought about where you wanna stay tonight?" I asked.

Rick shrugged again in his nonchalant way. "I'm a tall man to be fitting on that shitty couch of yours. I'll grab a hotel nearby. There anything close to you?"

"Not really, but the city ain't that big, man. I know you're a La Q fan."

"Don't knock my La Q predilection. Clean place. Reasonably priced."

"So many better places you could stay. So many!"

"Judge much, diva?"

"I just like my hotels free of potential infection, that's all. But you do you, man."

Rick got out his wallet and started counting bills. "I will. I'll get this, by the way. Least I can do."

"You better bring some more of that tomorrow. A shitload more. For the boys and expenses."

Rick fixed me with an inquisitive look. "Oh?"

I winked at him. "From what I hear, DFW tittehs don't come cheap."

8.

SHOPTALKIN'

The next day was Thursday. Mom called me early and woke me from a sound slumber full of dreams about Claudia Black in *Farscape* and the low-grade hangover fever you get from sugary margarita mixes.

"Yep-what?" I stuttered.

"Since you're unemployed, do you want to do your mother a favor?" I could hear Mom's smile through the phone. She always knew how to ask for something politely, Southernly, and in a way that was impossible to resist...which all might have been the same thing as Southernly anyway.

"Always."

"I need some help stuffing envelopes at the office. Two of my interns are missing."

"Missing? Shouldn't we be calling the poh-leese?"

"One of them's sick and the other one's from Texas Tech."

"Well, that explains everything."

"Can you help?"

"Sure. I'll be there in a minute."

Impossible to resist, but in any analysis, I didn't have shit else to do that morning. I showered, threw on another one of my short-sleeve button-ups over a black Pearl Jam T-shirt, legged into a pair of jeans without stains, laced up the Connies, and got moving. Having not committed to a specific time and still bleary-eyed at that ungodly hour, I detoured to Berry Street and collared a bag of breakfast tacos and the biggest coffee they'd give me at Fuzzy's. Berry and University was far out of the way, and there were plenty of the usual Starbucks and Dunkin's along the route from Bryce House to Downtown, but Fuzzy's dog whistled me. I struggled not to make a mess as I munched on a bean, potato, and cheese taco with one hand while piloting the Camry through Downtown Fort Worth's sometimes confusing one-way streets.

No parking spaces showed their ass to me as I prowled around Jones Street near the FWPD Central District building, so I backed into a wide area one street over next to a fire hydrant. Taco gripped firmly in one hand, the other fished out a placard from my glove compartment that I hung on the rearview mirror, its bright blue and white lettering declaring, "SPECIAL CITY TRANSPORTATION." I didn't like to use that thing often, but overcome by tacos and day-old margarita brains, I made an exception. I'd found that hanger at an event Mom had invited me to a few months back, one hosted by the city, so there were plenty of "special exceptions" all over the place. One of the valets outside the convention center had kept a stack of those in his back pocket for guests, and I swapped him one of Preacher's joints for one of the placards. With a little luck, it would fool the parking enforcement folks on their bikes—they never looked hard enough to find the tiny date on the back of the placard.

The building was an old lodge, marked of the dark red brick build typified by classic Fort Worth construction. Inscribed in a concrete-gray slab along the side of the building where Grove Street turned into East 6th was a chiseled notation that read "FORT WORTH LODGE NO. 2144." The lodge numeration belonged to the Grand United Order of Odd Fellows, a 19th century fraternal organization whose founders and members principally included African-Americans. The order had organized to give black folks safe places to meet, share ideas, and work together, something direly required for the burgeoning black businesspeople in 1926 Fort Worth, when the building had been erected. I loved that my Mom's work was headquartered in such a historic place.

At some point, No. 2144's deed had passed into the hands of an aging white developer whose children wanted to use the building for their own businesses, including a public relations agency that currently leased most of its office space to Fort Worth Sister Cities. The building had undergone many renovations over time but few structural changes aside from the addition of a parking lot in the back that serviced the police department's growing motor pool. This one blemish on the building's otherwise historic profile could only be seen from that parking lot where the city had erected a black fence to ward off would-be police car thieves, the likes of which had literally never been seen in Fort Worth since Harry "Nickel Tooth" McGillicuddy stole Marshal "Longhair Jim" Courtright's horse in 1877 (and they hung that son of a bitch for horse thievin').

Nothing stirred on the first floor of the building; all its space was dedicated to storage. A small cubed foyer gave way at the main door to a steep set of stairs leading to the second floor where the offices lay. I waved hello to the receptionist, didn't check in, and scooted past an office or two till I found Mom in the main conference room that occupied the center of the floor.

"I brought breakfast tacos!" I announced upon entering the room.

Mom and two other people were working in an assembly line fashion signing letters, folding them, sticking them into envelopes, licking them closed, and affixing stamps. The others were a volunteer and another Sister Cities employee whom I did not recognize. Mom fixed me with a determined grimace and put her hands up in the air.

"I can't eat no tacos, I've got pledge letters to sign!" she squawked.

"Whaaat?" I intoned, mildly interested in the task at hand, more interested in finding ice for my coffee.

"It's for the annual summer fundraising drive. We have to get these letters out to our donors from last year so they'll send us some more money this year." Mary-Margaret furiously signed her long-ass name on the letters in a patented loop-de-loop style, handing them over to the volunteer who owned the folding-and-stuffing task. The other person, a younger woman whose name I remembered as Lisa, looked like she was about to throw up from licking so many envelopes and stamps.

"Why don't y'all ever buy the sticky stamps?" I said, putting the tacos down and handing my coffee to the woman. "Here, can you find some ice for this? I'll take over for y'all now."

Lisa looked to Mary-Margaret for approval, but before either her or the volunteer—a big ole' sumbitch that looked like he'd been storing possums under his shirt—could say anything, Mary-Margaret said, "Y'all go. You have other things to do right now, and that's why I called Jackson. Thank you for your help!"

The volunteer and Lisa both traded "you're welcomes" with Mary-Margaret and got out of there, Lisa grabbing the giant Styrofoam cup of coffee I'd offered her. I unwrapped another taco, bit half of it off, and through a mouthful of chorizo and egg said, "You sign, I'll stuff."

"Watch those dirty hands, please," Mary-Margaret said in her director's voice. I didn't get any slack just for being the president's son in that joint.

"Yes'm."

"What are you up to today?" my Mom asked me as we worked. "Still looking for jobs?"

"Haven't really found time for that yet." I wiped my hands on my jeans and got to work triple-folding letters for fast deposit inside pre-addressed envelopes. This wasn't the first time Mom had volun-told me. Nonprofits like Sister Cities are often criminally understaffed and underfunded, but Mary-Margaret McDowell liked to run her ship tight and effective. Many were the Sundays that she dragged my sister and I to the office to finish some urgent volunteer task before some main event the next day.

"Rick's in town," I found myself saying.

"Really? What's he up to? Is he staying at your place?"

"He's working a case. Brought him to the area. He actually asked me for some help with it." I knew what was coming next, so I said, "It's not really a job-job. More of a favor."

"Well, that's good you get to see him. How is he doing?"

The shuffling papers made swishing sounds as they passed between callused fingers.

"Still in Austin. Still doing his thing. Working for that company that represents exploited children."

"Good for him. I couldn't believe it when you told me he left the FBI. I thought that was his thing. After so many years of y'all watching *Twin Peaks* and *The X-Files*!" Mom cackled in a staccato pattern as she often did when remembering good times, and there had been a few.

"Yeah, well, nothin's ever cracked up to be what you think it might."

I hadn't meant for it to happen, but the apprehension from the evening prior had crept into my voice. Mom heard it, too. That's the thing about moms: they can sniff out a problem sometimes before you know it's there yourself. Mine certainly could.

"Did something happen?" she said.

"I don't know. Maybe." I hedged. "He did a favor for me a while back, and I can't help shaking the feeling that it may have... *contributed* somehow to why he left the Bureau."

Mary-Margaret finished signing the last letter, set down her ballpoint pen, and moved to the other side of where I was stacking envelopes so she could begin licking them closed and affixing stamps. Lisa returned and set my coffee—freshly iced—down on the conference table near me, and I thanked her.

"Y'all aren't having problems, are you?" Mom said. "You and Rick? You haven't seen him in a while, right?"

"I wouldn't say we're having problems, per se," I said, admonishing my mother with a smirk. "And we're not married."

She blinked at me and straightened her mouth into a thin line, still gregarious but with a slight intonation toward the annoyed. "Don't I know it," she said. Mom had been married twice, once to my father, which would have been enough bullshit for anybody, bless their heart.

"What did y'all do? Something bad?" she said.

I averted my eyes and hid behind a long sip from the newly-iced coffee.

How do you tell your mother you killed somebody?

Fleeting, as if in jumbled images from a DVD movie whose disc reader malfunctioned, I saw in my mind the bullet enter Finley's forehead, the splash of chunky crimson on the wall behind him, his flummoxed expression frozen forever as he sank to the ground...the shock washing over his daughter as she found him dead and the gun in my hand. Intermixed with this macabre cinema were flashes of imagination from scenes I could not have witnessed yet still found recurring: Pussy Control shooting her stepbrother...Roger Hulen's legendary shootout with a drug smuggler in Weatherford...point blank gunfire that ended the lives of so many more wiseguys, wannabe gunfighters, and shitbirds.

All of this exploded in my subconscious in a nanosecond, as if deposited directly into my psyche via transporter beam. It didn't consume me, though. Didn't grip me. The cold thing didn't even happen to my gut this time or quiver up into my throat the way it did before I killed it with booze. Even here under the random scrutiny of my mother, the seconds-long thought barely gave me pause.

Did that worry me? Was that an emotion I was ready to ascribe to this crime? *My* crime? *Alleged*, my consciousness advised from the depths. *And never suspected, much less charged...* And if so, what did that mean? Was I all right with it? I certainly had been at the time.

"You know me, Mom," I said, grinning. "I'm always up to something bad."

My mother, Mary-Margaret McDowell, God bless her, rolled her eyes at me and licked another stamp. "You *better* not, I'll wear you out."

Having folded and stuffed the last envelope, I set about helping Mom seal them and give them their stamps.

"Yes, ma'am," I said.

It took me a while to find Roger Hulen's number buried in an ancient address book that folded into a gold-reflective magnetic business card holder with the inscription "DPI - DOOLEY PETROLEUM INTERNATIONAL" on the front and "I.L.D.S."

on the back. Another tchotchke from my uncle's propane business, double branded between the name and Carter Dooley's infamous personal motto, "I Love Dis Shit." He had given it to me as a young man, and I had filled it only with the most important names, addresses, and numbers I could think of as an adolescent. Hulen's had been one of the last additions before the novelty address book ended up in a drawer full of junk that followed me around through the years. I had found it wedged between a Huey Lewis CD and a clasp of collector coins from the Boy Scouts.

The number no longer rang Hulen directly but instead connected the main reception line for Texas Rangers Company B in Garland, bypassing the usual robot answering machine reserved for the suckers struggling to get through to the local DPS branch about expired drivers licenses, insufficient proof of insurance, identity validation. Surprisingly, Hulen was in at that moment; I always figured him for mobile in the preponderance of his working day. I walked him through what I needed and he told me to meet him closer into the Metroplex. Garland sat northwest of Dallas outside the 635 loop, the first clear, small Texas suburb free of the DFW rat race. Getting to that side of the area would run out the hours of my day, and Hulen was kind enough to oblige me a neutral rendezvous that thankfully prevented me from having to drive into or through Dallas. Midpoint in the Metroplex made it easier for him to accomplish the ask I had for him, so his even bothering to meet me there was a good sign.

He wanted to chaw the rag at a Shipley's of all places, and I was damned if I was gonna pass that up. You can take your Dunkin' Donuts and your Krispy Kremes all day and all ways, but give me Shipley's or give me death. Shipley Do-Nuts might be proof of actual God on planet Earth. I'd grown up anticipating Saturday mornings in Longview with the fervor of a crack addict because of Shipley's. My Dad would take me there, just me, before everyone else got up, and we'd *mug down* on the tastiest, lightest, melt-in-your-mouth, most deliciously perfect doughnuts ever. You could get glazed and chocolate covered back then; that was it. So that's what we did. Some of each plus donut holes and a chocolate milk. Sometimes we brought them home to eat so I could watch cartoons (*Starblazers* had just been imported from Japan), but I was equally enthralled watching the white-uniformed Shipley's people make the doughnuts through a glass window in the shop's small eating area. Absolute magic, lemme tell ya.

I was fortunate to have a Shipley's in Longview growing up. I got doubly lucky upon moving to Hattiesburg for college where an older Shipley's location stood with its 1960s-inspired arches and signage. Few of those originals remained in the South, but one of them was on East Abram Street in Arlington, not too far from the main Lone Star Comics store at which I had trained before taking over the Fort Worth branch. Serendipity, thy name is Shipley's. Or to put more fine of a point on it by stealing a better metaphor: luck—it follows fools, little children, ships named *Enterprise,* and dudes named Dooley.

We landed close to closing time. I held out a vain hope that the little Asian girl to whom I'd found myself irrevocably attracted when I started at Lone Star was still working the counter. The staff of this unapologetically classic doughnut shop was indeed Asian but of the geriatric demographic, unfortunately. What was that girl's name...?

The facade of the shop retained sixties-era style with the big "GREATEST NAME IN DO-NUTS!" sign and double three-dimensional Shipley Do-Nuts logos twinned to the front corners of the roof. The drive-thru sign, red letters on white background, still looked original, having been painted over again and again but never updated. The asphalt parking lot had long since faded to burnt-out white, holes peeking through to earth where crusted pieces broke underfoot. There was even still a newspaper dispenser next to the door.

Hulen and I greeted each other, and I could not help but be swayed again by his true Texan presence. He wore the exact same getup as I'd seen on him last at The Aardvark with the exception of a new shirt that looked crisp and freshly-pressed, even after a day of armoring a Texas Ranger from whatever it was he did all day. Hulen also wore a more obvious gunbelt now with his service pistol clipped tight to his left hip, butt pointing forward, indicating his preference for drawing across the body instead of directly from the right hip. His Texas Rangers badge shone brightly from where it was clipped to the belt on the opposite hip. Even the old Asian man behind the counter bowed respectfully as Hulen walked in, cowboy swagger intact, took off his sunglasses, and tipped his hat.

He ordered coffee and a single chocolate covered doughnut. I ordered the same plus two more regular glazed and a bag of two dozen donut holes to give to the boys later. We posted up at one of two tables and started jawing.

"So tell me again what you need, Jack," Hulen said, fiddling with his coffee but looking at me.

"I'm helping an investigator friend of mine look for someone," I said, sliding a copy of Tayona Parker's photo across the table to him. "This girl. Tayona Parker. She's likely dancing at one of the strip clubs somewhere in the greater Metroplex."

"That's a big area to be lookin'," Hulen said, picking up the photo to study it as he sipped his coffee. "She done something wrong?"

"Well, it's possible she kidnapped her own kid. Kid's named Arthur or Artie. Tayona's on the run from her husband in Austin."

"On the run?"

"Family drama. The husband is my friend's client."

"So your friend's private?"

"Yes."

"I know him?"

"Don't think so. Works for a firm in Austin that specializes in cases dealing with children. Kids that go missing, get exploited, that kind of thing. KidSmart."

Hulen shook his head as he lay the photo down on the table carefully and reached for his doughnut. "Yeah, doesn't ring a bell. The client file a missing persons report?"

"Not yet. No official call for either the girl or the kid. Yet. I get the impression the husband wants to keep things quiet. He's got money."

That made Hulen smile, and I watched the edges of his big ole' mustache smooth out when he did. "That's usually what does it, cases like these."

"I'm beatin' feet with my buddy lookin' for the girl tonight," I said, taking a quick respite for a bite of the smoldering glazed donut. I almost didn't come back from it. It's literally better than sex. *Some* sex. When I regained my composure, I said, "I know it's a big area to be lookin' for one stri—*dancer*, so I was hoping you could pass this photo around and get some of the local law to keep their eyes open. *Unofficially.*"

Hulen regarded me with a direct stare as he sipped his coffee, not a hostile one but a serious one. "If this woman's committed a crime, Jack, and I show this around, officers might be obliged to bring her in. Kidnapping's a serious offense."

"*If* charges are pressed and one parent is the clear custodial guardian," I countered, giving the glare back, doughnut in cheek. "So far, no charges have been pressed, and by the letter of the law, *both* of the parents have custody because they're still married and neither of them has technically filed for divorce. And we're not talkin' APBs here. I'm just askin' if you could disseminate the photo to a few folks whom you *might* know that *might* be in the area of the kinda joints this girl's likely to be workin' tonight."

Hulen's otherwise long eyes brightened, expanding to display more of the aging hazel, sunsetting light refracting the prisms and the rods and cones. "You know your kidnapping law, huh, Jack?"

I shrugged. "I may have done some reading."

"Often times, investigators get in a hurry. Forget to look at the contours of the case. Just knowin' what yer talkin' about from the get-go is a good place to start."

Absurdity incarnate. I munched on my last doughnut and gave Hulen a dismissive look. "I ain't an investigator."

Hulen's gentle smile crept into his visage again. "Okay, okay. Whatever you say, Jack."

"Look, can you help me out or not?" I didn't mean to get short with him, and I don't think it came off as such right away. Maybe I was just in a horn-tossin' mood from impatience. I needed a drink.

Hulen picked up the photo of Tayona Parker gingerly and slipped into the breast pocket of his shirt. "All bacon, no sizzle. Yeah, I'll be happy to, Jack. Your cell number a good way to get in touch?"

"So long as you're screening the calls, Mister Hulen," I said with a wink, a tad paranoid suddenly realizing many, many officers of the law would have my number.

He fixed me with a stare again. "Don't go swallowin' nails and spittin' up corkscrews now, Jack. All right? I don't mean to come down on you. Just a friendly observation."

I grasped his outstretched hand and felt the years in the calluses, the road leather in the whorls. Hulen knew the deal. If he knew too much more though, like say, a killing a couple years back in Jackson, Mississippi...

"Time to heat up the bricks," I said.

Imagine you're trying to do something important. Something potentially life-changing that requires careful attention to detail and scrupulous care. Something whose import carries weight, meaning, *gravitas*. Imagine all the tasks involved, the calculations for execution, the metrics for success, the resources required, the contingencies, the perils, the potentialities.

Now imagine you ask Preacher and Tex to do it for you.

That reaction you're having right now is right about the same as Rick's when we came together Thursday night at The Chat Room to plan the canvas. Except Rick sat there looking at all three of us mouth agape and with possibly the most disbelief I'd seen in his demeanor since Yoda threw Palpatine's guards against the wall in *Revenge of the Sith.* I don't know you so I dunno if you look like that or even care about *Star Wars,* you philistine.

We were sitting at one of the picnic tables outside on the bar's porch, cigarettes idling in tin trays, cans of Dos Equis and Miller Lite and Coors Lite already piling up. Preacher and I had steadily fed the jukebox all the loose change we could find without breaking into the singles we knew we'd need for later in the evening, and a combative competition of '90s rap and grunge fought for purchase over the loudspeaker-like amps pumping music to the porch. In fact, "Porch" was one of the songs I'd bought, and I'd bought it ten times just to piss off Preacher because he hates that song. The Chat Room is your everyday Fort Worth dive bar, just as accommodating to the hipsters as it is to the metalheads, the bikers, and the preps filtering in from a slowly gentrifying neighborhood in Fairmount. You could still smoke inside, and I had no idea how. Probably somebody paying somebody else off. It was the last place in Fort Worth that felt like the kind of dive you'd fall into in New Orleans: ripped barstool cushions, smoke-stained pool tables, sticky floor, cheap beer, better cocktails, barely functional jukebox from a bygone age. I loved it.

Rick clearly did not love it. To be fair, dive bars are generally not his thing. They are more so not his thing when he has to suffer The Three Idiots in a cloud of smoke, distorted music, and other Funkytown regulars. Every couple of minutes, something would nudge his anxiety button, and he'd set about adjusting his glasses just to fidget. Subtle but extant.

"Uhh," he started.

"Listen, these guys are *solid*," I said, pinning my brother from another mother with a knife-hand that also brandished a cigarette. "Trust me."

"Oi, I love tits," Preacher said.

"See? He loves tits."

Rick could not help the roll of his eyes at that point, and he placed his elbows on the table so that he could interlace his fingers in each other and find some semblance of calm in the shitshow that was Us.

"I'm not *not* grateful for the help," he said.

"Who better to blend in?" I smacked Preacher on the back and switched knife-handing toward Tex, who sat on the other side of the picnic table with Rick. "Go in, look around for our girl, spend a few singles, ask a few questions. How hard can it be?"

"No one at this table except for *me* is trained—"

"How hard is it to ask a question? 'Excuse me? Know this girl? Worried about her kid getting nabbed.' Done. Tex'll even do it with more panache than that, girls love him so much."

Tex was wearing his cowboy hat that night, the gray Stetson with the thin bolo band with intricate, detailed leatherwork and a tiny silver buckle. That and his usual white T-shirt, jeans, and a pair of square-toe Lucchese boots. He offered Rick a small smile, laconic.

"Okay, I hear what you're saying, and I appreciate it," Rick said, his jaw setting so rigidly I could practically hear it cracking under the stress. "I suppose we're not exactly interviewing people tonight. Right?"

"Right," I said.

"Right," Tex said.

"Aye," Preacher said.

"So let's just see what kind of responses we get, okay?" Rick looked at all of us in turn. "Hit the places on the list, show the photo, see if anyone's heard of Tayona Parker. If anyone asks why you're asking, just tell them that you've heard about her show and you want to catch it. You get a bite, call me as soon as you can."

"Where we all headed?" Tex said and held up the piece of note-pad paper that I had handed him. "Just these joints?"

"Yes, those places are clustered closer to each other so it'll be easier to move around between them," Rick said. "Look out for faces you've seen before. If you see someone in a crowd that you've seen before, chances are high they might be following you."

"Why's anybody following us?" Preacher said. "The lass don't know we're sniffin' around, wha?"

"She could know," I said. "We visited her mother yesterday. They could have talked. She could have enlisted help."

"Help?" Tex said with a questioning raised eyebrow.

"Dudes do stupid shit sometimes if a lady flashes the right amount of skin in front of 'em," Rick said. "Just be careful is all I'm saying."

He started counting out bills from a wad of cash that suddenly appeared in his hands from under the satiny, black button-up shirt he wore, part of Rick's method of blending in even though I didn't think he would need to worry about that in the places we were all headed. I did note that Rick had a disproportionate amount of nicer gentlemen's clubs on his list than the rest of us, but that likely had more to do with his chosen territory in central Dallas versus some of the scrubs the rest of us would be hitting up. I had changed into a long-sleeve button-up of my own, a paisley patterned dark blue number with the cuffs rolled up. Preacher sported decades-worn laced boots and one of his thinned-by-time flannels, one with a red and gray design that would have been in-step for the Pacific Northwest.

Rick handed each of us a stack of bills, about a grand each. "You'll want to make singles wherever it makes sense. Don't be flashing this kind of cheddar where you're going. Keep whatever you don't use tonight. We'll regroup later and compare notes."

Tex took his allowance and stuffed it in his pocket. "Hey, I just wanna say thanks for letting me in on this," he said. "I'm kinda outta work right now and could use the scratch."

Rick nodded to him. "Well, we'll relook things if you run out of what I just gave you. Don't spare the bread if the mustard's spreading, knowhumsayin?"

Tex returned the nod and polished off his Coors Lite.

"What else?" I said.

"Let's all trade numbers." Rick said.

"Preacher's got a flip phone. Be wary."

"Always makin' fun of me fookin' phone, Cajun..." Preacher grumbled as he struggled to enter the numbers.

"Let's get after it," Texas said, standing up and crushing his last beer can between massive palms. "See y'all later."

Preacher ambled off after Tex, eyeing Rick as suspiciously as Rick had been eyeing him if not moreso. Rick and I left the porch area together headed down the side street perpendicular to Magnolia back into the lush grasses of the Fairmount bungalows before which we'd parked our cars.

"I ain't gonna complain about the help, but *Jesus*, Jack..." Rick said in a quick exhalation that sounded like he'd been holding in for a while.

"I just thought it'd help to—"

Rick shook his head a little too hard and cut me off. "No, no. Too late now. You and your friends." His next shake seemed to throw off the apprehension with which he practically dripped. "How'd your other connection wind up?"

"Roger Hulen. Texas Ranger around these parts. Known him for years. He's passed around Tayona's picture to all the local street beats he can, and he'll call me if he gets a hit."

Rick made a face like he was impressed, but in the darkening evening I couldn't tell if it was placating or genuine. We stopped at my car first, and he held out a hand as I opened the driver's side door, the dome light inside casting a warm glow to one side of our faces. I gripped Rick's hand firmly, felt the same firmness shaking back.

"Good luck, bunk," he said. "Do whatcha gotta do."

"Same," I said, mustering a smirk and a wink that somehow I didn't feel.

9.
THE CANVAS

Look anywhere you want on the internet, nowhere will tell you how to find people in meatspace. Sure, there's plenty of tell-alls and cash-ins from retired cops, bounty hunters, and dubiously successful private investigators. Even a couple of really good manuals and textbooks that legit P.D.s issue to freshman detectives. But the majority of that stuff covers procedural-type look-sees: where to start when you're looking somebody up on public records or what steps to take in what order for properly processing a crime scene. Little effective content exists for self-directed learning in real world manhunting. No "how-to" manuals for locating those that don't want to be found. That's why fugitive search squads like those in the U.S. Marshals are so specialized. Their methods become precious after a fashion, and to dish them openly is to only arm bad guys with more advantage in skipping the law. Dummies' guides, however, litter the "true crime" shelves of your average half-price bookstore, dog-eared and endlessly recycled by armchair enthusiasts, amateur detectives, and shitbirds too stupid for white collar work.

I knew. A stack of such books and manuals to that effect lay piled in a cardboard box back at my apartment, dutifully awaiting trade-in at Half-Price Books for a sliver of store credit that I'd eventually spend on a Hunter Thompson tome. I'd graduated from fiction to reality since Jackson, and for some reason, accounts of dicks both private and badged rarely captivated me anymore. Instead, in the intervening years, I'd found myself gravitating more toward educational nonfiction about murder. Why? Well...*Jackson and New Orleans.*

These things being equal that late Thursday night (or early Friday morning), I found myself ill-equipped to hunt Tayona Parker, wherever she was. I'd made it sound easy to the boys, but after the first few joints, showing her photo and asking questions, I'd begun to twig the difficulty. I made sure to buy a drink here and stuff some singles in garters there, but it didn't take long for a burly sumbitch at each of those first strip joints to sidle up and ask me to take a hike if I wasn't spending more. At one place, I even dropped a hundo on a girl for a dance in the back since she told me she knew Tayona, and when we got back there and she got busy, I quickly discovered that anybody'll say anything for a C-note in most skin joints. But I guess it didn't take a calculus professor to figure that out.

My swath of the canvas included I-20 and south across the Metroplex. Lots of territory, even after striking out quickly at the first cluster. I grabbed an iced coffee to prop up the eyelids. I found plain blocks of concrete dropped into the middle of pockmarked, bombed out parking lots and seedier, broken down shacks covered in neon, advertising those three X's to heaven and gone. There were plenty of places to trawl.

Between fruitless probes of smoke-filled, flesh-humid rooms, I found no new messages or missed calls on my phone. I wondered how the rest of the boys were making out at that late hour. Confessionally, Preacher was probably an awful choice for this job. More than likely he was laid out at a VIP table spending Rick's money on champagne and private dances with bumps out of his personal stash. Tex I wasn't so worried about. You could count on that guy for a lightning strike if you needed one.

Something kept nagging me as I inhaled coffee and listened to Rage Against the Machine in the Camry to stay awake. A feeling about the Parkers bothered me. Ted Parker didn't exactly sound like the kind of guy that would be too upset by Tayona running off given her background. I could have understood it if Ted Bible-thumped his way into Rick's office, compelled by the Lord to do the right thing for the few squirts he had pumped into Tayona...but neither of those things could even be true given what I knew about Tayona and Artie. Maybe Ted just felt like he owed the kid better than his mother could give him. Honorable, I suppose. But if that was the case, and Deckhead's info on Artie's upbringing was solid, then Ted didn't know a key detail about his own family ties, a detail that could ruin his chances for custody of the kid in divorce court.

Ted Parker wasn't Artie's father.

Rick had made it sound like Ted and Tayona married shortly after their tryst in San Antonio and Artie had come along shortly thereafter. The truth was, however, Tayona had been rejected from an abortion clinic in Vegas due to inebriation and suspected drug use, an incident that had been reported to police but never went anywhere because she had fled Vegas shortly thereafter. So she had been pregnant *before* she got to San Antonio and met Parker. So the kid couldn't be his. Deckhead had the police report to prove it, too.

Rick must not have known about Artie because Parker didn't know himself. As far as Parker was concerned, he banged Tayona, she started showing, and they rolled with the punches.

So given the douche vibe I was feeling off this guy I'd never met, would he even care about getting Artie back if he knew the truth?

Or...*did* he know? In which case...*what the fuck*?

Questions chewed at my shit brain as I guided the Camry toward my next targets.

"Cajun! Yeh have to help me! I'm fookin' done for!"

I had just finished casing another fine establishment full of working women when Preacher called. The coffee was wearing off, and for once, I was thankful for watered down drinks and sleazy bartenders.

"Preacher, calm down," I said into the phone. "Where are you? What's going on?"

"Oi, fook, Caje, this may've been a bad idea." Preacher sounded more ruminant than I'd ever heard, even a little despondent. "Yeh know how I get when I'm off me head, wha."

"What have you done, Preach?"

"Just come'n get me, Caje! It's too much temptation fer me. I love it so much."

I rolled my eyes and hit the back of my head against the headrest. I should have known. For whatever reason, women found Preacher almost as irresistible as much as they did Tex. That often played against the odds of his bizarre relationship with his girlfriend, sometimes for the best, sometimes not. It was a weird situation that I could never explain. You just had to know them. For Preacher to pull the rip cord like this, the right mix of chemicals and willpower must have swirled together in the goulash of his Preacher brain to sound red alert.

"Where are you?"

"Big Six's."

"Okay. Stay there. Don't drink anything else. Don't *do* anything else. Just hang on, and I'll be there in a minute."

The line went dead.

The Camry struggled against its four cylinders and Japanese heritage to accelerate past the pokey line of cars on the freeway at that hour. Its engine roar sounded less threatening and more like a hoarse old woman scream-vomiting. I hadn't bought it for the pickup. Twenty minutes later, I found Big Six and came to a squealing stop in its pavement lot.

The phone rang into voicemail every time I'd tried calling Preacher back, which worried me. At the door, a big ole' bouncer held a hand up to check my ID and collect the cover charge. My heart was racing as I dug out the singles and paid up. Could Preacher have gotten rolled? Was he in worse trouble than he'd let on and I just didn't catch it on the phone?

Big Six's was a much nicer establishment than any of the ones I had come across. Its neon signs proudly admitted its trade, calling truckers and citizens alike to answer the siren song of almost fully nude girls and specialty acts of vice. There was more plastic in the humans inside than the barware. The carpeting was newish and clean, at least, and no haze of secondhand smoke hung like pallor. A muscular redhead was working it onstage, doing flips and leg bends and all kinds of crazy positions as she flung herself around the pole.

I scanned the dark corners of the club for signs of my idiot friend to no avail, so I started moseying around, looking at people in booths and tables and trying not to be weird about it. One group of men clustered in a large booth with an equal group of dancers, and I caught one of them running a rolled dollar pipe down the table to snort a white powdery substance.

Preacher wasn't in any of the booths or at the bar. The bathroom contained the usual poorly managed facilities and some freak jerking off in the corner. I even sweet-talked a waitress to let me stick my head in the ladies room and look around, howls notwithstanding. The only places left had to be the dressing and office areas in the back and the rooms they had blocked off for private shows. The latter lay off a corridor down one side of the main room, velvety walls and curtains shimmering in crimson under strobes. I braced myself, looking around for more bouncers and finding, thankfully, none.

With quick flips of my arms to fling aside the curtains hanging in front of each private cubicle, I darted down the corridor of private rooms, peering in quickly to see if I recognized anybody. Many were empty, a few contained the usual writhing bodies, none offered up Preacher. There was a door at the end of the corridor that grew larger as I progressed. It had a sign in black and white that read "VIP." When I pushed on the door's handle, it gave easily, and I braced again. Other bouncers could be right behind there, waiting for some asshole like me to barge in somewhere I wasn't welcome and give them the excuse they were looking for to put their overpaid krav magra classes to practicality. Images of Preacher's bony ass bouncing up and down on some collection of platinum blondes with chest balloons passed through my skull, and I girded my turning stomach as I stepped into the room.

Inside, it was dark, lit only by a number of low-lumen lamps in old French architectural styles arranged throughout the room. A matching couch or bench or something like that sat in the center of the room. Hidden smoke machines pumped out a low, incense-scented haze of obscurity to cloud full vision. I waved my hands in front of me to clear as much of it as I could to see what the hell was going on.

And then I did.

"Preacher...are you sucking a guy's dick?"

10.

UM, YES. YES, HE IS.

Preacher gargled, the tranny's cock slipped out of his mouth, and he twisted against the discomfort of the handcuffs binding his hands behind his back.

"Aye," he said.

11.
SAVES THE DAY

We didn't say a word to each other as we left Big Six, not even after the tranny unlocked Preacher's cuffs or after Preacher slinked down the corridor to the exits. We didn't meet eyes; just walked out of there. I could feel the tranny's stare burning two Superman-style heat vision holes in my back as I got the hell out, even through the closing doors and the "Have a nice night, fellas!" platitude offered by the doorman. We didn't say anything as we got into the Camry, nor when I started her up, nor when I guided her carefully out of the parking lot and onto the highway service road.

Eventually though... "Preacher."

"Aye, Cajun?"

"Do we exist in some post-Lynchian world where you can explain to me what was going on back there? 'Cause it looked—*it looked*!—like you had spent all of Rick's money on a tranny hooker to tie you up and feed you her—his—*their* junk."

Preacher rolled down the window and retrieved a gnarled joint from one of the pockets of his flannel shirt. "Aye, that's about the right of it, wha."

"What the fuck are you thinking? Unless that tranny knew Tayona Parker...?"

He lit up the joint, took a long slow hit, and said, "No, I don't think so."

"You don't think so?! You don't *think* so?! Preacher, what the hell, man?!"

"I got a weakness about that shite, Caje, I'm sorry, alright?"

"Oh, you got a tranny weakness now? Izzatright? Am I hearing you right?"

"They don't like yeh to use that term anymore, I don't think," Preacher said as he exhaled a long slow stream of marijuana smoke.

"Preacher!"

"I'm *sorry*, Caje. I'd just had some of this real sweet bud an' yeh know I like to get up t'some freaky things sometimes an' I never directly had the pleasure before..."

"What is Mikayla going to say about this?" I said, finding myself sounding like the lamest bro ever or possibly that trombone-voiced teacher on Charlie Brown.

"Well...we have an...an understandin' I guess yeh'd call it."

"Is that true? Are you fuckin' with me right now, Preacher? You called me to come get you!"

Preacher waved a hand to dissipate his next exhalation. "I know, I know. Oi, fook, yeh think she's gonna be pissed?"

I looked over at my friend with wide eyes and a slack jaw. "What else are you on, man?"

He dug around for a moment in his pockets with the expression of a man from the nineteenth century who had just awoken in modern times, which was to say Preacher might well have been panning for gold in those beat-ass pockets. When his hands did come away, one featured a few coins—a couple Canadian ones, at that—and two gumdrop-sized baggies of some shit you could not find on any usual candy aisle. In his other hand, he gripped a wad of dollar bills crinkled with lube. Awesome.

"I'm not sure what this does," Preacher said, indicating the baggies.

"Put that way, you fucking maniac." I blew out an exasperated breath. "Rick is gonna have my ass."

"Imma have your ass, Jack! No, fuck that—Imma have *this* asshole's ass!"

We were somewhere on the other side of the Metroplex, Planoway, in Rick's swathe of canvas territory. You could always count on a 7-11 to stand to as a meet-up site, and the eastern Dallas area only drew out the street racing enthusiasts at that hour. A couple tricked-out Toyota hatchbacks rested in the lot near us, their wannabe drivers comparing notes on the evening's competitions over Slushees and vape pens. They could not help glancing sidelong at the reedy black man reading two schlubby pricks the riot act nearby.

"How much of the money did you blow?" Rick demanded, poking a finger into Preacher's chest. Preacher, thankfully, was flying just high enough after the latest joint and whatever else was in his system to sway listlessly in recoil from the finger-poke. He offered the remainder of the lube-drenched cash in his pocket to Rick.

"Oi, I brought yeh change, lad."

Rick wasn't one to easily lose his composure, and the sticky gunk that ran off the bills onto his hand set him off even more. His eyes blew up behind his rectangular glasses, the whites offset by the night and his glistening black skin.

"*Mother-fucker!*"

"Hey-hey-hey!" I said, stepping in between the two with palms raised in a heartfelt approximation of placation. "Listen. Bad choices have been...chosen. We all admit that."

"Jack, you're the one makin' bad choices. With this fuckin' guy," Rick said.

"That's the black callin' the kettle pot, wha," Preacher whined between puffs on a cigarette.

Rick looked at me. I looked at him back. We both looked at Preacher. Preacher just stood there swaying in an imaginary current, smoking his cigarette, looking down at the pavement and kicking at pebbles, oblivious to the race war he was on the verge of causing.

"Okay, fair criticism," I said, stepping in to rescue Preacher before Rick throat-chopped him. "But listen: it sounds like none of us are really making headway on this canvas tonight. Right? Are you?"

Rick narrowed his eyes at me, sensing the redirect I was attempting but hearing righteousness over the din, as was his gift. "I ain't found shit."

"Me neither! So maybe we should rethink it."

"What about your other connection? The ones with badges and no predilection for tranny cock?" Rick sneered at Preacher, and Preacher made a hurt face in slow motion.

"They don't like to be called that anymore—"

"The *hell* you say."

"I ran into a couple cops here and there, and they got the word," I said. "Local P.D.s, state troopers, enough. Tayona's photo is circulating. If she materializes, I'll get a call."

Rick shook his head, and I could see his shoulders vibrating, the frustration radiating off him. "How hard is this to figure out, Jack? I ain't askin' for help covering up a killing."

That lanced through me like a hot needle through a blister. I looked at Preacher to have an excuse not to look at Rick for a moment. "Preacher, can you give us a minute?"

I didn't even hear what Preacher said in return as he wandered off. Heat spread across the back of my neck and arced up into my face as I squared off with Rick again. His demeanor had not changed since the barb.

"That's a goddamn low blow and you know it," I said, voice tightening.

"You said you owed me one, right?" Rick replied, outright hostile now. "I mean, all I did was aid and abet a *murder*, so how hard can a little recon be? Really fuckin' hard apparently."

"You didn't tell me one goddamn time to stop," I said, bringing a finger of my own to poking position. "I laid it out. I took responsibility. You fell right in on it. Hell, *you* bought the gun."

"You didn't take responsibility for shit! Are you fuckin' with me? You sailed out of that situation skippin' and singin', man. Thanks to me. So where the fuck are you now?"

Now it was my turn for the outrage to flame, and my own eyeballs grew wide and revealing of strained blood vessels swirling about the light brown irises. I stepped in closer to Rick and jammed two fingers, index and middle, into his chest. "Perhaps you've forgotten about the shit that sonofabitch did to me, to my family. Finley got everything that was coming to him, and you helped me plan it. So get the fuck off your steed there, Sheriff, and suck it up. You called. I'm repaying the favor. You don't like it, see ya 'round...bro."

With my other hand, I shoved the remaining wad of cash I had on me into the right front pocket of his trousers. It's not a good idea to antagonize someone who's bigger than you and can kick your ass with disciplines you've only seen in movies like Brazilian *jiu-jitsu*, but I seemed to be getting used to that lately. The only thing keeping Rick from popping me one right there was likely the racers with their phones, visible to Rick over my shoulder. Even if he had thrown a haymaker—and I had every confidence that it was coming—I don't think I wanted to or could have fought back. Every white hot iron of honesty that Rick threw at me right then was spot-on.

Rick the Investigator, Rick the FBI Agent had evolved with many a technique and training for conflict resolution, behavioral analysis, and hand-to-hand combat. He had exited Quantico with high marks in every standard requirement for a Bureau man and then some, leaning into those depictions of our favorite fictional law-men to inform the kind he wanted to exemplify. He could meditate in real time, and not knowing a lot about the cases on which he worked prior to leaving the Bureau, I wondered for a split second if I was turning out to be the worst confrontation of his career. In the back of my mind, I realized that in my selfish, inward staring world, I barely knew what Rick could do because I had never asked him. And right then, as we simmered together in a boil of fuckery, that stung me worse than any four knuckles on the jaw ever could.

He ended up taking a step back from me, and I could almost see the variegated radiation patterns exude from his form as he processed the encounter. His mind and his being worked invisibly while I hammered him with silent, shitty terribleness: loathing, exasperation, and jealousy all wrapped up into a Dooley-sized glare missile. Rick's training must have kicked in, or some lesson from some Tibetan meditative technique subsumed the anger that had sparked our clash. Dale Cooper assessing Joe Hallenbeck and denying him the punishment he subconsciously craved. *Smile, you fuck...*

"I've got work to do," Rick said in a flat tone, putting the stake in the ground. He backed away again, turned, got in his Explorer, and drove off into the night.

Every one of his barbs meant something. Every one landed on me. Every one flew true.

That still didn't prompt my dumb ass to forgive him.

Preacher appeared at my side with a phone in one hand and a freshly lit joint in the other. "Oi, Tex has been callin' yeh, Caje. Where've yeh been?"

I snatched the joint from him and took a deep hit, head swimming quickly from both the bud brand and the vacuuming of oxygen from my brain in the extended inhalation and hold. There wasn't even any smoke left when I breathed out again.

"What?" I said.

"Tex. He said yeh've not been answerin' yer phone, yeh daft fooker."

I looked at Preacher. "Ya *think*?"

He held up his phone. "'Ere he is."

I grabbed the phone and held it to my ear, taking another, sharper toke on the joint. "Well, how's your night, Sunshine?"

"I think I've got something," said the best of us.

Tex's canvas unfolded nearer to the hub of Dallas. Arguably more progressive than Fort Worth, Dallas sure does have a lot more sin strips. Somehow, I had gotten jammed with the crappier ones on the outskirts, the sticky trucker places. Tex was rolling in high cotton on his beat.

Preacher and I joined Tex at Molly's, the "gentlemen's" club at which his lead had apparently turned up. Molly's resided on a literal strip of strip clubs in the warehouse district, blending in with divey saloons, tattoo parlors, and biker bars over a few ugly, concrete-laden blocks. Tex met us in the parking lot where we caught each other up and shared another of Preacher's delights, this one carefully rolled from a baggie labelled "The Bubonic Chronic." It evened Preacher out and brought him down from his light-footed perch in the clouds, and the hits I took picked off the sharp edges left by my argument with Rick. Tex, ever stalwart, changed not a whit as he accepted his turn on the puff and filled us in on his evening.

"There's a girl here knows Tayona," he said, forming up in a tripod with us in front of his truck in the parking lot. I sure was seeing a lot of parking lots tonight. "Recognized the photo. Said she would talk to me more later after she was finished dancing for the night. I guess they have shifts here."

"When's that gonna be?" I said.

Tex shrugged.

"Well, shit." I wasn't even sure I wanted to keep working this case at that point.

"The drinks aren't that pricey inside nor are they watered down," Tex said, plying me with the right excuse to keep at it.

"I could certainly use some of those," I said, clapping Tex on the shoulder. "Let's go. Preacher can tell you all about the dick that he sucked earlier this lovely evening."

We hit it hard. Tex had already warmed the place up with generous tips, and all the girls zeroed in on him immediately as his big, lumbering manliness returned to claim a table in the pit just away from the main stage. Tex introduced me and Preacher and faded into the background, demurring from the ladies politely but quickly. Before a pasty-decorated waitress could even ask, we had a round of drinks and some pickleback shots lined up. Picklebacks are great. It's first a shot of whiskey, as shitty as you want because as that shitty whiskey pinches your face and burns your throat, you shoot some pickle juice right behind it. The pickle juice washes away any trace of the whiskey, and you can just keep on doing that. It has the effect of tricking you into thinking you have not been taking a lot of shots. That's where we *started*.

We couldn't smoke inside Molly's, so the nic fits set in after the first drink, and we cut it with more shots. One jiggly waitress tried to sell us tubes of Jaegermeister from a serving tray that looked like it came from a junior chemistry set. Preacher laughed at her and demanded a whole bottle of Jameson's, "a man's whiskey!" That went pretty quick too. When I found out they had spicy mixed nuts at the bar, I tossed some singles at the 'tender to send over the whole supply. Preacher and I suffered mad cases of the munchies from The Bubonic Chronic, and we decimated those nuts like a couple squirrels digging for acorns under a field of live oaks.

When I say we hit it hard, I mean it went down as one for the records: three ornery sonsabitches tying one on as if an asteroid was about to hit the planet. Even Tex—usually so even-keeled—got in on it with us, especially as Preacher regaled him with tales of uncut transexual penises. I guess Tex was still dealing with the end of his sports career. I thought a little T&A would help him even out, but the big guy had more of an eye for me and Preacher than anything else happening around us. Things worsened when we started mixing drinks, at one point ordering a bucket of cheap Tecates because the beer felt pretty good cleansing our whiskey-soaked palates.

We were drinking and bullshitting so much that we hardly paid attention to the stage. High quality skin frolicked under multicolored stage lights and bass-thumping music, but we could not be bothered. Don't get me wrong, eyes strayed from time to time, but we had more important things to do, like lie about how awesome we were and pitch peanuts into empty shot glasses. It must have been the twenty-thousandth time Texas, Preacher, and I had drunk ourselves stupid like that, telling tall tales common to our folk and consistently one-upping each other in outrageousness and verve. We retold stories that we had shared a million other times between us, and we laughed and shouted ourselves hoarse like they were new. This is the nature of a Texan's bullshittery, I suppose. It's also in the Dooley genes.

As it usually happened, Tex and I could not keep up with Preacher's never-ending, stream-of-consciousness hullabaloo. He launched into a tirade about some shit, probably butts and assholes because that's where we end up going as the nights grow long. If it's one thing I appreciate about Preacher, it's that the guy, no matter how full of shit he can be, can always compel me to raucous laughter. He was into an expletive-laden description of the worst shit he'd ever taken when I laughed so hard I pissed myself a bit. This prompted a quick respite to the restroom, at which time I noticed Tex had left the table. Neither Preacher nor I recalled how long he'd been gone nor could we see straight enough to check our phones for texts or calls. I had to deal with the piss stain expanding on my inner thigh, and Preacher fell in time with a dubstep groove with rapt and fluid dance moves of the smoldering high, so we ignored Tex's disappearance.

The great thing about heavy drinking is that you can always pull the trigger and reset your clock when you need to. I had resisted this impulse for years, managing nausea with food and lower power drinks before the brothers of my college fraternity twigged me to the benefits of a good mid-drunk vomit. However, I have a terrible habit of scream-vomiting. I can never just ralph surreptitiously or with suave. As soon as I pitch over to evacuate stomach contents, I wail like Jabba the Hutt dying in *Return of the Jedi*. I don't know what that is: it's like I have to exorcise some shamanistic spirit in addition to the expulsion of substances mixing in my gut. Sometimes, if you honk hard enough, your asshole opens up a little and you fart, and God help ya if you've got a bullet in the chamber. It no-shit sounds like the end of the world whenever the urge takes me, and it did that night in Molly's restroom as I was struggling to blot whiz off my jeans. It was bad. I painted those stall walls like they needed it (they didn't). If we had spent any less money at our table that night, I'm sure one of the bouncers would have tossed me out as I had tossed my cookies.

Panic gripped my topsy-turvy stomach as that thought crossed my mind, the panic of the blitzed drunk worried that he had done or said something to warrant physical violence. This situational fear propelled me out of the restroom and through the exit in search of fresh air, sweating and reeking of puke. Paranoia seized me as I met eyes with the club's staff at every step of the way. Would they sense it? How could they not? If I exhaled, they would surely smell the rot that issued from my drunk gut. And if I stumbled once, made one misstep, the game would be up. Muscled security would identify me as a drunken idiot that needed booting. Luckily, none of these things happened, and I slipped outside with a knowing smile to the doorman. I played it cool, walking away from him in a half-jog to get around the corner of the building where I could double over and spew another bile-filled explosion of alcoholic ejecta onto the pavement. I barely controlled the screaming that time but was unable to fight the massive, earthquaking fart that manifested as gas, thankfully, instead of mass.

I felt like I had run a marathon, had survived an obstacle course, had competed in an extreme workout game of some kind. I sunk against the wall in the back of Molly's, catching my breath. A ginger ale would have helped immensely, but there was no way I was going to find one in that state. Through the haze of tears, sweat, and other fluids, I saw Tex's white T-shirt come into focus in the distance, his cowboy hat bobbing up and down in rapid syncopation as he ran toward me. I only briefly wondered where he was coming from and why before he skidded to a stop next to me, his Luccheses scratching an asphalty noise as he came to rest.

"Cajun, you okay?" he said, and either my hearing was slurred or his speech was. Or both.

I blinked several times to try and right my ship. As I focused on Tex, I could see various light-colored stains on his otherwise white T-shirt. We were not clean drunks, the three of us.

"'M fine," I dribbled. "Where you go?"

"It's about time to find Elaynea." I had no idea what Tex was talking about. Weren't we just drinking? He saw the confusion on my face and patted my shoulder. "The dancer I told ya about earlier. Listen, no big deal. I'll go get her and we can all meet out here. Is Preacher still inside?"

I could only manage a heavy-lidded nod. Tex patted my shoulder again and stood from his squat. "Try to get your wits about ya, Cajun. You're the investigator here."

That sparked a guffaw in me. As Tex ambled off around the corner, I snickered to myself but not so that I felt any humor or any emotion at all for that matter. If I was the investigator in this situation, then God save the Queen.

Texas and Preacher came stumbling back around the corner a few minutes later, Tex guiding Preacher with one arm on his back while Preacher navigated the flat lot like it undulated beneath him. As they drew in closer, I tried to slide up the wall by backing my feet and legs up and pushing against it, whiskey legs fighting gravity in shakes. Tex reached for my arm and steadied me, hands on both of us.

That's right. Get ready, mokes. We got this.

Preacher doubled over and threw up on my shoes.

Tex guided us around back of the strip mall till we were directly behind Molly's. A janitorial person was emptying trashcans in a dumpster, the door behind him open to Molly's back office area. A girl would walk out of that door, clad in coats and other modest vestments that belied the work inside. Sometimes one or more would be accompanied by one of the musclebound bullet-heads from security. The glow of morning was starting to radiate in the background behind us. It must have been close to four or five.

"Hey-ey, big cowboyyyyeee," someone catcalled in more syllables than was required of the words, a girl. One of the dancing girls, of course, it took me a moment to reason. Preacher and I were still trying to maintain our balance, and I had the added indignity of the puke on my shoes. Tex had lit a cigarette and was waving to the source of the catcall.

"Hey, Elaynea," Tex said, tipping his hat at her. "Have a good night?"

"Damn, boyee, you need'a come back and see me again. Don't be givin' all dat paper to those bitches and hoes in there." Elaynea sported a calf-length white trench coat replete with faux diamonds and textures, itself matching a white leather bodysuit and knee-high boots she wore with it. Her skin was cow-leather brown but glistening and soft, framed by straight black hair pulled back into a tight ponytail. I couldn't remember if she had looked like this on stage earlier that evening. Hell, I couldn't remember any of the dancers.

"Well, if we weren't spendin', they mighta made us leave," Tex replied in that easy drawl of his, adding a cowboy's smile to it that caused Elaynea to inch up closer to him, pluck his cigarette out of his hand, and take a sensual drag on it herself.

"I woulda hated that, cowboyeee," she said, blowing smoke out of the side of her mouth.

"You were gonna tell us about Tayona. Tayona Parker."

Elaynea's eyes strayed to where me and Preacher were struggling to stand straight. Preacher had even given up and bent over to put his hands on his knees, exhorting a low growl. "Dayum, what's wrong wit' dat mufuh?"

"Oh, these are just friends of mine," Tex said. "They've had a bit to drink."

She made a noise in the back of her throat to accompany the judgey stare she was giving us. "White boys can't hold they liquor." She took another drag off Tex's cigarette and turned back to him. "So whatchu wanna know, cowboy?"

"Tayona Parker. You said you knew her."

"Damn right I know that bitch." Elaynea spat on the ground. "Cunt keeps takin' my cheddah, y'feel me? Come outta nowhere with her priss-ass pussy suckin' dick and gettin' the prime stage time 'round here. She *must* be fuckin' the owner to get the time she be gettin'."

"So she's been hornin' in on your territory," I said. She was coming into focus now. I hoped I would not throw up on her. I was definitely struggling to not shit myself.

"Right!" Elaynea said, brandishing the cigarette at me. "Girl come outta *nowhere* and start dancin' top-level, you know? Ain't no new pussy get to do that."

"Has she been dancing anywhere else?" I asked. "We didn't see her tonight."

"Yeah, I hear she be throwin' her ass all over the place. She old school trash. I seen her at Breakers, at Top 10s, Fannie's, all dem places 'round here. In fact, I *know* her trick ass gonna be at Whiskey Jim's tomorrow night 'coz my sistah Nonna tole' me she lost her spot on the main stage cuz of that cunt takin' it away. Trick-ass bitch."

Elaynea tossed the cigarette angrily to the ground and stamped it out. I traded glances with Tex. *Jackpot*, I thought.

"Whiskey Jim's, huh?" Tex said, offering Elaynea a roll of cash. I couldn't make out how much but trusted Tex's judgment. If only Rick had hung around him that night instead of Preacher.

"Yeah, you find her there on the primetime, shugah," Elaynea said, smiling sweetly at Tex as she took the money and started counting it. "She prob'ly get there late, shake her ass, and then trick the rest of the night. Jim's got dem high-payin' muhfuhs, you know? Sheeit, yeah, you know, baby. Look at dis stack of paper you gimme!"

Tex winked at her and offered up another of his trademark gentleman's grins. "Not really lookin' for that kinda party."

"What is you lookin' fo' though?" Elaynea said, casting another suspicious leer at me and Preacher, who had taken the opportunity to lean against the nearest wall.

"Just gotta ask her some questions is all," I said. "We're a little worried about her kid. You haven't seen her with a kid at all, have you?"

Elaynea twisted her ample lips into a grimace. "Naw, I ain't seen him, but I know she got him. Can't fuckin' shut up about him. Tellin' all the club owners she need that paper to take care of him." She made a dismissive noise, a long hiss between her teeth. "Like we ain't got people to take care of too! My momma got the lung cancer, an' I gotta make sure she don't die. You know how much those breathin' machines and tanks cost? Sheeeeiiiiiiit."

I nodded. Employers like Molly's didn't exactly issue health insurance options and benefits packages, and I could bet a good chunk of change that Elaynea wasn't exactly trading on a law degree in her free time. People had to make life work for them sometimes.

Like maybe Tayona was doing.

Tex kindly avoided Elaynea's continued attempts to get him to come with her: even at five in the morning, she wanted to shake her ass for fun instead of money. Tex did allow her a sloppy wet kiss, and she tipped the gray Stetson back on his head while she slurped on his lips. That's Texas for you. She didn't even bat an eye at me, and Preacher likely left her care-orbit right around the time he found that wall to hold up with his skinny ass.

When she'd left, we lit cigarettes, and Tex made a face at me. "Well? Is that something?"

"It's more than cock-gobbler here got for us," I said, jerking a thumb at Preacher.

"Oi, fook off, yeh shite," Preacher retorted. "Yer a right twat and so's yer friend."

"Blow me. Well, we know what we're doing tomorrow night. Should we celebrate with some Ol' South?"

"I like the sound of that," Tex said.

At that moment, a brazenly drunk collection of meatheads crashed into Tex's back and caused him to stumble into us. I caught him but Tex's bulk threw Preacher directly on his ass with a "What the fook?!" When we looked back, the meatheads offered douchey grins that matched their douchey haircuts and uniform polos. Security guards for Molly's tanked to the green zone on bennies, leftover shots from the closing bar, and whatever 'roid that ballooned up their bis and tris. They had stumbled down the iron staircase on the backside of the club, out of the door to the back office where the janitor was looking over his shoulder with a murderous glare that said the three douchebags had accosted him too. I remembered that look as the guy went inside and closed the door.

"Yo, this place is closed, *bro*," the lighter haired of the trio said, his demeanor hard in that professional way that intimidated most people but leaked cuntiness to assholes like me, Texas, and Preacher. As a matter of life, the bros must carry such cuntiness, and such bullshittery must narrow them into their own silos, not unlike the one in which we all probably thought about the janitor or even Elaynea.

"Yeah, skip on outta here, boys," the dark-haired security bro said. He was equally douchey and just as annoying as the first one but he had not descended to the highest possible prick puff-up of the third security bro with his completely shaved white head and lack of neck.

Preacher had clambered back up to his feet, all traces of drunkenness gone and the countenance of private madness intensifying in the one eye that ogled permanently larger than the other. Tex swiveled slowly around to face the douche bros once he made sure Preacher and I were okay. He regarded the bros with the calm, non-threatening carriage of a rancher counting the cattle in the morning, knowing where the cattle must go to make market. I let out a breathy sigh as I realized I had dropped my cigarette.

"I like my pancakes with a squirt of douche," I said.

"Gross," Tex said and hit the first guy so hard in the face that he shit his pants and landed in its squishy mess as unconsciousness and pavement greeted him...all precursor to Tex's brothers launching off the starting block with substance-fueled mad craziness in our fists.

12.

TAYONA GONNA GETCHA

The hangover claimed me like a psychotic madman, abetted by bruises, contusions, and a split lip. I couldn't remember how I'd gotten back to the apartment, but there I was: splayed out on the couch with vomit- and piss-soaked jeans down around my knees, crusted mucus sealing one eye shut and sticky across the throbbing in my face, likely mixed with blood and bile. My shirt was torn in three places on the floor, and I had thrown up on it, possibly to avoid soaking the carpet. I didn't feel like I had shit myself but remained still until I could confirm or deny. Movement prompted worse pain and dizzying nausea anyway, so I just lay there in my pool of sick until I could regain some sense of cogency.

The TV displayed the run-on menu from the *Clerks* DVD, a perennial late-night favorite for gradual drunken pass-outs. A stupor of alcohol, marijuana, head trauma, and damn knows what else last night had not prevented me from returning to familiar habits in the haze.

The downed pants could have been evidence of an unsuccessful attempt at masturbation, a numb-fingered handling of quivering sausage instead of the confidence of the strong shafted and genuinely horny. When I rolled over at last, falling to the floor on barely functional hands and knees, hammers pounded inside my skull. At least, by that time, I had worked out that no actual feces had slipped from my anus to stain an otherwise tobacco-redolent couch. No, the drunk shits would take me later alongside hours of bargaining against a burbling stomach seeking to continue a trend of evacuation. Shits that would require much more spatter-inducing attention to detail than I could provide with common cleaning products. I needed help. I needed *housekeeping*.

Cats would have to suffice for the time being. In stumbling inside my apartment, I had failed to shut and latch the door, leaving a sliver passage open for the neighborhood kittens to get in. Small, furry balls of feral might had invaded in the early light of morning. They were scattered across the apartment, nestled into the corners of the big maroon reading chair or sprawled out in rays of sunshine encroaching from between blinds. A particularly ferocious gray and white bastard kitten was halfway inside a bag of Doritos in the kitchen, crunching orange-crusted snacky goodness of a type sure to knock off one of its lives.

The tiniest of the litter—a puffy version of a Russian blue—had hidden itself inside the torn shirt on the floor and mewled at me as I struggled into my pants. He sensed inevitable eviction perhaps. Or maybe he just wanted to damage my throbbing head even more. Regardless, I snarled and groaned, leading the whole gang of floofs to jump, skip, and raise their hackles. I threw the bag of Doritos outside the apartment door and waited for the mocking sons of bitches to prance their feckless way out. The little Russian blue took his time, giving me a kitten's snarl and stretch before bopping outside to munch with his brothers and sisters next to where I'd deposited Preacher-vomit encrusted Converse. Lazy ass cats.

As my brain pieced itself and the night prior together, I spent the next several hours cleaning myself up and seeking coherence. My phone was riddled with messages upon which I could draw no focus. I winced as it rang in my hand, and even the simple act of responding to the caller pulsed knives into my forehead.

"What...?" I stammered.

"We gonna eat or what?" Tex said. When I did not respond right away, he said, "Don't worry. I bet you've got a slight case of the cocktail flu. I'll come getcha."

The rim of the toilet seat was cold.

"Gimme an hour," I said.

"I'm pretty sure we need to seek professional help, y'all," came crawling out my scratchy-ass throat a few hour later.

"Why?" Preacher said. He lay in the corner of the booth, sprawled as best his body would allow, head angled against the window. We both wore sunglasses to combat the afternoon glare. Sweat soaked Preacher's flimsy flannel and beaded on his forehead. I slumped in a similar fashion across the table from him, and Tex sat next to me hunched over.

"What, no snappy patter?" I said. "You *are* hung over."

"Not gonna lie, I shite meself."

"I can smell it," Tex said, rubbing the bridge of his nose. "Did you even bother to shower?"

"Shower? I didn't bother to change pants."

We were propping up the east wall at J&J's Oyster Bar, chosen for its copious fried food, a sure solution to the bubble guts. To take the edge off, we had opted for Bloody Marys, extra bacon and a fat Gulf of Mexico shrimp affixed to the lip of each glass. We were currently demolishing an appetizer basket full of gator tail and hush puppies. It was helping, but Preacher had already sprayed the bathroom with hangover leavings, and the paranoid in me couldn't help but feel that our welcome at that delightful establishment was slipping away.

A college girl in a J&J's T-shirt knotted at the waist delivered baskets of shrimp, crawfish, oysters, a po-boy, and more appetizers. It looked like she was about to smile and offer us some chatter to prompt a tip, but as soon as she got close, the look and stench of us assaulted her, and she scrunched up her nose in revulsion, deposited the food, and scurried away. We didn't care. We needed relief.

Tex sported a fresh shiner on his jaw, repercussion of the single clip one of the douches from last night managed to land. I gestured to it with my chin and said through a mouthful of fried oysters, "The ladies like a man knows how to handle himself."

"Fucker tagged me, didn't he?" Tex said, rubbing his jaw.

"You did drop that first one like panties on a Galveston hooker, Tex," said Preacher. "Not that those sonsabitches didn't fookin' deserve it."

"Sideswipin' faggots," I said.

"Hey, watch your mouth," Tex said, fixing me with a glare that I wasn't expecting. Sometimes Tex tended to look over someone... or through them...like they weren't really there or like he was seeing something else that nobody else could. Right then, Tex pinned me directly with his eyes. I felt it. Even behind my sunglasses, I couldn't meet his gaze, and my eyes darted nervously.

"What, Tex, what?" I said, putting a fry in my mouth to chomp.

"You shouldn't use that word." He paused firmly then returned to taking a big bite out of his oyster po-boy.

"Fuck do you care?" I said, inadvisably.

"Because I'm gay, dumbass."

You know the feeling you get right before you go off on a bungee jump? Like you're not sure if the line is safe? Or, for those of you who have the privilege, the same way you feel the first time you skydive? Like the pit of your stomach suddenly realizes it's its own gyroscope and then goes haywire because gravity reorients? That's the way I get every time I say something stupid and someone calls me on it. In my callous youth, I would continue pressing the effrontery in an effort to spin it toward some humorous outcome that mitigated my idiocy and prompted everybody to remember how much they loved me. This is what I attempted presently.

"What? Come on. I thought Preacher here was the only one of us with a penchant for gargling cock."

"Well, if it's all the same to you, Jack," Tex said, slowly speaking around a mouthful of po-boy, "don't knock it till you've tried it."

Preacher lit up and brandished his Bloody Mary at me in one hand, lifting his sunglasses with the other to reveal a pair of manic and bloodshot yet knowing eyes. "Y'see? Don't knock it, yeh fooker."

I pitched my own sunglasses up onto my head and narrowed eyes at Tex. The guts of a fried shrimp fell onto my basket as I failed pitching it into my mouth. "Tex, are you fuckin' with me?"

"Where do you think I went last night? That gay bar Herrod's was right across the street from Molly's. It's strictly 'dudes only,' if ya get my drift."

"Tex, I've known you for years. You crushed more pussy in high school than the whole athletic department combined. There's standing warnings of how difficult it is to run leg in your presence. How did I not know about this?" I blinked, looking away, hangover forgotten. "What is happening right now? Is this reality?"

Preacher sipped on the straw in his drink and regarded me with a neutral expression that I would look back on as patronizing. "Cajun, if yeh havenae noticed, yeh can be kind of a daft arsehole sometimes."

"It's been simmerin' for a while," Tex said, slurping his own Bloody Mary. "I mean, I guess I've always known what I've been into and whatnot. Still more of a pitcher than a catcher."

"But what about the ladies, Tex, *the ladies*!" I had dropped my food and held the sides of my head as if witnessing a black hole forming in the far wall. "You—you run more leg than anybody!"

"Ran, past tense," Tex said with a shrug. "Takes some time to figure out who ya are is all, I suppose."

I kept blinking. *Tex is gay?* It was like finding out that Malcolm X polished white men's shoes for spare change. Like Keith Richards cut every white substance he ever took with laxatives. Like Kermit the Frog started his own TV show just to prey upon children, Michael Jackson-style. Doctor Who couldn't stop the glue in the spacetime continuum from melting.

"Wait," I said, pointing at Preacher. "Did *you* know this?"

Preacher shrugged. "Oi, I don't think Texas and I ever had what ya'd call a heart-to-heart over it, but an oul' sod like me can see." To Tex, he said, "I think I woulda asked yeh for some tips on fellatio."

"I have a few," Tex said.

"What *planet* am I on right now?" I felt the dull throb of my hangover headache return. "Am I really that much of an asshole?"

"Hey, we all have our character flaws," Tex said. "But let's not dwell on it. Here, eat some of my po-boy."

I gamely took Tex's unfinished quarter of the po-boy. It was good. Slaw was just right. Oysters were perfectly fried. French bread was super fresh.

"Shit, man," I burbled through a mouthful, still not landing on where I really needed to be, which was apologizing to my friend. But that's me, I guess.

Tex patted me on the back with one of his oversize paws, jaw cranking through some popcorn crawfish tails and displaying a quintessential Texas-like half-smile.

"'S'all right, Cajun. We ain't all perfect gods."

The texts were going through but Rick wasn't answering. I even called him a couple times, getting no more than a terse identification on his voicemail. Through the hiss of post-beep recording static on each call, explanations eluded me, and all the platitudes I could think up sounded empty and juvenile. Maybe that was fall-out from Tex's bombshell earlier and a slow realization of just how deep my assholery sank. In either case, nothing sounded right in my head, and I knew Rick's silence justified itself.

A few more drunk shits and a nap got me right enough for Friday night's stakeout. Despite the communication breakdown with Rick—he was probably just following up on his own leads, I told myself—I still wanted to see the thing through with Tayona, if anything for the sheer mental satisfaction of determining exactly what the broad was all about. The nap helped. Nothing like dozing off on your couch in the daylight and awakening in pitch black darkness, unsure of the time or day, internal clocks askew, blessed confusion nursing your buzzing skull, and arms numb from curling up into yourself for hours.

The TV had turned itself on with the commencement of an Adult Swim block on The Cartoon Network: *Cowboy Bebop*, a hi-fi sci-fi epic imported from Japan with a jazz-funk soundtrack that could rouse a bear in hibernation. Mellow strings and piano keys stirred me, Yoko Kanno compositions executed in perfect synergy amongst a musical cast of characters that would make Damon Albarn and Jamie Hewlett jealous. There were worse ways to enter consciousness.

I tried Rick again to no avail. His refusal to pick up didn't worry me so much as it pissed me off. Least the guy could do was give me a warm shoulder brush-off.

Naptime worked out for everyone. Clocks scored midnight by the time we got our shit together. Tex drove, and we hit Whiskey Jim's just in time to see a particularly plastic Asian-American (could have been straight Asian for all I know what with the trafficking hub that was Dallas) bobble off the main stage. I side-eyed Tex as we found a table near one of the two smaller stages. He just seemed like regular old Texas, post-coming out. I guess that's just how it is.

Whiskey Jim's catered to a better crowd than most of the central Dallas joints we had already canvassed. Dark crimson velvet covered the floors and the walls. Thick ropes separated the casual areas from bottle service tables and VIP booths where high rollers got the touchy-feely treatment that went against the rules, in plain view of everyone else so as to elicit the upsells sought by management. One of the side stages was actually a gold-lined shower with glass walls. The servers dressed in uniforms: tight-fitted tuxedo tops and fishnets modeled from the old Playboy bunny acts of yesteryear. Servers were off-limits to the grubby hands of the customers, but the garters around their thighs bulged with cash tips from those that sought to try.

Hangovers in check, Preacher started us up again with a round of picklebacks and light beers. Before walking in, he had offered me a bump off his knuckle, a quick snort to combat fatigue from the previous night and another potentially long one. You've got to watch cocaine. People with addictive behaviors like me are usually the most susceptible to picking it up as a compulsive habit, which is damn difficult to come down from. If you're careful and selective with it though—or mix it just right with the kaleidoscope of other drugs Preacher supplied—it can hyper-tune every sense in your body. You hear all these stories about stockbrokers and finance geeks getting strung out on coke and decrying its befouling effects when they lose everything or crash hard against divorce or some other domestic melodrama. You never hear about the ones who *manage* it. The hard seekers, the everyday salarymen, the weirdos, the artists, and the freaks. They use it because it's fun, because it sharpens them, because they can control the desire to flatten out on it. Or they're idiots like me and Preacher who just cut the worst effects with more drugs.

A little bit of coke goes a long way, and Preacher's bump zeroed me in on the evening's task like I was peering down a perfect sniper scope to plug a twelve-point buck. My heart immediately ramped up to pound like the Flash kicking off nightmares in his sleep. The picklebacks helped stabilize. Now it would just be a matter of controlling the amount of booze I would inevitably suck down in half-remembered attempts to balance out the upper.

Tex asked after Tayona at the bar to no avail. Every time our server delivered us another round, we would add a wad of tens and fives to her nursing school fund. A few drinks in, she told us that she had never heard of a dancer named Tayona but the owner always had new girls coming in and out of the place. We kept drinking.

"Sex worker, sex worker, gimme some skin," Preacher started singing to the tune of "Matchmaker" from *Fiddler on the Roof.* He wasn't singing to anyone in particular, and in fact, he stared straight down into the preparation of a fresh fatty as he warbled.

"You should sell that theme song to these girls," I said.

"Aye, they got it hard enough, Caje, fer shoor. Our Zatanna trynna get her R.N. The lass last night got her mum to take care o'." He licked the straight edge of the rolling paper and folded it into an appropriate tubular shape. "Fookin' hard livin' down here, wha."

"You said it, Preach," Tex said, taking a long slow sip off his beer.

"'S'nae just them, 's'all of us," Preacher continued, tenderly handling his Bob Marley. "What kinda shite we got to look forward to, huh? Tex gettin' rolled off the Rangers. Cajun doin' silly work like *this* shite. And whatever the fook I'm doin'."

"What *are* you doin'?" I said.

Preacher ran the completed joint under his nose from tip to stern, inhaling its essence as if testing the vintage. "Survivin', Cajun. Survivin'. I mean, technically it *is* yer arsehole friend's money we're spendin' tonight..."

I facepalmed involuntarily. "Oh, that's right. Jesus, Rick's gonna kill me if he ever talks to me again."

"He hasn't been in touch?" Tex asked.

"No. He got a little...perturbed...with me and Preacher last night."

"Welcome to my world."

"You don't get perturbed with us." I blinked, remembering our earlier conversation. "Do you?"

Tex inclined his head with an easy demeanor. "It's hard being the even-keeled one in this trifecta."

Preacher laughed suddenly, ork-orking deep in his throat like a choking pig. "Tex, yer about as even as Joe Cocker wankin'!"

Tex winked at us both. "Cheers to that."

Clearly, more beer was warranted.

Whiskey Jim's didn't allow smoking inside—hazardous to the health of the employees, of course—so we broke to crush Preacher's joint in the parking lot. He had brought The Bubonic Chronic again, and its herb-infused, earthy aromas blended perfectly with the coke high and the beer buzz. It was that perfect climate, the perfect twist. I could focus razor-keenly on any detail I wanted while at the same time relaxing into a cushion of succor. It was like some mystical higher plane of existence that you only get to one time with the right dedication to meditation and psychedelics, although we had purposely stayed away from mescaline and other trip-inducing fun that might have winnowed us away from the night's task.

It was not to last, alas, as the usual series of one-upmanship commenced. I lamely switched to liquor, Crown and sevens, and Preacher decided to try the tequila. Tex stayed on the beer as he saw us twist, as the table became awash in the usual decay of our typical rager: sticky drink contents splashed about soaked napkins, spilt beer cans, and discarded lime husks. Preacher laid out another line to snort on the table, and I stuck my fingers in the ephemeral remains, rubbing coke dust on my gums and feeling the welcome tingle of numbness.

We could have gone on down that windy road of badness, but I tipped up early to get to the toilet. I could not find the bathrooms easily so I tottered outside and around the back to find a secluded corner in which to piss. That corner turned out to be just inside the loading dock in back where the establishment took delivery of its supplies. A lone light shone down from a cluster of three spots on a roof-mounted rod, the other two broken. It was still plenty of light to avoid the river of piss cascading down from the wall on which I relieved myself. You just had to dance a little to remove your feet from the flow: one foot back, one foot to the side, widen, repeat.

Something cold and hard prodded me behind my left ear and stayed there, digging into the skin and hair. The force of it surprised me, and I pissed all over my hands as I struggled to maintain my balance. My wet hands reflexively went palms-first on the wall to prevent a fall. The cold hard cylinder stayed fixed to my head, and I could sense the outline of the perfect cavity in its center.

"Why you lookin' for me, muthafucka?" Tayona Parker hissed into the other ear.

13.
HICKS IS MY FAVORITE

"You have me in a bit of a...*delicate* situation," I said, dick out.

"Answer my question, bitch, or I'll delicate yo' ass." Tayona pushed the gun barrel deeper into my skull, eliciting a wince.

"Whoah, easy there," I said in the most placating, slur-free voice I could muster, which was not. "I'll tell you everything you want to know, Tayona."

"How you know who I am?" She didn't move and neither did the gun.

"Who else would be jackin' me up out here after I've been asking around about you for the last couple nights?"

"Whatchu *want*, muthafucka?"

"Look, here's the straight dope, Tayona: your husband hired a friend of mine to track you and your boy down. Says you've kidnapped him against his will."

"Bullshit. Friend of a friend shit. You workin' for Ted!"

"I am not working for Ted." I raised my hands up higher. "I'm just looking for you. That's all."

"Well, you found me now." Tayona spat on the pavement next to my shoes. "You found my momma too, huh? Why you wanna fuck with my momma?"

"She was easy to find, that's all. You, not so much."

"Boy, I oughtta blow yo muthafuckin' head off—"

I rolled my eyes. "Well, this is turning into a great big cliché."

A stab of pain circulated from behind my ear to the middle of my skull. The gun butt rebounded off it but with little force. Tayona wasn't a fighter. I squealed a bit all the same, an emanation to show that she had been effective, what she wanted to hear. I put one hand to the spot where she'd hit me and leaned against the wall with the other.

"Is that how this is gonna go?" I said. "Why don't you just shoot me?"

Tayona didn't respond, and I knew I'd gotten into her thoughts. In the critical space, I turned slowly so I could see her, hands still up to convince her I was no threat. She wore a leather jacket over a T-shirt and ripped jeans with a pair of half-calf leather boots. Her straightened hair glistened so reflectively in the single light I thought it might be a weave, but I'd later learn that was all Tayona. She glared at me with dark eyes and lips compressed into a thin line, hiding their fullness. Those lips all of a sudden turned up at the corners, and she said with plenty of sarcasm, "Nice dick, white man."

At least the drunk blush on my face hid my chagrin. I didn't dare move my hands.

"You gonna shoot me? Shoot me. Otherwise, we can talk about the lengths your hubby is taking to find you and Artie. The kid's name is Artie, right?"

Tayona pulled the hammer back on the six-cylinder Smith & Wesson. "Ain't nobody gettin' they hands on my boy. You hear me, muthafucka?"

I held up my hands shoulder high, palms up. Gross. They were still wet with urine.

"Okay, okay. I hear you." I downshifted into a lower, slower tone. "You've got to know, though: Ted's got lots of resources to find you and your son. Lots of people looking for you."

"Ted don't care 'bout being no father!" Tayona shouted, shaking the gun at me. "He ain't even Artie's real dad! He just want Artie! Wanna plug him up into his goddamn computers and shit. If Artie wasn't special, Ted wouldn't give a shit."

Something in my head clicked.

"Artie's special, huh?"

"Yes, he is, but that ain't none of yo' business!"

"It could be. Tell me why Ted wants Artie. Huh? What's this about plugging the kid into computers?" The soothing lilt in my tone continued modulating. "Why are you running, Tayona? What's really going on?"

She kept the gun trained on me, but her posture told me she was beginning to soften: her stance narrowed, and she switched the gun to another hand. *Ambidextrous...*

"I ain't tellin' you shit if you lookin' for me. Lookin' for my boy!" She didn't shout that time.

"Look, I'm nobody, Tayona," I said, oozing calm. *Thanks, drugs.* "I'm not a cop. I don't work for Parker. I'm just a dude, okay? I might be able to help you, too."

She scowled at me. "How *you* gonna help me?"

My eyes darted left and my eyebrows popped up. "Uh. I haven't worked that out yet. But I could. Let's just say there's help on the way."

Texas and Preacher took that moment to round the corner, a fresh joint lit and propped between Preacher's fingers. They took in the scene: girl, gun, me, my dick. A pregnant pause engulfed us.

"Yeh think *I'm* into some weird shite, Cajun?" Preacher said.

If I was going to get shot, so be it, but it wasn't going to be with my dick hanging out. I had enough embarrassment to carry me out of this world. I zipped up, ignoring the ignominy of my mediocre man-stick's shriveling in the night air before a badass woman holding a gun on me.

Tayona swiveled the gun toward Tex and Preacher. "Who the fuck you two? Oh, wait..." She regarded Tex as he held his big hands up, biceps stretching against the cuffs of his T-shirt. "You that big cowboy muthafucka askin' round bout me."

"Ya got me, sheriff," Tex said, flashing that easy grin of his.

"Then who you?" Tayona said, training the gun on Preacher.

Preacher put one hand up in the air and proffered the joint to her with the other. "Just yer friendly neighborhood road man, luv. Yeh care for a toke?"

She eyed Preacher, hardening from the relaxed position Tex and I had charmed her into. She glanced sidelong back at me, lowered her pistol, and cautiously stepped toward Preacher.

"Fuck, now I *know* y'all ain't no cops cuz that shit smell goooood."

"Aye, that's a good lass," Preacher said, handing her the joint.

Tayona took a quick puff and rolled the smoke around in her nasal cavity before sucking it down. "Where you get this shit, man?"

Preacher flashed a set of crooked, nicotine stained teeth when he smiled. "I never reveal me sources, luv."

"Are we all sufficiently calmed the fuck down now?" I said, finally lowering my hands and wiping them on my jeans.

"This the help you talkin' 'bout?" Tayona said, jerking a thumb at Tex and Preacher.

"We're a triple act," I said, motioning with my fingers for her to come closer. "Here. Puff, puff, give, yo. I got to calm my nerves."

"You looked pretty calm there with your dick hangin' out, Jack," Tex snickered.

"Ha, ha," I said, taking a big hit.

"That your name?" Tayona said. "Jack?"

"That's me," I said, breath holding a delightful pot buzz down in the cockles of my lungs. I exhaled a thin stream of smoke and said, "Those are my friends. Tex is the big one. Preacher's the stoned one."

"How're yeh?" Preacher said, all smiles. Tex just saluted with a couple fingers from the brim of his cowboy hat when I called his name.

Tayona looked back and forth between the three of us.

"Y'all crazy," she said.

"I got this theory. You've seen *Aliens*, right? Great movie. Well, who's your favorite character? Ripley, right? You're gonna say Ripley. Most folks gravitate to Ripley because it's *her* story, yeah? *She* does all this insane shit to beat her fear of the alien and make up for the loss of her daughter by substituting Newt and so on and so on. And Sigourney totally deserved the Oscar for that performance.

"But really, who is the one character that you love the most in *Aliens*? Who you pick tells a lot about who you are."

"That's your theory?" Tex said.

"It is," I said, passing the spliff to Tayona. "So, take Hudson, for example. Hudson's comedy relief, he's imminently quotable, maybe a bit of a spaz."

"I love Hudson," Preacher broke in. "'Game over, man!'"

I gestured to Preacher. "My point exactly."

"Who your favorite?" Tayona said, passing the joint to Preacher.

"Who me?" I adjusted my squat perch. "I'm a Hicks man."

"Yeah, I am too," Tex said. "But for different reasons."

"Yer just loopy for Michael Biehn, yeh daft bastard," Preacher said.

"Hicks is still my favorite."

"Hicks the only other one that makes it to the end?" Tayona said.

"Yeah, the guy that gets the acid burn in the face," I said. "'Somebody wake up Hicks.' Cool as shit."

"Yeah," Tayona said. "He okay."

"Who's your favorite?"

Tayona made a face at me as if it was the stupidest question in the world. "Who you think? Ripley, obvi."

We had found egg crates on which to perch outside the loading dock behind Whiskey Jim's. Preacher's first doobie had gone down well, warranting a second.

I paused. "You ready to talk some more about Parker?" I asked Tayona.

"Look, I only ran away with my son because that man crazy," she said, clasping her hands together. "When we first got Artie diagnosed, Ted was all like 'I'm done.' He didn't wanna have nothin' to do with Artie. Piece of shit."

"Diagnosed with what?" I asked.

Tayona looked down. "They say he on the spectrum. That's the nice way to say it. He got autism."

My eyes involuntarily widened. "Really?"

"Yeah, but he *so smart* though." Tayona's eyes narrowed with pride as she looked back up at me. "He like a prodigy or somethin'. They call his kind 'savants.' *That's* why Ted want him."

"Does Ted know Artie's not his biological son?"

"Naw. I ain't gonna lie: I *liked* what I got with Ted. He put me up in a nice house, got me a nice car, spendin' money on anything I want." She shrugged, looking down. "Whole lot better than where I'm from, you know? And he may have been disappointed with Artie, but he didn't kick him out. He kept payin' the bills."

"So what changed?"

"Artie a good kid. I mean, yeah, he got problems, but he *crazy* smart. That boy can do things with numbers and computers and code. When he was five, he was taking apart calculators and puttin' 'em back together again. When he was six, he took the SAT math test and got a perfect score. That's when Ted started takin' notice. They got all these puzzles and tests on the internet, like millions of numbers in a code."

"Cryptography," I said.

"Somethin' like that. Artie love doin' those. He started finding new ones on his own. Beat every one. One of the doctors tested him on some complex math equations, and Artie figured every one out. Stuff that people in college can't solve. After a while, he started *making* his own."

"He's got *that* kind of autism," I said. "The *Good Will Hunting, A Beautiful Mind* type."

"Yeah. Artie got a beautiful mind, a'ight. He great at it."

"And you said Ted became interested in Artie once he started displaying those characteristics?"

"One time, I woke up at night and couldn't find nobody in the house." Tayona squinted as she recalled. "Ted keep this computer setup in his basement, like his workspace for his company. He got all kinds of big computers and things down there. I look all over the house for him and Artie, and then I go down to the basement. Ted got him on one of his computers doing some weird shit with all that code stuff Artie so good at. Ted say Artie solving problems that he couldn't solve, problems from his company."

I had begun to write details from her story down in a notepad from my back pocket. I'd taken to carrying one with me since meeting Rick at Ol' South. It proved handy.

"What kind of work does your husband's company do, Tayona?" I said, trying to not sound like a cop. It didn't matter. Tayona was nice and lit from The Bubonic Chronic, and our easygoing natures had lulled her into this cozy fireside chat. It had taken time, but we were winning her trust. Rapport-building. I could feel it.

"Com-puters," she said, emphasizing the second syllable with round lips. "Software. Engineering. I don't know about all that. He just got lots of computers at home and at his work."

"And a lot of money," Tex intoned.

Tayona eyed him. "I ain't gonna lie. Dude pulled me out of some rough patches. I was dancin' in San Antonio when he come in and sweep me off my feet. I already knew about Artie for a few weeks by then. That's why I left Vegas. I just got lucky with Ted. Man knew how to treat a woman right." Her eyes floated, unfocused. "Once upon a time."

"Is there anything else you can tell us about Ted's work? What he does in his free time when he's not with you or Artie?" I didn't know what I was fishing for, but I knew there were trout in the river. Something still stank about the whole situation, but I needed more to argue with, especially if I was going back to Rick.

Tayona didn't meet my gaze, purposely looking away. "I think he into some bad stuff," she said. "I don't know for sure, but I think he some kinda criminal on computers."

"How do you know that?"

"One time, he had a bunch of people from his company over to the house for a party. After while, it turned into work. 'Brainstorming session,' he told me. Ted told me to leave them alone but I overhear them talkin' 'bout hackin' and codes or some shit like that."

"Everybody's a hacker these days," Preacher said.

"Yeah, but I been around some bad dudes before," Tayona said, fixing him with a heart-dead glare. "Dudes do bad shit to people, rob people, kill people. And Ted sounded like *them* when he talked about this stuff. He sound like...I dunno. Like he rippin' someone off or something. He sound *criminal*."

I traded glances with Tex and Preacher. Tex lifted his eyebrows briefly, silently confirming the buzz in the back of my head. Preacher just ogled me with his one regular eye and his one big one. I could never tell what that fucker was thinking.

"So tell me watchu want from me," Tayona said, moving her glare to me. "I tell you what I know. You gonna take me now? You gonna take Artie? 'Cause *I tell you*, I shoot you all right here before I let that happen."

"Let's...not and say we did," I said, winking at her. "Look, all we wanted to do was talk. How 'bout this: I check into Parker and see what the deal is. Okay? Maybe I can talk to some people and see if we can't resolve all this without Artie getting in the middle of things. Sound good?"

Tayona's glare increased and she laughed, an incredulous whiff of air through her teeth. "Shit, you don't know shit, man. You gonna go tell whoever you saw me, and Ted gonna find me. He prolly hired all kindsa people to come find me. That's why I'm layin' low, ya muthafucka."

"If he's hiring other people, then you should be worried," I said. "Because we're the nice guys."

"Oi, the nice guys!" Preacher said.

"You got good weed, that's for sure," Tayona said as she got to her feet. She pulled the Smith & Wesson out of her jacket and held it against her thigh. Her stony countenance softened again, and I could sense real anguish in her.

"Yo, I'm *tired*," she said. "I gotta be thinkin' 'bout Artie. Y'all might be legit, but I don't know."

"Tayona," Tex said, getting to his feet. "Let me take you home. If there's others out there looking for you, Jack's right. They might not be so nice. At the very least, I can make sure you get home safely. If you don't want to see us again, we won't bother you."

She tried to summon her hard face, but fatigue crept into the borderline despair, likely playing havoc with emotions that were ready to accept Tex's charm. Tayona had been on her own for a while, even before Artie was born. Like Preacher had said, it's different for people down there. Down *here*.

"Why you actin' all chivalrous and shit, big man?" she said, a whisper of a grin on one corner of her mouth.

Tex winked. "Well, I sure as shit would hate to see anything bad happen to a lady as pretty as you."

She thought it over for a moment, precious seconds of haze passing as blocks clicked into place. Preacher's chronic had settled my nerves, and the coke kept me frosty, but I hung on the exchange with pulse racing.

"A'ight, big man." Tayona gestured toward the parking lot. "I'm over here. But no funny stuff, y'hear? I don't truck none of that shit. And you can't come in when we get there."

"Yes, ma'am," Tex said, tipping the brim of his cowboy hat. He exchanged glances with me and walked off with Tayona. We couldn't have planned it better.

Preacher and I waited for a while for the scene to clear. I struck up a cigarette, reviewing new details. Tayona may have indeed taken the boy away from his father, but she wasn't doing it nefariously. She was genuinely frightened for the kid, probably moreso with the autism angle. She had surrendered a suspicion or two that lined up with those that had been tickling the back of my neck for the past couple days. The right lawyer could probably prove her side of the story in divorce court. That Parker may have been doing something illegal on the internet was a new wrinkle for which I had just the ironing board. I just needed to find the starch.

Preacher stood and stretched his lanky body.

"Yeh know," he said; "I think Hicks is me favorite, too."

14.
DOTS DON'T CONNECT THEMSELVES

Saturday afternoon, I burned the Camry's four cylinders as hard as they would pick up to get to The Jetfire. That's not very fast, for all you slowpokes. Four cylinders on any car has all the pickup of a crack addicted sloth trying to get to the bottom of a honey jar.

Summer beat down hard, the first real heat of the season. That and the DTs provoked sweat as soon as I popped outside, cool shower be damned. Fort Worth tricked you with the weather. It's technically considered North Texas, but that didn't preclude humidity seeping in from the south. We rarely got the kind of ass crack bisque found in Houston and the grosser territories near the Gulf, but crazy thunderstorms that often funneled down from Oklahoma brought the wet in sufficient quantities to mildly annoy the citizenry. We would complain about that for a few weeks, and then the droughts would set in for the hard summer, and people would complain about that. Fort Worth is a fickle bitch, but I love her.

I'd tried my best to clean up after days of hard drinking and substance abuse. The shower helped. The sun did not. I craved a cold brew at The Gym, and Pussy Control didn't let me down.

"You look like shit," she said, watching me guzzle her homemade coffee concoction. Shit's good, y'all.

"I'm fairly certain my good days are behind me, P.C.," I said, sounding more like a gasp than acceptable speech.

"Let me guess: you've been carousing with Preacher again."

"And Tex."

She regarded me with a thoughtful gaze, the same way a normie would freshly painted fingernails. "I thought he'd be more of a stabilizing influence on you two."

I considered asking Pussy if she knew Tex's Big Gay Secret, a term I instantly copyrighted in my head for later presentation to Tex as a potential new business venture involving alcohol, mescaline, and alpacas. Still wrestling with my big friend's casual accusation of assholery, however, I shelved that particular conversation, not sure if it was my place to tell others yet or even if it mattered. What did I know? *Not shit.*

"Hey," I said, wiping beads of sweat off my tanning forehead. "I've got something I want to talk to y'all about. You ever hear of a dude named Ted Parker?"

The corners of Pussy's lips tugged downward as if in imitation of the grumpiest grandma in the world. That's how she indicated negativity instead of a head shake. Damn, she was beautiful.

"Aside from the stuff you asked us to check on the other day?" she said. Her eyes slid right and down. "Not much."

I caught the tell. Pussy was not one to prevaricate.

"Come on. You know if you don't tell me I'll just go ask Deck."

Pussy blew an amused laugh from behind a Cheshire smirk and admonished me with eyes that revealed exactly how much she put up with my dumbshittery. "Are you fucking with me, Jack?"

I held my hands up palms forward in apology. "Okay, okay, fair. People keep tellin' me I'm an asshole, I'm liable to believe 'em."

Pussy made a small noise, almost imperceptible, in the back of her throat and tilted her head, eyes looking left as her smirk intensified. Goddammit.

"Why don't we go backstage?" she said. "And don't joke, little boy."

"Yes'm."

She lead me back to The Gym's back office, that cockpit of cyberpunkery and computational badassery. Things had changed since my last visit. Huge sheets of paper had been draped from the walls, each depicting massive systems and flow charts, annotated in multicolor hacker scribble that would take ethnographers decades to untangle. Towers of computer equipment hummed as internal fans spun to keep up with energy demands from millions of lines of code being written, rewritten, and deployed. It was at least ten degrees warmer than normal, and the crew inside wore shorts, flops, tank tops, and other light clothing to fight off the heat. Deckhead was sunk into a huge leather cushioned chair set before three big HD monitors, bare chested and covered in sweat as his fingers danced across two keyboards. He sported a beautiful multicolored tattoo on his right breast, a giant bird of prey spearing a devil-demon through its chest, the spear clutched between highly detailed talons. Must have taken weeks to get the ink right on that thing. Beautiful.

"Too hot in the hot tub!" I sang.

"Behave," Pussy said, whapping me on the side of the head with an open palm. "I said no jokes."

"Jackpot!" Deck shouted, not looking back at me, keeping his focus entirely on the code-monkeying emblematic of his finger dances. "Brotha-what-you-need-I-got-weed!"

"Little-green-leaves!" I sang back.

"Nope," Pussy said, popping me another one. "We're working today, boys."

"Yes, ma'am," Deckhead said.

"What's this, the Tr1pw1re run?" I said, rubbing the fiery wound left on my skull.

"Intel," Deck said, still focused on his tasks on the screens. Lines and lines of code and gibberish that nauseated me slightly in their rapid writing and disappearance.

"Testing," Pussy corrected, joining me to look over Deck's shoulder. "Hypotheses. Benchmarks. Firewall capacities. Sockpuppets. The usual."

"Lordamercy," I said, fumbling for a cigarette. "This have anything to do with my guy?"

"Parker?" Pussy said. "Soooo..."

"If you hadn't asked us to look into that girl earlier, we never woulda found it," Deck noted.

"What?"

"I'll try to explain it in first grader terms," Pussy said, reaching for a whiteboard on wheels.

"Hey. You're giving first graders a bad name."

"For sure." She drew a series of concentric circles on the board, each with a number. "When you're looking for vulnerabilities in somebody's defenses, they usually fall into specific categories. Not always, but usually. Power. People. Infrastructure. Money." With each one she mentioned, she wrote its first letter in a circle. "*Money* is the common one. Everybody's got money...or wants it."

"Okay, I'm following. And agree."

Pussy drew a smaller series of circles around the bubble labeled "M." "Money is one of the best networks to crack because it reveals everything else about the target. Money pays for the power. Money pays for people. Money gets earned and spent."

She started drawing arrows between the circles, each directionally pointing from the big "M" bubble to the little ones. "Now think about all these little bubbles as the *interceptible* links between the target and their money."

"Links in the chain that you can cut," I said.

"Or *control*," Pussy said, adding a slow emphasis to that second word. "The goal is to expose Tr1pw1re, not just shut him down."

"And he who controls his pipes—"

"Controls his universe," Deck finished, still tapping away.

"I love it," I said, applauding golf-style, cigarette clenched between lips, smoke fluttering my eyes narrower. "So what?"

Pussy drew a thicker line from the "M" bubble to one of the smaller ones and then labeled the smaller one "First National Bank of The State of Texas." A long label, to be sure, but supremely relevant given what she was about to reveal.

"The first place you start is banks," she said. "Banks with ass security."

"Banks with vulnerabilities," I said.

"You infiltrate banking computers first to see who's using them and in what quantities of money," Pussy continued with her lesson. "Under a certain amount, you can rule out. Those are your farmers, workers, regular people. It's the big guys you wanna be on the lookout for. More than that, it's the big guys that claim they're one thing and then spend like another."

"I don't follow."

"Keep up, First Grade. Farmers don't receive payments of a million dollars at a time," Deck said over his shoulder to me. "Shit, they don't get hundreds of thousands in most cases unless they're selling."

"Or unless it's cattle season," Pussy said. "See? It's all about context. People wouldn't be spending or receiving big paydays at certain points in time."

"But bad guys might," I finished.

"*Maybe.* We have to prove it all out because otherwise it's just taking money from people who don't deserve it."

I shook my head briefly, lost. "What does this have to do with Ted Parker?"

Pussy flashed me a smile and two devilish eyebrows ticked upwards as she pointed with a black polished fingernail to the bank she had written on the whiteboard. "Bank-baby-bank-baby, one-two-three-four."

My eyes widened, and I joined in with Pussy's rhythm. "Bank-baby-bank-baby, *one?*"

"Zoom, zoom!" Deck crowed with a cackle.

"So Parker's in Tr1pw1re's orbit?" I asked.

"*Maybe,*" Pussy repeated, holding up an index finger at me. "I just find it really coincidental when things collide in ways they probably would not have without the grace of us."

"Well, shit." I stubbed out my cigarette in an ashtray. "Color me intrigued. I was just gonna ask y'all what else Parker was up to because his soon-to-be-ex-bride could not *be* more afraid of the dude, *and* it turns out her kid is autistic."

"You found Tayona Parker?"

"Tex did. Hey, didja know that—"

"Does she have any of his other financial info?" Pussy pressed. "Checks? Debit cards? Anything?"

"Er, maybe. I may have forgotten to ask her about that." Okay, so drugs don't always make you the best detective. Gimme a break.

"Can you find out?" Deck asked.

"Maybe. Tex followed her home last night. She seemed to like him a lot more than me and Preacher. Maybe we can get him to ask."

"Imagine that," Pussy snickered. "I'll give him a ring. If you don't mind...? Are you still working this thing for your friend?"

I shrugged, honestly not sure. "I don't know."

"Well, we got shit to do, Jackpot," Deck said, again over his shoulder, eyes trained on whatever massive hack he was perpetrating. "We gots to confirm or deny, *djoo-know*?!"

"Awright, awright. Do whatcha gotta do, man. But...one ask."

"Name it," Pussy said, capping her marker.

"I need poop on Ted Parker quick-like. Here's the deal: he's only into Tayona for the kid, Artie. Apparently, Artie is autistic but the kind of autistic where you can crack Fibonacci crypto like it's ripe Mississippi pecans. Y'get me?"

"In HD," Pussy said, again smirking in her way.

I tapped my Zippo on the table in two quick raps and winked at her. "Holla atcha."

"So you found her," Roger Hulen said, sipping from a steaming mug of coffee. How somebody could suck down hot coffee like Roger in summertime Texas heat eluded my simple sensibilities.

"I ain't even gonna tell ya how," I said, waving my own very cold cold brew around with a cigarette delicately perched between two fingers. "I don't think I'm cut out for being an investigator though, that's for damn sure."

"You'd be surprised, Jack. There are worse sportin' badges 'round these parts."

"Worse? Jesus. No wonder the state don't pay you guys shit."

We were posted up at a weathered picnic table outside near a coffee shop. I was sweating like I'd swallowed a bag of ghost pepper tamales. Hulen, goddamn him, wasn't even fazed as he sat there in an oversize, blue pinstriped Leddy's dress shirt that concealed a bulletproof vest, a craggy-valleyed Scully leather vest over *that*, and heavily starched Wranglers. To top it off, the mustache on that sonofabitch could have smothered a kraken, and he looked and smelled like he had just stepped out of the shower. Sturdier breed, he was. Meanwhile, trickles of Jack-sweat cascaded down my back into a swampy ass crack, propelling me toward a detective's conclusion that one of us at this table was going to have to change clothes three more times that day.

"Anybody on my end of the law help out?" Roger said.

"I ran into a couple regular police that were looking. Thanks for getting that word out, by the by."

"Of course."

"I do have another favor to ask."

"I'm all ears."

I produced an envelope and slid it across the grayed wooden picnic table to Roger. Inside, two Moleskine pages full of carefully written details had been folded up, prepared meticulously earlier to include only the information I wanted Hulen to have.

"I need a background check on a Ted Parker. All the details are in here. Looking for stuff not ordinarily available to the public. Criminal database searches, sealed court documents, that kind of thing."

"If they're sealed, Jack, I'm pretty sure we can't unseal them without a warrant," Roger said, expressionless as he often was while attempting to teach me a lesson.

"Whatever you can find then," I said, impatient. "This is the girl's husband, and I'm feeling a little hinky about him."

"So you want to check him out before turning the girl over?"

I lit up a cigarette, puzzling out the pathway's twists and turns briefly before meeting Roger's eyes again. "Yeah."

"He have a record?"

"As far as I've been able to determine? No."

Roger dipped the corner of his jaw down and to the left, admonishing me with a careful sidelong eye. "Might not have cause then. If I reckon correctly, you've got to turn over this girl because she's taken this Parker's son."

I paused. "They are technically not yet divorced, and he has not yet filed a formal complaint with any law enforcing authority."

"That's just a matter of time and place."

"Maybe. But it also doesn't mean that the guy is legit." I shook my head, cobwebs creeping back in. "Look, I'm worried if I turn Tayona and her son over to the firm that Parker hired, the kid might get unfairly separated from his mother. That's all."

Roger regarded me with the same gaze. "Abuse?"

"Not of the kind you're thinking. Artie's autistic. Challenges communicating and integrating with world, but he's also apparently a whiz on the computer...which is what Parker maybe really wants him for."

"'Maybe really'...?"

Roger was goading me, but he was making a good point too. What did I know from Shinola?

"Look, Tayona left because she was frightened for the kid. Why didn't she go to the police or a social worker? Who cares? She doesn't exactly come from the privileged side of the tracks that you and I did, so maybe she uses different tools than you and I would to crack nuts. Right? Also, the kid isn't really Parker's, so how's that paternity test gonna affect his case in divorce court?"

Roger conceded with a gentle couple of nods and took another pull on his coffee mug. "Sometimes a feelin's all you get in the investigation business, Jack. Evidence never adds up how you want it to. Ya just gotta follow it and see where it leads. Prosecutors want certain things to look right before they go to court. Bosses want quotas hit. But people lie, too, Jack. All the time. Sometimes just to buy time."

I smirked at Roger and showed him another card. "That's why I've got Tex Cochrane keeping an eye on her and the kid."

"Way I see it then, you've got to be careful with who knows that. If Parker goes to the police and makes a formal complaint of kidnapping, an APB might go out statewide, and I'd be obliged to bring her in." He winked at me as he sipped his coffee. "Were I to see such an APB."

"So maybe do me a solid and get me some dirt on Parker before that happens," I countered with wide eyes.

Hulen drained the mug and smacked his lips, sucking on his upper lip in a fell motion to dry any remaining beads of caffeination from the saggy hair of his mustache. He tapped the envelope with two fingers before scooping it up and stuffing it into a vest pocket marked by the tributary patterns of decades-weathered leather. As he leaned back on the bench, I could see the Texas Ranger badge on his hip, gleaming in the sunlight and framed by similarly worn leather and cord. His boots scraped the gravel ground under us as he made to rise, and his Stetson blotted out the sun as he ascended higher into my field of vision.

"Lemme see what I can do," he said.

———

A sopping, icy Dos Equis awaited me at Fred's Texas Cafe, the perfect cure to the intruding summer heat. Even in the open air eating area, wooden fans and cold drinks could keep you sated while you chowed on one of the juiciest burgers in town. Buzzing in my fingers and lips reported either the onset of a brain tumor or easement from the obsessive hard drinking in which I had engaged over the past few days. Sure, I could have tuned down with a gallon of water and a few sweat-soaked naps on the couch, but a greasy Fred's burger sounded better, and it sounded *even* better with a couple glistening schooners of delicious Mexican beer.

Rusted vintage signs from the sixties hung from rain-bronzed lumbered walls: Corona, Budweiser, Lone Star, Citgo, Coca-Cola, even an old Gulf gas station sigil. Everything looked better in the sixties, as Darwyn Cooke once sagely remarked. The signage, the fishtails on cars, the clothes, the haircuts. Streamlined, slipstreamed everything. High and tights. Skinny ties. Original Ray-Bans. Fred's exemplified a lot of that old sixties design chic, even though it had been erected in that dusty lot in the seventies. We always look backward, I suppose.

Early enough in the day and on the right day of the week, Fred's featured live music, local warm-uppers for bigger acts at night. A four-piece rockabilly band spouted baleful murder ballads from the stage as I mugged down on tortilla chips and queso. The lead guitarist and singer picked careful, harmonic squeals from a shiny red 1975 Fender Telecaster with a black pick guard and gold hardware. The bassist leaned into a huge stand-up bass, towering like Mario Cipollina from Huey Lewis and the News with similar bushy sideburns and thick sunglasses. A withering old geezer bent crustily over a pedal steel, sliding into back and forth wailings across the strings. The drummer kept time with a combination of brushes and rimshots, punctuating the soup-making on his snare head with occasional deep cracks in four-three. They all wore matching silvery jackets and dark pants and sang into Super-55 microphones whose brushed nickel plating defeated sunlight glint. I didn't catch their name but dropped a couple bucks into their tip jar on my way back from the shitter. Happy hour acts usually played for the opportunity instead of cash, and these cats deserved better.

As I bit into my burger, greasy grill juice spurted out and trickled down my chin. I let it, unself-conscious. The pins and needles in my phalanges faded in time. As advertised, the beer was the coldest-assed in the city and transformed my heat death into a comfortable haze.

Rick's phone continued to ring straight to voicemail, and texts went unanswered. Who knew what he was up to or how really pissed he was at me. Maybe he thought he'd found a different lead on Tayona on his own. Little did he know.

Tex had texted earlier, indicating that he still had eyes on Tayona, having tracked her to an apartment complex in Haltom City northeast of Downtown. The big man had apparently posted up in his truck overnight, periodically waking himself to ensure Tayona was still inside the apartment and checking the area to make sure no one else was surveilling her. He said he'd call if he needed help. I trusted him.

As the Fred meat worked its magic on my insides, I contemplated the meetup with Tayona. Who could blame her for being schizo about her son? A stripper, former hooker, and likely former drug addict, she would get almost zero sympathy from most of the conservative judges in the state during any custody hearings with Ted Parker. That likely contributed to her flighty skittishness and predisposition toward stealth. Again, how else would a mother act in that situation? And if what she said about Parker was true, would it not give any other mother the same creepy vibe?

I desperately wanted to reason all of it out with Rick. I knew if we could just sit down and talk again that it would make sense, that he could see Parker's angle even in spite of the lack of physical evidence. Why not just talk to that guy directly and see what he was about? Rick was better at that than me on any given Sunday.

"People lie," Roger Hulen had said.

"No shit," I said to myself and took another big bite out of the burger, dripping melted cheddar and mustard but leaving no quarter for the onions.

Parker's name showing up in the records of First National Bank of The State of Texas didn't immediately induce suspicion, or at least not at the level that had tweaked Pussy Control. Everybody gotta bank. He could be up to his own shady shenanigans independent of the Tr1pw1re run. Why would there be any connection? Timing? It didn't mean anything, and it might be unfairly influencing my own perception of a guy I had never met and had no real legit reason to think ill of. Could just be lazy links.

Whatever it was, if it was anything at all, Pussy and Deck would confirm or deny. Between that and a full-on criminal background check through state and federal systems to which Roger Hulen had access, there should be plenty paint to cover the barn.

Right?

Two schooners in, I switched to Lone Star tallboys as happy hour began. The cans glistened ice sweat under the fans and tasted just as good. The duck's assed Telly-wielder onstage belted a long slow lament about a lady suffering a beat-down from her husband, who just gets away with it in the end. Around me, Fort Worth regulars sauntered in for after-work relief, rancher jeans mixing with cargo shorts and T-shirts and the odd business casual. Everyone hip to the non-customary live music emanating from the stage. Funkytown at its best.

My phone danced across the table as it buzzed. I swallowed a cheek full of beer and fished it out of the melted ice water on the tabletop, wiping a wet thumb across the screen to identify the number. An involuntary smile burgeoned on my face as I recognized it. I clicked the answer button and held it to my head.

"Talk to me," I said, and the lilt of my speech slipped into Cajun roots.

"Where ya at, Big Shot?" Duke Dooley crowed into my ear.

15.

AN INTERLUDE WITH THE DUKE

The Worthington Hotel excelled as a convention venue. Despite its heritage as one of Fort Worth's nicest Downtown hotels, its conference rates kept out-of-towners coming back as did its location. Dallas hotels often up-charged because that's just what Dallas people did. Everything in between might have been more cost-effective but nowhere near as cool. No, The Worthington was the perfect site for the annual Texas Liquid Petroleum Gas Association convention.

I met my father in the hotel bar where he was already nursing a Crown and seven. A collection of characters surrounded him, mostly dressed in khaki pants with polo shirts tucked into leather belts, an assortment of shoes and boots to distinguish one another. Duke, of course, wore a polo of his own with an outlandish multicolored floral pattern against a navy blue background. His big Dooley belly curved down from sternum to waist, perfectly visible from the tight tuck of the shirt into Dillard's blue jeans that went out of style years ago. What made Duke stand out, however, was his consistent refusal to wear socks. With any outfit. Favoring well-worn loafers, Duke maintained a perpetual state of comfort wherever he went. Those sockless loafers lasted through mild Mississippi winters and resisted even the trendiest of dad-wear to blend in perfectly with the oblivi- ous appearance of your average Cajun son.

Duke cut his salt-and-pepper hair short with a skullcap-like grip on his head. He had let it grow out a little on this trip, likely because women kept telling him it looked better that way, and there would be a few at this convention. Duke's hazel-green eyes looked at you like you were telling him a good joke, and they rested in comfy bags that belied a lifelong addiction to cigarettes, good drinks, and many smiles. Unlike his son, he kept a clean shaven face at all times, smooth and evocative of a newscaster from his bygone era. The freckles common to our lineage shone lightly off his tan skin, products of decades' worth of exposure to beaches, boats, and lazy days in rivers and hammocks.

His favorite author was Jimmy Buffett. He only read books on audio and bought cars with tape decks and CD players that could replay all his old audiobooks, from Tom Clancy thrillers to *Star Trek* shorts I'd begged him to buy me as a kid. He smoked Vantage Ultra-Lights, the weakest cigarettes around, made only for those lying to themselves about their hopes to quit smoking.

When he wasn't belting out old tunes with his band or inspect- ing bobtail trucks, Duke spent a lot of his time fixing up an old Plymouth GTX in a garage tucked into the shallows of the largely empty warehouse where he rented an office. He had once owned a

GTX called The Blue Max in his youth, a growling muscle car that ate slower cars up on the road. Alas, he had loaned it to a friend who had wrapped *The Blue Max* around a tree one night. Duke had been crushed and thought he'd never have the opportunity to own a muscle car again. Thankfully, upon his return to Hattiesburg years later, Duke's brother—my uncle Carter—had introduced Duke to a mechanic that serviced Carter's own classic car passion. The mechanic—Dell Weyland, the sonofabitch—hid a 1970 GTX under a tarp, and Carter had spied it one day while relieving himself behind the garage after a long day of drinking cold beer while Dell worked on his '55 Chevy. Duke haggled like he was in an Arabian souk until he got Dell to sell him the GTX. Ever since, Duke worked on the car in every spare minute he could find, touching up green and yellow paint, cutting out a new interior dashboard mount in wood grain that matched the original, finding authentic wheel lug nuts in good enough condition to replace the old ones that Dell had let go to shit.

On a clear, sunny weekend, you could find Carter and Duke at the clearing off Highway 49 South on the outskirts of town where the Hattiesburg city council had debated building a community center. The Dooley brothers and those friends of theirs with similar passions for old cars and bullshit would gather with coolers full of cold beer to swap yarns and race through the dusty tracks of the clearing. Duke won often, and nearby citizens would prick up their ears when he stamped on his GTX's gas pedal, belching forth a rumbling roar that signaled his intent to whip somebody's ass on the makeshift racecourse. Good times.

Duke was a safety consultant, an expert in understanding the baffling, Byzantine regulations the Department of Transportation levied upon motor carriers, hazardous materials transporters, and other industrial for-profit organizations that hauled stuff with big ole' eighteen-wheelers and smaller bobtails. The LPGAs of Texas,

Louisiana, Mississippi, Alabama, Florida, and Georgia hired him every year to provide federally mandated HazMat and substance abuse training to their members at discounted prices adjunct annual convention dues. This became a lucrative racket for both Duke and the associations as it drove up attendance and guaranteed Duke a certain amount of income from each event. He also used the opportunity to book new business away from his competitors in each state, usually mom-and-pop operations who were price gouging mom-and-pop propane suppliers and distributors. Ideal competitive space for a guy like Duke who would swoop into an LPGA convention, take a hundred people out to get boozed up one night and drug test them in them morning poolside while serving signature Doo-Lada concoctions.

He called me in periodically to supplement him when work got heavy. I retained my DOT training certification through Duke's consultancy, so whenever he needed me, I could jump in a car, meet up, and we'd execute a double act on stages both professional and entertaining. Hence the reason for Duke's call. It was a welcome distraction from Rick's work and, even better, Duke was paying me.

"Hey, hey, hey!" my father said, sliding his freshly ordered Crown and seven down the bar to me. "My much better looking partner's here!"

I matched Duke's grin with an exact replica and hugged him tightly, arms encircling, pounding backs twice. He smelled like Old Spice, just like he had for years. "Hey, Pop."

He introduced me to a couple of the convention-goers standing about, names I would forget over the weekend. We all shot the breeze for a hot minute, aging Texan middle-class businessmen lubed up with beer and cocktails, paunchy stomachs poking over pant lines. The art of the bullshit strong in our family, Duke and I synchronized the centrality of the gathering with knowing winks and off-color ribaldry common only to male-dominant conventioneers kicking off a long weekend away from wives and kids. People were more likely to buy when they were having a good time.

At a break in the conversation, I asked Duke, "So what are we up to?"

"The usual," Duke said, draining his third Crown and seven. "Training and business development, baby. They got that Texas money over here."

"What, them Mississippi propane shops too skint for ya, Pop?"

"Sheeeeeiiit, man. It's only a lifestyle business if the lifestyle perpetuates. You still got your chops, Big Shot?"

I winked at my father. "Learned from the best."

The workshops started up the next day and ran parallel with the convention's main schedule. Duke and I took turns delivering the safety briefings in hourlong increments, tap-dancing our way through monotonous PowerPoint slides with stories about tragic accidents on the road and horror shows everyone in the transportation business would like to avoid. Every session, some guy would invariably complain about invasion of privacy when we got to the substance abuse seminar. Duke always had the answer: "Well, you can piss in this here cup or I can go out to my car and get that broomstick with a pine cone on the end." Surefire laughter and compliance, every time.

Duke had not prepared the appropriate certification paperwork for the people who completed the training. His printer had died on him, and the association had not even given him the names of his attendees ahead of time. A problem for the younger of the Dooley dual act. I sweet talked a front desk attendant into giving me access to the good printer in their back office, not the crappy one in the business center that coughed up multicolored ink like a cancer patient reacting poorly to chemo. The girl—as expected, a TCU maiden working her way through a sports medicine degree—demonstrated susceptibility to accents even more country than her own, so I let my Cajun-by-way-of-Mississippi drawl return in full, redneckery hiding just behind the veneer of a well-to-do salesman. She gave me a passkey to the back office where I posted up, doctored a few official-looking graduation certificates from the questionable accreditation authority of Dooley Consulting Services, and scooted back to the conference room where Duke was training. We set out the certs on a back table with a bunch of Dooley swag—mostly forgotten plastic drink cups and pens with the DCS logo—and started circulating through the rest of the convention to let people know they could pick up their certs when they wanted.

It wasn't totally a ramshackle operation. We took attendance at each class so Duke could later input them into a database, a formality really, but one required by DOT in case one of his graduates ever got into an accident. And they did, often. Duke fielded calls from DOT and NTSB investigators weekly seeking paperwork and certifications that his clients' drivers had lost, and those clients paid mightily to have that security with Duke. Duke could smell opportunity in a phone call, and the first time a concrete hauler called him in a panic over one driver that had run over a drunk at two in the morning, Duke started offering on-demand accident representation. For a slight up-charge, of course.

It wasn't quite a scam, but it felt like one. Doing someone else's work and charging them for it had not yet caught on globally in the way that virtual assistants and task management teams would in the future. People paid Duke not just for his gregarious attitude but also for his time, which I guess is interrelated.

There were women at the convention. Not in the same numbers of the men, but some of the moms from the mom-and-pop shops came singly or with their husbands, wheeling and dealing alongside suppliers and big operations. Some attendant businesses adjunct to the transportation industry like insurance and legal would show up as sponsors, and those usually brought with them tradewomen seeking to curry accounts from competitors. Every one of them knew and loved Duke. He couldn't even get down an aisle of the trade show floor without some babe with resplendent cleavage hugging and kissing him, exhorting how she hadn't seen him in God knows how long. That would invariably lead to a sudden recognition of me in Duke's wake and some shit about how much we looked alike. Duke kept a Photoshopped picture in his wallet of a boy with an elephant dick that he showed to people, claiming it was his baby picture. The girls liked to ask if I took after my dad. You know, in *that* way. Wink, wink.

I probably could have crushed some of those cougars had I been feeling it, but recent events had me less interested in making small talk with people I didn't care about. I was having more fun just hanging around in Duke's shadow, throwing back to being a kid when he'd make me tag along to all the conventions he worked in the summertime.

The first day of the convention ended with a happy hour sponsored by one of the big motor carriers, the guys that hauled everything from gasoline to industrial grade milk. We got very drunk, smoked a whole lot of cigarettes, and traded business cards with clients new and old. Duke walked back to his hotel room that night with a hundred new leads to follow up on.

The massive amount of Crown we had consumed slurred my words and stumbled my legs, so I decided to crash in Duke's room instead of driving home. His sleep apnea produced godawful noise once we drifted off, one that destroyed any chance of real sleep. So I stole the covers off my bed and drunkenly folded myself up into the bathtub, kicking the bathroom door shut and eventually dozing off to the low rumbles of Dooley snores, Duke's and my own...those deep-throated, air-stunted log-saws that thundered through walls and floors like cyclones.

The next day unfolded much like the previous one, but slower in our post-drunk haze. Eventually, we had to clean ourselves up for the big association dinner where awards would be granted, speeches made, and hyperbole thrown. There was always a band scheduled, and this year's Texas LPGA did not disappoint, promising a 9-piece Motown/Top 40 cover act plucked from the professional depths of party band heaven. Duke and I dressed in navy blue sports coats, khakis that did not quite match (we didn't want to look too alike), and he wore his usual loafers sockless while I went with a newer pair of topsiders that could pass for dress shoes. Duke wore a solid yellow polo shirt under his jacket while I opted for a plain and crisp blue button-up made of soft Egyptian cotton with a faint herringbone pattern. We looked like the kind of people Mississippi rednecks would call high class and definitely standouts from the Texans' boots and bolo ties.

We got to the dinner early so we could scope out the band's setup. Both of us were musicians, and we loved to see what kind of gear other players used. This particular group brought with them a legit six-piece Ludwig drum kit in sequined silver and a Toca percussion setup that would make The Grateful Dead jealous. Gearheads like us geeked on stuff like that, so we had a ball smoking cigarettes, drinking Crown and sevens, and pointing out the finer peculiarities of conga heads and cymbal selection.

"What else you been up to, boy?" Duke asked me at one point as convention-goers started filtering in for the dinner. "You workin' at all?"

I blew out a breath, idly picking at cigarette ash that had fallen on my sport coat. "Dad, I gotta tell ya. I don't think I'm doing so good."

"Whatcha mean, man?"

"Bouncing around between real jobs. Wasting time pretending I'm some kinda investigator and not getting paid for it. Having way too many of these lately." Ice cubes in my Crown and seven glass rattled as I shook its emptiness for emphasis. "Shit, I haven't even been able to sing right lately."

"What, you got a frog in your throat?"

I looked at Duke with the first serious glare I'd given him in some time. "You know what I mean."

Duke's eyes widened ever so imperceptibly, and he said, "Oh. *Finley.*"

Before I could say anything, my father pinned me with two fingers clutching a cigarette. "You did the right thing, son," he said in a low voice. "That sonofabitch hurt us. Hurt your uncle. He got what he deserved, the sonofabitch."

I couldn't meet his eyes. "You hear anything lately about Liz? Elizabeth?"

"His daughter? Not in *The Hattiesburg American*. Every so often, I check the local news in Jackson. Last I heard she was still in that institution."

My hand felt rough and leathery on my face as I rubbed away a trickle of sweat. "Her lawyers still trying to appeal?"

Duke looked around to see if anyone was nearby, the way you do right before telling an off-color joke. "She went down for killing her father. Story's been told, Jack."

The funny thing was, the worry that usually caused a butterfly swarm of panic in one's stomach when confronted with the outing of heretofore concealed information did not subsume me. Behavior aside, maybe I was getting right with Mississippi. That didn't sound right though. In truth, I didn't feel anything...and as time went on, I felt less.

How's that for a hero?

"Look, man," my dad said, tapping the table and lowering his voice. "You did what you had to do. That fuckin' guy needed killin', and his bitch of a daughter fucked you over too. Fuck 'em. You need to lighten up."

I couldn't help but laugh. My Dad. He could always boil things down to laughter, the need for it and the causes of it.

"My predilection for the substances you teach people to avoid and the loss of my singing voice say otherwise," I protested with a mocking grimace.

Duke winked at me. "We'll fix that."

Our *tête-a-tête* cut short as folks filtered into our table. Those who sat with us included a woman and her husband who owned a small propane delivery service in Abilene, two brothers who co-owned a major petroleum supplier in Houston, and a lady named Debbie from Shreveport with whom Dad had once been friendly. Everybody knew Duke, and Debbie probably knew him biblically.

Verbal *jiu jitsu* cranked up again with the awards gala, Texan country folk shouting faux insults across the room to their competitors and lady-folk wolf whistling the skinny-jeaned young men selected to present. Finally, the boredom of strangers patting themselves on the back abated, and the band took the stage. Seven men and two women, all black, took positions behind microphones and instruments, and with a quick downward swing of the arm in an axe-chop, the band leader kicked off the first song: "Saved."

The dance floor filled quickly, sun-kissed people from the Hill Country outside Austin mixed with wannabe Cajuns from Southeast Texas and the hootin', hollerin' people from the Piney Woods of East Texas. As country as many of those folks were, none of them could resist the allure of an authentic Motown group, especially one as good as this band. They covered Aretha, Marvin Gaye, and Wilson Pickett within the first twenty minutes, and asses shook at greater volume and temperament with each aural elevation. Even Duke got pulled out by ladies single and otherwise to bump hips in time with the music.

At the first set break, I shot up to the stage from where I'd been hiding in back near the bar. Appropriately jazzed, I felt the need to shake hands with musical groups so in the pocket as Millie Wilt and The Sixers—so named for mysterious encounters with the devil that musicians who supernaturally wooed their audiences sang about. Millie herself was already kissing on Duke by the time I got up there.

"Boy, I seen you shakin' yo' ass out there on that there dance floor," she was admonishing my father. "You got the devil up in dem hips."

"Ain't all I got, baby!" Duke said to a howls of laughter from Millie and her Sixers.

"Y'all oughtta get the Duke here to get up there and sing!" came a shout from a drunken passerby, one of the LPGA officers that had presented the association's awards earlier. As the man ambled on by Duke and patted his back, Millie's second-in-command, a tall lanky man in the Sixer tuxedo uniform leaned in.

"You got some pipes on ya?" the man said.

"Help ya out with yer percussion too, baby," Duke said, catching my eye and pointing at me. "Me and my boy."

"This here your boy?" The man grasped my hand and pumped it like a butter churn. "I'm Frankie Fix, boy, what's your name? What you sing?"

"Uh, Jack. I'm just here to make him look good," I said, pointing back at Duke.

"Brother, let's get y'all up there inna next set," yet another Sixer interrupted, this time the drummer, replete in that tuxedo and dark sunglasses.

"Shit, man, you got some sweet chops up there, sir," I told the drummer. "Love what you're doing."

This went on for a while, some of the Sixers responding to requests from the conventioneers while others shot the bull with me and Duke. We flagged down waiters to bring us drinks and got appropriately lubricated. I tried to disentangle myself from what was about to happen, but Duke kept pulling me back in. Before I knew it, the next set was kicking off and both of us were onstage next to the percussion set accepting tambourines and maracas shoved at us by the Sixers.

Duke negotiated with the percussionist to get behind the congas and bongos right away, his usual play-spot. He played on a set of bright wood-grain Toca congas just like the Sixers'. In fact, as he could not help but spill to Millie and Frankie, Duke's congas were famous. You know that live album The Neville Brothers released in '94? They're playing on Duke's conga and percussion setup, timbales to chimes. Apparently, before that show, the Nevilles' got their shit broken into and stolen outside Tipitina's in New Orleans, and the manager knew Duke had a similar rig. Duke happened to be nearby in Slidell and rolled in with minutes to spare, setting up that huge collection of chrome hardware and burnished wood just in time for showtime. So that's Duke shit you hear on that album, and he's hanging out just offstage watching the show. I think you can even hear him cutting up the wood blocks at one point on "People Get Ready."

We sang backup as Millie launched into "Take Me to the River," and I hid behind the mic we shared so as not to screw up too badly. It was easy just to shake that tambo and pretend to be a Sixer. Duke's crooner's voice mixed well over the Sixers' rhythms anyway. It felt weird though because usually me and Duke can harmonize pretty well on anything. Even to the most discerning ears, it's difficult to pick out who's who when we've sung together in the past. As such, Duke detected almost instantly my reticence.

When we got to the end of "Midnight Hour," he shouted at Millie and Frankie through the microphone, "Hey! Y'all wanna hear this Dooley boy up here cut it up?!"

The audience cheered a rousing positive, but Millie—ever the show-woman—cocked a hip, armed a fist on it, pointed at Duke, and said through her mic, "What y'all got cookin' back there, young man?" I think she was talking back to Duke and not me. She must have been eighty years old.

"Millie, dis man play wit' de Neville Bruddas in N'Orleans!" the Sixers' percussionist shouted, playing to the crowd of whiteys with a bit more patois than he had when we'd met him at the break.

"Oh, we gon' do some Nevilles," Frankie said. "'Love the One You're With!'"

The Sixers busted into a rendition of "Love the One You're With" that matched The Neville Brothers' from that same '94 show about which Duke loved to brag. Frankie took the lead, and one of the Sixer backup singers shoved wireless mics into mine and Dad's hands. I reacted without thinking, falling into a familiar pattern of *"shoo-doo, doo-doo, doo-doo, doo-doot"* alongside the multi-harmony voices of the whole band, finding purchase at an octave I had not expected. Duke and Frankie took turns singing lead on this one, matching the pattern of Cyril and Arthur Neville exactly.

When the last verse wrapped, and the Sixers' drummer brought it down with a sharp scatter on his snare, signaling a pivot directly into The Rolling Stones' "You Can't Always Get What You Want," perfectly in time as the Nevilles had executed. All the singers repeated the lyric, prompting everyone not currently dancing to fill the floor with barely rhythmic but fully enjoyed moves. As the song careened to the first verse, Duke kicked me out in front of him to the front area of the stage, and the Sixers parted to envelope me, and I knew I was fucked.

Something clicked though, and I recovered the transition with only fleeting panic that I had misremembered the words to one of the best songs from both the Stones' and the Nevilles' oeuvre. The key was such that it didn't put too much strain on my vocal cords, lying perfectly within a register that I could hit with little to no effort... and it was just there. That feeling that I'd missed from singing in the crowd at The Aardvark suddenly popped back into me, righting my ship and slipping my bip. The song was safe enough that I could meander through it with a modicum of success, and with a laser-like focus, I managed to string the proper notes together to bring us all down in a beautiful crescendo.

The crowd erupted in applause, and Millie held her hands out to me as if offering an embrace or a welcome to some golden state whose cleansing glow had just bathed me. Before I had a chance to approach her or even wave thanks to the crowd, the band suddenly exploded with a horn-screeching intro to "Hold On, I'm Comin'," and I realized the fucking had only just begun. Looking back over my shoulder, I saw Duke trot toward me, one hand reaching for my shoulder, the other lifting his mic to deliver the first verse in Sam's register.

I couldn't help but double over from the laughter inspired by this sight, this sound. Duke had taught me how to sing with this song, first through repeated viewings of *The Blues Brothers* and later through performing it live with each other's bands in Hattiesburg. My father had always been a Motown fanatic, but he instilled upon me similar respect for the Stax sound. Both flavors of soul tasted great in your mouth, and it was hard to choose just one, which was why the best party bands made sure to cover each just as Millie and The Sixers were doing.

I managed to harmonize with Duke on the high parts in the chorus, then diving into the second verse—Dave's verse—with an involuntarily hop dance that Millie, Frankie, and Duke mimicked in time with me, inadvertently creating the one thing people from the Texas LP Gas Association convention would be talking about from that year forward, thereby guaranteeing The Sixers' booking for future years.

Hard not to feel something with perfect syncopated melody blasting all around you.

I didn't have any trouble sleeping in Duke's room that night.

The next morning, I helped him pack up and load his big green Chevy Yukon for the drive back to Mississippi. He had four stops along the way for new clients in Tyler, Gilmer, and Terrell, Texas, not to mention an outlier in a central Louisiana backwoods called Coushatta. There wasn't shit in Coushatta but that didn't make no nevermind to Duke Dooley. He'd find ya.

"See ya later, Big Shot," Duke said in the valet drive, offering me a hand pump that collapsed into embrace.

"You got enough to listen to on the way back?" I said. "Need a new audiobook?"

"Naw, shit, man. I been listenin' to Tom Clancy again. Jack Ryan flyin' planes into the White House."

"I'm pretty sure that's not how that one went..."

"Check your bags." He backhanded my balls, a family move akin to grabass but more painful. I'd avoided it plenty over the years and easily deflected, but not without a worrisome urking noise that defeated whatever cool I may have been extruding.

"You sonfoabitch," I said.

"Don't talk about your grandmother that way." Duke jumped into the Yukon and rolled down the window to offer me a smile. "I'm proud of ya, boy. Get your shit together though, huh?"

I mock saluted my father. "Yes, sir."

"And holler at me after I get home in a couple weeks. I met a friend in the Army who said he might be able to offer you a job sometime if you want it."

I made a face. "In the Army? Do you really see me dress-right-dressing, Pop?"

"Nah. But there's more to it than monkeys in pickle suits." He gunned the Yukon's engine. "Love ya, son."

"Love you too, Pop."

With that, he roared off, mazing through blocks of concrete and brick until he was at last set free upon the plains and flora of North Texas, speeding east to where the trees shed pine needles and bent under humid skies toward the ground.

16.

MOM-AND-POP KOLACHE SHOP

The text read, "**PARKER'S SHADY A.F. S#!^ DON'T ADD UP.**"

The source number was actually a twenty-seven digit alphanumeric hash, meaning it was from Deckhead and/or Pussy Control. It came at me just as Roger Hulen was handing me a manila folder through the driver's side window of my Camry.

"Hope you find what you're lookin' for, Jack," Hulen said, tapping my windshield twice with a knuckle before leaning back to allow me to drive on. I thanked him and got moving.

I hadn't had a drink in about twenty-four hours and was fighting the buzzing in my extremities with water and Lifesavers. I'd slept a hard ten hours of that at Bryce House where, once again, I'd had to clean off the cats infesting my balcony entrance. As soon as I'd nudged them aside with my feet though, I'd felt bad about it, and I left four open tins of sardines outside in hopes of making amends.

I pointed the Camry at Haltom City, stepping on it to meet up with Tex. En route, I scanned pages from Hulen's folder, which amounted to barely comprehensible ASCII text from ancient, government-issue, first generation dot matrix printers. Still, within the blue spits of ink on green hued lines, I found a couple data points of interest.

First, Ted Parker had indeed been probed by the FTC for moving too fast with businesses acquiring or merging with each other. Nothing had generally been found to be out of the ordinary except a short blurb on one auditor's report indicating surprise over how much money Parker's first business had amassed, been valued at, and then sold for. That business apparently had something to do with internet security protocols and had been gobbled up by one of the major tech companies that now put software on most computers before they went in the box.

Second, Parker had been charged with, indicted for, and eventually defeated a federal grand jury inquiry for tax evasion a few years prior. The records were public but Hulen's report looked like a state query to a federal database with more esoteric information like evidentiary lists that included assets discovered. From what I could discern at a stoplight, those assets included money in various offshore banks moved between Parker's accounts and others that either were not identifiable or purposely anonymized. The account numbers didn't make any sense to me, but I knew they would to Deck and Pussy.

The last bit was a Texas state law enforcement database entry on Parker that listed him as being charged with domestic abuse. The dates didn't match up with his marriage to Tayona though.

In fact, the charge had been levied many years earlier and seemingly expunged from the public record by order of a judge in Travis County. I performed some poor arithmetic that took way too long and calculated that the incident in question had to have happened when Parker was only in his late teens. Domestic abuse. A history of?

After the stoplight turned to green, I folded up the papers back into their container and finished poking my way to Tayona's apartment complex. I passed by the front entrance once at a slow clip, looking around the block for signs of surveillance. Nothing jumped out at me: no weird vans or cars occupied by people sitting there frying in the heat. Tex's truck was on the corner, and I rounded it to park on the other side of the apartment's block in the most inconvenient place but concealed from anyone that would be trying to surveil the complex. I walked around the sidewalk opposite the way I'd entered the neighborhood and found an unlocked side entry gate. A quick couple of stair climbs and some heavy breaths up those steps took me right up to Tayona's door.

The door cracked open only a sliver to reveal Tex's baleful eye, and when he confirmed it was me, he opened the door to allow me inside and shut it fast. The interior of the apartment was scattered with brightly colored plastic toys and cheap, used furniture. It wasn't quite a shithole, but I'd never live there. Preacher sat on a sagging couch with Tayona taking hits off a bong whose glass had seen enough pot water to turn it a sickly shade of translucent brown. A thin haze of pot smoke hung over the room, which tripled as a living area, dining area, and open concept kitchen.

"How long has he been here?" I asked Tex.

"Oi, don't judge," Preacher interrupted. "Our lovely lass here has had a hard couple nights."

I kept my gaze on Tex. "Oh?"

"She wanted to work last couple nights while you were out," Tex said.

"Girl need the paper," Tayona said.

"Yeah, I hear you. How is everything? Y'all okay? No creepy-crawlies skulking around?"

"If by that you mean 'bugs,' let's not get into it," Tex said, leaning against the door. "If you mean creepy-ass dudes lookin' to do some bad shit to Tayona here, we ain't seen nothing. I went with her to her...place of employment...and I called Preacher to come over and watch Artie."

I did a double take. "You called *Preacher* to watch a *kid*?"

Preacher beamed, handing the bong back to Tayona. "We're like fookin' family here, Cajun. The oul' lad's a good one, aye."

"He's here now? He's okay?"

Tayona rose after exhaling her bong hit and gestured for me to follow her. "He's okay. C'mere."

I followed her around the corner of the single hallway from the one part of the apartment to the next, which housed only a bedroom and a bathroom. I peered around the corner into the bedroom where a young boy was crouched on the floor looking up at a TV screen, holding a game controller in one hand and typing furiously on a keyboard with the other. The peripherals connected via wires to a computer of unknown brand under the TV. The kid wore a plain gray sweatshirt of thin material, its sleeves cut off at the shoulder and a hood dangling from the neck over his back. Jeans covered his legs, and a pair of sneakers sat nearby his socked feet. Brown hair flopped over his forehead, which was the smooth color of blended ancestry, the kind of glistening beauty unique to biracial children. His dark brown eyes stared actively at the screen, retinas dancing back and forth in engaged fury.

"So that's Artie," I said. "You make cute kids, Tayona."

She grinned at me, suddenly self-conscious and embarrassed. "Why you gonna play me like that?"

"Sorry. Didn't mean to. He okay?"

"Yeah, he is. He gets plugged into that computer and he can go for hours." She called to him. "Artie! You wanna come over here and say hello to Mister Jack?"

The boy stood up, placed his controllers on the floor carefully, then walked up to me, eyes intent on my midsection. When he stopped, he told my stomach, "Hi, Mister Jack." Then he turned around, sat back down where he was, and started fiddling with the controllers again.

"Don't take it personally," Tayona said. "That's just Artie."

"That's just perfectly fine. He's kickass," I said. "Tayona, do you have access to any of Parker's financial accounts? Debit cards, credit cards, account numbers, anything like that?"

Her eyes vibrated in the sockets, gears crunching together. "I tried not to use none of that when I left. Thought he might track me that way, you know? But I took a bunch of papers, too. Maybe bank statements or some shit. I was kinda in a hurry and I just started grabbin' stuff."

She led me over to a bureau in the bedroom where she started rooting through drawers. Following, I got a better look at what Artie was up to on his computer. It looked like computer code, the same type of stuff I'd seen at The Jetfire Gym. Artie's work, however, split on one half of the TV screen into a terminal window for the coding and a second one that looked like a game environment of some kind. Digital mushrooms, trees, and animals roved through the game screen, some in various states of coherence, their skins de-rezzing into pixels and rebuilding themselves with new colors and textures. It took me a moment to realize, but Artie was playing that game while also rewriting its source code, changing things in the game world's rendering engine in real time as he played. Like a post-Matrix god, altering reality as he saw fit while experiencing the story through whatever multilevel kaleidoscope his disorder had equipped him with. My mouth dropped open, stupefied as realization hit me.

"Here you go," Tayona interrupted, handing me a folder with not very much paper in it. My attention stayed focused on Artie's gameplay.

"He's really something, isn't he," I said in a low voice, not a question.

I missed Tayona's slow smile, a color to her dark cheeks as they curved upward with obvious pride. "Ya damn right he is."

I offered her a smirk and playfully thwapped her with the folder. "Thanks for this. It might help."

"Why you helpin' me, Jack?" Tayona said.

I shrugged. "I dunno. Maybe I'm not the asshole everybody thinks I am."

She rolled her eyes. "Sheeeeiiiiiit."

We both chuckled, mine more of an amused and nervous titter as we walked back into the other half of the apartment. I put Tayona's folder inside the one Roger Hulen had given me. Entering the living area again, I handed the whole package of paper to Preacher, smacking him in the side of the face with the folder edge.

"You up to help out on another task, Preach? Fair warning: no penises involved except yours."

"Oi, that's all yeh need," Preacher said, snapping out of his weed haze and handling the papers I'd just shoved at him. "What've yeh here, Cajun?"

"Can you get those over to Deck and Pussy?"

"Aye, I got me hooptie-mobile right around the corner. Yeh need 'em to do somethin' specific with it?"

"Just tell 'em that stuff is Parker stuff. They'll know what to do with it. But make sure one of 'em calls me after they've had a chance to do their thing with it."

Preacher jumped to his feet and stretched, lanky body cracking as the kinks popped out of joints. An amiable smile overtook his face, possibly fallout from the weed binge, but with Preacher you never really knew. He had probably been high all day and was just in a good mood.

"I'm off," he said, ambling out the door.

"Want me to go with him?" Tex said from a dining table chair.

"No, I want you to stay here with Tayona and Artie," I said. I dug out a wad of cash from my jeans pocket and peeled off a few twenties. "You okay with that? Need anything?"

"This'll do." Tex took the proffered money. "We'll order a pizza or something. Everything here is pretty self-contained." He nodded at Tayona. "Despite some weird rules."

Tayona pinned him with a glower. "Ain't no drinkin' or hard drugs round my baby, y'hear?"

"I owe you one, Tex," I said. "Thank you for doing this."

He jerked his head in the direction of the door through which Preacher had just gone. "Make sure you thank that one, too. He's a shitshow, but he's our shitshow."

I couldn't help the grin that overtook my face. "Truer words..."

The phone clicked over into a familiar voice that said, "Hello?"

"What, you don't have caller ID?"

"I'm trying to be polite. You know, like our parents used to be?"

"That mean I'm in trouble?"

"He's in a pretty bad mood."

"Would it help if I said I was sorry? Again?"

"I don't know what'll help at this point. I haven't seen him like this before."

"Well, shit. How 'bout I come down with flowers and a box of chocolates?"

"Make it migas and tacos and it'll be a start. You close?"

"Still in The Fort. Should make it by dinner time. Maybe don't let Rick know I'm coming...?"

An exasperated sigh. I could feel the eye-roll. She stayed silent. "Nia, just keep him home. I'll be there as fast as I can."

"Okay, Jack. See you soon."

It's a three-hour drive from Fort Worth to Austin, give or take some bitch-ass time for rush hour and bad drivers. The grasslands jump out to envelop you as soon as you clear Cleburne on I-35W. No matter what time of year, Texas vegetation waves at you in lazy wind-swept unison over miles and miles. Wheat fields, corn, even the few patches of trees you come across all seem to catch the northern wind and sway at you, enticing you to slow down and take a hot minute to see the horizon so far off in the distance where the first slopes of the Hill Country begin.

I always stop in West, Texas, about halfway down, for one purpose: kolaches. Depending on your source, kolaches might be better grabs than brisket in some Texas subcultures. Poor ones resemble pigs in a blanket: dehydrated, wrinkly mini-sausages overcooked into hard dough that your mother used to make alongside jars of yellow mustard to mask the taste. No, the true kolache was gifted to us by an incredible influx of Czech immigrants who settled first in central Texas then spread out all over the state.

A perfect kolache relies on the bread. Good ones appear and taste like the best dinner roll you ever had, usually at a size sufficient to hiding the goodness inside, which could be anything from slow cooked jalapeño sausage to ham and cheese. The Czechs adopted the taste-making of their new home, and Texas BBQ could be found in many kolache menus. There were even jelly and fruit marmalade-filled kolaches for the breakfast crowd and damn near any other type of filling you could dream up.

West, Texas—not West Texas for all you comma-challenged Philistines—is ground zero for the Czech immigration wave into the Great State. Depending on who you talk to, there are a few different Czech kolache joints that claim firsties for introducing this delicious pastry to Texans. The most obvious is Slovacek's, which you can see from miles away coming in either direction, north or south, on 35. It's evolved into a modern monstrosity of side-highway allure, a mecca to all things tacky and required for your average road trip, right down to the multi-level rest stop atmosphere and neon signs. Slovacek's success was capitalized on a smart business pivot from a mom-and-pop kolache shop to its current form by expanding into onsite BBQ and gas, two key things every Texan needs when traversing its wide open spaces. In fact, I'd wager that Slovacek's likely draws more business from its incredible BBQ than the classic kolaches in its bakery.

All due respect to Slovacek's, but this here Texan always ties his horse up at The Czech Stop. Situated on the opposite side of the interstate from Slovacek's, The Czech Stop is smaller and more rustic than its competitors. Its simple yellow signs evoke classic diner fare, and its cramped parking lot always overflows from morning to night. The line goes out the door at every hour. People know the deal. The Czech Stop offers more variations on the classic kolache formula, and I swear their bread is so perfect that it makes you high when you smell it for the first time. Every chance I get to drive to or from Austin, I usually stop in for two kolaches—a jalapeño sausage and a pulled pork—and a Big Red to satiate the appetite and get me on down the road.

Not long after foraging for kolaches in the Texas wild, Deckhead called me up. I put him on speakerphone so I could continue delicately plying into kolache dough and sausage while leisurely piloting the Camry down the road.

"Whataboutcha, Deck?" I greeted, mouth full.

"That stuff you had Preacher drop off was money, yo," Deck crowed back at me, his Mexi-melt voice all the more tinny emanating from the shitty mobile's speaker.

"You got something?"

"We're still confirming but get a load of this: there's a definite connection in timing between large influxes and movements of cash to Parker's bank accounts...and *heists* of those same banks."

"Wait, whaaaat? You talking like stick-ups?"

"No, man, *cyber*-heists! Why you so slow, man? We're talkin' serious operations here, succotash. And guess how we got wise to that connection?"

He couldn't see me shrug over the phone but I did anyway and stuffed the rest of the last kolache in my mouth. I tried to respond but...kolache.

"These heists are *Tr1pw1re's*, man!"

"Wait. Back up. You telling me Parker's movin' money through banks that are being ripped off by your mythical mamma-jamma at the same time?"

"Saint, it's firm," Pussy Control's voice sublimated Deckhead's. "Now, if you match up his software engineering firm's financials with this activity, you can see some correlations that might make this look a little less suspicious. Like, big cash drops enter Parker's accounts after his company cashes invoices from a big software contract with one of the major tech companies."

"So he uses his business to hide the influx of cash that's been stolen from the same bank?" I said, trying to puzzle it out.

"Maybe. When we plotted the heists on a timeline and connected the financials from the accounts you sent us, the pattern becomes too clear to be coincidental. To me, at least. Saint, this guy Parker might be employing Tr1pw1re at one of his consultancies. Maybe even enabling his ops."

"How sure are you?"

A pause. They must have been deliberating. Then they said at the same time, "Seventy percent."

"Good enough for a showdown, but no good for the law."

"Agreed," Pussy said. "We're still working it. We're going to get into personnel records of Parker's employees, investors, all those other possible linkages."

"Hit me up if you find something more," I said. "I'm on my way down to Austin and possibly right up this Parker guy's ass."

The door swung open fast, betraying the tension in the knuckles gripping the knob. Rick kept his hand on that knob as he regarded me, blocking entry into the apartment.

"Nia told me you'd be coming over for dinner," he said tersely. "It's a little out of your way, isn't it?"

"Well, considering *some*body skipped town without saying goodbye, I figured you owe me din-dins at least." I held up a six-pack of Big Red. "Truce?"

Rick regarded me with that same emotionless, indefatigable glare that had served him so well. Before he could relent, the door was pulled open further by a pair of immaculately manicured hands. The woman who wedged herself into the space between Rick and I was no stranger, but it was always a surprise to see her given how often she altered her appearance. Today, Nia Sears wore a patterned dress that ended just shy of the knee, something of African heritage as evinced by the bright colors and fabric print. She also wore two enormous hoop earrings that framed a wide-cheeked smile that pursed into a smooch against my cheek.

"Don't leave him just standing out here, Rick," Nia said, pulling me into their apartment. "Dinner's on!"

"Great to see ya, Nia," I said. "I love your hair. Last time I saw you it was braided down to your knees."

Nia ran her hands through her short, poofy hair and giggled. "Why didn't y'all tell me short hair kept you cooler in this Texas heat?" She said it accusingly to both Rick and I, and I could see Rick deflate a little as his wife chided him.

"It's simple chemistry, hon," he said.

Nia waved her hands in flitting motions, a bundle of energy as she floated around the roomy apartment, drawing us to the dinner table where bowls of sweet-smelling deliciousness awaited. "Y'all make up or whatever. No wine till you make up."

Rick looked at me in his way, and I shrugged, feeling more like an idiot than I ever had before. "I'm sorry, brother. The Preacher situation was totally uncalled for, and I'm sorry."

Nia cleared her throat, forcing Rick to look into her wide eyeballs. He looked at her then looked back to me.

"I suppose I could have answered a phone call or two," he said.

We all sat down at the table once Rick and Nia had put their dogs at bay. Even the spaciousness of the two-bedroom apartment seemed claustrophobic with the Sears' killer dogs jumping around. They're not killers, they're sweethearts. I'm just partial to cats is all. Belle, the shepherd, Sarge, the schnauzer, and Honey, the bulldog, all wanted a piece of me, and I acquiesced to quick scratches behind their ears while Nia pulled them into a fenced off section of the living area. Nia fussed over her house like every southern woman you've ever heard of. From mother to wife to grandma, she filled the archetype and ruled the roost. It was a perfect balance to Rick's stolid demeanor. I had always been glorified that they had found each other.

"Salad, pasta, chicken teriyaki and vegetables from the wok," Nia said, pointing everything out on the table. "Dig in!"

"Smells amazing," I said, always happy to fill my ever-expanding belly.

"What brings you to Austin, Jack?" Nia said as we filled plates. She looked at Rick when she said it though, and he caught it even though he didn't meet her stare. They had clearly argued about it earlier.

"Well, to tell my brother Rick here that the thing he asked me to do, I did it." I winked at them.

"You found Tayona?" Rick said.

"If you had picked up your phone..."

Rick held up a hand. "I got it. I got it." There was still an edge to his tone. "But you *did* find her?"

"Yep. Know where she is and everything." With my fork, I speared a broccoli from the pile of wok-fried vegetables and brandished it at Rick. "Even saw the kid."

Rick's eyes grew wide so evident was his surprise. "You saw Artie? Is he okay?"

"He's fine. They're both fine. I got some...friends keeping an eye on them." Probably best not to bring up Rick's least favorite person.

"You neglected to tell me the kid's autistic," I said, deciding instantly to play all the cards.

"Autistic *savant* is the right term," Rick said, nonplussed.

"You didn't think that was an important detail?"

"I don't see how it matters seeing as how all I wanted you to do was find them, not babysit." Tension rose to palpable levels as Rick dug into a pile of angel hair pasta and teriyaki chicken, his movements tightening again. " When can I see her?"

I held up a hand. "Rick...let's talk about that. Later. First, let's talk about your client."

Rick's jaw slowed down in mid-chew. "Oh?"

"You remember I told you how I felt about this guy Ted Parker, right?"

"I remember you had some vague opinions about him, sure." Rick shrugged. "He is my *paying* client, though."

"He ain't paying that much," Nia said under her breath as she reached for her wineglass, eliciting a barely controlled glare from her husband.

"Rick, listen. I been looking into this guy. He's *dirty*. Tayona's afraid of him. She left with Artie because she's scared Parker's gonna use him like an autistic crypto-kiddie in whatever computer baloney he's always up to."

"Use him?" Rick repeated. "Use him how?"

"Apparently, Artie is a whiz with coding. I even saw him do it. He was rewriting the rendering on a video game *as he was playing it*. The kid's a genius."

Rick shook his head violently. "Ted Parker is still paying KidSmart to find his son for him. The wife is probably just running stories on you to buy time. Where did you say she was?"

"Dude. She wasn't running stories." My fork clattered to my plate as I got more animated. "The guy could be abusive. And, oh by the way: did you know Ted *isn't* Artie's biological father?"

Rick blinked. "What? His name's on the kid's birth certificate."

"Tayona was already pregnant when they met. She just wanted a sugar daddy, and Parker was driving the slow bus that day."

"All the more reason to get the kid away from that rather destabilized personality," Rick said evenly, pointing his fork at me. "I can get him to a neutral, safe place,"

I smacked the table hard, not meaning to, but clattering the dishes and silverware enough to draw the Sears' ire.

"I already got that taken care of, man," I said. "Ain't nobody gonna come near that kid. Look, all I want is a face-to-face with Parker. A chance to sit down and interview *him* the same way you would Tayona. Right?"

Nia looked sidelong at Rick, and he struggled to ignore that look. It said, "Boy, you *better* be listenin' to ya friend on this."

"Why won't you tell me where she is?" Rick said. "Is it money? Do I need to go get my wallet? We're way past favors here, aren't we?"

"Well, you're not asking me to fucking shoot anybody, are you?"

"Would it matter if I did?"

"Boys!" Nia screamed in a short, authoritative admonishment. "Settle yourselves down right this second. You both been friends too long to be bullshittin' each other like this."

I wasn't hungry anymore. And I didn't let my gaze stray from Rick's stony countenance. He evaluated me with his cool, detached way.

"If I get you this interview with Parker," he said slowly, "will you tell me where she is?"

"Shit, man, I'll drive her down here for you," I said, smacking the tabletop with an open palm. "Listen, I'm really confident saying that I think you're on the wrong side of this. Every time I get a phone call from one of my buds about this dude, my Spidey sense goes off. Something ain't right."

Rick let out a long slow breath and clasped his hands together in front of him, resting his elbows on the table. Nia rubbed his muscular arm. For the first time that evening, his diffidence breached. He checked his wristwatch.

"Give me a few minutes," he said, rising from the table. "I need to make some calls."

Rick stalked off into another part of the apartment. I could feel tension and distress radiating in his wake, like the backwash from some Japanese monster wading destructively through a cityscape.

After he passed, I leaned back in my chair and drained the red wine in my wineglass. It felt good going down, stinging my throat slightly, oaky merlot and the alcohol beneath it shooting throughout my body from the contact points in my mouth.

Nia offered me a wan smile. "Did that go how you wanted it to?"

I shook my head, not in the negative, just to clear it. "I...I don't know what I wanted, Nia."

"He's been real bad since he left the Bureau," she said, her tone taking a dive into melancholy, which was not a word I'd ever use to describe this effervescent source of happiness in Rick's life.

"Like how?"

"He's depressed. Leaving the Bureau hurt him, I think. It happened right after he got back from seeing you in Mississippi."

I bit my lip. "He tell you anything about that?"

Nia offered me a sad smile. "Enough. Enough that it explains why he's been so morose. I'll tell you, Jack, whatever he got up to with you, it's changed him. He blames himself for whatever went down, and that stubborn FBI agent couldn't go on being an FBI agent with that weight you put on him."

I ran a hand over my face. "I know. I know. He didn't pull the trigger though."

"He didn't have to, Jack. He's still Rick Sears, you know?"

A wistful grin crossed my face, and I saluted Nia with a toast from my wineglass. "Yeah, I sure do."

Before it could get any more awkward, my phone buzzed in my pocket. I excused myself from the table, giving Nia a quick hug to show how grateful I was for whatever therapy was happening around her, and scooted to another part of the apartment to answer the phone. It was Tex.

"Cajun, we got problems."

"Talk to me, Tex."

"I was escorting Tayona to one of her clubs tonight. She really wanted to pull in some quick cash. I said okay as long as I went with her."

"Where's Artie?" Realization struck me in the pit of my stomach. "Tex, you didn't leave him with Preacher..."

"Honest, Jack, Preacher's kind of a prodigy with that boy. He came back over and started playing video games with the kid, and it's like they're both tuned into the same wavelength. I wouldn't have left them there together if—"

"I know, I know, Tex, I'm sorry," I interrupted, suddenly cognizant of the random judgement oozing from me. "Back to Tayona."

"She saw somebody at the club, a guy she recognized. She got spooked and made me drive her home. Said the guy may have worked for her husband."

"No shit. Anything else? Could she describe him?"

"White male, nondescript, probably late thirties. She called him a sleazebag, but whaddya know from sleaze in those places, huh?"

"Yeah. Where are y'all now?"

"Her place. I walked the perimeter a few minutes ago and didn't see anything. Might do it again here in a bit."

"Do that. Get Preacher to do it, too, if he's not too stoned."

"Got it. It's all good right now, Cajun, but Tayona's scared. Like, for real scared."

"I hear ya, brother. I'm workin' on it. Check in with ya later."

The phone beeped as I hung up, and began to puzzle through Tex's update as I turned to go back to the dinner area. As I whirled around, though, Rick's towering form lumbered into view, a statue of judgement and crankiness if I ever saw one.

"Who the hell was that? Your boys? Those dumbasses you brought into this?" The angry edge to his voice had returned.

I pushed past him. "It doesn't matter. Not right now."

He grabbed my arm as I made it halfway into the living area. His grip wasn't hurtful but it was tight. A low rumble emanated from the dogs as they surveilled the scene from behind their gate.

"Jack, it matters," Rick said. "I just set up that meeting for you. It's gonna happen. But ain't nothing happening if your idiot friends lose Tayona and Artie."

He was starting to come loose again, the same way he had in the parking lot with Preacher. I shook my arm loose from his grip, and his hand balled up into a fist. I backed up a couple steps. Nia was moving to intercept.

"Rick, listen," I said, holding my hands up again. "I know I hurt you, okay? I know you put your trust in me, and I fucked it up. I fucked it up by asking you to help me in the commission of a crime, and I'm fucking it up for your KidSmart case. But you gotta listen to me, man."

Rick leaned into me and shouted, drilling a finger into my face. "*You* listen to *me*, Jack! You're a sloppy piece of shit! You've *always* been! You don't pay attention to shit, and you get people hurt. And then what, you don't care? Or you try to pass off caring? Like you really give a shit about this kid?"

Nia was physically interceding between us now, batting at Rick's hands as he tried to come at me. I just stood there.

"Rick, stop it!" Nia shouted.

"I'll play your fuckin' game one more time, Jack," Rick shouted over his wife, oblivious to her attempts to settle him down. "One more time just to watch you crash. Just so you can *know* this bullshit about yourself. Ten A.M. tomorrow morning. The Driskill Bar. Parker will be there."

Nia got the upper hand and pushed Rick away from me but he ignored her still, his inflamed eyes drilling into me, his words finding hooks. I felt the cold thing happen to my gut again, the butterflies you get right before the fight. But this time, there was no accompanying motivation, no prompt to respond, no hackles raising on my back. This time, I just let the loathing wash over me. I couldn't tell if it was all Rick's either or a little bit of my own directed square into my soul, like a spear through a catfish.

"Now get the hell outta my house," Rick bellowed, pointing toward the door.

Nia screamed at him again. Neither of us heard her words. I walked to the door, opened it, and left. I didn't look back. I got in the Camry and drove away.

I found a bar on the east side of Austin that wasn't too hipster and drank. A lot. Having spent all my carrying-around money, and done with people for a bit, I later climbed into the backseat of the Camry and curled up into a fitful, uncomfortable sleep.

17.

PARKER, AND NOT THE COOL ONE

The Driskill stands in all its Old Texas glory in downtown Austin, a few blocks down from The Capitol. Its buttresses look over Austin's oddly matched collection of sheer office building windows, hip music joints, and a revolving door of eateries catering to every possible taste and whim. "Keep Austin Weird" adorns tie-dyed T-shirts for sale at every tourist trap on every corner for thirty bucks, a ripoff gladly paid by the non-ironic and copious numbers of non-Texans moving into Our Capitol. Austin's weirdness is no more perfectly encapsulated than at The Driskill, where at certain times of the year, you can find a variegated mix of cargo-shorted movie geeks, hooded tech nerds, Stetson-hatted cattlemen, acid burnouts from the sixties, wide-eyed college kids, and Republicans.

And, at least on this day, a former FBI agent, a fishy tech bro, and a wannabe investigator from Fort Worth.

I got there early to smoke some cigarettes outside the hotel's Brazos Street entrance, hoping to catch Parker and whatever entourage he may carry, but I ended up missing them. They must have gone into the hotel bar directly on 7th Street. I arrived in the bar late, "fashionably," I told myself. My clothes were rumpled from the overnight stay at the Motel Camry, and I couldn't have smelled very good with all those cigarettes.

I found them in the parlor hall that separated the main bar area from the towering, polished wooden columns of The Driskill's lobby. Plush, old world couches and chairs littered the long hall area, offering plenty of space for parties to spread out, chill, drink some drinks, and watch some live music. At that time of day, no one was playing on the small stage that connected the parlor to the main bar, which was a shame. You could usually catch some great small acts on that stage from rockabilly all-stars to country soloists. Rick had organized the group standing in the hall, not seated, and he beckoned to me with an upraised hand as I walked in.

Ted Parker stood at a similar height as me and looked like your average tech guy: black business jacket over an untucked black button-down shirt over stylish denims. His feet tap-tapped at the heels in a pair of Justin boots, ostrich skin, from the gleam of the boot cream glistening on the leather. Parker was supposed to be from Texas, but urban cowboys littered the state. Anybody with a couple hundred bucks could score a decent pair of boots, and most of the tech crowd in Austin did just that. It irritated me though that Parker's were Justins, which were made in Fort Worth.

He had a mild complexion and brown hair that was going to bald early, widow's peaks receding to a pattern that would make

James Spader jealous. He kept his hands in his jeans pockets as he rocked on his heels, impatient. He didn't look anything special, and I surprised myself that I was sizing him up. Too many nights kicking asses with Tex and Preacher.

Around Parker were three hangers-on, two of which I sorted right away as security from special operations muscles bulging against plain black polo shirts sporting a wagon wheel logo, khaki pants, and the coiled antennae of radios connecting earwigs in each of their ears to devices hung on their belts at their backs. I couldn't make weapons on either, which meant they likely carried hold-outs at their ankles. No security stud goes without a concealed carry in this state, and the fact these jokers wanted to make it less obvious made me want to find out what firm they worked for. Parker likely hired them for their imposing appearance, and don't get me wrong: anybody with a neck bigger than both of my thighs deserves to be reckoned with. Sometimes in the security world, a little intimidation is all you need to keep your principal safe. It's like an invisible outer ring of protection that only gets breached by the most committed of threats.

I'd have to remember that.

The third member of Parker's little troupe must have been his lawyer because the guy was decked out in a plain blue suit and a dazzling gold tie with hardware to match on the cuffs. Rick confirmed this immediately on introduction.

"Jack Dooley, Ted Parker," Rick said, getting right down to it. "His attorney, Michael Sackler."

"'Sup?" I said, gripping Parker's hand and ignoring the lawyer altogether. Nobody bothered to introduce me to the security bros.

"Rick's been telling me about you, Jack," Parker said, aiming an affable business smile my way. He may even have meant it.

"That can't be good," I said, aiming one of my own back at him.

"What's the deal, buddy, you have some questions for me or something?" Parker said.

"Yeah," I replied. "Do you mind?"

That's when the lawyer stepped in. "Mister Dooley, are you a licensed private investigator in the state of Texas?"

I turned my bullshit business grin to Sackler. "Does it matter?"

"It does if you're conducting an official investigation related to Mister Parker," Sackler said.

"What's official?"

Sackler produced a ream of paper from a briefcase. "Perhaps if we had you sign this nondisclosure agreement first..."

I looked at Rick who shrugged imperceptibly. "Forget it. See y'all later."

As I turned on a heel, Parker reached out and grabbed my shoulder. His expression faded to one more conciliatory than the dick-check happening before.

"Jack, please. I really just want to see my son. Rick tells me talking to you might help speed that along, right?"

"Sure. Don't need an NDA for that though, right?" I inclined my head at Sackler. "Maybe leave your legal eagle here at the bar, and me, you, and Rick can go post up somewhere private to shoot the bull for a hot second."

Sackler leaned into Parker's neck space and whispered, "I don't really recommend—"

"Mike, it's fine!" Parker said, waving him away. "Jack's right. Just a friendly chat."

"Right," Rick said. He ushered toward the lobby again. "We've got a conference room set aside right up here."

The security bros took up residence outside the room, and I made sure the door was closed tightly once we were inside. The conference table was round so the positioning of the players was less confrontational from the get-go. Good. I plopped into one of the plush cowhide chairs and pulled out a notebook and pen.

"Well, Ted, let's get down to it," I said. "I can call you *Ted*, right?"

Parker smiled amiably as he sat down in another chair, but his eyes were glued to a mobile device of some kind, distracted. "Of course, of course."

"Okay, so you've hired KidSmart to find your missing wife and son, right?"

Parker spared a glance at Rick. Rick nodded to him once. "Right."

"Why are they missing?"

"Didn't Rick already explain all this to you?" Parker said. "I thought you were working for him?"

The tell didn't feel combative or exploratory, more like a statement to gauge who knew what about whom. I couldn't be too sure what else Rick had told Parker about me, but he at least knew how I'd entered the picture.

"I'm a free agent," I said. "Why are you looking for your wife and son, Ted?"

"Tayona kidnapped Artie," Parker replied.

"Kidnapping is a major felony, Ted. People who kidnap kids go to federal prisons. Ted."

Parker smirked and offered me a shrug before turning back to his mobile. "If that's what's gotta happen, then so be it. I'm divorcing her anyway, and that'll surely help my custody claim over Artie."

"Provided Tayona *actually* kidnapped Artie," I corrected him. "Because for kidnapping to work as crime, someone's got to report it...and so far nobody has."

"I wanted to keep this quiet, you know? Get my son back, make sure he's safe. Then I could figure out the divorce proceedings."

"Cops are pretty good at finding missing kids in Texas. Funny you hired an independent nonprofit purpose-built for protecting children."

Parker's eyes pinned me but his body language stayed focused on his phone. "Is that a question?"

"I guess I don't understand why you'd hire KidSmart if Tayona could go to the police and claim you were abusing Artie."

The stinger pulled Parker back from his device, and he slammed it down on the table. Rick leaned over to me and said in a warning tone, "Jack..."

It had gotten Parker's blood up. His attention wavered no more, and he fixed me with a direct glare.

"I have never abused my son," he said in a low, spiteful voice. "Why the hell would you say such a thing to me?"

"Abuse can take many forms, Ted," I said, pretending to write some things down on my notepad but merely scribbling nonsense. "Notice I didn't say 'sexual.' Unless you have something else to confess, too. Ted."

Parker looked over at Rick, clearly annoyed. Rick blinked slowly, not meeting his gaze. Parker got the hint.

"Jack Dooley you said your name was?"

I grinned at him. "You know who I am."

"Jack, listen. The bottom line is that I am paying a vast sum of money to Rick here's bosses at KidSmart to find my son. If you happen to know where he is, I'd be happy to pay you a vast sum of money too. How does that sound?"

"It sounds like a fuckin' bribe...Ted," I said, spinning as much revulsion into his name as I could.

Parker's visage hardened, and I watched the faux playfulness in his demeanor vanish out of him in a slow drown. Rick saw it, too, but played it cool, choosing instead to clear his throat, lean forward in his seat, and pin me with his Stone Mountain stare. Parker carefully folded his hands in front of him, and when he addressed me again, the threat was apparent as fire in his glare.

"Jack...who the fuck are you?"

I couldn't help but grin. It was one of those showdown moments, the kind screenwriters bled for in Peckinpah movies. That alone gave me the gumption to keep on going. I'd caught this guy on a string.

"I hear you make a lot of money, Mister Parker," I said. "Software consulting. App engineering. Cryptography...?" I put an evaluative spin on the last word, making it interrogative.

Parker glared, careful now. "Your point?"

"Making money's no big deal, right? It's America, baby! Land of the get-all-you-can-while-you-can. *How* you do it, though..." I shrugged. "Gotta be careful, am I right? Banks, taxes...burgeoning fraud laws..."

Parker lost his cool in that moment and turned to Rick. It was a small thing, but his detachment from me and focus on Rick spoke volumes. Showing even a sliver of my cards prompted Parker to squirm.

"I thought this was going to help me get my son back, Mister Sears," Parker said flatly. "But it seems like I'm just wasting my time...and you're not upholding your part of our agreement with KidSmart."

Rick turned to look at Parker, pivoting ever so slowly while conveying that serene stillness in which he kept his own confidence. Even through that, though, I could see his left eyelid twitch, and I knew something had changed. He had seen it, too.

"I'm sorry, Mister Parker. We're exhausting all possible avenues of approach, of course. Jack is a specialist in the Dallas/Fort Worth area, where we think your wife might have taken Artie."

Parker narrowed his eyes at Rick and looked back and forth between him and me. "You don't say. Then why am I wasting my time answering stupid questions when you could be out looking for them?"

"I'm just curious what they might be running from...*Ted*," I said, again emphasizing his shit name.

Parker raised a finger and pointed it at my face. "I think I'm done with this. You can either help Mister Sears find my son or get out of the way before you find yourself the subject of an obstruction of justice charge."

I made a face, facetiously. "I...don't think that's how obstruction works...Ted. It's more of a...*tripwire*...people get stuck on sometimes, isn't it...*Ted*?"

He flinched, then stood up suddenly, knocking his chair back into the wall behind him and stalking over to the conference room door. Device still in hand, he jerked open the door and looked back to pin Rick with his eyes, seemingly ignoring me. I wished I'd had my sunglasses on me right then to pull a David Caruso and hear Roger Daltrey scream "YEEEEEEAAAAHHHHHH!!!!!!"

"I'll be talking to your seniors, Mister Sears. I suggest you get back to work and stop wasting precious seconds in the day with things that don't matter to this case."

Parker left the conference room in a rush, and I could see the security bros outside follow him as his business jacket fluttered in the breeze caused by his departure. The lawyer wasn't far behind them, and he let his eyes sweep through the conference room quickly and with no expression as he went.

Rick turned to look back at me, and I fished a crushed pack of Marlboro Lights out of my jeans pocket, the cardboard box squished by the proximity of the ripped denim to a sweaty thigh. You weren't supposed to smoke in The Driskill. I knew I wouldn't be there much longer.

"That went well, doncha think?" I said through a toothy grin to my brother. "Buy you a slice?"

———

A few hours later, I gave into my inner tourist and took Rick out to Sixth Street for a bite before we parted ways. The sun beat down from an Austin skyline devoid of clouds, and both of us cowered behind sunglasses as we sauntered down the sidewalk. Rick wore the same pair of Huey Lewis-style Ray-Bans he'd favored since we were kids. I was on my third pair of convenience store shades this month, cheap knockoffs of any brand name pair I could find that looked cool.

We looked like a pair of Austin regulars on our prowl. Rick had worn a solid black short-sleeve button-down shirt over one of his thousand plain white Tees, an attempt to thwart the rising heat of the central Texas summer. His khaki slacks were pressed and straight but not snappy, moving with taut legs in a billowy breeze. The butt of a handgun created an extrusion in the small of his back from where it was stuck into his waistband. He looked like Adonais, and still no one noticed him as he strolled.

My jeans were years old, faded and softened by too many nights under tables and chairs. I hadn't even tried to dress up for the Parker meet, opting instead for dark navy short-sleeve button-up with golden paisley patterns. The fabric soaked up and hid the sweat stains under my arms, which spread even in spite of my Dooley swagger, a genetic inheritance from my father and his father before him that caused us to lead with our stomachs and swish our arms in unnecessary swing patterns as we walked. My black hair was a mess of curls on top, greased by molding cream and faded on the sides, similar to the kind of cut you'd see in photos of dudes from the fifties. I'd opted for a bright red pair of low-top Connies for the Austin trip, too, the black ones still crusted with Preacher vomit.

Where Rick blended in, I stood out. Given our history, that was pretty on target.

Roppolo's Pizza always makes for a great late-night drunk bite with its greasy, crispy slices. That time of day, though, no one was waiting in line at the small serving window cut into the building into which it was sandwiched by a country music saloon and a cafe. Roppolo's slices were as big as your back, cut from immense pies perfectly baked in whatever flamethrower engine hid behind the counter. You could order a full pizza if you wanted and stand around interminably waiting for it to finish, but the best bet was grabbing a couple slices from the pizzas they kept in the serving window, freshly prepared, fragrant with pepperoni and a galaxy of toppings, and perfectly crisped from a few short minutes in the prep oven. I bought Rick a single slice of plain pepperoni and two for myself along with a pair of Big Reds. Roppolo's is fucking awesome.

We stood on the corner of Sixth and San Jacinto, munching on pizza that drooled red grease onto sop-preventing paper plates and napkins, our cans of Big Red glistening in condensation from perches on a brick windowsill. We didn't talk for a short while, enjoying the pizza, washing it back with the soft drinks, watching Austin street people perambulate around us. Occasional burnouts and bums would ask us for change, which we provided in small handfuls, taking turns.

"You know I love you, man," I said after swallowing a massive bite from my second slice. "But I think you're on the wrong side of this one. Parker's dirty. Like a pair of shit-shorts on the back end of a chili pepper binge."

"He's my client, Jack," Rick said, still slowly chewing his pizza, his jaw clicking with each grind.

"That don't make him right. You saw him in there. He's a shifty little fucker."

"Yeah..." Rick exhaled hard as he finished the slice, crumpling up the pizza juice soaked paper plate in one big fist. "Yeah, he is. That true what you said about him not being Artie's biological father?"

"Tayona's a lot of things but she ain't a liar." I burped as I polished off my second slice and crushed my own plate. "Whaddya wanna do, brother? You want me to walk away from this shit? Just leave it alone? Let 'em sort their own shit out? 'Cause if you do, my next call is gonna be to get Tayona a lawyer she can trust to protect her and Artie from that fuckin' guy."

Rick took my crumpled leavings, smashed them into a ball with his, and dunked them into a nearby trash can. We both sipped off Big Red cans, lounging against the shade of the brick building on the corner, taking refuge from the enhancing heat.

"A feeling isn't proof, Jack, and you know that," Rick said. "KidSmart needs more than an unlicensed investigator's opinion on a subject before reconsidering representation of one of their highest paying clients. Whatever it is you think he's doing, you need evidence."

I lit up a cigarette, feeling the sharp crackle of the Zippo gas flaming across lingering pepperoni tickles in my mouth, breathing in the deep flamey feel to coat my throat with its stinging joy.

"How long have I got?"

"Twenty-four hours. After that, I'm officially reporting Artie as a kidnapping victim to state and local police, putting out an APB on Tayona and Artie in the DFW area." He crushed his empty Big Red can between his palms. "And on your friends Tex and Preacher, too."

18.

IT'S A CRUEL SUMMER

I drove back to Fort Worth that afternoon, beating Austin's afternoon traffic exodus. The Camry made it in record time, avoiding speed traps in Waco and a broke-down, jackknifed truck in Cleburne by skipping over a flat shoulder and onto the side road. En route, I called Tex, Preacher, and Deckhead and Pussy Control. Everyone was to meet up at The Jetfire.

The drive offered me time to marinate the steak, so to speak. Thinking about steak made me hungry again, so I detoured through Charley's Old Fashioned Hamburgers on my way to The Jetfire and sprung for a bag of burgers for the crew.

It was around seven in the evening when I skipped into The Jetfire Gym. Business was booming. Customers occupied the rental terminals. Kids who were too young to drink camped over mochas and lattes at the tables. In back, burly neckbeards in cargo shorts and black T-shirts gambled over *Magic: The Gathering* tournaments. Pussy greeted me with a low nod from behind the counter and led me to the back room without a word. The smell of marijuana was thick inside, the haze high enough to create an electric fog through the ambient light of the computer screens. Deckhead, Preacher, and Tex were seated at the conference table passing a joint. The burgers and fries could not have come at a better time.

"I hope you got something stronger than that, Preacher," I said, handing him one of the Charley's bags and taking the inch-left roach from him for a hit or two of my own.

Preacher started feeling his pockets down. "What yeh need, Cajun? Wanna ride the lightning? Got a sweet tooth for some nose candy? Hankerin' for a little mescalito-coolito?"

"Lay them lines, baby. We got work to do."

"What's happenin', Jack-Attack?" Deck said.

"I just got face-to-face with Ted Parker."

Pussy showed her eagerness with two wide, anime-babe eyes, and she licked her lips. "*Well*???" she demanded.

"He's dirtier than my asshole on any given day," I said, taking a chomp out of a Charley's burger. "I dropped the word 'tripwire' on him in an interview, and he looked like he was gonna shit out of his eyeballs. He knows the guy."

"Well, while you were fuckin' off in our Great State's Capitol," Deckhead said, "we kept drilling. Guess what we found?"

"Some bubblin' Texas crude?"

"Parker doesn't just *know* Tr1pw1re," Pussy said. "He *is* Tr1pw1re."

I paused mid-munch, forgetting my long-distant manners and speaking through a mouthful of burger and bacon. "Are you fucking kidding me?"

"The bank accounts, the financial histories, the movement of money from banks that got hit in those cyber heists," Pussy counted each one off on her fingers. "Jack, he launders everything through his tech businesses and investments. The links match. We can draw a timeline from prep before the heists take place where an offshore account gets established by Parker for one of his funds, it grows steadily over the course of months after the heist from other bank accounts *he owns*. And get this: how does he transfer the heist money? So it can't be traced? *Cryptocurrency*!"

My face must have betrayed an obvious flummox, because Deckhead laughed at me and said, "Internet money, Bitcoin, you dumb shit. It's perfectly anonymous if you set it up the right way, use the right software, and buy from the right crypto-market. Hell, there's an escrow service on the dark web that even *specializes* in that kind of finance anonymity."

"Shut the front door," I said, incredulous. "What *will* they think of next? Can you prove that Parker used it?"

"Not yet," Deckhead said, smoke in one hand, burger in the other. "But it's just a matter of time to find the right wallets. The blockchain's 100% public, so even if the wallet doesn't have any identifying information on it, you could still theoretically match the transaction histories with the amounts of boosted dough and *boo-yah*."

Preacher, through all this, had been carefully cutting up ten different lines of cocaine on the conference table, chop-chop-chopping with the edge of a credit card to transform his fine white powder into finer white powder suitable for sensitive noses. "Fookin' crypto-fiver shite!" he ejaculated presently, punctuating his syllables with additional taps on the white lines. "Usin' fookin' unreality money for reality shite. What happened to the feel of cold hard moolah in yer fookin' hands, wha? Laundry sacks of nondenominationals, thick rubber bands bindin' yer spoils, *fat stacks*, yeh ballacks! Yeh ain't got no ownership over all this digital bullshite. No fookin' skin inna game. Cheesin' fer fookin' photo ops with cunts...cunts yeh can't take back! Lyin', piece o' shite cunts! Oi, I was there in the shite when me fookin' forebears were movin' money under mahogany bars and barracks, fundin' the truncheons of hell and damnation! Black and Tans, yeh shites! *Black and Tans!*"

All of us had at one time or another been sermonized by Preacher's rambles, and they often engendered a certain entertainment value amongst friends. Nine times out of ten, nobody had any idea what he was talking about though, but it was fun to listen. He was headed off one of those cliffs now, prompted by the longest line of coke he could have snorted off the table, and I knew if we didn't head him off at the pass, he'd be lecturing us on the finer points of The Troubles and his tenuous genetic connections to such an insurgency's prosecution by forces legitimate and foreign.

I stuck a burger in Preacher's mouth as he recoiled from the coke hit, plugging the hole before it could spew forth another round of invective. "Thank you for that Black and Tan report, Preacher. Now, let's get back to the task at hand."

"Parker," Tex said. "And not the cool one."

"Right." I turned to Pussy. "How solid is your data? Would it stand up in court?"

Pussy traded looks with Deck. I could tell Deckhead had concerns, evidenced by his shifty eyes and immediate reach for a coke straw. Pussy pursed her lips, forehead scrunching in concentration before she looked back at me.

"How important is it that it's court-viable?" she said.

I made a face and leaned over to take a line of my own, ready for the heart-explosions to ramp up the crash of the comedown I had begun to feel. The Charley's burger, while tasty and perfect, had tipped me over into food coma territory, and I needed that bump if I were to keep cracking on what felt like a sure wave of progress. I snorted half of one line, just enough to jumpstart me but not enough to bring on the heart murmurs.

"If you can't prove it, you can't do anything about it," I said, wiping stray particles off my nostril. "At least not from a law enforcement perspective."

"But we *can* rip the *pendejo* off," Deckhead said. "If we finish enumerating his accounts, find out where all his money is...we take that shit and retire."

"He doesn't strike me as a multi-millionaire. Am I wrong about that?"

Pussy shrugged. "He's at *least* a millionaire. How much else he's got stashed away? We're still finding it."

"So that's the run," I said, a statement, not a question. I locked eyes with Pussy first then Deckhead. "Ripping Parker's fuck-ass off and then turning all this evidence over to the authorities? To go straight like you guys wanted?"

"Seems problematic stealin' from a fella then sellin' him up the river to the cops for the same thing," Tex said. He lounged in his chair, boots up on the lip of the table as he munched leisurely on a burger.

"The oul' git deserves it, Tex," Preacher said. "Fooker's terrorizin' his girl, his kid. Wants to plug that kid into The Matrix like a fookin' cyborg."

"He does what?" Deckhead said.

"Parker's kid is an autistic savant. A virtuoso with computers, code, cryptography," I said. "Tayona took him away because she thinks Parker wants him for that aptitude. If you're in the hacking business and you can get a resource like Artie, a resource that doesn't cost you anything because he's your son..."

"Weird we missed that," Deckhead whispered, more to himself than anyone else. He looked away with a perplexed grimace and a furrowed brow as he contemplated this new information.

"What a fucker," Pussy said. "Now I *want* to kick his ass."

Deckhead popped his knuckles and winked at his girl. "Then let's do it, baby."

"Hey, guys!"

The interruption came from Poquito, Deckhead's young team-mate. She was posted up in one of the computer cradles, hidden by humming towers and buzzing screens, illuminated by the glow. She poked her teeny bopper head—replete with *Sailor Moon* poofs in shock platinum hair—out from her pod and caught our attention with a high-pitched wail that screeched through the back office.

"Five-oh, five-oh!" she wailed.

Deck and Pussy shot to their feet, crowding around Poquito's cocoon. I ran over to join them. Preacher frantically wiped the cocaine off the table, cursing himself for wasting it as he did so. Tex slowly got to his feet.

"Who is it?" Pussy said, leaning over Poquito to look at one of her screens, a monitor that showed four feeds from closed-circuit TV cameras stationed inside The Gym. There were, of course, no cameras in the back office.

"Don't know," Poquito said. "But I know five-oh when I see 'em."

When I peered over their shoulders, all of us save for Poquito recognized the newcomer.

"Shit," Deck said. "What's Hulen doing here?"

"Shut everything down," Pussy said gravely.

"We got shit running!" Poquito protested.

"It can wait."

"There's P.D. on the street and out back," Deck said, an elevated worry in his voice as he checked a separate monitor that displayed camera feeds from the exterior of the building.

Pussy looked at me. "Stall him?"

"On it," I said. "Tex!"

Tex and I exited the back office, leaving behind a frantic Preacher who was scooping up drug paraphernalia into a bag to either flush or burn. Deckhead had an iron trash can in the back made for just such an eventuality, and he pushed Preacher toward it while the rest of his and Pussy's team started unplugging things.

Roger Hulen was talking to a fresh-faced kid behind the coffee bar when we navigated past the *Magic: The Gathering* crowd. That Saturday's traffic in The Gym was uncommon, so I felt somewhat on edge as my eyes hunted the faces of many strangers. Our history with Hulen kept me from panicking, but the cocaine coursing through my veins and the proximity to the Parker problem made me jumpy. Tex's sobering presence behind me, however, provided a reassuring crutch on which to lean as we closed in on the Ranger.

Hulen was dressed in his usual leather vest, Leddy's shirt, pressed jeans, and Stetson. His eyes found us as we approached, circumventing the line of high schoolers and summer vacationers seeking cold coffee and sweet tea after hours of exploring Sundance Square. Hulen walked away from the kid at the counter, an eighteen-year-old Pussy paid legitimately to man the coffee service, one of many kids whose lives would have turned out unluckier had it not been for The Jetfire Gym. This kid had no idea what was going on in the back room, and that was for the best.

"Roger," I said, offering an ears-wide grin as we approached. "Good to see ya. What's happening?"

"Jack," Hulen breathed, his downturned face seeming more mopey than usual. He oriented his body toward us, his hips pointing the Ranger badge directly at us. He put his hands on the gunbelt, one on the butt of his holstered sidearm, the other hooked above the badge, drawing attention to both. "I was hopin' y'all wouldn't be in today."

"Why's that, Mister Hulen?" Tex said, inclining his head to tip the brim of his own Stetson. Roger returned the salute.

"Cochrane." Hulen took a few steps to close the distance between us. "What do y'all know about people using this establishment as a front for cybercrime?"

My eyebrows, ever expressive, gave it away immediately, and I blushed. Hulen caught it, which made my next few words all the weaker. "Pretty sure I don't know nothing about that, Roger."

"Cybercrime ain't really a Ranger's jurisdiction, is it?" Tex said, folding his arms over his wide chest.

"Well, the deed takes us to where we need to be, I reckon. I'm guessing y'all are still friendly with Jeri Hernández and Domingo Reyes?"

"You likely already know the answer to that if we're here, Roger," I said. "What's going on?"

Roger kept his lawman's gaze on us both. "Are they here, fellas?"

"What's this all about, Mister Hulen?" Tex said, stalling.

"I don't really wanna have to bring you two in on this thing, so it would be best if you told me what you know right now."

"I don't even know what we're talking about right now," I blurted, and a sliver of panic speared me through the chest.

Deckhead and Pussy Control came out of the back office at that point, weaving through the card-playing crowd to join us. They would not have appeared had the back office been insufficiently sanitized. Poquito must have snuck out a different way. Preacher was in tow behind Deck, nervously looking around and none too subtle about it.

"What's the trouble?" Deck said, not combatively but directly enough and without preamble to set expectations, to maintain escalation. "Ranger."

"Domingo, Jeri, good to see y'all again," Hulen said, reaching behind his back. "There anybody else with y'all back there?"

"Sir, I think you need to tell us what's going on before we answer any questions," Pussy said. "Unless you're here for a friendly cup of coffee?"

"Or maybe to throw down some *Magic* manna, wha?" Preacher crowed.

"I'm gonna need to get into that back room y'all just came from," Hulen said evenly, undeterred, but not angrily. In fact, his voice was barely audible over the din of the crowd in The Gym. He produced an envelope from behind his back with an official seal of the State of Texas on it. "This here's a warrant to search the premises."

"On what grounds?" Pussy said. We had formed a protective wall between Hulen and the direct route to the back office, and there were more than thirty clueless nerds and geeks in the way too. Pussy wasn't stressed, and I could tell from her easygoing demeanor that we had provided ample time for them to do what they needed to back there.

Hulen ignored the question, grabbing a walkie talkie with his other hand, holding it upside down, speaker first to his mouth. It made a little squawking noise as he depressed the talk button, and he said into it, "Six-one-Charlie, clear to proceed."

The front door of The Gym burst open as multiple men in dark blue and brown uniforms filed inside. They began clearing the clientele immediately, ordering individuals to produce identification, lining them up against walls, divesting them of bags or anything else they happened to be holding. One fellow tried to run, taken off-guard at his computer terminal, and when he attempted to slip past the cops, one of them tackled him vertically against the wall, commanding the man with a shout to surrender. Cops with "FWPD" written on their vests mixed with the brown-shirted, cowboy-hat adorned men of the Tarrant County Sheriff's Office, all professional peace officers with a remit to subdue those on site. They worked cleanly and methodically, separating people into groups as zip ties were produced and plainclothes officers and detectives entered to begin sorting through the assemblage.

Preacher was about to throw a bottle of Coca-Cola at the cops when Tex restrained him with big biceps encircling his neck to cut off the wild vituperation sure to come from his addled throat. With this commotion, Hulen drew his sidearm, a silver pearl-gripped Colt six-shooter that glinted in the light when it brandished in our direction. Behind him, a couple detectives approached with handcuffs open. Hulen looked almost hangdog and put upon when he said what he said next.

"I'm sorry, boys, but y'all are under arrest."

19.
LAWYERS, GUNS, AND MONEY

People believe every cop show trope on TV. Somebody's a good cop. Somebody's a bad cop. Interviewees are more than eager to ignore their rights and babble on to the Pembletons and the Mackeys, confessions to authority in excess libre. Chicago accents. Rough promises that it'll go easier if you just cooperate. Big ole' mustaches.

In The Fort, it's a different story.

The mustache part is true enough. Each of the detectives that appeared in my small little interview room sported proper cop lip hair, which any of them would tell you was more of a product of their Texas heritage, not their police brotherhood. Fort Worth investigators, and by extension those of the Tarrant County Sheriff's Office, are perfect ladies and gentlemen. They are well-dressed, smoothly groomed, and eminently polite. Every conversation with a Tarrant County detective begins and ends with empathetic respect, kindness, and Texan manners. Their words are caressed by the same rural accents you'd hear on Weatherford ranches or Longview lakes, clipped only by the few times they need to admonish their suspect with knowledge of a lie. They're the type of folk you'd want to sit and have a beer with, anytime, and it wouldn't surprise me if they'd been able to coax a confession or two through just that method here in Fort Worth.

Five different investigators came at me. It began with a balding fraud detective sweating through his short-sleeve shirt and tie. In this, he upheld the cop stereotype. He seemed overworked, tired, and out of his depth as he asked me question after question about how easy I found it to steal other people's money on the internet. It was this cop's scattered questioning that tipped me off to the score from the get-go. The rest were easy. He was a nice guy and offered me a Coke, talked about his son, generally affable rapport-building. I kept quiet and looked at him till he left.

Next, two TCSO detectives tried to put the squeeze on me with more varied and aggressive interrogation techniques, extolling the virtues of confession, how good it would feel to let it all out. I farted, loudly and stinkily, filling the room with my insides. I didn't say a word. They finally left.

The next one was a state guy, DPS. He told me I'd be looking at twenty years in prison if charged. I asked him what I was being charged for. He demurred and told me I could mitigate my sentence if I admitted what Deckhead and Pussy Control had done, except he used their real names. I farted again and told him I'd only talk to Roger Hulen.

Roger was the fifth and final lawman to interrogate me, and honestly, they should have led with him. I only found out later the reason he didn't come in first was because he'd been talking to the rest of my friends. He shut the door to the interview room and sat in the chair caddy-corner to me. A camera whirred in a corner where the ceiling met walls. No two-way glass in shabby old Fort Worth.

"Roger, what the fuck am I doing here?" There was no anxiety in my voice, no judgment. I was more annoyed than anything by that time. It was well into the evening now by my estimation. I didn't wear a watch, and there wasn't a clock in the room. Another common police interview tactic: sublimate the subject's inherent need to fixate temporally. I'm sure it worked fine on other *hoi polloi*.

"Jack...I'm sorry," Hulen said slowly, and I could hear genuine regret in his scratchy tenor. "If I'd known you were into this as much as you are, I'd probably have talked to you earlier outside of here."

"Little late for regrets, Roger. What's going on?"

"You're here under suspicion of computer fraud charges. Either in direct commission or aiding and abetting, we're still not saying."

"Who's 'we'?"

"Special state task force on cybercrime. We've got a new prosecutor got his eye on the D.A.'s seat when the term comes up."

"And he thinks cybercrime is his ticket?" I couldn't help a chuckle of incredulity. "How does that work? Enough old country biddies complaining about getting rolled by Johnny Mnemonic?"

"Those old biddies bank at state institutions that have been getting breached pretty regularly, Jack." Hulen looked at me differently at that point, with a discerning, piercing stare devoid of cloudiness. He *was* interrogating me.

"Have I been charged?" I pressed.

"Not yet," Hulen said. "Right now, you're here as an accessory since we scooped you up at the cafe. It's really them that the prosecutor is after. So, I'd like your cooperation in talking about Domingo and Jeri if you don't mind."

There it was. The stateys were after Deckhead and Pussy Control.

"Your friends are all here, Jack," Hulen continued, sensing my pause but not sure of its source. "Cochrane too. They're gonna drug test the Irish one. What do you think will happen when those results come back? You can practically smell the reefer on him as it is. Should we test you, too?"

"He's not Irish," I said, giving him something, but nothing. "He's just Preacher."

"Jack, help me out here, man." Hulen lowered his voice and leaned closer to me. "Domingo and Jeri are gonna go down for capital fraud and God knows what else once Techt is through with them. He needs headlines to wave in front of voters."

Hulen wasn't off-base. Deck and Pussy had pulled more jobs online than even I knew about. It would be a misrepresentation of their pedigree to call them ethical hackers, too, at least as far as general society was concerned. They stole, sure, but they followed rules. They never stole from individuals unless they had a good reason. They sometimes pulled political stunts, anonymous ops aimed at shady organizations or shitbirds that deserved it like pedophile artists. Those wouldn't fall under the fraud case that the prosecutor was building though, so I had to wonder what evidence the state was working with. If there was a special task force as Hulen had said, they were woefully out of their depth on general principle. The state could barely pay for officers' cell phones much less the kind of counter-hackers whose skills would be required to detect traces of Deck's and Pussy's work. It didn't add up.

Maybe that was the point.

I needed to see more of the state's cards.

"I want my phone call," I said. "In fact, I just want Preacher to make *his* phone call."

———

I wasn't there when it happened, but I'm told that when they hand-ed Preacher the phone on one of the detectives' desks, he dialed a number and said very calmly into the receiver, "Cluster-cluster-cluster. TCSO. Love yeh."

Less than hour later, one of the baddest asses in the Fort Worth legal world strode into TCSO in a black suit with a skirt that hugged her hips, the longest legs you've ever seen on a Hispanic lady, and heels that clicked so loudly and in such perfect time that people who heard them sat up a little straighter. Mikayla Castañeda carried no briefcase, only a small handbag over her shoulder, itself plain black leather that matched her outfit and the void-like hairdo that encircled her taut face. She had one mole on an otherwise unblem-ished brown cheek, and people tended to focus on that initially, not realizing that she purposely wore a lipstick shade and mascara to match the birthmark's coloring, all of it complexion control enabling her dominance of opponents on sight.

When they came to get me, Roger was still trying to get me to talk, holding out hope that the hours in confinement would wear me down. I didn't blame him for the tactic. I figured of the whole crew, I was the easiest target, save possibly for Preacher who could say or do God knows what at any given time. A sheriff's deputy opened the door to my interview room to let Mikayla in, and she walked right on through as if she owned the place. She pinned Hulen with the type of expression one reserves for delivering bad news, like, "You have ass cancer, buddy. Tough luck."

"Ranger Hulen? Mikayla Castañeda. I'm representing Mr. Dooley, Mr. Cochrane, Mr. Reyes, Ms. Hernández, and Mr. Cornish. If there are no charges, I'd like them released right away."

Hulen crossed his arms as he regarded Mikayla, leaning against the wall near me and not moving. "Well, ma'am, we can release Jack, Cochrane, and the...excitable fella, but we're gonna charge Reyes and Hernandez for computer fraud. Prosecutor's working up the papers now."

"Jack, let's go," Mikayla said, ignoring Hulen and turning on a heel to leave. I jumped up and followed her, and Roger pursued, his gait instantly speedier than I had seen of the old man.

"Miss—" he started.

"It's *Ma'am*," Mikayla said as she walked with purpose down the hall, searching room numbers.

"Ma'am, it'd be good if we had a chat before y'all up and skedaddle out of here."

"Good for whom, Ranger?" She said it as a statement, not a question or at least not one she was expecting him to answer. Before Hulen could even attempt to respond, Mikayla banged into another interview room, using her shoulder to push the door open as she twisted the knob. Inside, I could hear Preacher.

"—it's fookin' Hicks, wha? Are yeh followin' me, lad? Oi, hi, luv."

He had been speaking to a clueless deputy assigned to keep an eye on him when Mikayla burst in. I couldn't see her face but it must have been as impassive as it was when she entered the building because Preacher sidled out of the room to offer me a look not unlike Winnie-the-Pooh in trouble with Christopher Robin again for eating all the honey.

"Hang on," Hulen said, barring the hallway before us. "This one might need a drug test before we can release him."

"Ranger, if you're not going to charge my client with anything, then he's going home," Mikayla said. "And you have no grounds to even suggest that."

She sidestepped Hulen, making her way to the next interview room where she retrieved Tex. The big man ambled out of his interview room, thumbs in his pockets, taking it all in, none too bothered.

"Hey, Mikayla," he said.

"Good to see you, Tex," Mikayla replied softly with a wink and a slight smile. Even she was not immune to the panty-curdling Tex imbued.

Hulen was striding up the corridor, just in time to receive another volley from Mikayala. "Where are the others?"

"I said they're going to be charged," Hulen said.

Mikayla's eyes narrowed. "That's not what I asked you, Ranger."

"What the fook's goin' on here?" Preacher exhorted.

I grabbed him around the neck and put my hand over his mouth. "Zip it, bud."

"We're not going to release these two," Hulen said. "The prosecutor—"

"Yes, I heard you the first time," Mikayla cut him off. "Take me to them anyway. They have a right to counsel, and I am that counsel. Do you need to see my certificate, sir?"

Hulen looked around to see all of us staring back at him. The corridor was open on one side, allowing a view into a squadron of office cubicles where deputies and TCSO employees peeked around partitions for an eyeful and an earful of this disruption, likely the most interesting thing in their day. The scene was on the precipice of turning into A Thing, and Hulen knew it. Not taking his eyes off hers, he lightly reached for her arm and pointed her in another direction.

"Why don't we discharge your other clients here first?" he said.

"They can come with," Mikayla said, shrugging out of his hand. "And I can walk myself just fine, Ranger, thank you."

Preacher made a long sizzling noise behind my clamped hand that must have been Preacher-code for *"Burrrrrrrrnnnnn!"* I gripped him harder and offered a guilty grin to both Hulen and Mikayla who regarded us, The Idiot Triplets, with a mix of dismay and derision. I suspected Preacher was going to have a lot to make up for later. Hulen's mouth twitched and his mustache rippled as he moved his tongue around inside, something I'd never seen him do and likely an indicator of annoyance. He gestured down another corridor.

"This way, please," he said.

Police, sheriff's office staff, and deputies all turned their noses up at us as we marched. Preacher had not showered in a couple days, and that, combined with his ever-present weed stench, elicited looks of disgust and loathing. Authority can be a tricky, fickle mistress. Some of us defer it to it, though disrespect may be bred in their bones. Others respect it absolutely, intently, and fully. The rest of us just hoped never to be ice cream for the long tongues of the law. They don't always get their man, but when they do, there's always a reckoning with natural justice.

They had Deckhead and Pussy Control in two different interview rooms, these ones higher-end versions of the ones in which Tex, Preacher, and I had been stashed. Two-way mirrors facilitated anonymous review of the rooms' occupants in addition to a camera feed from inside piping to a DVR setup right outside. A deputy was questioning Deck, and Pussy was alone. The viewing area outside the interview rooms featured a small card table and folding chairs for observers, all of which were full of law enforcers in various uniforms and suits.

One guy looked like he was about to pounce through the glass at Pussy. He wore a sharp, satiny suit of steel blue, tailored tight around the limbs and chest, accentuating his slim but powerful build. His brown hair was streaked with natural blond strands and cut short, almost into a fade from top to sideburns. He wore a red power tie with geometric pattern shapes and faux golden hardware on his cuffs and tie clip. A Texas flag pin adorned his lapel. His eyes were round and bright, determined but not hard.

"Mister Techt," Hulen said as we filed into the interview area. "Reyes' and Hernández' attorney has arrived."

"Mikayla Castañeda," she introduced herself, sticking her hand at the man in the suit. "You must be Dakota Techt."

"Assistant State's Attorney Dakota Techt," the man replied, taking Mikayla's hand and pumping it once. "Your clients are—"

"Not being charged with anything as of right now, correct?"

Techt put his hands on his hips as he turned to her, his face neutral. "The paperwork is on its way."

"The charge?"

"Char-*ges*. Multiple violations of the Computer Fraud and Abuse Act—"

"Those are federal statutes. You can't prosecute them in state court."

"We have a federal judge in our circuit that's telling us we can."

"I'd like to see that affidavit, please."

"Of course, I'll have it sent over to your office."

"I'd like to see it *now*, please."

Techt looked slightly taken aback, the initial dance revealing the partners' steps for adequate measure between each, a tango few could master. The state's attorney snapped his fingers at an assistant law clerk, a young man in an ill-fitting linen suit and glasses who sat scribbling furiously on a legal pad, and he darted out of the room like a rat sensing cheese.

"We've also got them on grand theft, fraud, conspiracy to commit such, and a few other minors that we'll likely negotiate down at arraignment, right? We'll charge tonight, probably see the judge first thing in the morning," Techt said, flashing perfect teeth in a smile that seemed too genuine. "Will there be anything else?"

"My clients will not be answering any more questions today," Mikayla said. "Please move them to the secure conference room on the second floor where there aren't any cameras or other recording devices so we can all have some privacy."

Techt noticed the rest of us scattered around Mikayla and folded his arms in seeming amusement.

"Are these your law clerks?" he said with a teasing grin.

"Oi, I'll clerk yer fookin'—" Preacher started, but I slipped my hand over his mouth again.

"He's just tired," I said by way of explanation before any of the cops in the room could close in on us.

"You're Jack Dooley, huh?" Techt said. "Heard about you. Say, can I see your P.I.'s license?"

"Put it back in your pants, counselor," Mikayla said with a laughing snarl that startled everyone. "The conference room, please. And make sure Mr. Reyes and Ms. Hernández make the journey *without* handcuffs. And while you're at it, make sure those affidavits annotate your probable cause and evidence *perfectly* otherwise I'll sue you for entrapment and unjustified prosecution."

As deputies began escorting us out of the interview chamber, I pulled my hand off Preacher's mouth and whispered in his ear, "Will you please shut up before your Superhero Girlfriend Lawyer decides she's made a terrible mistake and kicks us all to the curb?"

Preacher grinned like a schoolboy. "She's a right lovely lass, ain't she?"

———

"Can we get some sandwiches? Do yeh want some sandwiches? I'm bleedin' famished."

Mikayla grabbed Preacher by the ear and tweaked it just enough to prompt him to twist uncomfortably in his chair, freezing in place as she leaned in to speak directly into one ear at a volume we all could hear.

"You are not to speak anymore until I say otherwise, *capice?*"

Preacher squeaked an acknowledgement, and she let him go. As he relaxed, she leaned over and kissed him fully on the lips, a great smacking noise that made me blush.

"Such an endearing family," I said, wiping fake tears from the corners of my eyes.

"Watch it, buster, you're next," Mikayla warned, setting her brief-case down on the conference room table. She quickly evaluated the room, moving from corner to corner, running her fingers over light fixtures, panels, bookshelves, and the door, checking for listening devices. Mikayla knew the room, of course. She had represented a client or two in her time there, and as a young attorney-in-training, she had clerked for a former sheriff at TCSO. In addition to her stellar attention to detail and reputation, her firm had picked her up for all the connections she still maintained at Tarrant County, Fort Worth, and other Metroplex court systems.

I held my hands up pleadingly and said, "I'm innocent."

"Get your fucking private investigator's license, for God's sake, Jack," Mikayla said, taking a seat. "It's a hundred question test and some letters of recommendation. That would keep people like Dakota Techt from using it against you in situations like these and maybe—*MAYBE*—cover your ass for the actual investigating you seem to be doing lately."

"Yes, ma'am," I said, appropriately cowed.

"Thanks for coming to get us, Mikayla," Pussy said, reaching across the table to squeeze her hand. "It really means a lot."

Mikayala smiled for the first time since entering TCSO and squeezed Pussy's hand back with both of her own. Pussy's ghost white hand disappeared in the brown gold of Mikayla's. "Anytime,

P.C. How you doing? Whatever perfume you're wearing smells amazing."

Pussy smiled and winked at her. "Thanks, babe. Do you want some? When I get my things back, I've got some in my bag."

"Okay, okay, okay, *mamacitas*!" Deckhead interrupted, tapping his fingers and hands nervously on the table. "Enough jaw-jackin'. What the fuck is going *on*?! One minute we're doin' our thing and the next we're gettin' scooped up in a fucking *raid*? By the P.D?"

"By FWPD, TCSO, *and* DPS," I said. "State task force on cyber-crime? Does such a thing even exist?"

"It does now," Mikayla said. "I heard what Hulen was saying about Techt, and he's right. That guy is looking at making a name for himself before the next D.A. election, and cybercrime is a bespoke issue in the district. Enough big businesses around here have suffered breaches, and we've got some of the biggest insurance firms in the state right here in Fort Worth who are paying out millions to clients in the wake of those breaches."

"That's a lot of politics to motivate an up and coming D.A.," Tex said.

"Exactly. So for the sake of the matter, we're assuming he's going HAM on this. He'll string up Deck and Pussy, he'll subpoena the rest of you, he'll make you get drug tested and put you on the stand, every trick in the book to make waves for the press."

"I still don't understand *how* they found anything about us," Pussy said. "A raid like that usually takes weeks or months to set up. How were they on us so fast?"

"Yeah, I've been talking to Roger Hulen about this Ted Parker thing for a while now," I said. "I'd be surprised if he didn't warn me to walk or at least ask some more innocuous questions about Deckhead and Pussy, but he didn't."

Mikayla was flipping through the affidavit that contained the warrant for arrests and list of charges against Deck and Pussy. "They keep referring to an investigative source provided by a private cyber threat intelligence firm. I've never heard of it. Clean Wheel Security Solutions?"

"*Motherfucker*," Pussy, Deck, and I said at the same time looking at each other.

Mikayala looked up wide eyed. Tex and Preacher were similarly entranced.

"Don't keep us in suspense," Tex said.

"Clean Wheel was one of the nodes in the analysis we working on right before we got popped," Deckhead. "It's owned by Ted Parker."

"It's where he gets his security bros from, too," I said. "When I saw him in Austin, he had two goons with Clean Wheel logos on their polos. Holy shit. How fast was that?"

"Too fast," Pussy said. "A regular guy like him wouldn't just pull that investigative report together in a day to submit to the state. He had to have been working on it for a while."

Deckhead had grabbed the papers from Mikayla and was flitting through them himself. "Holy fucking shit. Pussy, they got us fingered for jobs in here that we were never close to. Higganbotham, the RNC fund hack—"

"Jobs we were only looking at for one reason," Pussy said. "*Tr1pw1re.*"

"Fuck me, he even flinched like a little bitch when I slipped the word on him," I said. "Ted Parker *is* Tr1pw1re."

Preacher smacked the table as if he were playing a Liberace crescendo and provided the sound effects to boot. "*Dun-dun-DUNNNNNN!*"

"Wait," Tex said; "are you saying he's been running some kind of counter-surveillance operation on y'all the whole time?"

"He must have been," Pussy said. "The whole purpose of attributing Tr1pw1re was to give this very kind of evidence to state and federal authorities. He must have picked up some chatter about it, or got clued from malware on the bank networks we were looking at—"

"Or he's got someone inside The Gym," I said, grimacing at Deckhead. He caught the look and was befuddled for a moment, but then he looked at Pussy who groaned and sank her head into her hands.

"Poquito," Deck said.

"Any of the rest of them?"

Deckhead shook his head. "She's new enough to fit the infiltration timeline. Also...she was the one working background on the Parkers, so that's why nothing ever came up about Artie's autism: Poquito filtered it." He slammed a fist on the table. "I can't believe we got played like this!"

Pussy lifted her head up, forlornly regarding him. "We weren't careful enough, babe. We got sloppy."

Mikayla interceded by slapping her yellow legal pad on the tabletop. "Okay, do I need to know any of this geek-speak to get you guys off?"

Preacher raised a hand. "You can get me—"

"*Preacher!*" everyone shouted, shutting him up.

"If we can discredit Clean Wheel Security by connecting them to Parker and Tr1pw1re, then the state's case has to be thrown out," I said. "Right?"

"There's also the matter of the jobs called out in the report that are attributed to Deck and Pussy," Tex said. "You'd have to refute every one even if the report is bullshit. And if those are really Tr1pw1re's jobs—"

"Then we need to get The Gym back up and plugged in," Pussy said. "Mickey, how much did they tear out of there?"

Mikayla looked at another piece of paper. "A lot. I can send someone by to do an assessment, but I'd assume anything that looked like a computer got confiscated."

"Fuck!" Deckhead shouted. "Can we get it back?"

"We may not need to," Pussy said, a thoughtful, faraway look in her eye. "Mickey, can you get us out of here? Tonight?"

Mikayla smirked at Pussy and cracked her knuckles. "I've been training for this *my whole life*."

20.

LIVIN' WITH WHAT I BEEN GIVEN

Chaos reigned the next day when arraignment and bail hearings were expedited. Mikayla's firm was one of the more lower key legal outfits in Fort Worth, mostly representing high-net worth individuals and corporations in criminal cases like wrongful deaths, insurance fraud, embezzlement, and domestic abuse. As such, the partners avoided advertising and making too many waves publicly, unlike many of their peers. Fort Worth pumped blue blood through its veins, and there wasn't a local magazine or newspaper that didn't hit the stands without some law firm or doctor's office underwriting that month's publication. Mikayla's firm went the other way, and their clients appreciated the discretion. Conversely, their name made state and municipal attorneys jumpy: their win rate was higher than their settlement rate, a fact that turned off state's attorneys from prosecuting anything they didn't have locked up from the jump.

That was the tack Mikayla was going to take with Deckhead and Pussy Control. Mikayla called one of her senior partners and got the bail money, no questions asked. Techt argued for a denial of bail but lost on argument from Mikayla that the defendants would submit to daily checkins with authorities, backed up by one Roger Hulen, with whom I'd had a recent heart-to-heart. Hulen agreed to be responsible for checking in on the two, and that seemed to satisfy the judge and Techt.

Hulen wasn't a fraud or cybercrime Ranger. His specialty was catching bank robbers and shooting down gunmen in the streets. He was also getting to the end of his walking days in the Rangers, and he carried an unusual affinity for we Paschalites who were just struggling to get our shit together. In our chat, I sensed Roger was regretful about being assigned to Dakota Techt's task force, not just because cyber finance wasn't his thing but also because his badge was being used to squash people he actually cared about in some weird way. He had done me plenty of favors already. I asked him point blank to do me another one and enable Deckhead and Pussy Control some space to do what we needed to do.

The strategic strike Parker had deployed against us left me paranoid, so I dispatched Tex to check on Tayona and Artie. Preacher and I got stuck surveying the damage at The Jetfire Gym, which had been roped off with police tape and virtually gutted. Everything resembling a working CPU had been taken. Every laptop packed out, even a couple of the screens got nabbed, likely victims of over-zealous cops who didn't know the difference between high power processors and monitors.

Hulen followed Mikayla to The Jetfire Gym after Deck and Pussy made bail. Deck was still sore at the whole situation, so he offered Hulen only diffidence and a stiff lip when signing for his daily checkin. Pussy was more gracious, a product of her innate serenity, and she even shook Roger's hand when they parted. I think I even saw Roger look at his boots with a sad, regretful stare after he let go of her hand, almost like he could feel the right in her, which thus forced recognition of his own biases. He packed up in his government-issue Bronco and rolled off, leaving us all at The Gym.

"We have two priorities as I see it," Pussy said, providing us an assortment of drinks from the fridge. "Number one: Poquito. I'll handle that. Number two: reconstituting the Tr1pwl1re data."

"How do we do that if A, we can't trust that one of your people didn't sabotage the analysis," I said; "and B, all your shit is in lockup at TCSO?"

Deckhead whistled like a loony bird, drawing our attention as he slowly arced a single finger up into the air. He was sitting behind the coffee bar, and his finger descended like a targeted nuclear warhead, heading for a small, unobtrusive button on the wall next to the espresso machine. From any vantage point, it looked like an emergency shutoff switch, a labeled warning button that enabled the barista to shut off the heat or the water or something like that. When he touched it though, a portion of the wall next to him detached from invisible creases hidden by the crown molding design and slid inside itself. He then pushed the false wall back and to the right, revealing a hidden compartment drilled into the hollowed out brick and concrete of the building in which The Gym sat. That wall separated The Gym from the tourist shop next door and retained its thick construction from the building's original founding in the 1930s. Deckhead and Pussy had hollowed out a secret space in there.

That something, Deckhead showed us, was a stack of solid state core drives linked to independent batteries in an off-the-grid configuration right next to a pineapple-looking device that I knew was a network scanner. Hackers used pineapples like that to scan for vulnerable networks in a mobile fashion: driving by places with poor network security and gaining access via penetrating programs. This particular one was set up in a reverse fashion: an always-on backup CPU and database. Deckhead explained as much as he flicked a switch on the core deck.

"Cloud computing my ass," he said. "*Pendejo putas* don' *know* security."

"Everything's encrypted in there so it'll take some time to parse," Pussy said. "And Poquito didn't know about it, so it should be virgin."

"Unless she poisoned the well a different way," I said.

Pussy cracked one knuckle on hand by intertwining her fingers together and squeezing them down. "I'll be sure to ask her."

"Number three," I said, "is making sure Tayona's safe. She might be able to offer testimony in this too. Tex is on his way to her place now, and he'll ask her about Clean Wheel. What else can we do to help?"

Deckhead cracked his own knuckles and pecked Pussy on the cheek. "Stay out of the way. For now."

"Oi, s' a golden moon day, fer sure," Preacher said, leaning casually on the coffee bar. "Might I interest anybody in a twink of the wacky tabacky to settle yer nerves?"

I shook my head and smirked at Mikayla. "What do you see in this guy?"

Mikayla smiled fondly at her boyfriend, kissing him on the cheek. "He's got certain...talents."

When you undertake professional skeet shooting, you don't issue your own commands to pull the trap. No, part of the challenge is anticipating the pull, listening for the trap mechanism to click imperceptibly in the nanosecond it takes to launch the target into the sky. Then you still have to hit it.

Mary-Margaret McDowell is a champion skeet shooter. She carries at least two different shotguns in her trunk in the off chance that she might get a hankering to drop by the range and squeeze off a few rounds. She won the co-ed Fort Worth Invitational Skeet Shooting Competition three years in a row, skipping the past year because she bored of winning. The first few years she competed, she did so because she genuinely liked it. Then she discovered how great it felt to own all the stodgy old dudes with whom she shot, competitively or just fun on weekends between cocktail hours and golf outings. My mother's a helluva competitor in everything she does, and damn can she shoot, too.

I, on the other hand, did not inherit the skeet genes. Three rounds in and my side ached from holding the weight of the shotgun up, tracking the sky trying to blow away clay pigeons. She was currently up on me by five, and the sweat of the mid-afternoon sun was sapping my will to live. Mary-Margaret, however, casually unloaded her two-buckshot rifle with every score, calmly chambered in another couple shells, and resumed her stance for the next flight.

"If you did this more often with me, you'd get better at it," she said, blasting a target within nanoseconds of its release.

"I don't wanna get better at it," I said breathlessly, taking aim, firing, missing. "I wanna get better at sitting on my ass. Watching movies. Drinking expensive cocktails prepared for me by beautiful women. Smoking incredibly hard-to-find strains of marijuana."

"This is why you don't have a job!" She didn't mean to shout. She just does every once in a while with that piercing voice of hers.

"I'm not actively looking!" I shouted back.

"Do you want to be? What are you looking for?"

I ejected spent shells from my shotgun and retrieved a couple fresh ones from the belt bucket affixed to my waist. "I dunno, Mom. I've been toying with getting a private investigator's license."

"What? Who's gonna pay you to do that?"

"I dunno. People."

"People 'round here don't pay for private investigators, honey. It's Fort Worth. There's not enough business for it."

"Huh," I said under my breath. "You'd be surprised."

"Now, I just met a guy at a publishing company downtown," she said as she reloaded. "He's hiring editors. That's probably something you can do."

"What kind of editors?"

"I think they do tax and accounting manuals."

I pulled the trigger, scoring a hit. "Oh, that sounds just lovely, Mom. Not boring at all."

"Hey, it's a good paying job with benefits, baby. You should at least go interview."

"Yeah, maybe."

She heard the downturn in my speech, and I involuntarily let the rifle sag in my arm, completely not paying attention as two targets went flying in front of me. Mary-Margaret toed the launch mechanism to its pause setting and set the stock of her shotgun on the ground, holding it by the barrel. With her other hand, she lifted her safety glasses and stuck them in the folds of her short, straight, brownish-black hair.

"You seem a little down today, baby. What's going on? Wasn't your father just in town? Y'all usually have a good time when you get together."

I opened the chamber of the rifle, pulling out the two fresh shells, clearing the chambers, and setting the open weapon in the crook of my elbow. I pulled off my own safety glasses and looked at my Mom.

Then I told her everything.

To her credit, Mary-Margaret didn't bat an eyelash, didn't sink into herself with shame, didn't wail in anguish as I laid it all out. We took seats on the hay bales that acted as benches in front of the shooting range, perfectly alone with the occasional crack of a rifle puncturing the air around us. She listened intently as I started with Hattiesburg, Uncle Carter, Jackson, Finley, and Rick, a mishmash of confessions tumbling out of me like plot vomit in a bad soap opera. I even told her about pointing that gun at Finley and squeezing the trigger, about watching him die, about setting up his daughter to take the fall for it, and Duke's news that she was spending her days in an asylum as a result.

"Jackson," my mother breathed slowly, quietly, once I'd finished. "Oh, my God."

"I know, Mom." Strangely, I could look her right in the eye. The confession didn't unburden me of any creeping guilt I'd been harboring, didn't lift the zero I'd been carrying with me, didn't do anything really. I wish I could say that it felt good to get it all out, especially to the one person who objectively had no idea I'd been capable of all that in the first place.

But I didn't feel anything.

I just felt like me.

Mom was quiet for a long moment, atypical for her and scary. I had essentially confessed to a murder, and if she did nothing about it, she'd be an accessory. I didn't need to remind her of that; she was sharp. But she was also family, and sometimes that tends to be sharper.

"So is it...fixed? For good?" she asked. I could tell she was genuinely interested from a procedural point of view and not just selfishly, as if anticipating blowback.

"I think so," I said. "It's fixed enough. Dad and Carter have been doing their thing in the background to see it stays that way."

Mary-Margaret offered me a judgmental glare. "Your father isn't exactly Mister Details, you know."

"Come on, Mom..."

"Okay, okay. I know you don't like to hear us snipe about each other. I'm sorry. I just want to make sure you're covered."

"As much as I can be, I suppose."

"Are you...okay?" Mom leaned forward, inquiring with squinting eyes, trying to see into me more than she ordinarily could in that way only mothers could. "I mean, Jack...shooting someone..."

"Honestly, it hasn't bothered me that much." I shrugged.

"You *have* been drinking a lot lately. And don't think I don't see those bruises on your face and your knuckles. You never have been a brawler."

I couldn't help but grin sheepishly. "Well...I have been hanging out with Tex and Preacher a lot lately."

Mom admonished me with one of her stern eyebrow lifts. "Have you been provoking these fights?"

"Well...shit follows us around sometimes. And we've been working this case with Rick—"

"Tell me how he fits into this whole thing," she said, tossing her legs on the hay bale and leaning in even more. "You've been working for him on finding someone...?"

"Kind of. It's complicated. He's in private security for a firm down in Austin that specializes in protecting children." I shrugged again. "He says I owe him since he...*helped out* with the Finley thing. And he's not wrong. I do owe him big time."

"But it's not going well...?"

I stared off into the distance, looking past the green fields of the shooting range to the rows of trees and hills in the western distance. "It is most definitely not going like it should."

Mary-Margaret leaned forward and patted my knee. "Well... fix it."

My face contorted. "Just like that? Fix it? What kinda sage parental advice is that?"

"You know. Just fix it," she said, pinning me with a matronly stare. "Rick is family, too."

I looked at my shoes. "Yeah. Yeah, he is."

My mother patted my knee again and then got up to go, collecting her gear. "You've got to learn to keep your elbow up when you shoot, Jackson. It only hurts you in your side because you don't maintain your posture."

A smile crept onto my face as I too rose and fell in step with my mother. I threw an arm over her shoulders and pecked her on the cheek.

"I know, Mom. Thanks."

The range was on the way out to Granbury on Highway 377, so it took me a little while to get back to the city. On the way, my phone bleated, and I answered it to hear an atypically panicked Tex on the other end.

"They got Artie," he said.

I broke every speed limit fishtailing through west Fort Worth to get to the hospital. Fort Worth has a robust medical industry from standard hospitals to children's hospitals to all kinds of specialty practices. It's sometimes confusing to find the one building you want where your loved ones are receiving care. I had to call Tex back a couple times to pinpoint the right one, and it turned out both he and Tayona had been admitted to the emergency room at Harris Methodist. En route, I called Preacher, told him to mobilize the rest of the gang.

When I arrived, it took me half an hour to figure out where they were holding Tex and Tayona. Police barred the door to the emergency wing of the ICU and wouldn't let me in, pushing back and telling me that Major Crimes detectives were inside and needed time to question the victims. Oh, by the way, who the hell was I?

I literally wailed in frustrated annoyance as my chest bounced off the stiff-wristed, obstructive cops and back into the waiting room. Preacher, Deckhead, and Pussy Control burst in minutes later and succeeded in calming me down, pulling me away from the confrontation that was brewing with the cops. The waiting room reeked of the unkillable acridity that you associate with sickness and death. It was driving me crazy.

"They won't tell me how either of them are doing," I told my friends. "Fort Worth detectives are here, and it sounds like they're Major Crimes, so that means gunshots."

"Holy shit," Pussy said. "But Tex called you, right?"

"Yeah, he was in the ambulance when he called, but the EMTs cut us off. It didn't sound like he was shot, but you know Tex."

"Oi, he could take a fookin' shotgun blast to the bollocks and right himself just fine," Preacher said, clapping me on the shoulder and surreptitiously producing a baggie full of bud to draw my attention. "Perhaps we should take a right nip outside wi' yer personal physician, wha?"

I let Preacher steer me outside. Pussy stayed in to talk to the nurses and try to learn more. Deckhead went with me. We found an alley behind the giant HVAC units that cooled the massive hospital, a hidey-hole marked by crushed cigarette butts on the asphalt. Preacher stuffed a pipe, lit up, and passed it around. I took more than my fair share only because whatever was in that kush started cooling me down immediately, and I liked the mellow haze that enveloped me, the fuzzy edges that smoothed out the wrinkles. My eyes turned bloodshot to match the comforting tingles behind them.

We came back in just in time to see Tex stumble out of the ICU doors. His white T-shirt was ripped at the neck and stained with blood. He had a bandage on his forehead, and his face was swollen purple with bruises that distorted his clean features. He had a cast on his left forearm, but it must have been more for precaution than anything else because he moved it normally, the hand and fingers gripping his dirtied and misshapen straw hat. Tex limped, favoring his right leg, and he uttered a slight hiss with every movement, betraying the agony wracking his body.

Pussy detached from the nurses' station and immediately came to Tex's side, meeting up with me and the rest of us to take his arms and help him into a chair in the waiting area.

"I'm all right, I'm all right," Tex said, grunting as he sat down. "Just got a dent in my fender is all."

"Jaysis-fook, Tex, yeh bobbed when yeh shoulda weaved," Preacher exclaimed.

"What happened?" I said.

"Must have been your security bros from Austin," Tex said. "They wore polos but no Clean Wheel logos. Pretty obvious it was them though. They were waiting for me when we got there."

"Where?"

"I picked up Tayona and Artie from Haltom City. Felt like it would be safer get them to someplace else. Went by my house to chill for a bit and call my sister to see if she would put us all up out in Azle for a few days. I didn't even have the phone off the hook before they came through the door. Like, ten of 'em. Masks and gloves, too."

"They were waiting," I said. "Shit, Tex. They had your place staked out."

"Yep. Stupid call. I shoulda just gone out to Azle and waited on my sister to get off work. Fuckin' sorry about that, Cajun. I fucked it all up."

I patted the big man on his back, eliciting a flinch that must have belied another patch of bruises. "Christ, what did they do to you, man?"

"Went to work on me while they rousted Tayona and took Artie. Tayona lost her shit, as you might expect. She stabbed this one in the eyes with her fingernails, and he drew down and shot her. They were workin' me over pretty hard so I couldn't get to her till they got out of there. She took two: hip and shoulder. I had to get her help or she wasn't gonna make it." His countenance became solemn with a thousand-yard stare. "I let Artie go..."

"It's okay, Tex, you did great, man. Did the detectives talk to you?"

"Yeah, I told 'em everything, even that they were likely from Clean Wheel, but they didn't seem so interested in that."

"Different department than the fraud task force," Deckhead said. "We should call Hulen, see if he's good for something."

I sunk into a chair next to Tex, smoked from the overnight stay at TCSO and everything else that had happened before anybody could jump Jimmy. A bubbling ferocity germinated in my gut. It was a familiar feeling. I'd last felt it in New Orleans and later in Mississippi right before I murdered the man who'd done harm to my family.

21.

SIDES STEPPED AND SWIPED

Rick picked up when I called. It was some time after the twenty-four hour limit he'd given me to produce evidence against Parker, but as we rapped, it turned out that didn't matter anymore.

"Parker let us go today," Rick said. "No official reasons, but I can guess."

"How about unofficial?" I said.

"He was less than pleased with your interview style."

"Did he mention if he had Artie back?"

"What? No, why would he?"

"Because about five hours ago, a bunch of douchebag muscle-butts matching Parker's security I saw at The Driskill beat the shit out of Tex, shot Tayona, and took Artie."

"*What*?!" Genuine surprise. Rick almost screamed. "Are you serious?"

"No lie, brother. Tayona and Tex gave statements to Major Crimes so unless the kid's other guardian comes clean, he's officially kidnapped. Just by the other parent."

"What jurisdiction?"

"Fort Worth. Whoever did it was watching Tex's place. Waiting. Sound like somebody you know?"

"Bunk, you gotta know I don't operate like that..."

"I ain't blaming you, brother, trust me. In fact, I think you got snowed over in all this just like everybody else who's touched Ted Parker. KidSmart was a means to an end for him. If it worked, great. If not, at least he got closer to finding the kid than he was before he hired y'all. You in trouble with your bosses?"

Rick blew out a guttural breath that I heard clearly through the cell phone speaker. "They are not too jazzed with me right now, I'll tell you that. You don't happen to have a Texas state P.I.'s license I can show them, do you?"

"Why does everybody keep asking me that? You want me to show you my left nut, too? Spoiler alert: it's bigger than the other one and prematurely grey."

A laugh escaped from Rick, something so rare to the past few days that it actually warmed my cold heart to hear. "Well...it doesn't matter anymore, I guess."

"Brother, I hate to turn this all back around on you," I said, steeling myself; "but if you wanna get right on this—for *Artie*—I could use your help."

"Tell me." No hesitation.

"You're closer to Parker than I am, at least geographically. If it was him that sent those goons after Tex and Tayona, he's got to have Artie back by now."

"You want me to look for him?"

"How fresh are your addresses?"

"Like banana boat mai tais, bunk. I'll call you when I've got something."

The line clipped dead immediately. There was nothing else to say.

Park Hill sits between the Fort Worth Zoo, the Trinity River, and University. It's a beautiful little neighborhood near TCU with immaculate lawns clipped to HOA specifications and huge, bushy trees that cast protective shade over some of the richest homes in the city. The neighborhood nestles into a secluded pocket of hills that makes it somewhat difficult to navigate or even locate if you're not a native. The houses tower behind the vegetation sporting flying buttresses, Spanish tiled roofs, and driveways packed with Jaguars, BMWs, and classic cars polished for boasting rights.

The first house Mom moved us to in Fort Worth was in neighboring Westcliff right off Stadium Drive, tucked into one of the clearings of oaks that flowed from Park Hill. You could see the stadium itself towering over the treeline, mere steps away from our backyard and its apple trees. Our house, a three-bedroom rental, seemed out of place in the vicinity of the stone manses around us. My sister and I would stare wide-eyed at these storybook legends as Mom drove us to school in the morning, and I would daydream absently about them as I walked past on the way home from school in the afternoons. I wondered who lived in each, what they did, how they could afford such extravagance and beauty. One of them had a DeLorean in the driveway once, and I would stop there every day to ogle its stainless steel perfection, its dripping signature of excess and privilege.

I never did meet anybody who lived in Park Hill.

Until Pussy Control took me to Poquito's house.

The house's facade reflected dark colored stone of varying size and pattern, held together with a brighter masonry that highlighted the disparities. A turret shot out of one corner near the immense front door, presenting the glamour of a castle entryway. The door itself was large, painted red, and dangled a circular knocker from a lion's mouth. Pussy knocked it hard against the iron lion three times and stood back a step while I held a rolled up newspaper over the peephole. We heard someone open the peephole's viewing door on the inside and then begin to fiddle with the locks. It came open only a couple of inches to allow its occupant space to peer, at which time I removed the newspaper and stepped out of the way.

"Oh, fuck," Poquito said.

Pussy kicked the door with the power and grace of Wonder Woman, like she was Jason Statham in any one of those movies where he forgot how to use doors. That day, she wore knee-high leather boots with reinforced soles, the right one of which created a perfect cracking noise as it impacted with the heavy oak door and snapped it into Poquito. It swung open inside the house's entry foyer as Poquito fell backward, toppling to the floor where she landed atop a plush Oriental rug, the only cushion for her backside. She began to bleed almost immediately from where the door struck her in the face.

Pussy's long arms held the door open to admit her, and she towered over Poquito, glowering down the length of her short nose. "Get up, you cunt."

She delivered a swift kick to Poquito's midsection, just hard enough to exploit the fear evident on the younger girl's face. Poquito scrambled to her knees, groaning and clutching at her stomach.

As she rose, Pussy grabbed her by one puff of anime-inspired hair and dragged her further into the house. I shut the door behind me, following.

"Hold on, hold on, hold on!" Poquito screamed as Pussy threw her down on the carpeted floor of the connecting den.

"After everything we did for you," Pussy fumed, her white skin consumed by blushing fire. I had never seen her angry before, or at least never this angry. She controlled the smaller girl's movement and proximity, ensuring she could not squirm away to grab a weapon or anything else.

"You're going to tell us all about your friend down in Austin," Pussy said, determined steel in her voice. "Or I'm going to kill you right here. With my bare hands."

"Wait!" Poquito screamed. "Wait! Please! How did you find me?"

Pussy kicked her again, and she screamed. "You've been talking about living in a house in Park Hill for months, you idiot. How hard do you think it is to look at property records around here? *'Melinda McQuarrie?'* Do you really think I'm that stupid?"

"I really am that stupid," I said, breaking in before Poquito could get a shot of her own off at Pussy. I squatted down between them, putting my body as an obstacle to keep Pussy from killing Poquito, an act that was looking more and more likely and one I knew P.C. to be perfectly capable of. Blood streamed from Poquito's face and bruises were beginning to form on her forearms. Anemic, probably.

"Since I'm that stupid, tell me everything about working for Ted Parker."

"Look, he gave me a shitload of money. He bought me this house!" Poquito said, crying now, likely from the rising pain of the bruises rather than contrition. "I met him over IRC."

"Did you know he was Tr1pw1re at that time?"

"Man, *nobody* uses that name," she spat. "It's a ghost name, bullshit he breaks off to mislead people from what he's doin'."

"Like futzing around with young girls on IRC?" I said.

"I do what I want! I ain't got no fam watchin' out for me."

Pussy cracked her knuckles. "You don't anymore, bitch."

"Fuck you!" Poquito hissed. "He gave me fifty grand right off the bat just to *talk* to him while you and Deckhead were penny-pinching from pension funds. You don't know *shit* about real action, Pussy!"

"Why did you get involved with Pussy and Deck then?" I said. "Did he send you?"

Poquito sneered at me. "Whatever, man, I'll send *you*."

Pussy sidestepped me in two strides, raised one leg up so that her knee almost came even with her jaw, and plunged it down again so that her boot heel crushed the tendon between Poquito's left knee and calf. Poquito screamed in a searing waver, reaching for the break with hands quivering from the torture. The crack made me flinch. Pussy remained calm.

"Answer the question or this is going to get messy," she said.

Poquito's reply leaked out between sobs and tears. "Pussy, I'm sorreeeeee! He gave me so much money! I wanted this house! I wanted a real place to live! Het got me all set! He said he needed access to your shit so he could make it look like you and Deck did a bunch of his jobs. He'd been following you guys online for ages! He knew all about you!"

"How? Why?" I pressed. "Does Parker have some kind of vendetta against Pussy and Deck? Why them?"

"They were just easy targets! It coulda been anybody. Teddy just needed pros close to his level that he could pin things on. It's like the opposite of bragging rights, man!"

"'Teddy,'" Pussy repeated, voice thick with revulsion. "Did you fuck him, Poquito?"

She responded by breaking into harder tears, curling up into her physical pain as her small frame was wracked by sobs. She was barely eighteen.

"Poquito," I said softly, calmly. "Did he hurt you? Did he force you?"

"I wanted to!" she cried. "He-he's handsome. And he took care of me!"

"I bet he did," Pussy said. "How compromised are our systems?"

"I put replicator cookies on everything. Up until the cops shut us down, Teddy was seeing every keystroke y'all made."

"'Us,' huh, Poquito? You still think you're one of *us*?"

She looked up at Pussy at that moment, bloody tears streaming down her face, her eyes puffy. "I'm still a...a..."

"You're *nothing*," Pussy said. "You get all that, Jack?"

I removed the micro tape recorder from my shirt pocket and held it up for everyone to see, switching it off with a sharp clicking noise from my thumb on the stop button. "In HDR," I said, getting to my feet.

"Poquito, the police are going to come arrest you soon," Pussy said calmly. "Do not leave this house. Go with them quietly and cooperate with them fully. Do you understand?"

Poquito struggled into a sitting position, wiping the tears out of her eyes as she looked up to Pussy. The distance seemed monumental, the little girl on the floor and the towering Amazon above her, all here in this stony aviary. I struck up a cigarette as I turned away and started looking for the ISP routers in the house.

"Yes, ma'am," Poquito said in a whisper.

"You are not to call anyone, talk to anyone, or do anything until the police arrive," Pussy continued. "Do you understand?"

"Yes, ma'am."

In a nearby closet, I found a router system and pulled all the cords from the wall. Gathering them up in a fist, I produced a pocketknife and sawed through the wires as one, cigarette perched between my lips, smoke making my eyes water. Once the ethernet and cable leads were severed, I cut the power cords, too.

Pussy's commanding voice ricocheted off stone walls of the den.

"If you have to urinate or defecate, you will do so right here on this carpet. Do you understand?"

"Yes, ma'am."

"If you are thirsty or hungry, you are to resist these urges. Do you understand?"

"Yes, ma'am."

"When asked, you are to tell the police and anyone else the truth about everything. Do you understand?"

"Yes, ma'am."

I walked back into the den and nodded at Pussy. She looked back down at Poquito. The teenager was on her knees, sunken, head down, tears all but stopped but still dripping onto her knees.

"You are nothing," Pussy said. "Do you understand?"

Poquito's voice cracked as she replied. "Yes, ma'am."

"Let's go," Pussy said to me.

We walked out of the luxurious Park Hill house and shut the door behind us. In my car, I lit up two more cigarettes and handed one to Pussy before starting up the motor.

"I'm sorry," I said.

"I get that a lot," Pussy replied.

We ran it through top to bottom with Mikayla, reviewing every piece of evidence, every potential insinuation, every last little strand of bullshit twisting in the prairie wind. She was hard on us, and we had to throw some stuff out, but we needed that to get bulletproof. Anything less would just be bloody meat to the sharks. When we had it all down, I called Roger Hulen.

"Where does Techt hang his hat?" I asked him.

"Tim Curry Center, Downtown. Criminal Division, Weatherford Street. Why?"

"Meet us there in twenty minutes and make sure he's available. Deckhead and Pussy Control are checking in with you there, and we've got an offer to make him. You'll want to be present."

"Who's 'we,' Jack? You're not under indictment or even wanted for questioning anymore. Maybe you should pray on that for a bit."

"Maybe you should just listen to me and get your shit together, Ranger."

I hung up.

We moved. Mikayla and I drove. Deckhead, Pussy, Preacher, and Tex. All of us saddled up. Preacher had self-medicated with Deck, but the rest of us opted to remain clear-headed. I especially wanted to ensure I was of sound mind and thought for what was coming. Don't get me wrong, I could have used a bump in the worst way, but walking into an assistant state's attorney's office with a headful of cocaine and a scheme like ours wasn't just brash, it was plain loco. Considering that, I almost asked Preacher for that hit until we got there.

Hulen met us downstairs and escorted us up to Dakota Techt's office. We filed past courtrooms, judges, cops in various uniforms, and every possible Texas citizen at odds with the law. People were paying traffic tickets, arguing against domestic abuse charges, and being dragged around by muscled cops for robbery beefs. The justice center had it all, and through the thin sheen of human-scented desperation permeating the air, you could detect the pallor of sadness that came with it, guilty or innocent.

Techt worked out of an investigator's office. Space came at a premium, and he didn't yet rate private chambers afforded high rollers like the D.A. That didn't stop him from lording over the office like it was owed to him, however. He made an assistant make us wait when we could clearly see him through an office with no door doing nothing more than reading a legal precis. I tried to be patient but Preacher's constant fidgeting set me on edge, and Mikayla pinched both of our elbows like we were a couple of children, which I guess we kind of are.

When he finally admitted us, we packed into his small office, and Hulen stood in the doorless entry way, hip cocked and shoulder on the frame. Techt was clearly annoyed to have his day interrupted in such a way, and he flashed Hulen that pique in a half-lidded eyefuck. By the time it made it around to me, I was grinning like I'd just scored a handy from Amelia Sheehy, the hottest cheerleader in high school three grades ahead of me.

"Ranger Hulen here says you all have something to say for yourselves," Techt said, butchering the proper pronunciation of the plural royal "you" and outing his nonstate heritage. "But I'm curious why *all* of you are here. Some of you aren't under suspicion of anything, despite my very strong instincts otherwise."

"How would you like to prosecute the biggest hacker in the country?" I said.

Techt smiled thinly, gesturing at Deck and Pussy. "I already am."

"So flattering," Pussy said, winking at Techt and eliciting a flush in his kid-like cheeks. He struggled to contain the fluster.

"What my clients are trying to say," Mikayla said, "is that clearly Mr. Reyes and Ms. Hernández are innocent of the charges you've filed against them because the crimes on which those charges are based were committed by a completely different party."

Techt waved his hands. "Ah, the old 'Somebody-Else-Musta-Done-It' play. Well, thanks for coming down, Miss Castañeda, but this is all better fodder for court."

"Have you ever seen the name *Tr1pw1re* before?" I said. "Hacker alias. Appears with numeric ones for the Is. What am I saying? Of *course* you have, right? You're the state's attorney that's breaking cybercriminals' asses."

Techt regarded me with thinly veiled derision but spoke as if lecturing a halfwit. "Mister Dooley. I have my defendants in this case. If there is other evidence, perhaps Miss Castañeda can introduce it during discovery. Unless this is all preamble to some kind of plea...?"

"It's a plea for you to do your fucking job instead of railroading my friends, you suit bitch," I said.

Techt turned redder. I was standing near enough to Hulen to know it was his heavy hand that clamped down on my shoulder as soon as I delivered the revilement.

"Easy, Jack..."

"Techt, we both know this trial isn't even going on the docket for another month at least," Mikayla said, opening her briefcase bag. "Let's quit two-stepping and get done what we need to get done so people can get on with their lives and you can be our new D.A."

She withdrew a stack of papers and a microcassette, the same one I had recorded earlier. She put it down on Techt's desk and said, "Two key pieces of evidence here the state should consider in this case before wasting anymore of the taxpayers' money squandering resources looking for answers that my clients have already provided. One, a sworn affidavit from my clients as to the true provenance of several cyber breaches that resulted in electronic bank robbery, data theft, fraud, and money laundering. Each of these breaches is attributable to one Ted Parker, a.k.a. Tr1pw1re.

"Two, a recorded statement from a witness employed by Mister Parker whom Parker directed to infiltrate my clients' legitimate business organization for the sole purpose of diverting attribution of the aforementioned cyber breaches from Parker to Mr. Reyes and Ms. Hernández. Furthermore, the witness is currently awaiting apprehension by law enforcement and will cooperate fully with questioning."

Techt's initial fury receded to neutral as he flipped through the documents. He eyed Hulen who offered up a look that communicated interest and dismay. Having Hulen in the room helped us sell it, I knew. A lawyer would go to trial with whatever evidence he needed to get to a plea deal, but a real lawman would always want to make sure they got the right man.

"Who is this guy Parker? Who is Tr1pw1re? I've never heard of him," Techt said.

"How long ago had you heard of Deckhead and Pussy Control?" I zinged him. "What, you're some kind of white hat counter-hacking all the boys and girls that wouldn't finger your asshole in college? Come on, man, you got twigged to these two because someone fed you a tip, and that someone is likely a girl who goes by 'Poquito.' And, oh by the way, you should probably go pick her up at this address." I handed a piece of paper to Roger.

"Your witness?" Hulen asked. I nodded, and he stepped outside the room to have a quick conversation with a nearby officer, passing off the note and some quiet instructions to have Poquito picked up.

Techt was growing restless, irritated again. He stood up and jammed a finger in my direction. "I'm not sharing the state's methods in discovery."

"Doesn't matter if you ignore evidence brought by the defense," Mikayla said. "Or maybe we could just go tell that to *The Star-Telegram*? 'Tarrant County prosecutor ignores evidence' equals front page news."

"Tr1pw1re's a big deal," I said. "And so would be the prosecutor that got him. Better story than going after two obviously innocent citizens who just run an internet cafe."

Techt looked at me with all the smarm of a schoolteacher on whom I'd tried to pull one too many fast ones to skip class and sneak ciggies in the bathroom. He looked at each of us in turn. When it finally came to be his turn for scrutiny, Preacher shouted, "I need to have a shite!"

Mikayla kept a straight face. Tex and I couldn't help but snicker.

The prosecutor regarded Deckhead and Pussy Control again, cinching up his pants by the beltline, puffing up his chest, making a show of magnanimity. Both of them remained silent but hawk-like in their countenance, severity in their still, grave demeanors. Techt looked back to me finally.

"Why are you in the middle of all of this?" he said.

I snapped open my Zippo with a flick of my wrist, having been fingering it in my pocket the whole time. I hadn't even noticed, but I'd unconsciously produced a cigarette as well, and it tipped from between my fingers to my lips in time with the scratch of the flint against the lighter's strike pad. You can't smoke in public buildings in Fort Worth. The cool heat of the nicotine subsumed my throat in the inhalation, and I didn't even feel it on exhale.

"I've got some land in Florida to sell ya, too," I said with a wink.

Despite the blatant disrespect on display from Preacher's gastric trauma to my smoker's delight, Dakota Techt went with it. He stipulated specific conditions that we would have to satisfy, namely that every charge currently levied against Deckhead and Pussy Control transferred cleanly to some evidence that clearly implicated Parker. The charges would stay for now until that evidence presented itself, the first tranche of which would involve Hulen and other investigators interviewing Poquito. Mikayla would be on hand to observe the interview and continue leaning on Techt until he had enough to dismiss the charges against Deck and Pussy. Having them brought back up against Parker would be a different hill to climb.

But we were going to take the long way 'round that hill anyway. Scores needed settling.

Rick rang as we were in transit. I answered the phone and said, "Go."

"He's at Steiner Ranch. Went by his office in Round Rock. Few employees there but nobody had seen him in a while. Got the stinkeye from a couple guys that must have been undercovers."

"Clean Wheel?"

"Likely. What's the play?"

"Lemme call you back."

We posted up at The Chat Room on Magnolia where Deckhead swapped shakes with a few of his Chicano partners and proffered some scratch. Beers came to us outside at the picnic tables in frosted glasses, and we swigged them down hard. Pussy sat next to me on a laptop, her thin fingers clacking away on keys.

"Steiner Ranch," I said. "North of Round Rock."

"Got it. There's a dedicated ISP tower out that way," she said. "Like the kind you see at a telecom campus. One of the big ones that guarantees bandwidth and connectivity."

"Wonder why you'd need so much internet way out at an old ranch?"

"Because yer a fookin' twat, that's why," Preacher said, slurping on his beer.

"Won't argue with that."

I craned my neck to see around the corner of The Chat Room's porch toward the parking area in back. Deckhead had been in negotiation with his boys back there for a while. "Is this taking too long?" I asked.

"Everybody's on their own timeline," Pussy said, eyes intent on her laptop. "What time do you want all this to go down?"

"Dusk. Which means we need to get moving soon."

"Sure you don't want to take our cars?" Tex said. "We got plenty of room between the two of us."

"Clean Wheel Security pricks are probably already familiar with our rides and will make us as soon as we get close to the ranch."

"Hey." Tex nodded toward the street. A low rumble had overridden the pub's outdoor speakers, blending not at all well with the Stone Temple Pilots wailing. It was Roger Hulen's Bronco sidling up the curb. Before he could get out, I hopped the fence around the picnic table area and jogged over to the truck. Hulen rolled down his window, and I leaned against its jamb partially to rap with him, partially to conceal his line of sight to the others.

"Funny how you keep showing up unannounced," I said, offering a hand. He shook it.

"Thing is, y'all pretty much keep to your patterns," Hulen said. "If you're not at one place, you're at another. We got the girl."

"Is she singing?"

"Not yet."

"She will."

"She looked a little beat-up, Jack."

I shrugged. "We all seem to be in uncomfortable business."

Hulen pinned me with a stare. "Domingo and Jeri should stay put, y'know. They're not out from under this yet, so maybe help 'em to realize they shouldn't be leavin' town."

I two-finger saluted him. "Whatever you say, Ranger. Hope you're enjoying your retirement."

A glimmer of a smirk peeked out from behind Hulen's bushy mustache. "A Ranger never really retires."

"What, too much to live for?"

"Well, there's always too much of somethin'. *Bravo too much.*'"

"What?"

"Bravo too much. Used to be, the Rangers were organized to fight Indians. Kept 'em from attacking outposts, camps, colonies and the like. It was a whole different frontier back then. Anyway, Indians started working with Rangers eventually, at least the ones who saw the writing on the wall. There's a story about one of 'em who worked as an informant for a Ranger down in South Texas, a real hard-leg sonofabitch who would jump half-ass into a camp full of Indians and shoot 'em all down till he was the last breathing thing in that place. His Indian friend told him that he was 'bravo too much.' That kinda became an unofficial motto for the Rangers."

The grin I offered Hulen was authentic, and it felt right. "One riot, one Ranger," I said.

"Amen." Hulen tipped his hat to me and put his truck in gear. "You be careful, Jack, y'hear?"

"As you say, sir."

Hulen's truck growled away down the street, and I looked after it for a brief moment. The sun gleamed through the window, shining through forward windshield, highlighting a Texan's hat in the glow. Seconds passed, and another engine rumbled at a lower pitch. I looked behind me to see Deckhead leaning out of the driver's side window of a plain, disheveled white van. Deck shot me a salute and winked.

"Doable?" he shouted over the grumbling engine.

I turned around and whistled loudly to capture the attention of the rest of the gang. "Okay, Team Jetfire: mount up!"

22.

THE PROMISE

A slow throb pulsed through a vein just below the meat of her left thumb, the hand curled weakly around mine. Tex held the other one between his big fishhooks. Preacher stood at the end of the hospital bed, one hand absently placed on her right foot, which poked up through the bedcovers like a small mountain in the snow. An ambient thrum of life support machinery hummed around us. A periodic beep notified a regular yet sparse heartbeat.

Tayona lay in a pool of exhaustion, eyes so puffy from crying that they seemed bruised from pummeling. Her shoulder was immobilized with gauze and bandages. Under the sheet, the bulge of more bandaging was visible atop her left hip.

When she looked up at me, her dark brown, irisless eyes penetrated mine, seeing through me as if I were an apparition. The whites of her eyes were bloodshot from inconsistent sleep and painkillers. There wasn't much left.

She had given up.

"Artie..." she whispered, comprehending our presence and closing her eyes against it, maybe trying to forget the reminder of our failure. Maybe preparing to grieve.

"We're going to get him," I said, squeezing her hand.

"We promise," Tex said.

"Fookin' aye," Preacher said.

23.
STRANGE TORPEDO

The taco stand was also a BBQ shack, replete with smokers and stacks of firewood collected from carefully felled trees whose burning bark filled the air with a mix of charcoal singed plumery. The owner, a knock-kneed old Mexican in a white T-shirt stained brown from decades of backwoods cuisinery, deposited stacks of foil-wrapped tacos on our picnic tables. Pulled pork and brisket juice seeped from the wrappings' corners in the Mexican's special sauce, a secret he advertised as "unique to *gringos*" on the single sign above the shack's serving counter. There was no other logo for the place, merely this claim that attracted copious foot traffic in a nouveau-suburban Austin/Round Rock niche.

McMansions and shopping plazas were popping up all around the shack as bourgeoisie crept further away from both city centers. It was still far enough off the main road to Steiner Ranch and Lake Travis that it retained a gravelly lot instead of pavement and an unincorporated forest in back from which the Mexican chopped his smoking wood. In another ten years, developers in artisan boots and their soccer mom wives would claim the area, and the Mexican would have to move on. For now though, our money was good, and his land offered a good staging ground for the coming operation.

I indolently watched the sky above the treeline turn pink and purple as the sun made to set, rippling cirrus and cumulonimbus clouds painting the oldest picture above. I wasn't hungry, and I didn't join the gang as they scarfed tacos and Mexican Cokes. I smoked a cigarette as I looked up at the encroaching dusk. After some minutes, Rick appeared at my side with two barely detectable crunches in the gravel.

"Did they let you go?" I asked.

"I haven't checked in since you told me about Artie," Rick replied. "But I can imagine an uncomfortable conversation is coming."

"Like about the first time you tried anal?"

"Maybe not that uncomfortable."

I clicked my teeth against the inside of my cheek and flicked the cigarette to the ground. "You just need some hot water and a distraction."

Rick grinned at that, a smile gracing his features the likes which he had not shown me in a while. "Ain't that the truth. Look, bunk...I owe you—"

"Not shit," I cut him off, looking from the sky to his eyes, devoid of bullshit now. Meaning it. Proving it. I clapped him on the back with one hand, making a loud slapping noise, and winked. "You know me. Let's get to work."

We walked to the picnic table in back of the taco stand where my other friends clustered. Preacher and Tex regarded Rick with neutral glares, the kind of laconic oversight that spoke alone. I introduced Pussy Control and Deckhead to Rick, and they all shook hands.

"Heard y'all are legends on the interweb," Rick said.

"Jack's a flatterer," Pussy said, offering Rick a warm grin.

"But he ain't wrong!" Deck said.

Rick eyed Tex and Preacher. They remained silent for a long moment. It wasn't quite uncomfortable, not quite awkward. But it was enough.

"Ted Parker's ranch is a compound," Rick said, unlimbering a folder wrapped in strong rubber bands from his waistband. He snapped the bands off and set it on the picnic table, withdrawing schematics, diagrams, and maps. "Apologies for all the paper, but I didn't want to leave any digital traces."

"Old school's the best school," I said. "Security?"

"I trust all y'all have heard of Clean Wheel?"

"To a degree," Tex said, growling. He fingered the cast on his left arm, itching the skin where his thick rancher fingers sprouted from the plaster and cotton.

"Probably five to ten men on premises," Rick continued. "The compound itself is wired for CCTV, motion activated sensors, and lights."

"Know all this," Deckhead said, looking through the papers for something of interest. "More interested in getting into his network. Hard hack. There a guardhouse?"

"There's something right inside the main gate." Rick pointed to a spot on one of the maps. "Big enough for a gun safe, a desk, possibly a computer."

"We sniffed plenty of wifi signals all over the property already," Pussy said, opening a laptop and tapping on its mousepad. "It would be best to get into something outside the property that's already logged into the network."

"Are y'all driving that POS over there?"

"Yeah, *ésé*," Deck said. "That's the Deck-mobile."

Rick looked at me. "Some of these guys likely know me. I could drive us in. At least get inside the perimeter so these two can get into the guardhouse."

"Why would they let you in?" I said, working the scenario. "In the wake of firing KidSmart..."

"I'm coming to apologize personally," Rick played into it. "I want to make up for the poor job I did finding Artie. Maybe make a play for a job. Either way, it should be enough to get us in."

"Why does Parker care about you now that he's got Artie?"

"Pride, maybe? Vanity? The ranch is far enough out here, away from everything else. It's an effort to come out in person. Maybe he does care. Worth a try."

"If they turn you away at the gate," Tex said; "and they're armed..."

Rick jerked his head back in the direction of his Explorer. "Good thing I have some leftover gear from the Bureau."

Preacher's eyebrows went up. "Shooty gear?"

Rick deadpanned it. "Well, I didn't bring it to pay your country club dues."

Pussy inclined her head at a steep angle, eyes widening as her chin descended. "Are we really bringing guns to a...a..."

"A gunfight?" I said, flipping my Zippo cover open and closed with a nervous clacking noise. "Looks like it."

A silent look passed between Pussy and Deckhead, partners' instincts passing between them. He would never tell her to stay away from a fracas in whose game she had skin. She would never back out. They looked back at me together and reached across the picnic table to each other, fingers encircling. Their gaze emanated rock-hard resolve, steadfast.

Tex and Preacher looked at each other then looked at me. Silence punctuated by heartbeats of loyalty passed between us, too. We then looked over to Rick who met our eyes each in turn with his stony composure.

"Another chance to get it right," my brother said.

The ranch was nestled behind a treeline and hillock, connected via a dusty dirt road flanked by tufts of grass and bush...natural Hill Country flora. The road bisected a fence composed of two thick wooden beams arranged equidistant between cream-colored brick and stone stanchions. The stanchions grew larger the closer in to the main gate they got until the last two blended into an artful portal through which vehicles could pass. The gate itself was smoothly finished with black iron rods and a Texas star in the center made out of the same material. The rods pointed skyward with arrowhead tips, an architectural anachronism often adopted by those who had never even seen a real bow and arrow. Completing the cultural appropriation was a longhorn skull affixed to the gate's stone overhang, the same one you could find on a hundred other rich people's gates in the county, likely purchased by an exterior design consultant at exorbitant cost from some furniture warehouse full of Chinese-manufactured products. It probably wasn't even real.

Rick drove the van right up to the gate with me in the passenger seat. The others lay in the back under blankets and tarps, tightly gripping weapons and portable computer equipment. None of them had uttered a single complaint on the bumpy ride over save for a periodic "Fook!" from Preacher.

The gate opened as the van approached, and two security guards walked outside holding hands up indicating that we should stop. They wore dark polos, cargo pants laden with tactical gear, and armored vests with SAPI plates. No-shit military-grade tactical gear. They drew their handguns and kept them pointed at the ground but clearly visible. Radio earbuds and jawbone mics dangled from their ears. They sported the rounded biceps, combat boots, and gelled hair of the security bros from Clean Wheel I'd seen at The Driskill.

Rick rolled his window down as he brought the van to a halt, and one of the guards ambled up to him. I saw the other one headed my way on the passenger side and rolled my window down, too. I lit a cigarette and held it smoldering at the window so that secondhand smoke would float into the guard's face.

"Rick Sears from KidSmart, here to see Ted Parker," Rick said to the guard on his side.

"You're not expected," the guard said.

"Maybe you should call your boss and check on that," Rick said. "He's my client."

"Not sure that's the case anymore, but okay." The guard tabbed his radio. "Base, Gate 1. Rick Sears, KidSmart, is here to see principal. Please confirm."

The other guard was covering me, looking at me but not coming too close. The first guard looked past Rick to see me, too, and said, "Who's this?"

"My assistant," Rick said. "We've got some paperwork to iron out with Mr. Parker."

"What's your assistant's name?"

"Uhhhh, Mister *Round*?" I said, leaning over Rick's lap to smile obnoxiously at the guard. "*Short* Round."

The guard was either not impressed or didn't get the reference. "IDs?"

Rick reached for his. I stayed where I was. "His, too," the guard said taking Rick's driver's license.

"Didn't bring it with me," I said. "That's why I'm the assistant."

The guard was about to say something when he touched his earbud. He looked over to the other guard, and they confirmed with a look and curt nods that they had both heard the same thing. They stepped back toward the gate and motioned Rick to drive forward.

"Drive forward and park inside the gate next to the roundabout. Then put the van in park and get out. Slowly. Keep your hands visible at all times."

It wasn't ideal. We had wanted stop right inside the gate and occupy the guards while Deckhead and Pussy slipped into the guardhouse. The roundabout that the guard indicated was further into the ranch's front lot, which retained the dirt and gravel ground that we had driven over on our way in. The ranch house sat on the other side of the circular roundabout where two other cars were parked: a BMW and a giant black H2 Hummer. I made a slow scan of the area as we rolled to a stop. I couldn't count all the other outlines of security guards across the ranch property, but there must have been at least ten. I tapped ten times on the van's door in a half-note progression then drummed my fingers quickly. This signaled the number of guards to the crew in the back, the drumming our pre-coordinated indicator of uncertainty.

We lucked out in that the security guys didn't bother to search the van. Had that happened, we would have had to go guns up right away. The two security guards that met us continued to escort Rick and I into the ranch house. I stole a glance back as we walked up old wooden stairs to the deck that surrounded the house and saw the outline of another security guy in the guard shack. It was a pretty good clip from the van. *Damn.*

The gate guards ushered us into the ranch house's foyer where two additional meatheads patted us down. Neither Rick nor I were carrying, but they pulled our cell phones and monkeyed around with them. Rick snatched his back after it became apparent that the guards would likely try more invasive techniques to unlock them, and this drew both the ire of the guard in question and enough time for me to have a look around. The interior of the ranch house boasted dark oaken floors and walls that curved too cleanly and shone too brightly to be classic originals. Modern decor adorned the connected living and dining areas in an open floor plan with large windows casting remnants of daylight inside. Everything was so *retro deco moderne* that I questioned whether the whole house had been constructed within the last ten years if not the last two.

"I don't think that's very nice," Rick was saying.

"Give me that back," the guard said, no traces of an accent. Likely an out-of-stater with those frosted tips.

"No," Rick said.

The other guard who had my phone drew his weapon again, the SigSauer clearing leather with the audible sigh handguns make when they're unsheathed. Rick looked at that one and said, "You gonna shoot me over my cell phone, boy?"

"Only if you don't—" the guy started to say, but then we were interrupted.

"Rick Sears!" Ted Parker squealed as he sashayed into the foyer, hands extended wide in the faux magnanimity I had come to expect, even after only a single meeting in person. "And your friend Jack Dooley. Interesting time for a visit."

"I had hoped to apologize for a couple things before your boys here decided to get antsy about cell phones," Rick said, eyes still on the guard. "Maybe you can tell him to give Jack's back."

"Jack's back," I cackled at Parker, offering him a stupid grin.

"You can understand we're all very conscious of cellular security around here," Parker said, nodding to the guard who had my phone. "I've been in software a long time, and you'd be surprised at the lengths to which competitors go to steal your secrets. Perhaps you wouldn't mind turning those phones off and leaving them right here on the foyer table while we talk...?"

"Sure," Rick said, thumbing the off button on his phone and setting it down where Parker had indicated. I followed suit once the guard who had pulled his gun gave me mine. Once this was complete, Parker—with a grateful smile—held an arm up, his hand indicating the living area. We filed that way followed by our guards, who took up positions behind us as we sat on a giant L-shaped plush sectional.

"You said something about apologizing?" Parker said, seating himself on the edge of one side of the sectional, folding a leg up under him. Not stressed. He wore canvas hiking pants and a flannel pattern shirt over a T-shirt, all with none of the physical exertion hinted by their brand. Tech bro costumery. The appearance of ruggedness.

"I've been told that you've terminated your contract with KidSmart," Rick said, leaning over to put his elbows on his knees and clasp his hands together. "I can only assume that's a result of my poor performance. So I wanted to express my apologies."

Parker sobered, almost playful though as he draped an arm over the back of the couch and regarded Rick. "In hopes of...what? Getting that contract back?"

"I'm pretty sure you don't need our help anymore."

"Well. I don't need *his*." Parker pointed his eyebrows at me, and I rolled my eyes. "*You* might be another story. Former FBI, right?"

Rick dipped his head respectfully. "Yes."

"Are you currently looking for work?"

"No, but...who knows what tomorrow might bring?"

Parker nodded curtly, the corner of one side of his mouth curving in a slight smirk. He looked at me. "And what do *you* have to say for yourself, Jack Dooley?"

"I don't think I have anything to apologize for," I said amiably, fishing my cigarettes out of my pocket. "You cunty douche rat fucker."

Parker blinked once. "Do not smoke in my home."

I smirked back. "Okay...Ted. Or should I call you Tr1pw1re?"

"Can't say as I know what you mean," Parker said evenly.

"Is that why you flinched like a little bitch at The Driskill when I said that name? Huh? *Ted*?" It felt good deploying his name as a taunt.

I could tell the guard behind me was getting restless. He must have signaled something because Parker looked above my head and shook his head in a short, two-shake motion. When he spoke next, he kept hardening eyes on me while addressing Rick.

"Your choice in partners doesn't really scream apology, Rick."

Rick made a clicking noise against his teeth, tsking in that way only African-Americans could with such rich expression. "He's never been subtle. But then again, he's also pretty on target about most things."

"Then I hesitate to make the offer I was about to make." Parker fidgeted, uncomfortable. "I can't fathom why you'd bring your little shit friend with you if you were truly interested in contrition."

"A mystery is different than a secret."

"In either case, we'll crack both apropos of your extracurricular activities," I said. "Or are they all just the same thing anyway? Innovation Apps Consultants. The other tech firms you've started up and sold. Just fronts for Tr1pw1re, right? Legit money hovels to funnel your hack loot through."

Parker looked back and forth between me and Rick. His fidgets became more pronounced: legs shifting, fingers interlacing, tense movements.

"You know," he said slowly, "my security does a lot for me out here. What I pay them, they're pretty good at hunting the vermin that skitter around the property."

"What you pay them must be awesome," I said, "for them to stake their name on a fake report attributing *your* jobs to *my* friends."

"Or shoot your wife and forcibly take your son from her," Rick said.

"Is that where we are now?" Parker said, and the timbre of his voice turned up a notch as he continued to speak. "Accusations? You're not police. You're not even in a position to report with any credibility to an authority of any kind. My businesses are just that: *mine*. As is everything else I—" He cut himself off.

"What's that, Ted?" I said, leaning back on the couch and twirling my finger in a circle near my head. "Everything else you what? Stole? You don't think there's a forensic record of that somewhere on your local network here? You got more infrastructure in this house than most small towns. I'd even a hazard a guess that—"

"Fuck it," Parker said, shooting to his feet and pointing at the guard behind me. "Take them outside, shoot them, and bury them on the back quarter." Then to me he said, "Fine. I *am* Tr1pw1re. And I'll do whatever I goddamn please."

"Cool," I said, and the lights went black.

All the things happened simultaneously.

My strange torpedo struck Parker's hull with perfect accuracy and effect.

First, the power to the house went out, making no noise, sending no signal other than a short flutter of the lights until darkness coated everything. I wouldn't find this out until later, but Pussy Control had indeed managed to get into the guardhouse, apparently waiting for security's attention to turn away from the van long enough for her to slip out and cross the dusty drive. Inside the shack, a Clean Wheel guard was seated at a desk keeping an eye on several monitors tied to the ranch's camera system. Pussy plunged a syringe into the guard's neck, delivering a massive dose of paralyzing, sleep-inducing sedative that incapacitated him. From there, the game really got on.

While Pussy had been in motion, Deck had been firing up mine and Rick's cell phones using a program he had filched and futzed with over the years with cyber-buds who possessed bigger skills in telecommunications hacking. He only needed one to function, but he used both on separate frequencies to scan the local network and log on using credentials Pussy acquired from the guard shack computer. In the space of a few minutes, Pussy and Deck got into the ranch's LAN and started their buttfuckery. Cameras powered down, comms links clicked off, and wifi signals bent to work only for them. They set some choice worms loose on that network to search for data while rerouting electrical grid controls.

As great as modern cyber warfare can be, sometimes the old ways are the best. That's why, next, Preacher scooted out of the van and rounded the side of the house as quietly as his thin form could take him. Not one for clandestine movement but inherently small and unnoticeable enough for it, he followed Pussy Control's instructions from the earwig she had equipped him with to find the main power generator on the back side of the house. He navigated around a couple more security guards guided by Pussy, who now managed the CCTV feeds in the guard shack. He threw the proper lever on the generator's circuit breaker panel and deactivated the power in as many rooms of the house as he could throw switches. Pussy barked at him to leave one particular circuit open: the one marked "Basement."

Preacher was never one to do anything right, or perhaps it was just the gravity of a situation that put us all in that place facing down professionally trained combat veterans. A guard caught him skulking his way back around front and squeezed off a couple of shots after a half-hearted command to halt. Preacher yelped and danced as he darted back toward the van, unlimbering the shotgun that he had appropriated from Rick's stash. Before he could return fire, though, his pursuer sprayed bullets in his direction, throwing him off balance.

The gunfire alerted others to the gang's presence as chaos began to unfold inside the house. Preacher was in trouble as another guard ran down the ranch house's front deck toward the sounds, drawing his own weapon. Ambush.

Before the guard could fire, though, three loud pistol reports punctuated the deepening dusk, catching the guard square in the back of his armored vest and knocking him unconscious into the side of the house. Tex stepped out from the door of the van where he had knelt, taken aim with the SigSauer P226 he'd selected from Rick's stash, and fired. As the guard chasing Preacher rounded the corner of the house, Tex pivoted and shot him square in the chest twice, aiming directly for the SAPI plate where knew the rounds would impact and distribute kinetic force. The guard flew backwards from the impact, arms waggling raggedly in shock, his weapon flying from his hand and landing in the dust.

I didn't hear this myself until later, but Preacher said as he hot-footed it to cover, "Texas! Yer a fookin' gunfightin' sumbitch, yeh big, bad bad-arse!"

And Tex said, "I may have hitched my horse up to this here trough a coupla times, Preach."

As Tex and Preacher linked up, landing back-to-back in a position to cover the area with the van on one side, shit was getting real inside.

The instant the lights went out, I twisted and punched the security guard behind me directly in the balls. They crunched against my knuckles with satisfying yet sickening force, like I had knocked a couple of overripe oranges. The guard didn't just howl, he screamed like that little whiny bastard Shinji in *Neon Genesis Evangelion*. But that's the beauty of going for the balls: the overreaction is so potent.

Rick didn't bother with a punch on his guard and simply reached over to crush the guy's nuts in one of his big black hands. That guy shrieked like a bitch, too, and the multiple cries sent a sympathetic pain through my own loins. I couldn't indulge that feeling long though. Rick and I flipped over the couch to search the guards, feeling along their bodies as our eyes adjusted to the dark. We found their weapons at about the same time, disarmed them, and then delivered kicks to the guards' faces, two each per prick.

I could hear Rick gripping his appropriated Glock 17 and whirling to point back at Parker. The dusk light hadn't quite intensified to night yet, and I could make out my friend's tall, lissome shape in combat stance pointing the gun in a direction where I could sense movement. Parker had cleared the couch and fled into the house, and I could make out his shape darting into the darkness.

"I'll lead, you follow," Rick said. "You got a nice grip on that Glock there?"

"I don't even know how this thing works, man," I said, gripping my confiscated Glock.

"Good. Keep your finger *outside* the trigger guard just in case, and point it at the floor. Not me."

"Yessir. I'm right behind ya."

Unbeknownst to Rick and I as we searched the house, the fracas outside was getting fricasseed. With two men down inside and three down outside, we had estimated another five Clean Wheelers on premises giving us the business. It turned out to be more like eight, and they had called in reinforcements. Apparently, Clean Wheel was renting a house up the road for more of its security bros, the ones who worked other shifts for Parker.

Tex and Preacher were already engaged in a gun battle with the seven who were converging on the van from various stations across the property. Preacher kept them at bay with ferocious, repeating reports from a tactical combat shotgun, which hit nothing every time but scared combatants away. Tex sighted along the hood of the van to drop targets one at a time with inhuman precision. Neither of them wanted to kill anybody, but if somebody walked away with a few pieces of steel in their limbs, they weren't going to complain.

The same could not be said of the Clean Wheelers, however. Their wadcutting rounds perforated the van, ripping tears in the dilapidated metal. Inside, Deckhead yelled curses in Spanglish frustration, trying to work on his laptop as he hunkered down between the van's seats for some semblance of protection even though any one of the ricocheting bullets ccould have torn into him as easily as the van.

Five more Clean Wheelers appeared as a truck came speeding into the roundabout parking area, skidding to a stop between the van and where the other security forces were taking refuge behind the Hummer and the BMW. Neither car was faring well as Preacher's shotgun rounds spidered glass, exploded tires, and holed metal chassis. The truck disgorged reinforcements, and these men brought to bear various semiautomatic rifles and submachine guns augmented by laser sights and flashlights on the barrels. In the space of this arrival, Deckhead jumped out of the van on Tex and Preacher's side, laptop underarm, and scurried toward the house as they covered him. Somewhere behind them, Pussy Control was taking cover in the guard shack.

Bullets from M-4 assault rifles ripped into the van's engine block with sharp zings. Tex grabbed Preacher in one thick hand and dragged him stumbling up the steps to the ranch house deck and then inside the front door, kicking it open with a powerful blow from one booted foot. Deckhead had scurried around the other side of the house and was nowhere to be seen. Tex slammed the door as he and Preacher dove in amidst the peppering of gunshots all around them.

"Jaysis fook, these wankers can't shoot fer shite!" Preacher squealed.

"Don't look a gift horse, you dizzy cunt," Tex said, ejecting the clip from his Sig and replacing it with a fresh one retrieved from his jeans pocket. "P.C.'s still in that guard shack."

Preacher peeked out of the window next to the door, eyes barely crossing the sill yet still drawing fire. He jerked back down as holes appeared in the glass. "Shite! What're we gonna do?"

Tex looked out another window and smiled broadly. "Wait for the cavalry."

The Bronco plowed through the ranch gate and into the round-about area, kicking up dirt that the Clean Wheelers' lasers and lights played across in semi-psychedelic dances. The truck hit two polo-shirted, armored security guards dead-on, pinning them with gut-wrenching force between the Bronco's grille and the back of the Clean Wheel truck in a bone-crunching, chassis-shaking crash. The two guards screamed and dropped their weapons as shock took them.

The door of the Bronco flew open and Roger Hulen stepped out smartly, Stetson framed in the headlights. He held his badge up high in one hand and brandished a pearl-gripped Colt Python in the other, a six-shooter so ridiculously custom in design and power that it would one day adorn a special place of honor in the Texas Ranger Museum in Waco.

"Texas Ranger!" he shouted. "Put down your weapons or I *will* shoot you!"

Split seconds after saying it, Hulen fired, and his .357 magnum rounds connected with Clean Wheelers. They dropped to the sandy ground with plumes of crimson exploding from impact points. Hulen harbored no reservations as he moved, closing the distance to the additional Clean Wheelers at astonishing speed. Tex and Preacher gawked from the windows inside the ranch house foyer as they watched Hulen wade into the gunmen, eventually putting his badge away so he could reload under cover of one of the vehicles and then drawing a Colt .38 Super Automatic from a second holster on the back of his belt. For every Clean Wheel shot fired, Hulen returned fire with such speed and precision that it felt as if a vengeful phantasm had manifested inside the rising dust cloud of the ranch house roundabout.

I know all this because Tex and Preacher told me about it later, and I'm sorry to say I missed it. Preacher even told me he'd considered going straighter than a Comanche arrow after seeing Roger Hulen in action.

Alas, I had other problems.

24.
OF STEEDS AND STERNER STUFF

A horrific scream emanated from somewhere inside the house, the kind that reaches inside you and destroys your heart because you know it's coming from someone so innocent that they have never known pain. A child's scream, but not the normal kind, the kind you'd expect from a kid who just had his ice cream taken away by force. It had to have been Artie.

Artie's autism must have exacerbated the fright the poor kid had experienced since the Clean Wheelers took him. Now lights were flickering off and his father was jerking him around like a wobbly old stuffed animal. Like a *thing*. Something to be controlled or owned. Not a boy. Not a son.

Rick honed in on the scream and shuffled through the kitchen, swinging his gun left and right as he cleared corners. Scrambling noises permeated the darkness as we tried to feel our way along the corridors. We had stalled Parker long enough with our bullshit, long enough for the crew to cut the power, but the diversion caused new problems as it solved the others. We had to feel our way down halls and kick blindly around doorjambs. All the while, the pop-pop-pop of gunfire outside peppered the edges of our ears. That worried me most. Even though we'd brought Rick's weapons for the eventuality, I hadn't counted on an all-out shootout with Clean Wheel.

I didn't have time to ruminate on this as I stayed on Rick's hip. We turned a corner and heard a screen door bang against a doorframe, seeing darkness clear for the last remaining light outside. Rick dove at the door, and I scrambled behind him. As we burst onto the back deck, we could see Parker taking off deeper into the ranch property on foot, Artie slung over his shoulder beating at his father's back with balled-up fists and crying, crying, crying.

"Shit!" I said.

"Let's go!" Rick said.

We took off after them, but Parker had a good head start on us. Rick broke off from my fat ass, his long legs propelling him toward the stable into which Parker disappeared. I began huffing as I fell behind, nicotine-laced lungs and my shitty, de-conditioned body betraying me. As Rick closed in on the stable door through which Parker had entered, gunshots exploded forth, dousing the half-closed metal of the structure and sounding a great ruckus. Rick ducked to the ground as the shots tracked downward, punching through the tin and raising puffs of dirt from the ground. He turned back toward me, stepping out of sight from the door, knowing it was useless to hide from bullets behind so thin a wall. I jerked to a stop next to him, and we danced around together like a couple of idiots as one more gunshot tore through the stable wall, eliciting panic.

We looked ridiculous pirouetting about like that, and I know Rick only did it because of my inexperienced, uncoordinated swivet.

"For fuck's sake!" I said, hopping from foot to foot. "What the fuck are we doing?!"

"Shhh!" Rick said, regaining composure and combat stance. He light-footed it toward the stable door, gesturing for me to follow. The Glock wound tightly into my palm, and I felt sweat grease the space between the skin and the handgrip. I fell in behind Rick, mimicking his stance as best I could in the darkening evening. He squatted and poked his head in the door.

A horse whickered, and I followed Rick into the stable as the clopping of hooves conveyed from within. We filed into the stable to see Parker riding horseback out the door on the other side, Artie clutched to the front of him. Parker had mounted up a riding horse in his private stable, one of many that still grazed in their berths neighing at Rick and I as we watched Parker's steed kick up soil in its wake, galloping further into the rolling hills of the Texas frontier.

"Goddammit," Rick said, looking around frantically.

I shoved the Glock into the waistband of my jeans and evaluated our surroundings with staccato, bird-like movements. There were four more horses in the stable. A row of tack was laid out across a big staging table: various saddles and saddle pads. I grabbed one of the saddle pads and made for the nearest mare.

"I'm going back for a car," Rick said. "There was a Hummer back there."

"No time," I said, placing the blanket on the horse's back and putting a slow hand on her mane. She was dapple gray with streaks of brown in her mane, and when I stroked that mane, she leaned into my hand ever so slightly.

A long time ago, Mary-Margaret McDowell had taken her two kids on an authentic cowboy trail ride in Abilene. Neither of those kids appreciated the trouble that hands-full single mom undertook that weekend to expose them to the glory of their native Texas heritage. They complained the entire time, but they suffered through horseback riding lessons that included instruction from real horsemen and women: those of the West who breathed fresh ranch air every day and rose with the sun to catch its first peek over ridgelines. Despite their complaints and to the credit of their teachers' patience, the Dooley kids kept that knowledge of tying tack and settling saddles.

It took me a hot minute, but I remembered.

The hardest part was just convincing the horse I was an okay guy. She was already broken, but you never knew with horses. Sometimes they only responded well to certain riders, and sometimes they broke weird. Sometimes you smelled like The Substances, and that could annoy any good girl, mare or otherwise. Parker had probably bought these horses already broken, and I hedged that if they could put up with that asshole, then maybe they could put up with me.

I lodged my right foot in the stirrup and slung my left leg over her back, standing up in the saddle as I pulled my bulk upright. She stumbled back a bit as I did this, coming to grips with the portly dude that had just climbed atop. I leaned over to pat her on the neck and scratch her, thanking her for not throwing me off right away.

"Good girl," I whispered.

"What the fuck are you doing?" Rick said, looking at me incredulously.

"Imma gonna go get me a Ted Parker, partner," I replied, putting a long-dormant drawl into my voice and wishing I had a proper hat. "Sure you don't wanna join?"

Rick looked like he had seen Jesus rise, and he was an atheist. "Sooooo...you know I don't know how to ride one of these things."

"Do whatcha gotta do, brother, and I'll..." I stuttered as I took up the reins. "Shit, I dunno. I'll figure it out when I get there. *Hi-yaahhh!*"

And with a couple of light kicks of my heels into the tucked pockets of her hide, my horse carried me off into the night.

The base rules of horseback are stand up in your saddle when loping or galloping, squeeze in to go faster, match your horse's pace though the soles of your feet in the stirrups, and give her plenty of time to come to a stop so that she doesn't lose her balance. Somebody could have told me that right then, and I *still* would have garnered the sore ass that plagued me for months after bouncing up and down on that bitch's back. She generally pointed the way I wanted her to, and she took off when prompted, but I'll be damned for an imbecile who can't remember how to comport himself in the saddle.

My tailbone bonked against the saddle and her back out of rhythm, bopping me like a son of a bitch. I tried another position and at least got into a bearable rhythm, but my choad would never be the same. Still, I kicked her on faster, pointing into Hill Country skies now being claimed by a clear patch of stars. The glow over the hills in the distance illuminated the path Parker had taken, one cleared artificially by groundskeepers and underpaid day laborers. Marcy and me thanked them for showing us the way.

I called my horse Marcy because it had to be better than whatever Parker had named her, if he had at all.

Artie's screams punctuated the night as gunshots receded behind me, and I saw plumes of earth puffing up waist-high ahead. Parker had not gotten far, likely due to difficulties with the boy. Marcy and me closed the distance fast. The trail twisted and turned into a manmade switchback, a trail for the sake of trailblazing, and the gritty path became consumed by tall bushes and trees. Tight pulls on her reins directed Marcy around these sharp corners, and with every pivot of her hooves, Artie's wails grew louder.

Parker's insistent curses cut the air ahead, and I emerged from the boughs of firs and pecan trees around the trail into a clearing that spread up to a great gulch whose edge dropped sharply into chasm. Parker must have known it was there because he had come to a stop on his horse, pulling back reins hard and slowing to a jog. If I had kept up at my speed, Marcy and I would have plunged over into the gulch and the bone-shattering grip of doom.

Parker's horse whinnied as he fought to control it, to get it stationary amidst the wailing, fidgeting form of the boy. He drew down on me as soon as Marcy and I exploded out of the path, and I cried, *"Oh, shit!"* as four warning shots from Parker's gun rang out, creating geysers in the sand and dirt ahead of me. The commotion frightened Marcy, who reeled back from the gunfire at the same time I jerked back on her reins, and I lost purchase on my steed. I tumbled over her back and landed on my side, the impact expelling all air from my lungs in a full-body punch. It happened too fast for me to take stock, and as I rolled around in the dust, I reached for the gun in my waistband, pulling it. I rolled around and away from Marcy as she clopped away from her stupid-ass rider. By the time I had come to a sitting position with the gun in my hands, Parker had me.

"Hold it, Dooley. I've got your ass," he said, weapon directed right at my head from his extended arm. He was even more ridiculous than I could have imagined for the armed tech bro: his hand could barely grip the double-barreled AF2011-A1, a handgun so over-engineered that it belonged in a Michael Bay movie. In Parker's lap, bound by his father's rein-hand, Artie sobbed uncontrollably, more from fear than anything else, and his little feet and hands kicked weakly against the horse's saddle and his father's legs.

Vertigo seized me from dazing activity to which I was unaccustomed, and I sat on my ass in the fine grained dirt looking up at Parker, framed by clear night stars atop his horse. I grimaced, folding my full lips into a hard thin line as I tossed my gun to the side and leaned forward, elbows on my knees. "Ya got me, you fucking asshole."

"You really did not need to get all up in my business, Dooley," Parker said in the selfsame tone of voice that conveyed bored derision with everything and everyone around him. Like it was chore to suffer through goddamn everything. "I was prepared to write you and your friends a hefty check *and* make sure the Tarrant County police dropped the case against Reyes and Hernández. After a fashion, of course."

"After you had moved your Tr1p1wire operation out of jurisdiction," I said, hands and fingers held loosely from their perches on my knees. I could feel a bloody nose coming, drips cascading out of one nostril. "Or maybe you would have just said fuck it."

"I *have* wasted a lot of time on this already. And time is something they aren't making much more of."

I shook my head, annoyed. "It's *land* they're not making more of, you dumb shit. *Land*. We got all the time in the world."

"Well, you don't." His gun made a clacking noise as he retrained it on me. "I'm going to have to get moving now, and I don't want you following me. Maybe I'll just shoot you in your legs and leave you out here to bleed out. I'm not really into the whole killing thing."

"That's why you hired Clean Wheel."

"They do offer a certain something over and above meatheaded door-watching." He cackled. "I don't even know how good a shot I am, to tell you the truth. This is a little different than shooting at ranges. Maybe you can stay real still for me."

"Tell me one thing," I said, not moving. "Why Artie? You don't strike me as daddy material. Tayona said it had to do with his gifts, but that doesn't sound like it outweighs the trouble you're taking right now, big boy."

"Well, had Tayona just shut up and been Artie's mama, none of this would have had to happen. Yes, Artie's a *god* on the keyboard. Maybe even better than me. I can shape him, help him find a mold into which he can grow...and make a shit-ton of money."

"Money for you," I spat. "You're gonna make *him* into Tr1pw1re."

"Works out great, right? He keeps bringing in the dough, I get to retire. And if anybody ever attributes us—"

"Artie takes the fall," I seethed. "You were going to turn him into a goddamn child slave."

"So judgey. And not 'were.' '*Are.*'"

"He ain't even yours anyway," I spat.

"What?"

"Tayona was already preggo when you married her, you dumb shit. You ain't Artie's real father."

Parker stiffened in his saddle. "Well, what does it matter now anyway, huh?" He clicked the dual hammers back on the AF2011-A1. "And now we need to go from mere flesh wounds to something a little less likely to preserve your mouth, Jack Dooley. Sayonara, shitbird."

Four shots exploded into the night, two each reporting from two different barrels. Two bullets took Parker's outstretched gun arm, creating fountains of blood against the starlit night and forcing his aim wide, his trigger finger to squeeze. He only got off the one shot and it burrowed into the ground next to me harmlessly. The other two bullets pierced both of his collarbones, whipping him back in his saddle and blasting blood and bone through the exit wounds in his back. He toppled backwards with a high-pitched shriek, falling off the horse, shit boots flipping up in the air.

Parker's fall propelled Artie off his lap and down the other side of the horse into a clump on the ground. As I scrambled up to get my bearings and head in his direction, I saw another horse canter into the clearing with Roger Hulen and Rick Sears riding bareback. Roger held reins in one hand and his six-shooter stretched out toward Parker in the other. Rick had one arm wrapped around Roger's midsection and his other arm extended in the same direction toward Parker, hand gripping the SigSauer he'd taken off the security guard. Both of their long arms, trained in perfect parallel unison, covered Parker's crumpling form as he came to a slump on the ground. Rick slid off Roger's horse and combat shuffled over to their prey, kicking aside the double-barrel and pointing his weapon on the moaning man. I couldn't see his state, but four on-target shots wouldn't be leaving that shit-fuck sonofabitch in any kinda condition I cared to ameliorate anytime soon.

I crab-crawled over to Artie, feeling the minuscule kinks and pinpricks of aches that would blossom into full-blown arthritic seizures later, but ignoring the pain as my heart raced, suddenly panicking over the kid's condition. I scooped Artie's light body up in my arms, my hands gripping his limbs and checking to make sure he hadn't broken any bones or was bleeding out anywhere. As I did so, the kid's tear-streaked face and big puppy-dog eyes looked up at me.

"Mister Jack, I had a bad day," he said with a quivering lip.

"I know, kid. Let's get you back to your mom, okay?"

"Okay."

I looked over my shoulder to where Roger Hulen was snapping a pair of handcuffs onto Parker's wrists, having rolled him over onto his chest to more shrieks, the kind of exhortations you'd expect from someone who had never been in a fight before much less taken a round or two. Or four. Rick stood over him, training his weapon on the man until Roger finished with the cuffs. Secured, Rick stuck his gun back in his waistband, and Roger removed his hat, rubbing sweat from his forehead with the wrist cuff of the same hand.

"Shit, Roger," I said. "What are you doing here?"

"Just lucky, I guess," Hulen said with a smirk.

Parker vacillated between consciousness and the pain-coma caused by multiple gunshot wounds, shrieks and moans spilling from his mouth. I stood over him next to Hulen and Rick, letting Artie down to kneel quietly on the ground where he could look up and inspect Hulen's horse. Rick fist-bumped me.

"I feel like you are owed some honors here," he said.

I unzipped my jeans, pulled out my dick, and disgorged a long, slow piss all over Parker, taking care to douse his head and wounds as completely as the golden stream would last. I let out a shuddering sigh as I felt pressure surge in my kidneys.

"Ahhh, serendipity," I breathed.

A few seconds later, Rick unlimbered his own dick and pissed on Parker, too. Not be left out, Roger Hulen cackled under his Ranger's demeanor and followed suit. Just three grown men with their dicks out, pissing on a real sonofabitch on a brambly Texas night.

25.
GET RIGHT, GET WISE

"And *this*," Mikayla Castañeda said, plopping a big ream of papers onto the desk with a *Moby Dick*-sized hard drive on top, "is every bit of data recovered from Parker's network and mainframe onsite. The raw data is in the hard drive and contains evidence of every hack, crack, and brag made about such online to which he can be attributed to Tr1pw1re for the past ten or so years. The papers are highlighted reports, network diagrams, and a summary written up by my clients to help guide the state through the evidence, step-by-step."

Dakota Techt held his hands up in protest as the docket joined several boxes of evidence that we had unloaded onto his desk. Each one was conscientiously labeled and numbered in block handwriting indicating sequence and contents. Roger Hulen stood nearby the desk, signing sworn statements that he had verified each box's contents, and as he finished each affidavit, he affixed it to the box's lid with duct tape and an ink stamp of the Texas Rangers.

We had staged the handover prior to showing up, and Hulen had been in on it. Deckhead had gotten so far into Parker's ranch house network, the pot was still roasting meat. While Hulen had been calling state crime scene support in the wake of the shootout, Deck and Pussy Control had been digging for and finding the gold that they were going to use to attribute Tr1pw1re to Ted Parker and clear their names for good.

Granted, Hulen couldn't comprehend everything Deck and Pussy were up to at the ranch, and when he had pressed them to wrap it up, Pussy had used her gentle way to convince him that the digital forensics would take a bit of time. While Hulen granted them that time under the stipulation that a state investigator join them to supervise their work, Deck and Pussy rewired a few key bank accounts to move funds that said investigator would never see. That state investigator, by the way, had to drive down from Dallas, so Deck and Pussy had engineered the output exactly the way they wanted it to appear to Techt. The zealous state's attorney would never see a million and change in offshore assets that the crew split up into child support for Tayona, an education fund for Artie, and a little drinking money for The Jetfire Skwad.

"With this," Mikayla was saying, "you now have a top-to-bottom case against Ted Parker." She counted off each thing she said next on a long brown finger. "You have data from Parker's mainframe proving he executed operations attributed to the hacker known as Tr1pw1re. You have witness testimony from Samarra 'Poquito' Franklin identifying Ted Parker having committed multiple crimes also attributable to Tr1pw1re, to include conspiracy to frame my clients for the commission of these crimes. You have eyewitness testimony from Jack Dooley and Rick Sears that Ted Parker tried to murder Jack Dooley." She inclined her head toward Hulen. "You have your own state investigator's testimony corroborating that as well. You have that same investigator's testimony that Ted Parker tried to kidnap his own son, backed up by witness statements from Jack Dooley, Tex Cochrane, and others."

Mikayla stopped when she noticed Techt wasn't listening anymore and had instead started clipping his nails. She clasped her hands in her lap and fixed him with a derisive glare.

"Clearly you believe me when I say we have provided enough evidence to clear my clients of the charges for which you had them arrested."

Techt threw one hand in the air absently. "Reyes and Hernández are free to go. We'll process today."

"Perhaps the state will be so kind as to remember that the reason they have all of this evidence so neatly collated in front of them is because of Mr. Reyes and Ms. Hernández," Mikayla said, gesturing to the boxes on Techt's desk with a slight smirk. "I'm not sure the state could have pulled together so clean a case on Ted Parker..."

Techt looked at her blankly. "What else do you want?"

Mikayla offered him a wink and slid a business card across the desk. It was one of the nice jobs, texturized super-cardstock, gold embossed font that indented just so. It read "JETFIRE SERVICES" and under that an email address and a phone number.

"Just a phone call in the event the state may find the need for cyber attribution services or consulting," she said with a grin. "I can guarantee they work affordably and with discretion."

Techt raised an eyebrow on his lawyer's face as he picked up and regarded the business card, rubbing it between his thumb and forefinger.

"I can attest to the efficacy of their services, Mister Techt," Hulen intoned as he pulled another strip of duct tape to place atop one of the evidence boxes. "Could always be good to have some investigatory support in this brave new digital world."

Techt did not conceal his eye roll as he set the business card atop the hard drive. "I'll take it under advisement. Anything else?"

Mikayla's delicate fingers reached inside her shoulder bag and withdrew a single typed sheet of paper. "I've drafted a letter that I would hope you would agree to endorse, Mister Assistant State's Attorney. I've been retained by Tayona Parker to represent her in divorce proceedings against Ted Parker. She is suing him to obtain sole custody of their son, Arthur. This note from a state's attorney would go a long way with the judge to complete those proceedings quickly and in favor of Miss Parker."

Techt snatched the letter out of the air and sped-read it. "Is this really necessary?"

"I'll be happy to sign one, Miss Castañeda," Roger Hulen said.

Mikayla flashed Hulen and knowing and somewhat playful grin. "Oh, don't worry, Ranger, your ask is coming."

Techt shook his head quickly, placed the letter on his desk, and signed it hastily. "There. That should conclude our business, wouldn't you say, Miss Castañeda?"

Mikayla looked at me and I nodded with a much-too-smug pursing of my lips and slow eye blinks, to which she grinned and looked back to Techt with a nod. "Thank you for your time, Mister Techt."

I patted the rails of the old wooden chair in which I was sitting next to Mikayla and made to stand. "And everybody lived happily ever after."

"You played this out like a boss, Dooley," Techt said, leaning back in his big leather chair, folding his hands behind his head, and kicking his feet up on the desk. He was wearing a blue power suit again, this time with dark brown leather Oxfords that would have been more at place in a Boston or a Chicago courtroom. "Maybe you should think about doing this full time...getting your P.I.'s license... hanging a shingle... Looks like you've already got some leads with ole' Mikayla's firm here."

I shot Mikayla a side eyed look, some kind of brief joke dancing in the silent giggle between us. "Law firms often need private investigators..." she said.

"Hang a shingle, huh?" I said, reaching for a pack of cigarettes and the trusty Spartan Zippo in the pockets of my khakis.

"Lot of work round these parts for a good investigator," Hulen intoned, half-sitting on the side of Techt's desk, his hip flashing the Texas Ranger badge and silvery sidearm. "Of the private type."

A cigarette found its way between my lips. "Izzatafactnow?"

"Just get your goddamn license, Dooley," Techt said, smirking himself now. "And get the hell out of here before you light that thing."

———

Mikayla slipped me one of her business cards outside the justice center and told me to call her whenever I wanted to get serious about the license. Texas had peculiarities about licensing investigators, and she didn't want to see me fall into black holes of my own making. Her firm had its share of criminal defense accounts, but Mikayla was making such a name for herself in those ranks, enough so that she was shaping a litigation agenda that could warrant her own practice one day. Being two of few people who knew and accepted the madcap of one Aloysius "Preacher" Cornish, Mikayla and I held a special bond. She followed a path all her own, seen things the rest of us had not, done things she merely blithely hinted at over drunken nights in Fairmount with Preacher weed. She was one of the best of us, and I'd lay down in traffic for her if she ever asked me.

I met Rick on the steps of the old Tarrant County Courthouse where Main Street dead-ended. The summer heat had intensified, and nowhere did it glisten more than on Downtown's pavement and brick. A sheen of sticky sweat developed in the small of my back as I hoofed it, and I resolved to somehow peel off a piece of the drunk fat that I was carrying. Months of drinking too much, chowing on unadulterated Tex-Mex, and sweetening each course with desserts from Preacher's all contributed to my body beginning to show its age. I puffed impermeably as I rolled up on the courthouse, feeling that old Dooley discomfort in the chest, the early pulling sensation that denoted the heart disease that had killed so many of the men in our line over the centuries. Maybe I'd do something about it.

Rick was seated on the courthouse steps when I arrived, leaning back against one row, long legs bent at the knee in khaki pants of his own. Huey Lewis Ray-Bans covered his eyes, and he wore a plain navy blue polo over a white undershirt that was no doubt sopping up his own Texas sweat. By the time I'd taken position next to him, sprawling on the steps, I was breathing hard.

"You know, they make twelve-step programs for what you got," Rick said, looking down at me.

"Too many steps," I said. "Jesus fuck, man, why do we live here?"

"On this planet?"

"In Texas. We ain't got much choice in the other."

"There's always a choice, bunk."

Each of us sat like we had just ridden horses...badly. My taint felt like a boulder was permanently lodged there. Rick's wide-legged perch also belied the tenderness left over from one too many bounces on Hulen's gelding.

"Remember when we used to sit out on these steps? Talkin' comic books and good movies. It's been an asteroidal age, man," I said.

"I haven't been to the show in a while. You should come down to Austin with me and Nia sometime, let us take you to The Alamo Drafthouse. They've got Lebowski Fest that's right up your alley."

"Sounds like my kinda deal, baby."

"Listen, Jack..." Rick started, leaning forward. He made to reach out and put a hand on my shoulder or my knee or some shit, thought better of it, opted to pull his shades up onto his head. "I owe you an apology, man."

I shook my head vigorously. "You don't owe me shit, brother. Said it once, I'll say it again. All is right with the world."

"It's really not. I should have listened to you when I first brought you into this. Your instincts were right."

A single breath of a guffaw escaped my mouth. "How often has that ever been true?"

"Well, it matters that they were this time. I was way off, man, and I'm sorry I didn't listen."

I patted his shoe. "All in the past, brother. It is what it is. You really wanna do me a favor, say all that to Preacher and Tex."

"I'm game for it."

"Buy you a coffee?"

"Too hot for that shit."

"I know where we can get something cold."

We walked to Sundance Square past booted business folk and big-haired mamas. Summer brought out the tourists, most of them visiting from elsewhere in Texas. We rounded the mural of the longhorns on the backside of the 95.9 FM radio station building just to see it, despite the sweat cascading inside our shirts.

The Jetfire Gym had reopened, but traffic was light. Only one juvenile seemed to have braved the remnants of police tape outside to pay rental fees and get after the pages and pages of hentai flavor he needed to mainline. He was a regular, and Pussy told him if she ever caught him jerking off in her cafe, she'd call the cops. He still showed up every day, furtively clicking and clicking, on the hunt for ever increasing levels of depravity in round-eyed, effervescent girls and tentacle dicks.

Tex, Preacher, Deckhead, and Pussy were cleaning up when we got there. Most of the computers and equipment had been returned by the police earlier that day, courtesy of Roger Hulen's continuing desire to do the right thing. Pussy and Deck wanted to get revenue-positive again, so Tex and Preacher were setting up computers in the library terminals, Deck was testing wifi signals, and Pussy was serving coffee behind the counter.

When Rick and I walked in, Pussy offered us a great big smile and waved. "Mickey just called and told us the news. We're back in business, baby!"

"Music to my ears," I said. "Hey, y'all remember my buddy Rick Sears, right?"

"How could we forget?" Deckhead said, coming up to Rick and grasping his hand hood-style, pulling Rick in for a light chest bump. "You doin' okay, *ése*?"

"I'll live," Rick said. "Thanks for asking."

"It's hot out, fellas. Y'all want something cold?" Pussy asked.

"I'll take a beer if you got one," I said.

"Soda's fine with me," Rick said.

"Oi, is it that time again?" Preacher said, walking up to the counter, ragged old Pink Floyd T-shirt marked by sweat and grime. Holes and rips marked a particularly ragged pair of jeans, through which I struggled not to look at one of Preacher's balls hanging free and unabashed. "One delicious pint o' some shite, please."

"How many times we gotta tell ya there ain't no pints of anything here, Preacher?" Tex said, also joining us.

Pussy handed a trio of Dos Equis bottles to me and the boys, an iced coffee for Deckhead, and a Sprite for Rick. The beer bottles clinked together as one. After a swig, Tex inclined his bottle at Rick.

"Ain't you late for work or something?" he said.

"Something tells me I'll be on the dole by the time I get back to Austin," Rick said. "My bosses are not too happy with me losing the Parker account, even if he *was* an asshole."

"Oi, mebbe yeh don' need 'em anyway, lad," Preacher said, clinking his beer bottle against Rick's glass of Sprite. "All good, wha?"

Rick let a small smile cross his otherwise stony face. "All good. Preacher, Tex...I need to apologize to y'all. I'm sorry I didn't—"

Tex threw a meaty arm around Rick's shoulders and hugged him to his chest. He had lost the cast and seemed no worse for the wear. "Friends of Jack's, friends of ours, man. Nothin' doin'."

"Aye, mate," Preacher said. "Are yeh hidin' a large pecker in them khakis, by the way?"

"Strangle a wrestler," Rick said.

"Fucking men," Pussy laughed, rolling her eyes as she often did to our antics and sipping a cup of sweet-scented chai tea.

"So I never asked about the closeout," Rick said. "State's attorney dropped the case?"

"Kinda hard not to when he saw that hard drive full of shit that Pussy and I cooked up for him," Deckhead giggled. "Every IP address, every intrusion record, every attribution technique, every goddamn thing we ever did was in there. On *top* of all the shit I got outta Parker's network at the ranch house. Muthafucka ain't gonna be seein' the light of day *ever* again with that mountain of shit."

"We pinned every job we ever did on him," Pussy said. "Turned it back on him, the shit he and Clean Wheel did on us."

"What about Clean Wheel?" Rick asked.

"Hulen arrested a bunch of them on site, but I think he's also got some state warrant lined up for the corporate leadership," I said.

"The company's toast, but the leadership will likely take plea deals to turn state's evidence on Parker since he was a part-owner in the company."

"And the wheel comes around," Tex said with a grin.

"'Round and around," Preacher said.

At that moment, the bell on the front door emitted its pathetic little ring as the door swung open. The squeaky noise drew our attention to Tayona Parker, who lead Artie in by a hand. She favored one leg and didn't move as quickly as she had, but she *was* moving. Artie held her hand absently and looked around with his wide, all-seeing eyes, perfectly calm.

Pussy came around the counter, pushed past us, and gave Tayona a big hug. "Hi! Jack's told me about you. You're Tayona, right? We spoke on the phone. I'm Pussy Control."

"Damn, girl, I ain't never gettin' used to that name," Tayona said with not a small amount of sass. "You should be dancin' with me."

"Girl, you see how white I am? I got no rhythm." Pussy leaned down and looked at the little boy. "Hi there! You must be Artie. How ya doing, fella?"

Artie didn't respond but instead kept looking around The Gym. "It takes him a while," Tayona said by way of explanation.

"It's okay. We got all the time in the world."

Tayona looked at the rest of us, accepting hugs and squeezes.

"Back on your feet again?" I asked.

"Slowly but surely. Ain't gonna be twirlin' 'round no poles no more though."

"I bet we could find you something else to do," Tex said.

"Why y'all so nice to me?" Tayona said, shaking her head. "P.C. been tellin' me all 'bout this money y'all got me and Artie. I mean... *damn*. Y'all don't know me."

"That's *your* money, *mamacita*," Deckhead said, nodding at her. "You and your boy earned it."

"How? By being around some asshole?"

"Spoiler alert, luv: yer still around a few," Preacher whispered. "Sorry."

"Look, you've got a nice nest egg to get settled with," Pussy said, holding Tayona's hands. "And there's likely going to be more after Mikayla finishes kicking Ted's ass in court. In the meantime, you can rest, relax, hang around here if you want."

Tayona looked around The Gym. "What y'all got goin' on here? Thought y'all was some kinda hackers, too."

"Reformed," Deckhead said. "We're actually gonna turn this place into a STEM academy for computer science. Kids can come here, study how things work, build their own programs, learn to write code. I'm even thinking about getting one of those 3D printing machines. It's going to be great." Deck squatted down to come to eye level with Artie. "Maybe little man here wants to come bang on some keyboards with ole' Deckhead, huh? Whaddya say to that, little man?"

Artie let go of his mother's hand, walked over to Deckhead, and—with no pretense—wrapped his arms around Deck's neck in a light and anxiety-free hug. Deck was caught off-guard and looked up at Tayona as Artie spoke.

"I like Xbox," he said.

"Well, little man, we'll get you an Xbox if your Mom says it's okay, okay?"

Artie disengaged and looked back to his mother. "Is it okay?"

Tayona's smile was big and tear-streaked. "Yeah, baby, it's okay."

I traded a look with Rick, and he knocked his Sprite bottle against my beer bottle.

"All good in the neighborhood," I said.

"Down on the upside," Rick said.

26.

FADING, FADED, AND FEYD

The band that night played covers mostly, pop-funk from the six-ties to the nineties, fitting in an original here and there, breaking frequently because the crowd at The Aardvark was light and who really gave a shit. Texas, Preacher, and I found a table with seats, one of the few spread to the outskirts of the bar's perimeter, opt-ing to sprawl out in typical man-fashion with a boot on the table here and knees akimbo there. Cigarettes intertwined with cans of Miller Lite (there was a special). The cans collected in a grow-ing tower of aluminum, a monument to American badassery and lite beer bullshittery. We ashed in the beer cans, having not found any of the thick, black plastic ashtrays since colonizing our table. Perhaps they were trying to outlaw smoking inside. Savages.

"Oi, lemme tell yeh the fookin' problem," Preacher started.

"Tell us the problem," I said.

Preacher pointed his cigarette at me. "There's fookin' poison in Miller Lite cans, wha."

"How do you know this?" Tex said.

"It's a fact, Texas. It's a fuckin' fact. Yeh drink out've a can like this, and yeh get the fookin' iron castor-oil taste on backwash."

"That's just Miller Lite," I said.

"Shut it. Nae, it's fookin' shite is what it is. Wankers workin' wiv the fookin' government to try and keep the fookin' intellectual clemency of the population down to manageable levels so's they can be controlled easier and faster when necessary in times of social unrest or riotous effrontery."

"You're telling us the government is feeding us Miller Lite to make us more *controllable*?"

"Exactly!"

"Preacher...how controllable have you *ever* seen *anybody* after drinking a case of Miller Lite?"

"Or any beer for that matter?" Tex said.

"Oi, that's not the point."

"And yet it is, Randy Quaid," I said. "For fuck's sake, Preacher, drink your beer and chill your shit out."

The silences between the bullshit never became awkward, not ever since we were kids. But there were still some things needed to be said.

"Hey, Tex," I said.

"Hey, Cajun," said Tex.

"Hey, man...I ain't never said sorry about...y'know. About the gay stuff."

Tex's eyes twinkled as he regarded me. My belly flopped. Shame?

"Cajun, it's okay. I didn't tell anybody for a long time. You shoulda seen my dad. He liked to have kicked me off the ranch... comin' from his uniformed tradition in the army and all." His eyes fluttered down to the beer can in his hand, propped up on the thigh of one leg that was similarly propped on the table. "Guess I just didn't wanna deal with all the disappointment, y'know? I'm sorry I didn't tell ya. Or you, Preacher."

Preacher smacked Tex on the shoulder and tried to shake him in a brotherly collision of flesh and muscle. He only succeeded in vibrating himself against Tex's immovable bulk.

"Oi, I love yeh just the way yeh are, Texas. I've slurped me share of shafts."

"I think I was actually offended at one point that you hadn't told me," I said. "But, shit, man, that just makes it about me, and that ain't fair to you. So, I'm sorry, man."

Tex winked at me. "If you give me a decent handy, all's forgiven."

The laughter came freely and easy, the way it's supposed to. Accentuated by good tunes and tasty beverages. We Three Wankers clinked beer cans, universal signals that everything was cool, that no further words were necessary. Three old bastards markin' time and watchin' stones roll. Security of a different type, brotherhood in bullshittery. It felt good to be back in that circle. Bent but unbroken.

We were having so much fun that we didn't notice when Roger Hulen appeared at our table. Preacher recoiled visibly once he saw the Texas Ranger and screamed loudly, *"Fookin' shite a ghost yeh berk!"*

"Not yet, young man," Hulen said with a laugh. "Y'all mind if I join ya for a spell?"

"Sure, pull up a chair, Ranger," I said, stamping out his cigarette hastily in deference.

"Ya don't have to stop smoking on my account, Jack," Hulen said, throwing his legs—Riker-style—over a chair and closed the distance to us, one hand gripping a can of Shiner. "I ain't gonna arrest nobody for smoking."

"Fer real?" Preacher said, wide-eyed.

"Well...not until possession becomes more of a state felony than something greenhorn black-and-whites chase around for their first collars." Hulen sipped his beer, ably avoiding foam on his sagging mustache. "I might be a few years removed from that."

"What's the good word, Roger?" I said, still comfortable with my Converse-covered shoe on one edge of the table. I was still sporting the reds since I hadn't yet figured out how to get Preacher vomitus off the blacks. "Slumming with us assholes? Something we should be wary of before we get too shitfaced and loose-lipped?"

"Boys, I ain't got nothin' for ya tonight. Just havin' a beer with some of the locals."

"Yer about as local as fookin' Josey Wales, yeh long arm of the law!" Preacher accused. "What've yeh done?!"

Hulen held his hands up with a gruff laugh. "Seriously, fellas, no agenda here. I was just hoping y'all would let an old lawman hang with ya for a little while and maybe buy you a beer or two."

"Hell, yes," I said, motioning for a server to come over and fill us up. "Unleaded, please."

"Ranger, that was a helluva showdown you brought down in Round Rock," Tex said with a warm, appreciating smile. "I ain't never seen nothin' quite like that."

"Kinda felt like I should have brought some backup, tell you the truth. You boys sure did open up a hornet's nest down there."

"One riot, one Ranger," I said with a grin and cheersed Hulen's beer can with my own.

"Amen. You know, Cochrane, you oughtta see about applying for the Ranger Academy. Maybe do a little SWAT or HRT work to build up to your star."

Tex's face opened up in surprise. "You think?"

"I saw you down there, too, son. You've got a helluva gift connectin' lead to those that deserve it." Hulen nodded his head at Tex, and the Ranger's hat bobbed over his bushy-eyed sight line. "I think you've got the moves. That noggin' any good at piecing together spare parts like your bud Jack's here?"

"Maybe so, sir. Maybe so."

"Just give it some thought, son. I'd be happy to sponsor your application."

"Oi, what about me?" Preacher said. "I was poppin' caps and splittin' wigs right next to oul' Tex here, I was."

Roger looked at Preacher deadpan. "Son, you didn't hit one goddamn thing with that scattergun you were clutchin' like it was your Linus blanket. And something tells me you wouldn't pass the drug test."

Tex and I roared. Preacher made a face and drained his beer can. "Just for that, Imma get right right in front of yeh, Ranger."

"Be my guest," Hulen laughed.

I clapped Tex on the shoulder. "One Texas Ranger team for another. Seems right, man. You oughtta do it."

"Yeah, sounds good," Tex said. "What about you, Cajun? You're a better detective than I am. Mister Hulen, you think Jack has what it takes?"

Hulen adjusted his position in his seat. "Jack's surely one hell of an investigator, Cochrane...but something tells me he'd never be able to pin on a badge." Hulen looked at me. "The weight and all."

I met Hulen's gaze and nodded slowly, toasting him in the air with my beer can. "Here's to the weight."

Preacher pushed a few orange-colored pills into the center of the table. "C'n I interest any of yeh in some mescaline?"

There were notes posted all over my door and the doors of my Bryce House neighbors. The landlord was tired of the cat situation. He threatened to have every animal on the premises scooped up and put down in the next week. They would send Animal Control or, worse, somebody's bucktoothed hillbilly cousin with a penchant for animal abuse armed with cattle prods and a shotgun.

The kittens were clustered around my door and wailing small cries. A few of them had already survived some kind of meat grinder, sporting cuts, bloody wounds, and fleas. I gathered them up into a cardboard box, dumping out the investigative books and journals that for months sat unread inside. I emptied a few cans of food into the box so the cats would have something to chew on for the few minutes it would take to get to the vet.

In Westcliff Village, I dropped them off with a friend, a veterinarian who had gone to high school with me and Preacher and Tex and Mikayla and Deck and Pussy Control. Babs. Babs told me to come back tomorrow with some money to cover the strays' accommodations, and I did. Babs said a couple of them had gotten pretty chewed up by someone or something.

Within the span of another day, every one of the kittens had been adopted. Babs could sweet talk anybody into helping out an animal in need, and it didn't take much for Fort Worthers to open their hearts to animals. Families came through the vet's office over the weekend, and the kitties' squeals were too much to ignore.

Except one. The Russian blue. He had taken a bad bite across his left hindquarters, and it had gotten infected. Green with maggots. Babs called again and told me she'd have to put him down if he didn't get treatment that cost a lot of money. I got the money and brought it to her.

A few days later, the blue kitten that looked gray to me had rehabilitated and was sending signals of thriving. He was loud and insistent. He loved milk. Babs called me back to check in on him.

I brought him back to my apartment with me, called my landlord's management company that if they came inside my apartment ever I'd turn them into the real estate board to audit their books. I got plenty of milk and sardines for the Russian blue.

I called him Feyd.

ACKNOWLEDGEMENTS

This second time around the sun, I owe huge thanks to my family for making me space in which to write *Bravo Too Much*. To my wife: I could not do this without your encouragement and patience, and I'm thankful you let me run around like an idiot doing idiot things like this.

To the people of Fort Worth, it has been an abject delight writing about you and our wonderful town. Folks like to say Fort Worth's still a small town where everyone knows everybody, but I keep meeting new folks all the time. It's been a lot of fun writing this book in my hometown these past months, being able to post up outside Will Rogers Coliseum or The Kimbell and feel the influence of this unique community. I can't wait to do it again and again.

For this novel, I often found myself retreating to the keyboard late at night while traveling during my day job. I am lucky to have found myself in Australia and Mexico during this course of this writing, and I feel like there's a little special something that filtered into me as I struck keys over spiced rum in Perth and between beers in Cancun. We seldom find the rarity of wisdom in our travels, and I am grateful for all those touchstones that have befallen me as I traipsed around the world this year. I am also forever grateful for the incredible people I've met in these travels that have prompted me to keep on writing. You will find me at that same café in Canberra sometime again, furiously beating out the best words I can find to describe a cocaine binge. I promise.

I could not have written *Bravo Too Much* without the gaggle of friends who made growing up in Fort Worth great, friends with whom I have had the honor and privilege of calling "old" now as we come together in these later years. To Ware, Danny, Jeremy, Robby, Shelby, Raleigh, Nathan, Victor, Laurel, Katharine, all my classmates from Paschal, and all of you close pals and gals from Funkytown: I pray thee never change, and thank you—and your significant others and your kids!—for indulging this old fart's novelistic wanderings.

As usual, to Warren Ellis for the daily inspiration in his newsletters and internet spatterings, and whose online community once yielded up the *Waiting for Godot / Waiting for Planetary* joke I shamelessly cribbed for Chapter 6. The Republic of Newsletters and the Isles of Blogging are real places, and you should visit them if you can.

To the incredible writing staff at *Texas Monthly* for producing continuing stories about Texas culture…I have taken a ton of inspiration and good humor from your words in 2018 and 2019. I tip my hat to you, Texanist, for your ongoing good-natured advice on gracefully dealing with out-of-staters.

To the boys from Soviet Space whose album I continue to spin. "Evidence for Running Away" tantalizes still today, even though you can't find it anywhere these days save for the "local artist" bins at Record Town and other fine used music shops in the Fort Worth area. If you're ever in Funkytown, try to find this CD. It's a gem. Alternatively, for all you younglings that can't fathom a CD player, hit me up via *du4writes.com*, and maybe I'll send you a carefully preserved digital file. You'll notice the Soviet Space songs appearing in this text show up on my Spotify playlist for *Bravo Too* Much, but because they are local files, I unfortunately can't stream them that way. Soviet Space was an incredible Fort Worth band. With a little bit of creative Googling, you can find some fun old *Fort Worth Weekly* articles about them.

I have the good fortune to be big brother to a sister with a much more creative eye, so it was a real thrill to be able to work with her to produce this novel's cover photo. Thank you, Sarah, for putting up with my insanely detailed asks. I really love what you shot, including those outtakes. I'd also like to thank my erstwhile brothers-from-other-druthers Sam and Tyson for acting alongside me as the models in these photos during what was a hectic and alcohol-infused Texas Christmas…as I suppose it always should be.

Again, to all the folks on the business side of things that helped make this happen: Erin Baehr for financial advice, and Michelle at Wide Sky Studios for cover and interior design services. Of course, no Du4writes joint would be complete without the recognition of my long-suffering editor, upon whose Atlas-like shoulders the weight of this entire author's literary fumblings are carried. I could not do this thing I love without you, O Editor, and I am forever grateful for you, your hard work, and your unending patience with my bullshit.

Of course, no acknowledgement could be complete without you, Dear Reader. It's really hard doing this on my own, but I love doing it, and you who brave these unkempt sentences feed my heart. I appreciate every one of your reviews, comments good and bad, and feedback.

Keep up with me at *du4writes.com* and sign up for my newsletter to stay current on what's next. Right now, newsletter subscription is the only way to get a special, exclusive short story that bridges *The One Star Goodnight* and *Bravo Too Much*. There may even be some new surprises for dedicated subscribers in the near future as I march on new novelistic adventures. Tall tales are still being told…

Chris Dufour
Fort Worth
January 2020

ABOUT THE AUTHOR

Christopher Dufour is the author of *The One Star Goodnight* and *Bravo Too Much*, each a self-published venture through Amazon Kindle Direct Publishing. He has also written a number of short stories, some featuring characters from The Jack Dooley Series, and others in various genres like science and speculative fiction. Almost no one buys his shit.

When not pouring out his soul to a manuscript, Dufour instructs in the art of open source intelligence and persuasion science. He is a noted national security consultant, disinformation researcher, and speaker. His nonfiction writing includes studies on digital data, information operations, disinformation, social media, strategic influence, and morale operations. Let that sink in for a moment.

His favorite comic book is *The Legion of Super-Heroes*, Giffen-era. He lives in Fort Worth, Texas with a cat named Roxy.

Jack Dooley will return in

CUBICLE STRATEGY

Coming soon.

www.ingramcontent.com/pod-product-compliance
Lightning Source LLC
Chambersburg PA
CBHW021526250626
47154CB00006BA/1993